Capitola The Madcap
Part II Of The Hidden Hand

by

Mrs. Emma D. E. N. Southworth

Capitola The Madcap
Part II Of The Hidden Hand
by Mrs. Emma D. E. N. Southworth

ISBN: 978-93-61156-94-6

Published by

DOUBLE 9 BOOKS

2/13-B, Ansari Road
Daryaganj, New Delhi – 110002
info@double9books.com
www.double9books.com
Tel. 011-40042856

ABOUT THE AUTHOR

Emma Nevitte was born on December 26, 1819, in Washington, D.C., to Susannah Wailes and Charles LeCompte Nevitte, a trader from Virginia. Her father died in 1824, and she was given the name Emma Dorothy Eliza Nevitte at his final wish. She attended a school run by her stepfather, Joshua L. Henshaw. She later described her youth as lonely, with her best times spent exploring Maryland's Tidewater region on horseback. During such rides, she developed a deep interest in the area's history and mythology. After attending her stepfather's school, she finished her secondary education at the age of 15 in 1835. In her works, her heroines frequently challenge modern ideas of Victorian feminine domesticity by demonstrating that virtue is naturally coupled with wit, adventure, and rebellion to fix any terrible situation. Though The Hidden Hand (1859) was her most popular novel, Southworth preferred Ishmael (1876).

CONTENTS

CHAPTER I
THE ORPHAN'S TRIAL

"We met ere yet the world had come
To wither up the springs of youth,
Amid the holy joys of home,
And in the first warm blush of youth.
We parted as they never part,
Whose tears are doomed to be forgot;
Oh, by what agony of heart.
Forget me not!—forget me not!"

—Anonymous.

At nine o'clock the next morning Traverse went to the library to keep his tryst with Colonel Le Noir.

Seated in the doctor's leathern chair, with his head thrown back, his nose erect and his white and jeweled hand caressing his mustached chin, the colonel awaited the young man's communication.

With a slight bow Traverse took a chair and drew it up to the table, seated himself and, after a little hesitation, commenced, and in a modest and self-respectful manner announced that he was charged with the last verbal instructions from the doctor to the executor of his will.

Colonel Le Noir left off caressing his chin for an instant, and, with a wave of his dainty hand, silently intimated that the young man should proceed.

Traverse then began and delivered the dying directions of the late doctor, to the effect that his daughter Clara Day should not be removed from the paternal mansion, but that she should be suffered to remain there, retaining as a matronly companion her old friend Mrs. Marah Rocke.

"Umm! umm! very ingenious, upon my word!" commented the colonel, still caressing his chin.

"I have now delivered my whole message, sir, and have only to add that I hope, for Miss Day's sake, there will be no difficulty thrown in the way of the execution of her father's last wishes, which are also, sir, very decidedly her own" said Traverse.

"Umm! doubtless they are—and also yours and your worthy mother's."

"Sir, Miss Day's will in this matter is certainly mine. Apart from the consideration of her pleasure, my wishes need not be consulted. As soon as I have seen Miss Day made comfortable I leave for the far West," said Traverse, with much dignity.

"Umm! and leave mama here to guard the golden prize until your return, eh?" sneered the colonel.

"Sir, I do not—wish to understand you," said Traverse with a flushed brow.

"Possibly not, my excellent young friend," said the colonel, ironically; then, rising from his chair and elevating his voice, he cried, "but I, sir, understand you and your mother and your pretty scheme perfectly! Very ingenious invention, these 'last verbal instructions.' Very pretty plan to entrap an heiress; but it shall not avail you, adventurers that you are! This afternoon Sauter, the confidential attorney of my late brother-in-law, will be here with the will, which shall be read in the presence of the assembled household. If these last verbal directions are also to be found duplicated in the will, very good, they shall be obeyed; if they not, shall be discredited."

During this speech Traverse stood with kindling eyes and blazing cheeks, scarcely able to master his indignation; yet, to his credit be it spoken, he did "rule his own spirit" and replied with dignity and calmness:

"Colonel Le Noir, my testimony in regard to the last wishes of Doctor Day can, if necessary, be supported by other evidence—though I do not believe that any man who did not himself act in habitual disregard of truth would wantonly question the veracity of another."

"Sir! this to me!" exclaimed Le Noir, growing white with rage and making a step toward the young man.

"Yes, Colonel Le Noir, that to you! And this in addition; You have presumed to charge my mother, in connection with myself, with being an adventuress; with forming dishonorable 'schemes,' and in so charging her, Colonel Le Noir, you utter a falsehood!"

"Sirrah!" cried Le Noir, striding toward Traverse and raising his hand over his head, with a fearful oath, "retract your words or—"

Traverse calmly drew himself up, folded his arms and replied coolly:

"I am no brawler, Colonel Le Noir; the pistol and the bowie-knife are as strange to my hands as abusive epithets and profane language are to my lips; nevertheless, instead of retracting my words, I repeat and reiterate them. If you charge my mother with conspiracy you utter a falsehood. As her son I am in duty bound to say as much."

"Villain!" gasped Le Noir, shaking his fist and choking with rage; "villain! you shall repent this in every vein of your body!"

Then, seizing his hat, he strode from the room.

"Boaster!" said Traverse to himself, as he also left the library by another door.

Clara was waiting for him in the little parlor below.

"Well, well, dear Traverse," she said, as he entered. "You have had the explanation with my guardian, and—he makes no objection to carrying out the last directions of my father and our own wishes—he is willing to leave me here?"

"My dear girl, Colonel Le Noir defers all decision until the reading of the will, which is to take place this afternoon," said Traverse, unwilling to add to her distress by recounting the disgraceful scene that had just taken place in the library.

"Oh! these delays! these delays! Heaven give me patience! Yet I do not know why I should be so uneasy. It is only a form; of course he will regard my father's wishes."

"I do not see well how he can avoid doing so, especially as Doctor Williams is another witness to them, and I shall request the doctor's attendance here this afternoon. Dear Clara, keep up your spirits! A few hours now and all will be well," said Traverse, as he drew on his gloves and took his hat to go on his morning round of calls.

An early dinner was ordered, for the purpose of giving ample time in the afternoon for the reading of the will.

Owing to the kind forbearance of each member of this little family, their meeting with their guest at the table was not so awkward as it might have been rendered. Mrs. Rocke had concealed the insults that had been offered her; Traverse had said nothing of the affronts put upon him. So that each, having only their own private injuries to resent, felt free in forbearing. Nothing but this sort of prudence on the part of individuals rendered their meeting around one board possible.

While they were still at the table the attorney, Mr. Sauter, with Doctors Williams and Dawson, arrived, and was shown into the library.

And very soon after the dessert was put upon the table the family left it and, accompanied by Colonel Le Noir, adjourned to the library. After the usual salutations they arranged themselves along each side of an extension table, at the head of which the attorney placed himself.

In the midst of a profound silence the will was opened and read. It was dated three years before.

The bulk of his estate, after the paying a few legacies, was left to his esteemed brother-in-law, Gabriel Le Noir, in trust for his only daughter, Clara Day, until the latter should attain the age of twenty-one, at which period she was to come into possession of the property. Then followed the distribution of the legacies. Among the rest the sum of a thousand dollars was left to his young friend Traverse Rocke, and another thousand to his esteemed neighbor Marah Rocke. Gabriel Le Noir was appointed sole executor of the will, trustee of the property and guardian of the heiress.

At the conclusion of the reading Mr. Sauter folded the document and laid it upon the table.

Colonel Le Noir arose and said:

"The will of the late Doctor Day has been read in your presence. I presume you all heard it, and that there can be no mistake as to its purport. All that remains now is to act upon it. I shall claim the usual privilege of twelve months before administering upon the estate or paying the legacies. In the mean time, I shall assume the charge of my ward's person, and convey her to my own residence, known as the Hidden House. Mrs. Rocke," he said, turning toward the latter, "your presence and that of your young charge is no longer required here. Be so good as to prepare Miss Day's traveling trunks, as we set out from this place to-morrow morning."

Mrs. Rocke started, looked wistfully in the face of the speaker and, seeing that he was in determined earnest, turned her appealing glances toward Traverse and Doctor Williams.

As for Clara, her face, previously blanched with grief, was now flushed with indignation. In her sudden distress and perplexity she knew not at once what to do—whether to utter a protest or continue silent; whether to leave the room or remain. Her embarrassment was perceived by Traverse, who, stooping, whispered to her:

"Be calm, love; all shall be well. Doctor Williams is about to speak."

And at that moment, indeed, Doctor Williams arose and said:

"I have, Colonel Le Noir to endorse a dying message from Doctor Day entrusted to my young friend here to be delivered to you, to the effect that it was his last desire and request that his daughter, Miss Clara Day, should be permitted to reside during the term of her minority in this her patrimonial home, under the care of her present matronly friend, Mrs. Marah Rocke, Doctor Rocke and myself are here to bear testimony to these, the last wishes of the departed, which wishes, I believe, also express the desires of his heiress."

"Oh, yes, yes!" said Clara, earnestly. "I do very much desire to remain in my own home, among my old familiar friends. My dear father only consulted my comfort and happiness when he left these instructions."

"There can be, therefore, no reason why Miss Day should be disturbed in her present home," said Traverse.

Colonel Le Noir smiled grimly, saying:

"I am sorry, Doctor Williams, to differ with you or to distress Miss Day. But if, as she says, her lamented father consulted her pleasure in those last instructions, he certainly consulted nothing else—not the proprieties of conventionalism, the opinion of the world, nor the future welfare of his daughter. Therefore, as a man of Doctor Day's high position and character in his sane moments never could have made such a singular arrangement, I am forced to the conclusion that he could not, at the time of giving those instructions, have been in his right mind. Consequently, I cannot venture to act upon any 'verbal instructions,' however well attested, but shall be guided in every respect by the will, executed while yet the testator was in sound body and mind."

"Doctor Rocke and myself are both physicians competent to certify that, at the time of leaving these directions, our respected friend was perfectly sound in mind at least," said Doctor Williams.

"That, sir, I repeat, I contest. And, acting upon the authority of the will, I shall proceed to take charge of my ward as well as of her estate. And as I think this house, under all the circumstances, a very improper place for her to remain, I shall convey her without delay to my own home. Mrs. Rocke, I believe I requested you to see to the packing of Miss Day's trunks."

"Oh, heaven! shall this wrong be permitted?" ejaculated Marah.

"Mrs. Rocke, I will not go unless absolutely forced to do so by a decree of the court. I shall get Doctor Williams to make an appeal for me to the Orphans' Court," said Clara, by way of encouraging her friend.

"My dear Miss Day, that, I hope, will not be required. Colonel Le Noir acts under a misapprehension of the circumstances. We must enter into more explanations with him, In the mean time, my dear young lady, it is better that you should obey him for the present, at least so far as retiring from the room," said Doctor Williams.

Clara immediately rose and, requesting Mrs. Rocke to accompany her, withdrew from the library.

Doctor Williams then said;

"I advised the retirement of the young lady, having a communication to make the hearing of which in a mixed company might have cost her an innocent blush. But first I would ask you, Colonel Le Noir, what are those circumstances to which you allude which render Miss Day's residence here, in her patrimonial mansion, with her old and faithful friends, so improper?" inquired Doctor Williams, courteously.

"The growing intimacy, sir, between herself and a very objectionable party—this young man Rocke!" replied Colonel Le Noir.

"Ah! and is that all?"

"It is enough, sir," said Colonel Le Noir, loftily.

"Then suppose I should inform you, sir, that this young man, Doctor Rocke, was brought up and educated at Doctor Day's cost and under his own immediate eye?"

"Then, sir, you would only inform me that an eccentric gentleman of fortune had done—what eccentric gentlemen of fortune will sometimes do—educated a pauper."

At this opprobrious epithet Traverse, with a flushed face, started to his feet.

"Sit down, my boy, sit down; leave me to deal with this man," said Doctor Williams, forcing Traverse back into his seat. Then, turning to Colonel Le Noir, he said:

"But suppose, sir, that such was the estimation in which Doctor Day held the moral and intellectual worth of his young protege that he actually gave him his daughter?"

"I cannot suppose an impossibility, Doctor Williams," replied Colonel Le Noir, haughtily.

"Then, sir, I have the pleasure of startling you a little by a prodigy that you denominate an impossibility! Clara Day and Traverse Rocke were betrothed with full knowledge and cordial approbation of the young lady's father."

"Impossible! preposterous! I shall countenance no such ridiculous absurdity!" said Colonel Le Noir, growing red in the face.

"Miss Day, Doctor Rocke, Mrs. Rocke, and myself are witnesses to that fact."

"The young lady, and the young man are parties immediately concerned—they cannot be received as witnesses in their own case; Mrs. Rocke is too much in their interest for her evidence to be taken; you, sir, I consider the dupe of these cunning conspirators—mother and son," replied Colonel Le Noir, firmly.

"Tut!" said Doctor Williams, almost out of patience. "I do not depend upon the words of Miss Day and her friends, although I hold their veracity to be above question; I had Doctor Day's dying words to the same effect. And he mentioned the existing betrothal as the very reason why Clara should remain here in the care of her future mother-in-law."

"Then, sir, that the doctor should have spoken and acted thus, is only another and a stronger reason for believing him to have been deranged in his last moments! You need give yourself no farther trouble! I shall act upon the authority of this instrument which I hold in my hand," replied Colonel Le Noir, haughtily.

"Then, as the depository of the dying man's last wishes and as the next friend of his injured daughter, I shall make an appeal to the Orphans' Court," said Doctor Williams, coldly.

"You can do as you please about that; but in the mean time, acting upon the authority of the will, I shall to-morrow morning set out with my ward for my own home."

"There may be time to arrest that journey," said Doctor Williams, arising and taking his hat to go.

In the passage he met Mrs. Rocke.

"Dear Doctor Williams," said Mrs. Rocke, earnestly, "pray come up to poor Clara's room and speak to her, if you can possibly say anything to comfort her; she is weeping herself into a fit of illness at the bare thought of being, so soon after her dreadful bereavement, torn away from her home and friends."

"Tut! tut! no use in weeping! all will yet be right."

"You have persuaded that man to permit her to remain here, then?" said Marah, gladly.

"Persuaded him! no, nor even undertaken to do so! I never saw him before to-day, yet I would venture to say, from what I have now seen of him, that he never was persuaded by any agent except his own passions and interests, to any act whatever. No, I have endeavored to show him that we have law as well as justice on our side, and even now I am afraid I shall have to take the case before the Orphans' Court before I can convince him.

He purposes removing Clara to-morrow morning. I will endeavor to see the Judge of the Orphans' Court to-night, take out a habeas corpus, ordering Le Noir to bring his ward into court, and serve it on him as he passes through Staunton on his way home."

"But is there no way of preventing him from taking Clara away from the house to-morrow morning."

"No good way. No, madam, it is best that all things should be done decently and in order. I advise you, as I shall also advise my young friends, Traverse and Clara, not to injure their own cause by unwise impatience or opposition. We should go before the Orphans' Court with the very best aspect."

"Come, then, and talk to Clara. She has the most painful antipathy to the man who claims the custody of her person, as well as the most distressing reluctance to leaving her dear home and friends; and all this, in addition to her recent heavy affliction, almost overwhelms the poor child," said Mrs. Rocke, weeping.

"I will go at once and do what I can to soothe her," said Doctor Williams, following Mrs. Rocke, who led him up to Clara's room.

They found her prostrate upon her bed, crushed with grief.

"Come, come, my dear girl, this is too bad! It is not like the usual noble fortitude of our Clara," said the old man, kindly taking her hand.

"Oh, Doctor, forgive—forgive me! but my courage must have been very small, for I fear it is all gone. But then, indeed, everything comes on me at once. My dear, dear father's death; then the approaching departure and expected long absence of Traverse! All that was grievous enough to bear; and now to be torn away from the home of my childhood, and from the friend that has always been a mother to me, and by a man, from whom every true, good instinct of my nature teaches me to shrink. I, who have always had full liberty in the house of my dear father, to be forced away against my will by this man, as if I were his slave!" exclaimed Clara, bursting into fresh tears of indignation and grief.

"Clara, my dear, dear girl, this impatience and rebellion is so unlike your gentle nature that I can scarcely recognize you for the mild and dignified daughter of my old friend. Clara, if the saints in heaven could grieve at anything, I should think your dear father would be grieved to see you thus!" said the old man in gentle rebuke that immediately took effect upon the meek and conscientious maiden.

"Oh! I feel—I feel that I am doing very wrong, but I cannot help it. I scarcely know myself in this agony of mingled grief, indignation and terror—yes, terror—for every instinct of my nature teaches me to distrust and fear that man, in whom my father must have been greatly deceived before he could have entrusted him with the guardianship of his only child."

"I think that quite likely," said the old man; "yet, my dear, even in respect to your dear father's memory, you must try to bear this trial patiently."

"Oh, yes, I know I must. Dear father, if you can look down and see me now, forgive your poor Clara, her anger and her impatience. She will try to be worthy of the rearing you have given her and to bear even this great trial with the spirit worthy of your daughter!" said Clara within her own heart; then, speaking up, she said: "You shall have no more reason to reprove me, Doctor Williams."

"That is my brave girl! That is my dear Clara Day! And now, when your guardian directs you to prepare yourself for your journey, obey him—go with him without making any objection. I purpose to arrest your journey at Staunton with a habeas corpus that he dare not resist, and which shall compel him to bring you into the Orphans' Court. There our side shall be heard, and the decision will rest with the judge."

"And all will be well! Oh, say that, sir! to give me the courage to act with becoming docility," pleaded Clara.

"I have not a doubt in this world that it will all be right, for, however Colonel Le Noir may choose to disregard the last wishes of your father, as attested by myself and young Rocke, I have not the least idea that the judge will pass them over. On the contrary, I feel persuaded that he will confirm them by sending you back here to your beloved home."

"Oh, may heaven grant it!" said Clara. "You do, indeed, give me new life."

"Yes, yes, be cheerful, my dear; trust in Providence and expect nothing short of the best! And now I dare not tarry longer with you, for I must see the Judge at his house this night. Good-by, my dear; keep up a good heart!" said the old man, cheerfully, pressing her hand and taking his leave.

Mrs. Rocke accompanied him to the hall door.

"My dear madam, keep up your spirits also for the sake of your young charge! Make her go to bed early! To-morrow, when she thinks she is about to be torn from you forever, remind her in her ear that I shall meet the carriage at Staunton with a power that shall turn the horses' heads."

And so saying, the worthy old gentleman departed.

As Marah Rocke looked after him, she also saw with alarm that Colonel Le Noir had mounted his horse and galloped off in the direction of Staunton, as if impelled by the most urgent haste.

She returned to the bedside of Clara, and left her no more that night. As the colonel did not return to supper, they, the family party, had their tea in Clara's room.

Late at night Mrs. Rocke heard Colonel Le Noir come into the house and enter his chamber.

Poor Clara slept no more that night; anxiety, despite of all her efforts, kept her wide awake. Yet, though anxious and wakeful, yet by prayer and endeavor she had brought her mind into a patient and submissive mood, so that when a servant knocked at her door in the morning with a message from Colonel Le Noir that she should be ready to set forth immediately after breakfast, she replied that she should obey him, and without delay she arose and commenced her toilet.

All the family met for the last time around the board. The party was constrained. The meal was a gloomy one. On rising from the table Colonel Le Noir informed his ward that his traveling carriage was waiting, and that her baggage was already on, and requested her to put on her bonnet and mantle, and take leave of her servants.

Clara turned to obey—Traverse went to her side and whispered:

"Take courage, dear love. My horse is saddled. I shall ride in attendance upon the carriage whether that man likes it or not; nor lose sight of you for one moment until we meet Williams with his habeas corpus."

"Nor even then, dear Traverse, nor even then! You will attend me to the court and be ready to take me back to this dear, dear home!" murmured Clara in reply.

"Yes, yes, dear girl! There, be cheerful," whispered the young man, as he pressed her hand and released it.

Colonel Le Noir had been a silent but frowning spectator of this little scene, and now that Clara was leaving the room, attended by Mrs. Rocke, he called the latter back, saying:

"You will be so kind as to stop here a moment, Mrs. Rocke and you also, young man."

The mother and son paused to hear what he should have to say.

"I believe it is the custom here in discharging domestics to give a month's warning, or in lieu of that, to pay a month's wages in advance.

There, woman, is the money. You will oblige me by leaving the house to-day, together with your son and all your other trumpery, as the premises are put in charge of an agent, who will be here this afternoon, clothed with authority to eject all loiterers and intruders."

While the colonel spoke Marah Rocke gazed at him in a panic from which she seemed unable to rouse herself, until Traverse gravely took her hand, saying:

"My dear mother, let me conduct you from the presence of this man, who does not know how to behave himself toward women. Leave me to talk with him, and do you, dear mother, go to Miss Day, who I know is waiting for you."

Marah Rocke mechanically complied and allowed Traverse to lead her from the room.

When he returned he went up to Colonel Le Noir, and, standing before him and looking him full and sternly in the face, said, as sternly:

"Colonel Le Noir, my mother will remain here and abide the decision of the Orphans' Court; until that has been pronounced, she does not stir at your or any man's bidding!"

"Villain, out of my way!" sneered Le Noir, endeavoring to pass him.

Traverse prevented him, saying:

"Sir, in consideration of your age, which should be venerable, your position which should prove you honorable, and of this sacred house of mourning in which you stand, I have endeavored to meet all the insults you have offered me with forbearance. But, sir, I am here to defend my mother's rights and to protect her from insult! And I tell you plainly that you have affronted her for the very last time! One more word or look of insult leveled at Marah Rocke and neither your age, position nor this sacred roof shall protect you from personal chastisement at the hands of her son!"

Le Noir, who had listened in angry scorn, with many an ejaculation of contempt, now at the conclusion which so galled his pride, broke out furiously, with:

"Sir, you are a bully! If you were a gentleman I would call you out!"

"And I should not come if you did, sir! Dueling is unchristian, barbarous and abominable in the sight of God and all good men. For the rest you may call me anything you please; but do not again insult my mother, for if you do I shall hold it a Christian duty to teach you better manners," said Traverse, coolly taking his hat and walking from the room. He mounted his horse and stood ready to attend Clara to Staunton.

Colonel Le Noir ground his teeth in impotent rage, muttering;

"Take care, young man! I shall live to be revenged upon you yet for these affronts!" and his dastard heart burned with the fiercer malignity that he had not dared to meet the eagle eye, or encounter the strong arm of the upright and stalwart young man. Gnashing his teeth with ill-suppressed fury, he strode into the hall just as Mrs. Rocke and Clara, in her traveling dress, descended the stairs.

Clara threw her arms around Mrs. Rocke's neck, and, weeping, said:

"Good-by, dear, best friend—good-by! Heaven grant it may not be for long! Oh, pray for me, that I may be sent back to you!"

"May the Lord have you in His holy keeping, my child I shall pray until I hear from you!" said Marah, kissing and releasing her.

Colonel Le Noir then took her by the hand, led her out, and put her into the carriage.

Just before entering Clara had turned to take a last look at her old home—all, friends and servants, noticed the sorrowful, anxious, almost despairing look of her pale face, which seemed to ask:

"Ah, shall I ever, ever return to you, dear old home, and dear, familiar friends?"

In another instant she had disappeared within the carriage, which immediately rolled off.

As the carriage was heavily laden, and the road was in a very bad condition, it was a full hour before they reached the town of Staunton. As the carriage drew up for a few moments before the door of the principal hotel, and Colonel Le Noir was in the act of stepping out, a sheriff's officer, accompanied by Dr. Williams, approached, and served upon the colonel a writ of habeas corpus, commanding him to bring his ward, Clara Day, into court.

Colonel Le Noir laughed scornfully, saying:

"And do any of you imagine this will serve your purposes? Ha, ha! The most that it can do will be to delay my journey for a few hours until the decision of the judge, which will only serve to confirm my authority beyond all future possibility of questioning."

"We will see to that," said Doctor Williams.

"Drive to the Court House!" ordered Colonel Le Noir.

And the carriage, attended by Traverse Rocke, Doctor Williams and the Sheriff's officer, each on horseback, drove thither.

And now, reader, I will not trouble you with a detailed account of this trial. Clara, clothed in deep mourning, and looking pale and terrified, was led into the court room on the arm of her guardian. She was followed closely by her friends, Traverse Rocke and Doctor Williams, each of whom whispered encouraging words to the orphan.

As the court had no pressing business on its hands, the case was immediately taken up, the will was read and attested by the attorney who had drawn it up and the witnesses who had signed it. Then the evidence of Doctor Williams and Doctor Rocke was taken concerning the last verbal instruction of the deceased. The case occupied about three hours, at the end of which the judge gave a decision in favor of Colonel Le Noir.

This judgment carried consternation to the heart of Clara and of all her friends.

Clara herself sank fainting in the arms of her old friend, the venerable Doctor Williams.

Traverse, in bitterness of spirit, approached and bent over her.

Colonel Le Noir spoke to the judge.

"I deeply thank your honor for the prompt hearing and equally prompt decision of this case, and I will beg your honor to order the Sheriff and his officers to see your judgment carried into effect, as I foresee violent opposition, and wish to prevent trouble."

"Certainly. Mr. Sheriff, you will see that Colonel Le Noir is put in possession of his ward, and protected in that right until he shall have placed her in security," said the judge.

Clara, on hearing these words, lifted her head from the old man's bosom, nerved her gentle heart, and in a clear, sweet, steady voice said:

"It is needless precaution, your honor; my friends are no law-breakers, and since the court has given me into the custody of my guardian, I do not dispute its judgment. I yield myself up to Colonel Le Noir."

"You do well, young lady," said the judge.

"I am pleased, Miss Day, to see that you understand and perform your duty; believe me, I shall do all that I can to make you happy," said Colonel Le Noir.

Clara replied by a gentle nod, and then, with a slight blush mantling her pure cheeks she advanced a step and placed herself immediately in front of the judge, saying:

"But there is a word that I would speak to your honor."

"Say on, young lady," said the judge.

And as she stood there in her deep mourning dress, with her fair hair unbound and floating softly around her pale, sweet face, every eye in that court was spellbound by her almost unearthly beauty. Before proceeding with what she was about to say, she turned upon Traverse a look that brought him immediately to her side.

"Your honor," she began, in a low, sweet, clear tone, "I owe it to Doctor Rocke here present, who has been sadly misrepresented to you, to say (what, under less serious circumstances, my girl's heart would shrink from avowing so publicly) that I am his betrothed wife—sacredly betrothed to him by almost the last act of my dear father's life. I hold this engagement to be so holy that no earthly tribunal can break or disturb it. And while I bend to your honor's decision, and yield myself to the custody of my legal guardian for the period of my minority, I here declare to all who may be interested, that I hold my hand and heart irrevocably pledged to Doctor Rocke, and that, as his betrothed wife, I shall consider myself bound to correspond with him regularly, and to receive him as often as he shall seek my society, until my majority, when I and all that I possess will become his own. And these words I force myself to speak, your honor, both in justice to my dear lost father and his friend, Traverse Rocke, and also to myself, that hereafter no one may venture to accuse me of clandestine proceedings, or distort my actions into improprieties, or in any manner call in question the conduct of my father's daughter." And, with another gentle bow, Clara retired to the side of her old friend.

"You are likely to have a troublesome charge in your ward," said the sheriff apart to the colonel, who shrugged his shoulders by way of reply.

The heart of Traverse was torn by many conflicting passions, emotions and impulses; there was indignation at the decision of the court; grief for the loss of Clara, and dread for her future!

One instant he felt a temptation to denounce the guardian as a villain and to charge the judge with being a corrupt politician, whose decisions were swayed by party interests!

The next moment he felt an impulse to catch Clara up in his arms, fight his way through the crowd and carry her off! But all these wild emotions, passions and impulses he succeeded in controlling.

Too well he knew that to rage, do violence, or commit extravagance as he might, the law would take its course all the same.

While his heart was torn in this manner, Colonel Le Noir was urging the departure of his ward. And Clara came to her lover's side and said, gravely and sweetly:

"The law, you see, has decided against us, dear Traverse! Let us bend gracefully to a decree that we cannot annul! It cannot, at least, alter our sacred relations; nor can anything on earth shake our steadfast faith in each other; let us take comfort in that, and in the thought that the years will surely roll round at length and bring the time that shall reunite us."

"Oh, my angel-girl! My angel-girl! Your patient heroism puts me to the blush, for my heart is crushed in my bosom and my firmness quite gone!" said Traverse, in a broken voice.

"You will gain firmness, dear Traverse. 'Patient!' I patient! You should have heard me last night! I was so impatient that Doctor Williams had to lecture me. But it would be strange if one did not learn something by suffering. I have been trying all night and day to school my heart to submission, and I hope I have succeeded, Traverse. Bless me and bid me good-by."

"The Lord forever bless and keep you, my own dear angel, Clara!" burst from the lips of Traverse. "The Lord abundantly bless you!"

"And you," said Clara.

"Good-by!—good-by!"

"Good-by!"

And thus they parted.

Clara was hurried away and put into the carriage by her guardian.

Ah, no one but the Lord knew how much it had-cost that poor girl to maintain her fortitude during that trying scene. She had controlled herself for the sake of her friends. But now, when she found herself in the carriage, her long strained nerves gave way—she sank exhausted and prostrated into the corner of her seat, in the utter collapse of woe!

But leaving the travelers to pursue their journey, we must go back to Traverse.

Almost broken-hearted, Traverse returned to Willow Heights to convey the sad tidings of his disappointment to his mother's ear.

Marah Rocke was so overwhelmed with grief at the news that she was for several hours incapable of action.

The arrival of the house agent was the first event that recalled her to her senses.

She aroused herself to action, and, assisted by Traverse, set to work to pack up her own and his wardrobe and other personal effects.

And the next morning Marah Rocke was re-established in her cottage.

And the next week, having equally divided their little capital, the mother and son parted—Traverse, by her express desire, keeping to his original plan, set out for the far West.

CHAPTER II
OLD HURRICANE STORMS

"At this sir knight flamed up with ire!
His great chest heaved! his eyes flashed fire.
The crimson that suffused his face
To deepest purple now gave place."

Who can describe the frenzy of Old Hurricane upon discovering the fraud that had been practised upon him by Black Donald?

It was told him the next morning in his tent, at his breakfast table, in the presence of his assembled family, by the Rev Mr. Goodwin.

Upon first hearing it, he was incapable of anything but blank staring, until it seemed as though his eyes must start from their sockets!

Then his passion, "not loud but deep," found utterance only in emphatic thumps of his walking stick upon the ground!

Then, as the huge emotion worked upward, it broke out in grunts, groans and inarticulate exclamations!

Finally it burst forth as follows:

"Ugh! ugh! ugh! Fool! dolt! blockhead! Brute that I've been! I wish somebody would punch my wooden head! I didn't think the demon himself could have deceived me so! Ugh! Nobody but the demon could have done it! and he is the demon! The very demon himself! He does not disguise—he transforms himself! Ugh! ugh! ugh! that I should have been such a donkey!"

"Sir, compose yourself! We are all liable to suffer deception," said Mr. Goodwin.

"Sir," broke forth Old Hurricane, in fury, "that wretch has eaten at my table! Has drunk wine with me!! Has slept in my bed!!! Ugh! ugh!! ugh!!!"

"Believing him to be what he seemed, sir, you extended to him the rights of hospitality; you have nothing to blame yourself with!"

"Demmy, sir, I did more than that! I've coddled him up with negusses! I've pampered him up with possets and put him to sleep in my own bed! Yes, sir—and more! Look there at Mrs. Condiment, sir! The way in which she worshiped that villain was a sight to behold!" said Old Hurricane, jumping up and stamping around the tent in fury.

"Oh, Mr. Goodwin, sir, how could I help it when I thought he was such a precious saint?" whimpered the old lady.

"Yes, sir! when 'his reverence' would be tired with delivering a long-winded mid-day discourse, Mrs. Condiment, sir, would take him into her own tent—make him lie down on her own sacred cot, and set my niece to bathing his head with cologne and her maid to fanning him, while she herself prepared an iced sherry cobbler for his reverence! Aren't you ashamed of yourself, Mrs. Condiment, mum!" said Old Hurricane, suddenly stopping before the poor old woman, in angry scorn.

"Indeed, I'm sure if I'd known it was Black Donald, I'd no more have suffered him inside of my tent than I would Satan!"

"Demmy, mum, you had Satan there as well! Who but Satan could have tempted you all to disregard me, your lawful lord and master, as you every one of you did for that wretch's sake! Hang it, parson, I wasn't the master of my own house, nor head of my own family! Precious Father Gray was! Black Donald was! Oh, you shall hear!" cried Old Hurricane, in a frenzy.

"Pray, sir, be patient and do not blame the women for being no wiser than you were yourself," said Mr. Goodwin.

"Tah! tah! tah! One act of folly is a contingency to which any man may for once in his life be liable; but folly is the women's normal condition! You shall hear! You shall hear! Hang it, sir, everybody had to give way to Father Gray! Everything was for Father Gray! Precious Father Gray! Excellent Father Gray! Saintly Father Gray! It was Father Gray here and Father Gray there, and Father Gray everywhere and always! He ate with us all day and slept with us all night! The coolest cot in the dryest nook of the tent at night—the shadiest seat at the table by day—were always for his reverence! The nicest tit-bits of the choicest dishes—the middle slices of the fish, the breast of the young ducks, and the wings of the chickens, the mealiest potatoes, the juiciest tomatoes, the tenderest roasting ear, the most delicate custard, and freshest fruit always for his reverence! I had to put up with the necks of poultry, and the tails of fishes, watery potatoes, specked apples and scorched custards—and if I dared to touch anything better before his precious reverence had eaten and was filled, Mrs. Condiment there—would look as sour as if she had bitten an unripe lemon—and Cap would tread on my gouty toe! Mrs. Condiment, mum, I don't know how you can look me in the face!" said Old Hurricane, savagely. A very unnecessary reproach, since poor Mrs. Condiment had not ventured to look any one in the face since the discovery of the fraud of which she, as well as others, had been an innocent victim.

"Come, come, my dear major, there is no harm done to you or your family; therefore, take patience!" said Mr. Goodwin.

"Demmy, sir, I beg you pardon, parson, I won't take patience! You don't know! Hang it, man, at last they got me to give up one-half of my own blessed bed to his precious reverence—the best half which the fellow always took right out of the middle, leaving me to sleep on both sides of him, if I could! Think of it—me, Ira Warfield—sleeping between the sheets— night after night—with Black Donald! Ugh! ugh! ugh! Oh, for some lethean draught that I might drink and forget! Sir, I won't be patient! Patience would be a sin! Mrs. Condiment, mum, I desire that you will send in your account and supply yourself with a new situation! You and I cannot agree any longer. You'll be putting me to bed with Beelzebub next!" exclaimed Old Hurricane, besides himself with indignation.

Mrs. Condiment sighed and wiped her eyes under her spectacles.

The worthy minister, now seriously alarmed, came to him and said:

"My dear, dear major, do not be unjust—consider. She is an old faithful domestic, who has been in your service forty years—whom you could not live without! I say it under advisement—whom you could not live without!"

"Hang it, sir, nor live with! Think of her helping to free the prisoners! Actually taking Black Donald—precious Father Gray!—into their cell and leaving them together to hatch their—beg you pardon—horrid plots!"

"But, sir, instead of punishing the innocent victim of his deception, let us be merciful and thank the Lord, that since those men were delivered from prison, they were freed without bloodshed; for remember that neither the warden nor any of his men, nor any one else has been personally injured."

"Hang it, sir, I wish they had cut all our throats to teach us more discretion!" broke forth Old Hurricane.

"I am afraid that the lesson so taught would have come too late to be useful!" smiled the pastor.

"Well, it hasn't come too late now! Mrs. Condiment, mum, mind what I tell you! As soon as we return to Hurricane Hall, send in your accounts and seek a new home! I am not going to suffer myself to be set at naught any longer!" exclaimed Old Hurricane, bringing down his cane with an emphatic thump.

The sorely troubled minister was again about to interfere, when, as the worm if trodden upon, will turn, Mrs. Condiment herself spoke up, saying:

"Lor, Major Warfield, sir, there were others deceived besides me, and as for myself, I never can think of the risk I've run without growing cold all over!"

"Serves you right, mum, for your officiousness, and obsequiousness and toadying to—precious Mr. Gray!—serves you doubly right for famishing me at my own table!"

"Uncle!" said Capitola, "'Honor bright! Fair play is a jewel! If you and I, who have seen Black Donald before, failed to recognize that stalwart athlete in a seemingly old and sickly man, how could you expect Mrs. Condiment to do so, who never saw him but once in her life, and then was so much frightened that she instantly fainted?"

"Pah! pah! pah! Cap, hush! You, all of you, disgust me, except Black Donald! I begin to respect him! Confound if I don't take in all the offers I have made for his apprehension, and at the very next convention of our party I'll nominate him to represent us in the National Congress; for, of all the fools that ever I have met in my life, the people of this county are the greatest! And fools should at least be represented by one clever man—and Black Donald is the very fellow! He is decidedly the ablest man in this congressional district."

"Except yourself, dear uncle!" said Capitola.

"Except nobody, Miss Impudence!—least of all me! The experience of the last week has convinced me that I ought to have a cap and bells awarded me by public acclamation!" said Old Hurricane, stamping about in fury.

The good minister finding that he could make no sort of impression upon the irate old man, soon took his leave, telling Mrs. Condiment that if he could be of any service to her in her trouble she must be sure to let him know.

At this Capitola and Mrs. Condiment exchanged looks, and the old lady, thanking him for his kindness, said that if it should become necessary, she should gratefully avail herself of it.

That day the camp meeting broke up.

Major Warfield struck tents and with his family and baggage returned to Hurricane Hall.

On their arrival, each member of the party went about his or her own particular business.

Capitola hurried to her own room to take off her bonnet and shawl. Pitapat, before attending her young mistress, lingered below to astonish the housemaids with accounts of "Brack Donel, dress up like an ole parson, an' 'ceiving everybody, even ole Marse!"

Mrs. Condiment went to her store room to inspect the condition of her newly put up preserves and pickles, lest any of them should have "worked" during her absence.

And Old Hurricane, attended by Wool, walked down to his kennels and his stables to look after the well-being of his favorite hounds and horses. It was while going through this interesting investigation that Major Warfield was informed—principally by overhearing the gossip of the grooms with Wool—of the appearance of a new inmate of the Hidden House—a young girl, who, according to their description, must have been the very pearl of beauty.

Old Hurricane pricked up his ears! Anything relating to the "Hidden House" possessed immense interest for him.

"Who is she, John?" he inquired of the groom.

"Deed I dunno, sir, only they say she's a bootiful young creature, fair as any lily, and dressed in deep mourning."

"Humph! humph! humph! another victim! Ten thousand chances to one, another victim! who told you this, John?"

"Why, Marse, you see Tom Griffith, the Rev. Mr. Goodwill's man, he's very thick long of Davy Hughs, Colonel Le Noir's coachman. And Davy he told Tom how one day last month his marse ordered the carriage, and went two or three days' journey up the country beyant Staunton, there he stayed a week and then came home, fetching along with him in the carriage this lovely young lady, who was dressed in the deepest mourning, and wept all the way. They 'spects how she's an orphan, and has lost all her friends, by the way she takes on."

"Another victim! My life on it—another victim! Poor child! She had better be dead than in the power of that atrocious villain and consummate hypocrite!" said Old Hurricane, passing on to the examination of his favorite horses, one of which, the swiftest in the stud, he found galled on the shoulders. Whereupon he flew into a towering passion, abusing his unfortunate groom by every opprobrious epithet blind fury could suggest, ordering him, as he valued whole bones, to vacate the stable instantly, and never dare to set foot on his premises again as he valued his life, an order which the man meekly accepted and immediately disobeyed, muttered to himself:

"Humph! If we took ole marse at his word, there'd never be man or 'oman left on the 'state," knowing full well that his tempestuous old master would probably forget all about it, as soon as he got comfortably seated at the supper table of Hurricane Hall, toward which the old man now trotted off.

Not a word did Major Warfield say at supper in regard to the new inmate of the Hidden House, for he had particular reasons for keeping Cap in ignorance of a neighbor, lest she should insist upon exchanging visits and being "sociable."

But it was destined that Capitola should not remain a day in ignorance of the interesting fact.

That night, when she retired to her chamber, Pitapat lingered behind, but presently appeared at her young mistress's room door with a large waiter on her head, laden with meat, pastry, jelly and fruit, which she brought in and placed upon the work stand.

"Why, what on the face of earth do you mean by bringing all that load of victuals into my room to-night? Do you think I am an ostrich or a cormorant, or that I am going to entertain a party of friends?" asked Capitola, in astonishment, turning from the wash stand, where she stood bathing her face.

"'Deed I dunno, Miss, whedder you'se an ostrizant or not, but I knows I don't 'tend for to be 'bused any more 'bout wittels, arter findin' out how cross empty people can be! Dar dey is! You can eat um or leab um alone, Miss Caterpillar!" said little Pitapat, firmly.

Capitola laughed, "Patty" she said, "you are worthy to be called my waiting maid!"

"And Lors knows, Miss Caterpillar, if it was de wittels you was a-frettin' arter, you ought to a-told me before! Lors knows dere's wittels enough!"

"Yes, I'm much obliged to you, Patty, but now I am not hungry, and I do not like the smell of food in my bedroom, so take the waiter out and set it on the passage table until morning."

Patty obeyed, and came back smiling and saying:

"Miss Caterpillar, has you hern de news?"

"What news, Pat?"

"How us has got a new neighbor—a bootiful young gal—as bootiful as a picter in a gilt-edged Christmas book—wid a snowy skin, and sky-blue eyes and glistenin' goldy hair, like the princess you was a readin' me about, all in deep mournin' and a weepin' and a weepin' all alone down there in that wicked, lonesome, onlawful ole haunted place, the Hidden House, along of old Colonel Le Noir and old Dorkey Knight, and the ghost as draws people's curtains of a night, just for all de worl' like dat same princess in de ogre's castle!"

"What on earth is all this rigmarole about? Are you dreaming or romancing?"

"I'm a-telling on you de bressed trufe! Dere's a young lady a-livin' at de Hidden House!"

"Eh? Is that really true, Patty?"

"True as preaching, miss."

"Then, I am very glad of it! I shall certainly ride over and call on the stranger," said Capitola, gaily.

"Oh, Miss Cap! Oh, miss, don't you do no sich thing! Ole Marse kill me! I heerd him t'reaten all de men and maids how if dey telled you anything 'bout de new neighbor, how he'd skin dem alive!"

"Won't he skin you?" asked Cap.

"No, miss, not 'less you 'form ag'in me, 'case he 'didn't tell me not to tell you, 'case you see he didn't think how I knowed! But, leastways, I know from what I heard, ole marse wouldn't have you to know nothin' about it, no, not for de whole worl'."

"He does not want me to call at the Hidden House! That's it! Now why doesn't he wish me to call there? I shall have to go in order to find out, and so I will," thought Cap.

CHAPTER III
CAP'S VISIT TO THE HIDDEN HOUSE

And such a night "she" took the road in
As ne'er poor sinner was abroad in.
The wind blew as 'twad blawn its last
The rattling showers rose on the blast;
The speedy gleams the darkness swallowed
Loud, deep and long the thunder bellowed;
That night a child might understand
The de'il had business on his hand.

—BURNS.

A week passed before Capitola carried her resolution of calling upon the inmate of the Hidden House into effect. It was in fact a hot, dry, oppressive season, the last few days of August, when all people, even the restless Capitola, preferred the coolness and repose of indoors. But that she should stay at home more than a week was a moral and physical impossibility. So on Thursday afternoon, when Major Warfield set out on horseback to visit his mill, Capitola ordered her horse saddled and brought up that she might take an afternoon's ride.

"Now please, my dear child, don't go far," said Mrs. Condiment, "for besides that your uncle does not approve of your riding alone, you must hurry back to avoid the storm."

"Storm, Mrs. Condiment, why bless your dear old heart, there has not been a storm these four weeks!" said Capitola, almost indignant that such an absurd objection to a long ride should be raised.

"The more reason, my child, that we should have a very severe one when it does come, and I think it will be upon us before sunset; so I advise you to hurry home."

"Why, Mrs. Condiment, there's not a cloud in the sky."

"So much the worse, my dear! The blackest cloud that ever gathered is not so ominous of mischief as this dull, coppery sky and still atmosphere! And if forty years' observation of weather signs goes for anything, I tell you that we are going to have the awfulest storm that ever gathered in the heavens! Why, look out of that window—the very birds and beasts know it, and instinctively seek shelter—look at that flock of crows flying home! See how the dumb beasts come trooping toward their sheds! Capitola, you had better give up going altogether, my dear!"

"There! I thought all this talk tended to keeping me within doors, but I can't stay, Mrs. Condiment! Good Mrs. Condiment, I can't!"

"But, my dear, if you should be caught out in the storm!"

"Why, I don't know but I should like it! What harm could it do? I'm not soluble in water—rain won't melt me away! I think upon the whole I rather prefer being caught in the storm," said Cap, perversely.

"Well, well, there is no need of that! You may ride as far as the river's bank and back again in time to escape, if you choose!" said Mrs. Condiment, who saw that her troublesome charge was bent upon the frolic.

And Cap, seeing her horse approach, led by one of the grooms, ran up-stairs, donned her riding habit, hat and gloves, ran down again, sprang into her saddle and was off, galloping away toward the river before Mrs. Condiment could add another word of warning.

She had been gone about an hour, when the sky suddenly darkened, the wind rose and the thunder rolled in prelude to the storm.

Major Warfield came skurrying home from the mill, grasping his bridle with one hand and holding his hat on with the other.

Meeting poor old Ezy in the shrubbery, he stormed out upon him with:

"What are you lounging there for, you old idiot! You old sky-gazing lunatic! Don't you see that we are going to have an awful blow! Begone with you and see that the cattle are all under shelter! Off, I say, or," he rode toward Bill Ezy, but the old man, exclaiming:

"Yes, sir—yes, sir! In coorse, sir!" ducked his head and ran off in good time.

Major Warfield quickened his horse's steps and rode to the house, dismounted and threw the reins to the stable boy, exclaiming:

"My beast is dripping with perspiration—rub him down well you knave, or I'll impale you!"

Striding into the hall, he threw down his riding whip, pulled off his gloves and called:

"Wool! Wool, you scoundrel, close every door and window in the house! Call all the servants together in the dining-room; we're going to have one of the worst tempests that ever raised!"

Wool flew to do his bidding.

"Mrs. Condiment, mum," said the old man, striding into the sitting-room, "Mrs. Condiment, mum, tell Miss Black to come down from her room until the storm is over; the upper chambers of this old house are not safe in a tempest. Well, mum, why don't you go, or send Pitapat?"

"Major Warfield, sir, I'm very sorry, but Miss Black has not come in yet," said Mrs. Condiment, who for the last half hour had suffered extreme anxiety upon account of Capitola.

"Not come in yet! Demmy, mum! Do you tell me she has gone out?" cried Old Hurricane, in a voice of thunder, gathering his brows into a dark frown, and striking his cane angrily upon the floor.

"Yes, sir, I am sorry to say she rode out about an hour ago and has not returned," said Mrs. Condiment, summoning all her firmness to meet Old Hurricane's "roused wrath."

"Ma'am! You venture to stand there before my face and tell me composedly that you permitted Miss Black to go off alone in the face of such a storm as this?" roared Old Hurricane.

"Sir, I could not help it!" said the old lady.

"Demmy, mum! You should have helped it! A woman of your age to stand there and tell me that she could not prevent a young creature like Capitola from going out alone in the storm!"

"Major Warfield, could you have done it?"

"Me? Demmy, I should think so; but that is not the question! You—"

He was interrupted by a blinding flash of lightning, followed immediately by an awful peal of thunder and a sudden fall of rain.

Old Hurricane sprang up as though he had been shot off his chair and trotted up and down the floor exclaiming:

"And she—she out in all this storm! Mrs. Condiment, mum, you deserve to be ducked! Yes, mum, you do! Wool! Wool! you diabolical villain!"

"Yes, marse, yes, sir, here I is!" exclaimed that officer, in trepidation, as he appeared in the doorway. "De windows and doors, sir, is all fastened close and de maids are all in the dining-room as you ordered, and—"

"Hang the maids and the doors and windows, too! Who the demon cares about them? How dared you, you knave, permit your young mistress to ride, unattended, in the face of such a storm, too! Why didn't you go with her, sir?"

"'Deed, marse—"

"Don't ''deed marse' me you atrocious villain! Saddle a horse quickly, inquire which road your mistress took and follow and attend her home safely—after which I intend to break every bone in your skin, sirrah! So—"

Again he was interrupted by a dazzling flash of lightning, accompanied by a deafening roll of thunder, and followed by a flood of rain.

Wool stood appalled at the prospect of turning out in such a storm upon such a fruitless errand.

"Oh, you may stare and roll up your eyes, but I mean it, you varlet! So be off with you! Go! I don't care if you should be drowned in the rain, or blown off the horse, or struck by lightning. I hope you may be; you knave, and I shall be rid of one villain! Off, you varlet, or—" Old Hurricane lifted a bronze statuette to hurl at Wool's delinquent head, but that functionary dodged and ran out in time to escape a blow that might have put a period to his mortal career.

But let no one suppose that honest Wool took the road that night! He simply ran down-stairs and hid himself comfortably in the lowest regions of the house, there to tarry until the storms, social and atmospheric, should be over.

Meanwhile the night deepened, the storm raged without and Old Hurricane raged within!

The lightning flashed, blaze upon blaze, with blinding glare! The thunder broke, crash upon crash, with deafening roar! The wind gathering all its force cannonaded the old walls as though it would batter down the house! The rain fell in floods! In the midst of all the Demon's Run, swollen to a torrent, was heard like the voice of a "roaring lion, seeking whom he might devour!"

Old Hurricane strode up and down the floor, groaning, swearing, threatening, and at every fresh blast of the storm without, breaking forth into fury!

Mrs. Condiment sat crouched in a corner, praying fervently every time the lightning blazed into the room, longing to go and join the men and maids in the next apartment, yet fearful to stir from her seat lest she should attract Old Hurricane's attention, and draw down upon herself the more terrible thunder and lightning of his wrath. But to escape Old Hurricane's violence was not in the power of mortal man or woman. Soon her very stillness exasperated him and he broke forth upon her with:

"Mrs. Condiment, mum, I don't know how you can bear to sit there so quietly and listen to this storm, knowing that the poor child is exposed to it?"

"Major Warfield, would it do any good for me to jump up and trot up and down the floor and go on as you do, even supposing I had the strength?" inquired the meek old lady, thoroughly provoked at his injustice!

"I'd like to see you show a little more feeling! You are a perfect barbarian! Oh, Cap! my darling, where are you now? Heavens! what a blast was that! Enough to shake the house about our ears! I wish it would! blamed if I don't!"

"Oh, Major! Major! don't say such awful things, nor make such awful wishes!" said the appalled old lady—"you don't know what you might bring down upon us!"

"No, nor care! If the old house should tumble in, it would bury under its ruins a precious lot of good-for-nothing people, unfit to live! Heavens! what a flash of lightning! Oh, Cap, Cap, my darling, where are you in this storm? Mrs. Condiment, mum! if any harm comes to Capitola this night, I'll have you indicted for manslaughter!"

"Major Warfield, if it is all on Miss Black's account that you are raving and raging so, I think it is quite vain of you! for any young woman caught out in a storm would know enough to get into shelter; especially would Miss Black, who is a young lady of great courage and presence of mind, as we know. She has surely gone into some house, to remain until the storm is over," said Mrs. Condiment, soothingly.

This speech, so well intended, exasperated Old Hurricane more than all the rest; stopping and striking his cane upon the floor, he roared forth:

"Hang it, mum! hold your foolish old tongue! You know nothing about it! Capitola is exposed to more serious dangers than the elements! Perils of all sorts surround her! She should never, rain or shine, go out alone! Oh, the little villain! the little wretch! the little demon! if ever I get her safe in this house again, won't I lock her up and keep her on bread and water until she learns to behave herself!"

Here again a blinding flash of lightning, a deafening peal of thunder, a terrific blast of wind and flood of rain suddenly arrested his speech.

"Oh, my Cap! my dear Cap! I needn't threaten you! I shall never have the chance to be cruel to you again—never! You'll perish in this terrible storm and then—and then my tough old heart will break! It will—it will, Cap! But demmy, before it does, I'll break the necks of every man and woman, in this house, old and young! Hear it, heaven and earth, for I'll do it!"

All things must have an end. So, as the hours passed on, the storm having spent all its fury, gradually grumbled itself into silence.

Old Hurricane also raged himself into a state of exhaustion so complete that when the midnight hour struck he could only drop into a chair and murmur:

"Twelve o'clock and no news of her yet!"

And then unwillingly he went to bed, attended by Mrs. Condiment and Pitapat instead of Wool, who was supposed to be out in search of Capitola, but who was, in fact, fast asleep on the floor of a dry cellar.

Meanwhile, where did this midnight hour find Capitola?

CHAPTER IV
THE HIDDEN HOLLOW

On every side the aspect was the same,
    All ruined, desolate, forlorn and savage,
No hand or foot within the precinct came
    To rectify or ravage!
Here Echo never mocked the human tongue;
    Some weighty crime that Heaven could not pardon.
A secret curse on that old Building hung
    And its deserted garden!

—Hood's Haunted House.

Cap was a bit of a Don Quixote! The stirring incidents of the last few months had spoiled her; the monotony of the last few weeks had bored her; and now she had just rode out in quest of adventures.

The Old Hidden House, with its mysterious traditions, its gloomy surroundings and its haunted reputation, had always possessed a powerful attraction for one of Cap's adventurous spirit. To seek and gaze upon the somber house, of which, and of whose inmates, such terrible stories had been told or hinted, had always been a secret desire and purpose of Capitola.

And now the presence there of a beautiful girl near her own age was the one last item that tipped the balance, making the temptation to ride thither outweigh every other consideration of duty, prudence and safety. And having once started on the adventure, Cap felt the attraction drawing her toward the frightful hollow of the Hidden House growing stronger with every step taken thitherward.

She reached the banks of the "Demon's Run" and took the left-hand road down the stream until she reached the left point of the Horse-Shoe Mountain, and then going up around the point, she kept close under the back of the range until she had got immediately in the rear of the round bend of the "Horse Shoe," behind Hurricane Hall.

"Well," said Cap, as she drew rein here, and looked up at the lofty ascent of gray rocks that concealed Hurricane Hall, "to have had to come such a circuit around the outside of the 'Horse Shoe,' to find myself just at the back of our old house, and no farther from home than this! There's as many doubles and twists in these mountains as there are in a lawyer's discourse! There, Gyp, you needn't turn back again and pull at the bridle, to tell me that there is a storm coming up and that you want to go home! I have no more respect for your opinion than I have for Mrs. Condiment's. Besides, you carry a damsel-errant in quest of adventures, Gyp, and so you must on, Gyp—you must on!" said Capitola, forcibly pulling her horse's head around, and then taking a survey of the downward path.

It was a scene fascinating from its very excess of gloom and terror!

It was a valley so deep and dark as to merit the name of the hollow, or hole, but for its great extent and its thick growth of forest, through which spectral-looking rocks gleamed, and moaning waters could be heard but not seen.

"Now, somewhere in that thick forest, in the bottom of that vale, stands the house—well called the Hidden House, since not a chimney of it can be seen even from this commanding height! But I suppose this path that leads down into the valley may conduct me to the building! Come along, Gyp! You needn't turn up your head and pull at the bit! You've got to go! I am bound this night to see the outside of the Hidden House, and the window of the haunted chamber at the very least!" said Cap, throwing her eyes up defiantly toward the darkening sky, and putting whip to her unwilling horse.

As the path wound down into the valley the woods were found deeper, thicker and darker. It occupied all Cap's faculties to push her way through the overhanging and interlacing branches of the trees.

"Good gracious," she said, as she used her left arm rather vigorously to push aside the obstructions to her path, "one would think this were the enchanted forest containing the castle of the sleeping beauty, and I was the knight destined to deliver her! I'm sure it wouldn't have been more difficult."

Still deeper fell the path, thicker grew the forest and darker the way.

"Gyp, I'm under the impression that we shall have to turn back yet!" said Cap, dolefully stopping in the midst of a thicket so dense that it completely blockaded her farther progress in the same direction. Just as she came to this very disagreeable conclusion she spied an opening on her left, from which a bridle-path struck out. With an exclamation of joy she immediately turned her horse's head and struck into it. This path was very rocky, but in some degree clearer than the other, and she went on quickly, singing to herself, until gradually her voice began to be lost in the sound of many rushing waters.

"It must be the Devil's Punch Bowl! I am approaching!" she said to herself, as she went on.

She was right. The roaring of the waters grew deafening and the path became so rugged with jagged and irregularly piled rocks, that Cap could scarcely keep her horse upon his feet in climbing over them. And suddenly, when she least looked for it, the great natural curiosity—the Devil's Punch Bowl—burst upon her view!

It was an awful abyss, scooped out as it were from the very bowels of the earth, with its steep sides rent open in dreadful chasms, and far down in its fearful depths a boiling whirlpool of black waters.

Urging her reluctant steed through a thicket of stunted thorns and over a chaos of shattered rocks, Capitola approached as near as she safely could to the brink of this awful pit. So absorbed was she in gazing upon this terrible phenomenon of natural scenery that she had not noticed, in the thicket on her right, a low hut that, with its brown-green moldering colors, fell so naturally in with the hue of the surrounding scenery as easily to escape observation. She did not even observe that the sky was entirely overcast, and the thunder was muttering in the distance. She was aroused from her profound reverie by a voice near her asking:

"Who are you, that dares to come without a guide to the Devil's Punch Bowl?"

Capitola looked around and came nearer screaming than she ever had been in her life, upon seeing the apparition that stood before her. Was it man, woman, beast or demon? She could not tell! It was a very tall, spare form, with a black cloth petticoat tied around the waist, a blue coat buttoned over the breast, and a black felt hat tied down with a red handkerchief, shading the darkest old face she had ever seen in her life.

"Who are you, I say, who comes to the Devil's Punch Bowl without leave or license?" repeated the frightful creature, shifting her cane from one hand to the other.

"I? I am Capitola Black, from Hurricane Hall; but who, in the name of all the fates and furies, are you?" inquired Capitola, who, in getting over the shock, had recovered her courage.

"I am Harriet the Seeress of Hidden Hollow!" replied the apparition, in a melodramatic manner that would not have discredited the queen of tragedy herself. "You have heard of me?"

"Yes, but I always heard you called Old Hat, the Witch," said Cap.

"The world is profane—give me your hand!" said the beldame, reaching out her own to take that of Capitola.

"Stop! Is your hand clean? It looks very black!"

"Cleaner than yours will be when it is stained with blood, young maiden!"

"Tut! If you insist on telling my fortune, tell me a pleasant one, and I will pay you double," laughed Capitola.

"The fates are not to be mocked. Your destiny will be that which the stars decree. To prove to you that I know this, I tell you that you are not what you have been!"

"You've hit it this time, old lady, for I was a baby once and now I am a young girl!" said Cap, laughing.

"You will not continue to be that which you are now!" pursued the hag, still attentively reading the lines of her subject's hand.

"Right again; for if I live long enough I shall be an old woman."

"You bear a name that you will not bear long!"

"I think that quite a safe prophecy, as I haven't the most distant idea of being an old maid!"

"This little hand of yours—this dainty woman's hand—will be—red with blood!"

"Now, do you know, I don't doubt that either? I believe it altogether probable that I shall have to cook my husband's dinner and kill the chickens for his soup!"

"Girl, beware! You deride the holy stars—and already they are adverse to you!" said the hag, with a threatening glare.

"Ha, ha, ha! I love the beautiful stars but did not fear them I fear only Him who made the stars!"

"Poor butterfly, listen and beware! You are destined to imbrue that little hand in the life current of one who loves you the most of all on earth! You are destined to rise by the destruction of one who would shed his heart's best blood for you!" said the beldame, in an awful voice.

Capitola's eyes flashed! She advanced her horse a step or two nearer the witch and raised her riding whip, saying:

"I protest! If you were only a man I should lay this ash over your wicked shoulders until my arms ached! How dare you? Faith, I don't wonder that in the honest old times such pests as you were cooled in the ducking pond! Good gracious, that must have made a hissing and spluttering in the water, though!"

"Blasphemer, pay me and begone!"

"Pay you? I tell you I would if you were only a man; but it would be sinful to pay a wretched old witch in the only way you deserve to be paid!" said Cap, flourishing her riding whip before a creature tall enough and strong enough to have doubled up her slight form together and hurled it into the abyss.

"Gold! gold!" said the hag curtly, holding out black and talon-like fingers, which she worked convulsively.

"Gold! gold, indeed! for such a wicked fortune! Not a penny!" said Cap.

"Ho! you're stingy; you do not like to part with the yellow demon that has bought the souls of all your house!"

"Don't I? You shall see! There! If you want gold, go fish it from the depth of the whirlpool," said Cap, taking her purse and casting it over the precipice.

This exasperated the crone to frenzy.

"Away! Begone!" she cried, shaking her long arm at the girl. "Away! Begone! The fate pursues you! The badge of blood is stamped upon your palm!"

"Fee—faw—fum" said Cap.

"Scorner! Beware! The curse of the crimson hand is upon you!"

—"'I smell the blood of an Englishman'"—continued Cap.

"Derider of the fates, you are foredoomed to crime!"

—"'Be he alive or be he dead, I'll have his brains to butter my bread!'" concluded Cap.

"Be silent!" shrieked the beldame.

"I won't!" said Cap. "Because you see, if we are in for the horrible, I can beat you hollow at that!"

> "'Avaunt! and quit my sight!
> Let the earth hide thee!
> Thy bones are marrowless! Thy blood is cold!
> Thou hast no speculation in those eyes
> Which thou dost glare with?'"

"Begone! You're doomed! doomed! doomed!" shrieked the witch, retreating into her hut.

Cap laughed and stroked the neck of her horse, saying:

"Gyp, my son, that was old Nick's wife, who was with us just this instant, and now, indeed, Gyp, if we are to see the Hidden House this afternoon, we must get on!"

And so saying she followed the path that wound half-way around the Punch Bowl and then along the side of a little mountain torrent called the Spout, which, rising in an opposite mountain, leaped from rock to rock, with many a sinuous turn, as it wound through the thicket that immediately surrounded the Hidden House until it finally jetted through a subterranean channel into the Devil's Punch Bowl.

Capitola was now, unconsciously, upon the very spot, where, seventeen years before, the old nurse had been forcibly stopped and compelled to attend the unknown lady.

As Capitola pursued the path that wound lower and lower into the dark valley the gloom of the thicket deepened. Her thoughts ran on all the horrible traditions connected with the Hidden House and Hollow—the murder and robbery of the poor peddler—the mysterious assassination of Eugene Le Noir; the sudden disappearance of his youthful widow; the strange sights and sounds reported to be heard and seen about the mansion; the spectral light at the upper gable window; the white form seen flitting through the chamber; the pale lady that in the dead of night drew the curtains of a guest that once had slept there; and above all Capitola thought of the beautiful, strange girl, who was now an inmate of that sinful and accursed house! And while these thoughts absorbed her mind, suddenly, in a turning of the path, she came full upon the gloomy building.

CHAPTER V
THE HIDDEN HOUSE

The very stains and fractures on the wall
Assuming features solemn and terrific,
Hinted some tragedy of that old hall
Locked up in hieroglyphic!
Prophetic hints that filled the soul with dread;
But to one gloomy window pointing mostly,
The while some secret inspiration said,
That chamber is the ghostly!

—Hood.

The Hidden House was a large, irregular edifice of dark red sandstone with its walls covered closely with the clinging ivy, that had been clipped away only from a few of the doors and windows, and its roof over-shadowed by the top branches of gigantic oaks and elms that clustered around and nearly concealed the building.

It might have been a long-forsaken house, for any sign of human habitation that was to be seen about it. All was silent, solitary and gloomy.

As Capitola drew up her horse to gaze upon its somber walls she wondered which was the window at which the spectral light and ghostly face had been seen. She soon believed that she had found it.

At the highest point of the building, immediately under the sharp angle of the roof, in the gable and nearest to view, was a solitary window. The ivy that clung tightly to the stone, covering every portion of the wall at this end, was clipped away from that high placed, dark and lonely window by which Capitola's eyes were strangely fascinated.

While thus she gazed in wonder, interest and curiosity, though without the least degree of superstitious dread, a vision flashed upon her sight that sent the blood from her ruddy cheek to her brave heart, and shook the foundations of her unbelief!

For while she gazed, suddenly that dark window was illumed by a strange, unearthly light that streamed forth into the gloomy evening air, and touched with blue flame the quivering leaves of every tree in its brilliant line! In the midst of this lighted window appeared a white female face wild with woe! And then the face suddenly vanished and the light was swallowed up in darkness!

Capitola remained transfixed!

"Great heavens!" she thought, "can these things really be! Have the ghostly traditions of this world truth in them at last? When I heard this story of the haunted window I thought some one had surely imagined or invented it! Now I have seen for myself; but if I were to tell what I have seen not one in a hundred would believe me!"

While these startling thoughts disturbed her usual well-balanced mind, a vivid flash of lightning, accompanied by a tremendous peal of thunder and a heavy fall of rain, roused her into renewed activity.

"Gyp, my boy, the storm is upon us sure enough! We shall catch it all around, get well drowned, beaten and buffeted here and well abused when we get home! Meantime, Gyp, which is the worst, the full fury of the tempest or the mysterious terrors of the Haunted House!"

Another blinding flash of lightning, a stunning crash of thunder, a flood of rain and tornado of wind decided her.

"We'll take the Haunted House, Gyp, my friend! That spectral lady of the lighted window looked rather in sorrow than in anger, and who knows but the ghosts may be hospitable? So gee up, Dobbin!" said Capitola, and, urging her horse with one hand and holding on her cap with the other, she went on against wind and rain until she reached the front of the old house.

Not a creature was to be seen; every door and window was closely shut. Dismounting, Capitola led her horse under the shelter of a thickly leaved oak tree, secured him, and then holding up her saturated skirt with one hand and holding on her cap with the other, she went up some moldering stone steps to an old stone portico and, seizing the heavy iron knocker of a great black oak double door, she knocked loudly enough to awaken all the mountain echoes.

She waited a few minutes for an answer, but receiving none, she knocked again, more loudly than before. Still there was no reply. And growing impatient, she seized the knocker with both hands and exerting all her strength, made the welkin ring again!

This brought a response. The door was unlocked and angrily jerked open by a short, squarely formed, beetle-browed, stern-looking woman, clothed in a black stuff gown and having a stiff muslin cap upon her head.

"Who are you? What do you want here?" harshly demanded this woman, whom Capitola instinctively recognized as Dorky Knight, the morose housekeeper of the Hidden House.

"Who am I? What do I want? Old Nick fly away with you! It's plain enough to be seen who I am and what I want. I am a young woman caught out in the storm and I want shelter!" said Cap, indignantly. And her words were endorsed by a terrific burst of the tempest in lightning, thunder, wind and rain!

"Come in then and when you ask favors learn to keep a civil tongue in your head!" said the woman sternly, taking the guest by the hand and pulling her in and shutting and locking the door.

"Favors! Plague on you for a bearess! I asked no favor! Every storm-beaten traveler has a right to shelter under the first roof that offers, and none but a curmudgeon would think of calling it a favor! And as for keeping a civil tongue in my head, I'll do it when you set me the example!" said Cap.

"Who are you?" again demanded the woman.

"Oh, I see you are no Arabian in your notions of hospitality! Those pagans entertain a guest without asking him a single question; and though he were their bitterest foe, they consider him while he rests beneath their tent sacred from intrusion."

"That's because they were pagans!" said Dorky. "But as I am a Christian, I'd thank you to let me know who it is that I have received under this roof."

"My name," said our heroine, impatiently, "is Capitola Black! I live with my uncle, Major Warfield, at Hurricane Hall! And now, I should thank your ladyship to send some one to put away my horse, while you yourself accommodate me with dry clothes."

While our saucy little heroine spoke the whole aspect of the dark-browed woman changed.

"Capitola-Capitola," she muttered, gazing earnestly upon the face of the unwelcome guest.

"Yes, Capitola! That is my name! You never heard anything against it, did you?"

For all answer the woman seized her hand, and while the lightning flashed and the thunder rolled, and the wind and rain beat down, she drew her the whole length of the hall before a back window that overlooked the neglected garden, and, regardless of the electric fluid that incessantly blazed upon them, she held her there and scrutinized her features.

"Well, I like this! Upon my word, I do!" said Cap, composedly.

Without replying, the strange woman seized her right hand, forcibly opened it, gazed upon the palm and then, flinging it back with a shudder, exclaimed:

"Capitola, what brought you under this roof? Away! Begone! Mount your horse and fly while there is yet time!"

"What! expose myself again to the storm? I won't, and that's flat!" said Cap.

"Girl! girl! there are worse dangers in the world than any to be feared from thunder, lightning, rain or wind!"

"Very well, then, when I meet them it will be time enough to deal with them! Meanwhile the stormy night and my soaked clothing are very palpable evils, and as I see no good end to be gained by my longer enduring them, I will just beg you to stop soothsaying—(as I have had enough of that from another old witch)—and be as good as to permit me to change my clothes!"

"It is madness! You shall not stay here!" cried the woman, in a harsh voice.

"And I tell you I will! You are not the head of the family, and I do not intend to be turned out by you!"

While she spoke a servant crossed the hall and the woman, whisking Capitola around until her back was turned and her face concealed, went to speak to the newcomer.

"When will your master be here?" Capitola heard her inquire.

"Not to-night; he saw the storm rising and did not wish to expose himself. He sent me on to say that he would not be here until morning. I was caught, as you see! I am dripping wet," replied the man.

"Go, change your clothes at once then, Davy,"

"Who is that stranger?" asked the man, pointing to Capitola.

"Some young woman of the neighborhood, who has been caught out in the tempest. But you had better go and change your clothes than to stand here gossiping," said the woman, harshly.

"I say," said the man, "the young woman is a God-send to Miss Clara; nobody has been to see her yet; nobody ever visits this house unless they are driven to it. I don't wonder the colonel and our young master pass as much as ten months in the year away from home, spending all the summer at the watering places, and all the winter in New York or Washington!"

"Hold your tongue! What right have you to complain? You always attend them in their travels!"

"True, but you see for this last season they have both been staying here, old master to watch the heiress, young master to court her, and as I have no interest in that game, I find the time hangs heavy on my hands," complained the man.

"It will hang heavier if you take a long fit of illness by standing in wet clothes," muttered the woman.

"Why, so 'twill, missus! So here goes," assented the man, hurrying across the hall and passing out through the door opposite that by which he entered.

Dorcas returned to her guest.

Eying her closely for a while, she at length inquired:

"Capitola, how long have you lived at Hurricane Hall?"

"So long," replied Cap, "that you must have heard of me! I, at least, have often heard of Mother Dorkey Knight."

"And heard no good of her!"

"Well, no—to be candid with you, I never did," said Cap.

"And much harm of her?" continued the woman, keeping her stern black eyes fixed upon those of her guest.

"Well, yes—since you ask me, I have heard pretty considerable harm!" answered Cap, nothing daunted.

"Where did you live before you came to Hurricane Hall?" asked Dorcas.

"Where I learned to fear God, to speak the truth and to shame the devil!" replied Cap.

—"And to force yourself into people's houses against their will!"

"There you are again! I tell you that when I learn from the head of this household that I am unwelcome, then I will retreat, and not until then! And now I demand to be presented to the master."

"To Colonel Le Noir?"

"Yes."

"I cannot curse you with the 'curse of a granted prayer! Colonel Le Noir is away."

"Why do you talk so strangely?" inquired Capitola.

"It is my whim. Perhaps my head is light."

"I should think it was, excessively so! Well—as the master of the house is away, be good enough to present me to the mistress?"

"What mistress? There is no mistress here!" replied Dorcas, looking around in strange trepidation.

"I mean the young lady, Colonel Le Noir's ward. In lieu of any other lady, she, I suppose, may be considered the mistress of the house!"

"Humph! Well, young girl, as you are fully resolved to stand your ground. I suppose there is nothing to do but to put up with you!" said Dorcas.

"And put up my horse," added Cap.

"He shall be taken care of! But mind, you must depart early in the morning!" said Dorcas, sternly.

"Once more, and for the last, Mother Cerberus, I assure you I do not acknowledge your authority to dismiss me!" retorted Capitola. "So show me to the presence of your mistress!"

"Perverse, like all the rest! Follow me!" said the house keeper, leading the way from the hall toward a back parlor.

CHAPTER VI
THE INMATE OF THE HIDDEN HOUSE

There is a light around her brow,
A holiness in those dark eyes,
That show, though wandering earthward now,
Her spirit's home is in the skies.

—MOORE.

Pushing open the door, Dorcas Knight exclaimed:

"Here is a young lady, Miss Black, from Hurricane Hall, come to see you, Miss Day."

And having made this announcement, the woman retired and shut the door behind her.

And Capitola found herself in a large, dark, gloomy, wainscoted room, whose tall, narrow windows afforded but little light, and whose immense fireplace and blackened furniture seemed to belong to a past century.

The only occupant of this somber apartment was a young girl, seated in pensive thought beside the central table. She was clothed in deep mourning, which only served to throw into fairer relief the beauty of her pearly skin, golden hair and violet eyes.

The vision of her mourning robes and melancholy beauty so deeply impressed Capitola that, almost for the first time in her life, she hesitated from a feeling of diffidence, and said gently:

"Indeed, I fear that this is an unwarranted intrusion on my part, Miss Day."

"You are very welcome," replied the sweetest voice Capitola had ever heard, as the young girl arose and advanced to meet her. "But you have been exposed to the storm Please come into my room and change your clothes," continued the young hostess, as she took Cap's hand and led her into an adjoining room.

The storm was still raging, but these apartments being in the central portion of the strong old house, were but little exposed to the sight or sound of its fury.

There was a lamp burning upon the mantelpiece, by the light of which the young girl furnished her visitor with dry clothing and assisted her to change, saying as she did so:

"I think we are about the same size, and that my clothes will fit you; but I will not offer you mourning habiliments—you shall have this lilac silk."

"I am very sorry to see you in mourning," said Capitola, earnestly.

"It is for my father," replied Clara, very softly.

As they spoke the eyes of the two young girls met. They were both good physiognomists and intuitive judges, of character. Consequently in the full meeting of their eyes they read, understood and appreciated each other.

The pure, grave, and gentle expression of Clara's countenance touched the heart of Capitola.

The bright, frank, honest face of Cap recommended her to Clara.

The very opposite traits of their equally truthful characters attracted them to each other.

Clara conducted her guest back into the wainscoted parlor, where a cheerful fire had been kindled to correct the dampness of the air. And here they sat down unmindful of the storm that came much subdued through the thickness of the walls. And, as young creatures, however tried and sorrowful, will do, they entered into a friendly chat. And before an hour had passed Capitola thought herself well repaid for her sufferings from the storm and the rebuff, in having formed the acquaintance of Clara Day.

She resolved, let Old Hurricane rage as he might, henceforth she would be a frequent visitor to the Hidden House.

And Clara, for her part, felt that in Capitola she had found a frank, spirited, faithful neighbor who might become an estimable friend.

While they were thus growing into each other's favor, the door opened and admitted a gentleman of tall and thin figure and white and emaciated face, shaded by a luxuriant growth of glossy black hair and beard. He could not have been more than twenty-six, but, prematurely broken by vice, he seemed forty years of age. He advanced bowing toward the young women.

As Capitola's eyes fell upon this newcomer it required all her presence of mind and powers of self-control to prevent her from staring or otherwise betraying herself—for in this stranger she recognized the very man who had stopped her upon her night ride. She did, however, succeed in banishing from her face every expression of consciousness. And when Miss Day courteously presented him to her guest, saying merely, "My cousin, Mr. Craven Le Noir, Miss Black," Capitola arose and curtsied as composedly as if she had never set eyes upon his face before.

He on his part evidently remembered her, and sent one stealthy, been and scrutinizing glance into her face; but, finding that imperturbable, he bowed with stately politeness and seemed satisfied that she had not identified him as her assailant.

Craven Le Noir drew his chair to the fire, seated himself and entered into an easy conversation with Clara and her guest. Whenever he addressed Clara there was a deference and tenderness in his tone and glance that seemed very displeasing to the fair girl, who received all these delicate attentions with coldness and reserve. These things did not escape the notice of Capitola, who mentally concluded that Craven Le Noir was a lover of Clara Day, but a most unacceptable lover.

When supper was announced it was evidently hailed by Clara as a great relief. And after the meal was over she arose and excused herself to her cousin by saying that her guest, Miss Black, had been exposed to the storm and was doubtless very much fatigued and that she would show her to her chamber.

Then, taking a night lamp, she invited Capitola to come and conducted her to an old-fashioned upper chamber, where a cheerful fire was burning on the hearth. Here the young girls sat down before the fire and improved their acquaintance by an hour's conversation. After which Clara arose, and saying, "I sleep immediately below your room, Miss Black; if you should want anything rap on the floor and I shall hear you and get up," she wished her guest a good night's rest and retired from the room.

Cap was disinclined to sleep; a strange superstitious feeling which she could neither understand nor throw off had fallen upon her spirits.

She took the night lamp in her hand and got up to examine her chamber. It was a large, dark, oak-paneled room, with a dark carpet on the floor and dark-green curtains on the windows and the bedstead. Over the mantelpiece hung the portrait of a most beautiful black-haired and black-eyed girl of about fourteen years of age, but upon whose infantile brow fell the shadow of some fearful woe. There was something awful in the despair "on that face so young" that bound the gazer in an irresistible and most painful spell. And Capitola remained standing before it transfixed, until the striking of the hall clock aroused her from her enchantment. Wondering who the young creature could have been, what had been her history and, above all, what had been the nature of that fearful woe that darkened like a curse her angel brow, Capitola turned almost sorrowfully away and began to prepare for bed.

She undressed, put on the delicate nightclothes Clara had provided for her use, said her evening prayers, looked under the bed—a precaution taken ever since the night upon which she had discovered the burglars—and, finding all right, she blew out her candle and lay down. She could not sleep—many persons of nervous or mercurial temperaments cannot do so the first night in a strange bed. Cap was very mercurial, and the bed and room in which she lay were very strange; for the first time since she had had a home to call her own she was unexpectedly staying all night away from her friends, and without their having any knowledge of her whereabouts. She was conjecturing, half in fear and half in fun, how Old Hurricane was taking her escapade and what he would say to her in the morning. She was wondering to find herself in such an unforeseen position as that of a night guest in the mysterious Hidden House—wondering whether this was the guest chamber in which the ghost appeared to the officer and these were the very curtains that the pale lady drew at night. While her thoughts were thus running over the whole range of circumstances around her singular position, sleep overtook Capitola and speculation was lost in brighter visions.

How long she had slept and dreamed she did not know, when something gently awakened her. She opened her eyes calmly—to meet a vision that brave as she was, nearly froze the blood in her warm veins.

Her chamber was illumined with an intense blue flame that lighted up every portion of the apartment with a radiance bright as day, and in the midst of this effulgence moved a figure clothed in white—a beautiful, pale, spectral woman, whose large, motionless black eyes, deeply set in her death-like face, and whose long unbound black hair, fallen upon her white raiment, were the only marks of color about her marble form.

Paralyzed with wonder, Capitola watched this figure as it glided about the chamber. The apparition approached the dressing-table, seemed to take something thence, and then gliding toward the bed, to Capitola's inexpressible horror drew back the curtains and bent down and gazed upon her! Capitola had no power to scream, to move or to avert her gaze from those awful eyes that met her own, until at length, as the spectral head bent lower, she felt the pressure of a pair of icy lips upon her brow and closed her eyes!

When she opened them again the vision had departed and the room was dark and quiet.

There was no more sleep for Capitola. She heard the clock strike four, and was pleased to find that it was so near day. Still the time seemed very long to her, who lay there wondering, conjecturing and speculating on the strange adventure of the night.

When the sun arose she left her restless bed, bathed her excited head and proceeded to dress herself. When she had finished her toilet, with the exception of putting on her trinkets, she suddenly missed a ring that she prized more than she did all her possessions put together—it was a plain gold band, bearing the inscription Capitola-Eugene, and which she had been enjoined by her old nurse never to part from but with life. She had, in her days of destitution suffered the extremes of cold and hunger; had been upon the very brink of death from starvation or freezing, but without ever dreaming of sacrificing her ring. And now for the first time it was missing. While she was still looking anxiously for the lost jewel the door opened and Dorcas Knight entered the room, bearing on her arm Capitola's riding dress, which had been well dried and ironed.

"Miss Capitola, here is your habit; you had better put it on at once, as I have ordered breakfast an hour sooner than usual, so that you may have an early start."

"Upon my word, you are very anxious to get rid of me, but not more so than I am to depart," said Capitola, still pursuing her search.

"Your friends, who do not know where you are, must be very uneasy about you. But what are you looking for?"

"A ring, a plain gold circle, with my name and that of another inscribed on it, and which I would not lose for the world. I hung it on a pin in this pin-cushion last night before I went to bed. I would swear I did, and now it is missing," answered Cap, still pursuing her search.

"If you lost it in this room it will certainly be found," said Dorcas Knight putting down the habit and helping in the search.

"I am not so sure of that. There was some one in my room last night."

"Some one in your room!" exclaimed Dorcas in dismay.

"Yes; a dark-haired woman, all dressed in white!"

Dorcas Knight gave two or three angry grunts and then harshly exclaimed: "Nonsense! woman, indeed! there is no such woman about the house! There are no females here except Miss Day, myself and you—not even a waiting-maid or cook."

"Well," said Cap, "if it was not a woman it was a ghost; for I was wide awake, and I saw it with my own eyes!"

"Fudge! you've heard that foolish story of the haunted room, and you have dreamed the whole thing!"

"I tell you I didn't! I saw it! Don't I know?"

"I say you dreamed it! There is no such living woman here; and as for a ghost, that is all folly. And I must beg, Miss Black, that you will not distress Miss Day by telling her this strange dream of yours. She has never heard the ridiculous story of the haunted room, and, as she lives here in solitude, I would not like her to hear of it."

"Oh, I will say nothing to disquiet Miss Day; but it was no dream. It was real, if there is any reality in this world."

There was no more said. They continued to look for the ring, but in vain. Dorcas Knight, however, assured her guest that it should be found and returned, and that breakfast waited. Whereupon Capitola went down to the parlor, where she found Clara awaiting her presence to give her a kindly greeting.

"Mr. Le Noir never gets up until very late, and so we do not wait for him," said Dorcas Knight, as she took her seat at the head of the table and signed to the young girls to gather around it.

After breakfast Capitola, promising to come again soon, and inviting Clara to return her visit, took leave of her entertainers and set out for home.

"Thank heaven! I have got her off in time and safety!" muttered Dorcas Knight, in triumph.

CHAPTER VII
CAP'S RETURN

Must I give way and room for your rash choler?
Shall I be frighted when a madman stares?
Go show your slaves how choleric you are!
And make your bondsmen tremble! I'll not blench!

—SHAKESPEARE.

It happened that about sunrise that morning Wool awoke In the cellar, and remembered that on the night previous his master had commanded him to sally forth in the storm end seek his young mistress, and had forbidden him, on pain of broken bones, to return without bringing her safe. Therefore, what did the honest soul do but steal out to the stables, saddle and mount a horse and ride back to the house just as Mrs. Condiment had come out into the poultry yard to get eggs for breakfast.

"Missus Compliment, ma'am, I'se been out all night in search of Miss Caterpillar, without finding of her. Is she come back, ma'am?"

"Lor', no, indeed, Wool! I'm very anxious, and the major is taking on dreadful! But I hope she is safe in some house. But, poor Wool, you must have had a dreadful time out all night in the storm looking for her!"

"Awful! Missus Compliment, ma'am, awful!" said Wool.

"Indeed, I know you had, poor creature, come in and get some warm breakfast," said the kind old lady.

"I dare'nt, Missus Compliment. Old marse forbid me to show my face to him until I fotch Miss Caterpillar home safe," said Wool, turning his horse's head as if to go. In doing so he saw Capitola galloping toward the house, and with an exclamation of joy pointed her out to the old lady and rode on to meet her.

"Oh, Miss Caterpillar, I'se so glad I've found you! I'se done been out looking for you all night long!" exclaimed Wool, as he met her.

Capitola pulled up her horse and surveyed the speaker with a comical expression, saying:

"Been out all night looking for me! Well, I must say you seem in a fine state of preservation for a man who has been exposed to the storm all night. You have not a wet thread on you."

"Lor', miss, it rained till one o'clock, and then the wind riz and blowed till six and blowed me dry," said Wool, as he sprang off his horse and helped his young mistress to alight.

Then, instead of taking the beasts to the stable, he tied them to the tree and hurried into the house and upstairs to his master's room, to apprise him of the return of the lost sheep, Capitola.

Old Hurricane was lying awake, tossing, groaning and grumbling with anxiety.

On seeing Wool enter he deliberately raised up and seized a heavy iron candlestick and held it ready to hurl at the head of that worthy, whom he thus addressed:

"Ah, you have come, you atrocious villain! You know the conditions. If you have dared to show your face without bringing your young mistress—"

"Please, marse, I wur out looking for her all night."

"Have you brought her?" thundered Old Hurricane, rising up.

"Please, marse, yes, sir; I done found her and brought her home safe."

"Send her up to me," said Old Hurricane, sinking back with a sigh of infinite relief.

Wool flew to do his bidding.

In five minutes Capitola entered her uncle's chamber.

Now, Old Hurricane had spent a night of almost intolerable anxiety upon his favorite's account, bewailing her danger and praying for her safety but no sooner did he see her enter his chamber safe and sound and smiling than indignation quite mastered him, and jumping out of his bed in his nightgown, he made a dash straight at Capitola.

Now, had Capitola run there is little doubt but that, in the blindness of his fury, he would have caught and beat her then and there. But Cap saw him coming, drew up her tiny form, folded her arms and looked him directly in the face.

This stopped him; but, like a mettlesome old horse suddenly pulled up in full career, he stamped and reared and plunged with fury, and foamed and spluttered and stuttered before he could get words out.

"What do you mean, you vixen, by standing there and popping your great eyes out at me? Are you going to bite, you tigress? What do you mean by facing me at all?" he roared, shaking his fist within an inch of Capitola's little pug nose.

"I am here because you sent for me, sir," was Cap's unanswerable rejoinder.

"Here because I sent for you! humph! humph! humph! and come dancing and smiling into my room as if you had not kept me awake all the live-long night—yes, driven me within an inch of brain fever! Not that I cared for you, you limb of Old Nick! not that I cared for you, except to wish with all my heart and soul that something or other had happened to you, you vagrant! Where did you spend the night, you lunatic?"

"At the old Hidden House, where I went to make a call on my new neighbor, Miss Day, and where I was caught in the storm."

"I wish to heaven you had been caught in a man-trap and had all your limbs broken, you—you—you—Oh!" ejaculated Old Hurricane, turning short and trotting up and down the room. Presently he stopped before Capitola and rapping his cane upon the floor, demanded:

"Who did you see at that accursed place, you—you—infatuated maniac?"

"Miss Day, Mr. Le Noir, Mrs. Knight and a man servant, name unknown," coolly replied Cap.

"And the head demon, where was he?"

"Uncle, if by the 'head demon' you mean Old Nick, I think it quite likely, from present appearances, that he passed the night at Hurricane Hall."

"I mean—Colonel Le Noir!" exclaimed Old Hurricane, as if the name choked him.

"Oh! I understood that he had that day left home."

"Umph! Oh! Ah! That accounts for it; that accounts for it," muttered Old Hurricane to himself; then, seeing that Cap was wistfully regarding his face and attending to his muttered phrases, he broke out upon her with:

"Get out of this—this—this—" He meant to say "get out of this house," but a sure instinct warned him that if he should speak thus Capitola, unlike the other members of his household, would take him at his word.

"Get out of this room, you vagabond!" he vociferated.

And Cap, with a curtsey and a kiss of her hand, danced away.

Old Hurricane stamped up and down the floor, gesticulating like a demoniac and vociferating:

"She'll get herself burked, kidnapped, murdered or what not! I'm sure she will! I know it! I feel it! It's no use to order her not to go; she will be sure to disobey, and go ten times as often for the very reason that she was forbidden. What the demon shall I do? Wool! Wool! you brimstone villain, come here!" he roared, going to the bell-rope and pulling it until he broke it down.

Wool ran in with his hair bristling, his teeth chattering and his eyes starting.

"Come here to me, you varlet! Now, listen: You are to keep a sharp look-out after your young mistress. Whenever she rides abroad you are to mount a horse and ride after her, and keep your eyes open, for if you once lose sight of her, you knave, do you know what I shall do to you, eh?"

"N—no, marse," stammered Wool, pale with apprehension.

"I should cut your eyelids off to improve your vision! Look to it, sir, for I shall keep my word! And now come and help me to dress," concluded Old Hurricane.

Wool, with chattering teeth, shaking knees and trembling fingers, assisted his master in his morning toilet, meditating the while whether it were not better to avoid impending dangers by running away.

And, in fact, between his master and his mistress, Wool had a hot time of it. The weather, after the storm had cleared the atmosphere, was delightful, and Cap rode out that very day. Poor Wool kept his eyeballs metaphorically "skinned," for fear they should be treated literally so—held his eyes wide open, lest Old Hurricane should keep his word and make it impossible for him ever to shut them.

When Cap stole out, mounted her horse and rode away, in five minutes from the moment of starting she heard a horse's hoofs behind her, and presently saw Wool gallop to her side.

At first Cap bore this good-humoredly enough, only saying:

"Go home, Wool, I don't want you; I had much rather ride alone."

To which the groom replied:

"It is old marse's orders, miss, as I should wait on you."

Capitola's spirit rebelled against this; and, suddenly turning upon her attendant, she indignantly exclaimed:

"Wool, I don't want you, sir; I insist upon being left alone, and I order you to go home, sir!"

Upon this Wool burst into tears and roared.

Much surprised, Capitola inquired of him what the matter was.

For some time Wool could only reply by sobbing, but when he was able to articulate he blubbered forth:

"It's nuf to make anybody go put his head under a meat-ax, so it is!"

"What is the matter, Wool?" again inquired Capitola.

"How'd you like to have your eyelids cut off?" howled Wool, indignantly.

"What?" inquired Capitola.

"Yes; I axes how'd you like to have your eyelids cut off? Case that's what ole marse t'reatens to do long o' me, if I don't follow arter you and keep you in sight. And now you forbids of me to do it, and—and—and I'll go and put my neck right underneaf a meat-ax!"

Now, Capitola was really kind-hearted, and, well knowing the despotic temper of her guardian, she pitied Wool, and after a little hesitation she said:

"Wool, so your old master says if you don't keep your eyes on me he'll cut your eyelids off?"

"Ye—ye—yes, miss," sobbed Wool.

"Did he say if you didn't listen to me he'd cut your ears off?"

"N—n—no, miss."

"Did he swear if you didn't talk to me he'd cut out your tongue out?"

"N—n—no, miss."

"Well, now, stop howling and listen to me! Since, at the peril of your eyelids, you are obliged to keep me in sight, I give you leave to ride just within view of me, but no nearer, and you are never to let me see or hear you, if you can help it for I like to be alone."

"I'll do anything in this world for peace, Miss Caterpillar," said poor Wool.

And upon this basis the affair was finally settled. And no doubt Capitola owed much of her personal safety to the fact that Wool kept his eyes open.

While these scenes were going on at Hurricane Hall, momentous events were taking place elsewhere, which require another chapter for their development.

CHAPTER VIII
ANOTHER MYSTERY AT THE HIDDEN HOUSE

"Hark! what a shriek was that of fear intense,
Of horror and amazement!
What fearful struggle to the door and thence
With mazy doubles to the grated casement!"

An hour after the departure of Capitola, Colonel Le Noir returned to the Hidden House and learned from his man David that upon the preceding evening a young girl of whose name he was ignorant had sought shelter from the storm and passed the night at the mansion.

Now, Colonel Le Noir was extremely jealous of receiving strangers under his roof, never, during his short stay at the Hidden House, going out into company, lest he should be obliged in return to entertain visitors. And when he learned that a strange girl had spent the night beneath his roof, he frowningly directed that Dorcas should be sent to him.

When his morose manager made her appearance he harshly demanded the name of the young woman she had dared to receive beneath his roof.

Now, whether there is any truth in the theory of magnetism or not, it is certain that Dorcas Knight—stern, harsh, resolute woman that she was toward all others—became as submissive as a child in the presence of Colonel Le Noir.

At his command she gave him all the information he required, not even withholding the fact of Capitola's strange story of having seen the apparition of the pale-faced lady in her chamber, together with the subsequent discovery of the loss of her ring.

Colonel Le Noir sternly reprimanded his domestic manager for her neglect of his orders and dismissed her from his presence.

The remainder of the day was passed by him in moody thought. That evening he summoned his son to a private conference in the parlor—an event that happily delivered poor Clara Day from their presence at her fireside.

That night Clara, dreading lest at the end of their interview they might return to her society, retired early to her chamber where she sat reading until a late hour, when she went to bed and found transient forgetfulness of trouble in sleep.

She did not know how long she had slept when she was suddenly and terribly awakened by a woman's shriek sounding from the room immediately overhead, in which, upon the night previous, Capitola had slept.

Starting up in bed, Clara listened.

The shriek was repeated—prolonged and piercing—and was accompanied by a muffled sound of struggling that shook the ceiling overhead.

Instinctively springing from her bed, Clara threw on her dressing-gown and flew to the door; but just as she turned the latch to open it she heard a bolt slipped on the outside and found herself a prisoner in her own chamber.

Appalled, she stood and listened.

Presently there came a sound of footsteps on the stairs and a heavy muffled noise as of some dead weight being dragged down the staircase and along the passage. Then she heard the hall door cautiously opened and shut. And, finally, she distinguished the sound of wheels rolling away from the house.

Unable longer to restrain herself, she rapped and beat upon her own door, crying aloud for deliverance.

Presently the bolt was withdrawn, the door jerked open and Dorcas Knight, with a face of horror, stood before her.

"What is the matter! Who was that screaming? In the name of mercy, what has happened?" cried Clara, shrinking in abhorrence from the ghastly woman.

"Hush! it is nothing! There were two tomcats screaming and fighting in the attic, and they fought all the way downstairs, rolling over and over each other. I've just turned them out," faltered the woman, shivering as with an ague fit.

"What—what was that—that went away in the carriage?" asked Clara shuddering.

"The colonel, gone to meet the early stage at Tip-Top, to take him to Washington. He would have taken leave of you last night, but when he came to your parlor you had left it."

"But—but—there is blood upon your hand, Dorcas Knight!" cried Clara, shaking with horror.

"I—I know; the cats scratched me as I put them out," stammered the stern woman, trembling almost as much as Clara herself.

These answers failed to satisfy the young girl, who shrank in terror and loathing from that woman's presence, and sought the privacy of her own chamber, murmuring:

"What has happened? What has been done? Oh, heaven! oh, heaven! have mercy on us! some dreadful deed has been done in this house to-night!"

There was no more sleep for Clara. She heard the clock strike every hour from one to six in the morning, when she arose and dressed herself and went from her room, expecting to see upon the floor and walls and upon the faces of the household signs of some dreadful tragedy enacted upon the previous night.

But all things were as usual—the same dark, gloomy and neglected magnificence about the rooms and passages, the same reserved, sullen and silent aspect about the persons.

Dorcas Knight presided as usual at the head of the breakfast table, and Craven Le Noir at the foot. Clara sat in her accustomed seat at the side, midway between them.

Clara shuddered in taking her cup of coffee from the hand of Dorcas, and declined the wing of fowl that Craven Le Noir would have put upon her plate.

Not a word was said upon the subject of the mystery of the preceding night until Craven Le Noir, without venturing to meet the eyes of the young girl, said:

"You look very pale, Clara."

"Miss Day was frightened by the cats last night," said Dorcas.

Clara answered never a word. The ridiculous story essayed to be palmed off upon her credulity in explanation of the night's mystery had not gained an instant's belief.

She knew that the cry that had startled her from sleep had burst in strong agony from human lips!

That the helpless weight she had heard dragged down the stairs and along the whole length of the passage was some dead or insensible human form!

That the blood she had seen upon the hand of Dorcas Knight was—oh, heaven! her mind shrank back appalled with horror at the thought which she dare not entertain! She could only shudder, pray and trust in God.

CHAPTER IX
CAP FREES THE CAPTIVE

Hold, daughter! I do spy a kind of hope,
Which craves as desperate an execution
As that is desperate, which we would prevent
And if thou darest, I'll give thee remedy!
Hold, then! go home, be merry, give consent
To marry Paris! Wednesday is to-morrow!

—Shakespeare.

As the autumn weather was now very pleasant, Capitola continued her rides, and, without standing on ceremony, repeated her visit to the Hidden House. She was, as usual, followed by Wool, who kept at a respectful distance, and who during his mistress' visit, remained outside in attendance upon the horses.

Capitola luckily was in no danger of encountering Colonel Le Noir, who, since the night of the mysterious tragedy, had not returned home, but had gone to and settled in his winter quarters in Washington city.

But she again met Craven Le Noir, who, contrary to his usual custom of accompanying his father upon his annual migrations to the metropolis, had, upon this occasion, remained home in close attendance upon his cousin, the wealthy orphan.

Capitola found Clara the same sweet, gentle and patient girl, with this difference only, that her youthful brow was now overshadowed by a heavy trouble which could not wholly be explained by her state of orphanage or her sorrow for the dead—it was too full of anxiety, gloom and terror to have reference to the past alone.

Capitola saw all this and, trusting in her own powers, would have sought the confidence of the poor girl, with the view of soothing her sorrows and helping her out of her difficulties; but Miss Day, candid upon all other topics, was strangely reserved upon this subject, and Capitola, with all her eccentricity, was too delicate to seek to intrude upon the young mourner's sanctuary of grief.

But a crisis was fast approaching which rendered further concealment difficult and dangerous, and which threw Clara for protection upon the courage, presence of mind and address of Capitola.

Since Clara Day had parted with her betrothed and had taken up her residence beneath her guardian's roof, she had regularly written both to Traverse at St. Louis and to his mother at Staunton. But she had received no reply from either mother or son. And months had passed, filling the mind of Clara with anxiety upon their account.

She did not for one moment doubt their constancy. Alas! it required but little perspicacity on her part to perceive that the letters on either side must have been intercepted by the Le Noirs—father and son.

Her greatest anxiety was lest Mrs. Rocke and Traverse, failing to hear from her, should imagine that she had forgotten them. She longed to assure them that she had not; but how should she do this? It was perfectly useless to write and send the letter to the post-office by any servant at the Hidden House, for such a letter was sure to find its way—not into the mail bags, but into the pocket of Colonel Le Noir.

Finally, Clara resolved to entrust honest Cap with so much of her story as would engage her interest and co-operation, and then confide to her care a letter to be placed in the post-office. Clara had scarcely come to this resolution ere, as we said, an imminent crisis obliged her to seek the further aid of Capitola.

Craven Le Noir had never abated his unacceptable attentions to the orphan heiress. Day by day, on the contrary, to Clara's unspeakable distress, these attentions grew more pointed and alarming.

At first she had received them coldly and repulsed them gently; but as they grew more ardent and devoted she became colder and more reserved, until at length, by maintaining a freezing hauteur at variance with her usually sweet temper, she sought to repel the declaration that was ever ready to fall from his lips.

But, notwithstanding her evident abhorrence of his suit, Craven Le Noir persisted in his purpose.

And so one morning he entered the parlor and, finding Clara alone, he closed the door, seated himself beside her, took her hand and made a formal declaration of love and proposal of marriage, urging his suit with all the eloquence of which he was master.

Now, Clara Day, a Christian maiden, a recently bereaved orphan and an affianced bride, had too profound a regard for her duties toward God, her father's will and her betrothed husband's rights to treat this attempted invasion of her faith in any other than the most deliberate, serious and dignified manner.

"I am very sorry, Mr. Le Noir, that it has at length come to this. I thought I had conducted myself in such a manner as totally to discourage any such purpose as this which you have just honored me by disclosing. Now, however, that the subject may be set at rest forever, I feel bound to announce to you that my hand is already plighted," said Clara, gravely.

"But, my fairest and dearest love, your little hand cannot be plighted without the consent of your guardian, who would never countenance the impudent pretensions which I understand to be made by the low-born young man to whom I presume you allude. That engagement was a very foolish affair, my dear girl, and only to be palliated on the ground of your extreme childishness at the time of its being made. You must forget the whole matter, my sweetest love, and prepare yourself to listen to a suit more worthy of your social position," said Craven Le Noir, attempting to steal his arm around her waist.

Clara coldly repelled him, saying:

"I am at a loss to understand, Mr. Le Noir, what act of levity on my part has given you the assurance to offer me this affront!"

"Do you call it an affront, fair cousin, that I lay my hand and heart and fortune at your feet?"

"I have called your act, sir, by its gentlest name. Under the circumstances I might well have called it an outrage!"

"And what may be those circumstances that convert an act of—adoration—into an outrage, my sweet cousin?"

"Sir, you know them well. I have not concealed from you or my guardian that I am the affianced bride of Doctor Rocke, nor that our troth was plighted with the full consent of my dear father," said Clara, gravely.

"Tut, tut, tut, my charming cousin, that was mere child's play—a school-girl's romantic whim. Do not dream that your guardian will ever permit you to throw yourself away upon that low-bred fellow."

"Mr. Le Noir, if you permit yourself to address me in this manner, I shall feel compelled to retire. I cannot remain here to have my honored father's will and memory, and the rights of my betrothed, insulted in my person!" said Clara, rising to leave the room.

"No—stay! forgive me, Clara! pardon me, gentlest girl, if, in my great love for you, I grow impatient of any other claim upon your heart, especially from such an unworthy quarter. Clara, you are a mere child, full of generous but romantic sentiments and dangerous impulses. You require extra vigilance and firm exercise of authority on the part of your guardian to save you from certain self-destruction. And some day, sweet girl, you will thank us for preserving you from the horrors of such a mesalliance," said Craven Le Noir, gently detaining her.

"I tell you, Mr. Le Noir, that your manner of speaking of my betrothal is equally insulting to myself, Doctor Rocke and my dear father, who never would have plighted our hands had he considered our prospective marriage a mesalliance."

"Nor do I suppose he ever did plight your hands—while in his right senses!"

"Oh, sir, this has been discussed before. I beg of you to let the subject drop forever, remembering that I hold myself sacredly betrothed to Traverse Rocke, and ready when, at my legal majority, he shall claim me—to redeem my plighted faith by becoming his wife."

"Clara, this is madness! It must not be endured, nor shall not! I have hitherto sought to win your hand by showing you the great extent of my love; but be careful how you scorn that love or continue to taunt me with the mention of an unworthy rival. For, though I use gentle means, should I find them fail of their purpose, I shall know how to avail myself of harsher ones."

Clara disdained reply, except by permitting her clear eye to pass over him from head to foot with an expression of consuming scorn that scathed him to the quick.

"I tell you to be careful, Clara Day! I come to you armed with the authority of your legal guardian, my father, Colonel Le Noir, who will forestall your foolish purpose of throwing yourself and your fortune away upon a beggar, even though to do so he strain his authority and coerce you into taking a more suitable companion," said Craven Le Noir, rising impatiently and pacing the floor. But no sooner had he spoken these words than he saw how greatly he had injured his cause and repented them. Going to Clara and intercepting her as she was about to leave the room, he gently took her hand and, dropping his eyes to the floor with a look of humility and penitence, he said:

"Clara, my sweet cousin, I know not how sufficiently to express my sorrow at having been hurried into harshness toward you—toward you whom I love more than my own soul, and whom it is the fondest wish of my heart to call wife. I can only excuse myself for this or any future extravagance of manner by my excessive love for you and the jealousy that maddens my brain at the bare mention of my rival. That is it, sweet girl. Can you forgive one whom love and jealousy have hurried into frenzy?"

"Mr. Le Noir, the Bible enjoins me to forgive injuries. I shall endeavor, when I can, to forgive you, though for the present my heart is still burning under the sense of wrongs done toward myself and those whom I love and esteem, and the only way in which you can make me forget what has just passed will be—never to repeat the offence." And with these words Clara bent her head and passed from the room.

Could she have seen the malignant scowl and gesture with which Craven Le Noir followed her departure, she would scarcely have trusted his expressions of penitence.

Lifting his arm above his head he fiercely shook his fist after her and exclaimed:

"Go on, insolent girl, and imagine that you have humbled me; but the tune shall be changed by this day month, for before that time whatever power the law gives the husband over his wife and her property shall be mine over you and your possessions. Then we will see who shall be insolent; then we shall see whose proud blue eye shall day after day dare to look up and rebuke me. Oh: to get you in my power, my girl! Not that I love you, moon-faced creature, but I want your possessions, which is quite as strong an incentive."

Then he fell into thought. He had an ugly way of scowling and biting his nails when deeply brooding over any subject, and now he walked slowly up and down the floor with his head upon his breast, his brows drawn over his nose and his four fingers between his teeth, gnawing away like a wild beast, while he muttered:

"She is not like the other one; she has more sense and strength; she will give us more trouble. We must continue to try fair means a little longer. It will be difficult, for I am not accustomed to control my passions, even for a purpose—yet, penitence and love are the only cards to be played to this insolent girl for the present. Afterwards!—" Here his soliloquy muttered itself into silence, his head sank deeper upon his breast, his brows gathered lower over his nose and he walked and gnawed his nails like a hungry wolf.

The immediate result of this cogitation was that he went into the library and wrote off a letter to his father, telling him all that had transpired between himself and Clara, and asking his further counsel.

He dispatched this letter and waited an answer.

During the week that ensued before he could hope to hear from Colonel Le Noir, he treated Clara with marked deference and respect.

And Clara, on her part, did not tax his forbearance by appearing in his presence oftener than she could possibly avoid.

At the end of the week the expected letter came. It was short and to the purpose. It ran thus:

Washington, Dec. 14, 18—

MY DEAR CRAVEN You are losing time. Do not hope to win the girl by the means you propose. She is too acute to be deceived, and too firm to be persuaded. We must not hesitate to use the only possible means by which we can coerce her into compliance. I shall follow this letter by the first stage-coach, and before the beginning of the next month Clara Day shall be your wife.

Your Affectionate Father,

GABRIEL LE NOIR,

C. LE NOIR, ESQ., Hidden House.

When Craven Le Noir read this letter his thin, white face and deep-set eyes lighted up with triumph. But Craven Le Noir huzzaed before he was out of the woods. He had not calculated upon Capitola.

The next day Colonel Le Noir came to the Hidden House. He arrived late in the afternoon.

After refreshing himself with a bath, a change of clothing and a light luncheon, he went to the library, where he passed the remainder of the evening in a confidential conference with his son. Their supper was ordered to be served up to them there; and for that evening Clara had the comfort of taking her tea alone.

The result of this conference was that the next morning, after breakfast, Colonel Le Noir sent for Miss Day to come to him in the library.

When Clara, nerving her gentle heart to resist a sinful tyranny, entered the library, Colonel Le Noir arose and courteously handed her to a chair, and then, seating himself beside her, said:

"My dear Clara, the responsibilities of a guardian are always very onerous, and his duties not always very agreeable, especially when his ward is the sole heiress of a large property and the object of pursuit by fortune hunters and maneuverers, male and female. When such is the case, the duties and responsibilities of the guardian are augmented a hundredfold."

"Sir, this cannot be so in my case, since you are perfectly aware that my destiny is, humanly speaking, already decided," replied Clara, with gentle firmness.

"As—how, I pray you, my fair ward?"

"You cannot possibly be at a loss to understand, sir. You have been already advised that I am betrothed to Doctor Rocke, who will claim me as his wife upon the day that I shall complete my twenty-first year."

"Miss Clara Day! no more of that, I beseech you! It is folly, perversity, frenzy! But, thanks to the wisdom of legislators, the law very properly invests the guardian with great latitude of discretionary power of the person and property of his ward—to be used, of course, for that ward's best interest. And thus, my dear Clara, it is my duty, while holding this power over you, to exercise it for preventing the possibility of your ever—either now or at any future time, throwing yourself away upon a mere adventurer. To do this, I must provide you with a suitable husband. My son, Mr. Craven Le Noir, has long loved and wooed her. He is a young man of good reputation and fair prospects. I entirely approve his suit, and as your guardian I command you to receive him for your destined husband."

"Colonel Le Noir, this is no time 'for bated breath and whispered humbleness.' I am but a simple girl of seventeen, but I understand your purpose and that of your son just as well as though I were an old man of the world. You are the fortune hunters and maneuverers! It is the fortune of the wealthy heiress and friendless orphan that you are in pursuit of! But that fortune, like my hand and heart, is already promised to one I love; and, to speak very plainly to you, I would die ere I would disappoint him or wed your son," said Clara, with invincible firmness.

"Die, girl! There are worse things than death in the world!" said Colonel Le Noir, with a threatening glare.

"I know it! and one of the worst things in the world would be a union with a man I could neither esteem nor even endure!" exclaimed Clara.

Colonel Le Noir saw that there was no use in further disguise. Throwing off, then, the last restraints of good breeding, he said:

"And there are still more terrible evils for a woman than to be the wife of one she 'can neither esteem nor endure!'"

Clara shook her head in proud scorn.

"There are evils to escape which such a woman would go down upon her bended knees to be made the wife of such a man."

Clara's gentle eyes flashed with indignation.

"Infamous!" she cried. "You slander all womanhood in my person!"

"The evils to which I allude are—comprised in—a life of dishonor!" hissed Le Noir through his set teeth.

"This to my father's daughter!" exclaimed Clara, growing white as death at the insult. "Aye, my girl! It is time we understood each other. You are in my power, and I intend to coerce you to my will!"

These words, accompanied as they were by a look that left no doubt upon her mind that he would carry out his purpose to any extremity, so appalled the maiden's soul that she stood like one suddenly struck with catalepsy.

The unscrupulous wretch then approached her and said:

"I am now going to the county seat to take out a marriage license for you and my son. I shall have the carriage at the door by six o'clock this evening, when I desire that you shall be ready to accompany us to church, where a clerical friend will be in attendance to perform the marriage ceremony. Clara Day, if you would save your honor, look to this!"

All this time Clara had neither moved nor spoken nor breathed. She had stood cold, white and still as if turned to stone.

"Let no vain hope of escape delude your mind. The doors will be kept locked; the servants are all warned not to suffer you to leave the house. Look to it, Clara, for the rising of another sun shall see my purpose accomplished!"

And with these words the atrocious wretch left the room. His departure took off the dreadful spell that had paralyzed Clara's life; her blood began to circulate again; breath came to her lungs and speech to her lips.

"Oh, Lord," she cried, "oh, Lord, who delivered the children from the fiery furnace, deliver the poor handmaiden now from her terrible foes!"

While she thus prayed she saw upon the writing table before her a small penknife. Her cheeks flushed and her eyes brightened as she seized it.

"This! this!" she said, "this small instrument is sufficient to save me! Should the worst ensue, I know where to find the carotid artery, and even such a slight puncture as my timorous hand could make would set my spirit free! Oh, my father! oh, my father! you little thought when you taught your Clara the mysteries of anatomy to what a fearful use she would put your lessons! And would it be right? Oh, would it be right? One may desire death, but can anything justify suicide? Oh, Father in heaven, guide me! guide me!" cried Clara, falling upon her knees and sobbing forth this prayer of agony.

Soon approaching footsteps drew her attention. And she had only time to rise and put back her damp, disheveled hair from her tear-stained face before the door opened and Dorcas Knight appeared and said:

"Here is this young woman come again." "I declare, Miss Day," said Cap, laughing, "you have the most accomplished, polite and agreeable servants here that I ever met with! Think with what a courteous welcome this woman received me—' Here you are again!' she said. 'You'll come once too often for your own good, and that I tell you.' I answered that every time I came it appeared to be once too often for her liking. She rejoined, 'The colonel has come home, and he don't like company, so I advise you to make your call a short one.' I assured her that I should measure the length of my visit by the breadth of my will—But good angels, Clara! what is the matter? You look worse than death!" exclaimed Capitola, noticing for the first time the pale, wild, despairing face of her companion.

Clara clasped her hands as if in prayer and raised her eyes with an appealing gaze into Capitola's face.

"Tell me, dear Clara, what is the matter? How can I help you? What shall I do for you?" said our heroine.

Before trusting herself to reply, Clara gazed wistfully into Capitola's eyes, as though she would have read her soul.

Cap did not blanch nor for an instant avert her own honest, gray orbs; she let Clara gaze straight down through those clear windows of the soul into the very soul itself, where she found only truth, honesty and courage.

The scrutiny seemed to be satisfactory for Clara soon took the hand of her visitor and said:

"Capitola, I will tell you. It is a horrid, horrid story, but you shall know all. Come with me to my chamber."

Cap pressed the hand that was so confidingly placed in hers and accompanied Clara to her room, where, after the latter had taken the precaution to lock the door, the two girls sat down for a confidential talk.

Clara, like the author of Robin Hood's Barn, "began at the beginning" of her story, and told everything—her betrothal to Traverse Rocke; the sudden death of her father; the decision of the Orphans' Court; the departure of Traverse for the far West; her arrival at the Hidden House; the interruption of all her epistolary correspondence with her betrothed and his mother; the awful and mysterious occurrences of that dreadful night when she suspected some heinous crime had been committed; and finally of the long, unwelcome suit of Craven Le Noir and the present attempt to force him upon her as a husband.

Cap listened very calmly to this story, showing very little sympathy, for there was not a bit of sentimentality about our Cap.

"And now," whispered Clara, while the pallor of horror overspread her face, "by threatening me with a fate worse than death, they would drive me to marry Craven Le Noir!"

"Yes, I know I would!" said Cap, as if speaking to herself, but by her tone and manner clothing these simple words in the very keenest sarcasm.

"What would you do, Capitola?" asked Clara, raising her tearful eyes to the last speaker.

"Marry Mr. Craven Le Noir and thank him, too!" said Cap. Then, suddenly changing her tone, she exclaimed:

"I wish—oh! how I wish it was only me in your place—that it was only me they were trying to marry against my will!"

"What would you do?" asked Clara, earnestly.

"What would I do? Oh! wouldn't I make them know the difference between their Sovereign Lady and Sam the Lackey? If I had been in your place and that dastard Le Noir had said to me what he said to you, I do believe I should have stricken him down with the lightning of my eyes! But what shall you do, my poor Clara?"

"Alas! alas! see here! this is my last resort!" replied the unhappy girl, showing the little pen-knife.

"Put it away from you! put it away from you!" exclaimed Capitola earnestly; "suicide is never, never, never justifiable! God is the Lord of life and death! He is the only judge whether a mortal's sorrows are to be relieved by death, and when He does not Himself release you, He means that you shall live and endure! That proves that suicide is never right, let the Roman pagans have said and done what they pleased. So no more of that! There are enough other ways of escape for you!"

"Ah! what are they? You would give me life by teaching me how to escape!" said Clara, fervently.

"The first and most obvious means that suggests itself to my mind," said Cap, "is to—run away!"

"Ah! that is impossible. The servants are warned; the doors are all locked; I am watched!"

"Then the next plan is equally obvious. Consent to go with them to the church, and when you get there, denounce them and claim the protection of the clergyman!"

"Ah! dear girl, that is still more impracticable. The officiating clergyman is their friend, and even if I could consent to act a deceitful part, and should go to church as if to marry Craven and upon getting there denounce him, instead of receiving the protection of the clergyman I should be restored to the hands of my legal guardian and be brought back here to meet a fate worse than death," said Clara, in a tone of despair.

Capitola did not at once reply, but fell into deep thought, which lasted many minutes. Then, speaking more gravely than she had spoken before, she said:

"There is but one plan of escape left, your only remaining chance, and that full of danger!"

"Oh, why should I fear danger? What evil can befall me so great as that which now threatens me?" said Clara.

"This plan requires on your part great courage, self-control and presence of mind."

"Teach me! teach me, dear Capitola. I will be an apt pupil!"

"I have thought it all out, and will tell you my plan. It is now eleven o'clock in the forenoon, and the carriage is to come for you at six this evening, I believe?"

"Yes! yes!"

"Then you have seven hours in which to save yourself! And this is my plan: First, Clara, you must change clothes with me, giving me your suit of mourning and putting on my riding habit, hat and veil! Then, leaving me here in your place, you are to pull the veil down closely over your face and walk right out of the house! No one will speak to you, for they never do to me. When you have reached the park, spring upon my horse and put whip to him for the village of Tip Top. My servant, Wool, will ride after you, but not speak to you or approach near enough to discover your identity—for he has been ordered by his master to keep me in sight, and he has been forbidden by his mistress to intrude upon her privacy. You will reach Tip Top by three o'clock, when the Staunton stage passes through. You may then reveal yourself to Wool, give my horse into his charge, get into the coach and start for Staunton. Upon reaching that place, put yourself under the protection of your friends, the two old physicians, and get them to prosecute your guardian for cruelty and flagrant abuse of authority. Be cool, firm and alert, and all will be well!"

Clara, who had listened to this little Napoleon in petticoats with breathless interest, now clasped her hands in a wild ecstasy of joy and exclaimed:

"I will try it! Oh, Capitola I will try it! Heaven bless you for the counsel!"

"Be quick, then; change your dress! provide yourself with a purse of money, and I will give you particular directions how to make a short cut for Tip Top. Ha, ha, ha!, when they come for the bride she will be already rolling on the turnpike between Tip Top and Staunton!"

"But you! Oh, you, my generous deliverer?"

"I shall dress myself in your clothes and stay here in your place to keep you from being missed, so as to give you full time to make your escape."

"But—you will place yourself in the enraged lion's jaws! You will remain in the power of two men who know neither justice nor mercy! Who, in their love or their hate, fear neither God nor man! Oh, Capitola! how can I take an advantage of your generosity, and leave you here in such extreme peril? Capitola, I cannot do it!"

"Well, then, I believe, you must be anxious to marry Craven Le Noir!"

"Oh, Capitola!"

"Well, if you are not, hurry and get ready; there is no time to be lost!"

"But you! but you, my generous friend!"

"Never mind me. I shall be safe enough! I am not afraid of the Le Noirs. Bless their wigs; I should like to see them make me blanch. On the contrary, I desire above all things to be pitted against these two! How I shall enjoy their disappointment and rage! Oh, it will be a rare frolic!"

While Capitola was speaking she was also busily engaged doing. She went softly to the door and turned the key in the lock, to prevent any one from looking through the keyhole, murmuring as she did it:

"I wasn't brought up among the detective policemen for nothing!"

Then she began to take off her riding-habit. Quickly she dressed Clara, superintending all the details of her disguise as carefully as though she were the costumer of a new debutante. When Clara was dressed she was so nearly of the same size and shape of Capitola that from behind no one would have suspected her identity.

"There, Clara! tuck your light hair out of the way; pull your cap over your eyes; gather your veil down close; draw up your figure; throw back your head; walk with a little springy sway and swagger, as if you didn't care a damson for anybody, and—there! I declare no one could tell you from me!" exclaimed Capitola in delight, as she completed the disguise and the instructions of Clara.

Then Capitola dressed herself in Clara's deep mourning robes. And then the two girls sat down to compose themselves for a few minutes, while Capitola gave new and particular directions for Clara's course and conduct, so as to insure as far as human foresight could do it, the safe termination of her perilous adventure. By the time they had ended their talk the hall clock struck twelve.

"There! it is full time you should be off! Be calm, be cool, be firm, and God bless you, Clara! Dear girl! if I were only a young man I would deliver you by the strength of my own arms, without subjecting you to inconvenience or danger!" said Cap, gallantly, as she led Clara to the chamber door and carefully gathered her thick veil in close folds over her face, so as entirely to conceal it.

"Oh, may the Lord in heaven bless and preserve and reward you, my brave, my noble, my heroic Capitola!" said Clara, fervently, with the tears rushing to her eyes.

"Bosh!" said Cap. "If you go doing the sentimental you won't look like me a bit, and that will spoil all. There! keep your veil close, for it's windy, you know; throw back your head and fling yourself along with a swagger, as if you didn't care, ahem! for anybody, and—there you are!" said Cap, pushing Clara out and shutting the door behind her.

Clara paused an instant to offer up one short, fervent prayer for her success and Capitola's safety, and then following her instructions, went on.

Nearly all girls are clever imitators, and Clara readily adopted Capitola's light, springy, swaying walk, and met old Dorcas Knight in the hall, without exciting the slightest suspicion of her identity.

"Humph!" said the woman; "so you are going! I advise you not to come back again!"

Clara threw up her head with a swagger, and went on.

"Very well, you may scorn my words, but if you know your own good you'll follow my advice!" said Dorcas Knight, harshly.

Clara flung up her head and passed out.

Before the door Wool was waiting with the horses. Keeping her face closely muffled, Clara went to Capitola's pony. Wool came and helped her into the saddle, saying:

"Yer does right, Miss Cap, to keep your face kivered; it's awful windy, ain't it, though? I kin scarcely keep the har from blowing offen my head."

With an impatient jerk after the manner of Capitola, Clara signified that she did not wish to converse. Wool dropped obediently behind, mounted his horse and followed at a respectful distance until Clara turned her horse's head and took the bridle-path toward Tip Top. This move filled poor Wool with dismay. Riding toward her, he exclaimed:

"'Deed, Miss Cap, yer mus' scuse me for speakin' now! Whar de muschief is yer a-goin' to?"

For all answer Clara, feigning the temper of Capitola, suddenly wheeled her horse, elevated her riding whip and galloped upon Wool in a threatening manner.

Wool dodged and backed his horse with all possible expedition, exclaiming in consternation:

"Dar! dar! Miss Cap, I won't go for to ax you any more questions—no—not if yer rides straight to Old Nick or Black Donald!"

Whereupon, receiving this apology in good part, Clara again turned her horse's head and rode on her way.

Wool followed, bemoaning the destiny that kept him between the two fierce fires of his old master's despotism and his young mistress's caprice, and muttering:

"I know old marse and dis young gal am goin' to be the death of me! I knows it jes' as well as nuffin at all! I 'clare to man, if it ain't nuff to make anybody go heave themselves right into a grist mill and be ground up at once." Wool spoke no more until they got to Tip Top, when Clara still closely veiled, rode up to the stage office just as the coach, half filled with passengers, was about to start. Springing from her horse, she went up to Wool and said:

"Here, man, take this horse back to Hurricane Hall! Tell Major Warfield that Miss Black remains at the Hidden House in imminent danger! Ask him to ride there and bring her home! Tell Miss Black when you see her that I reached Tip Top safe and in time to take the coach. Tell her I will never cease to be grateful! And now, here is a half eagle for your trouble! Good-by, and God bless you!" And she put the piece in his hand and took her place in the coach, which immediately started.

As for Wool! From the time that Clara had thrown aside her veil and began to speak to him he had stood staring and staring—his consternation growing and growing—until it had seemed to have turned him into stone—from which state of petrefaction he did not recover until he saw the stage coach roll rapidly away, carrying off—whom?—Capitola, Clara or the evil one?—Wool could not have told which! He presently astounded the people about the stage office by leaving his horses and taking to his heels after the stage coach, vociferating:

"Murder! murder! help! help! stop thief! stop thief! stop the coach! stop the coach!"

"What is the matter, man?" said a constable, trying to head him.

But Wool incontinently ran over that officer, throwing him down and keeping on his headlong course, hat off, coat-tail streaming and legs and arms flying like the sails of a windmill, as he tried to overtake the coach, crying:

"Help! murder! head the horses! Stop the coach! Old marse told me not to lose sight of her! Oh, for hebben's sake, good people, stop the coach!"

When he got to a gate, instead of taking time to open it, he rolled himself somersault-like right over it! When he met man or woman, instead of turning from his straight course, he knocked them over and passed on, garments flying and legs and arms circulating with the velocity of a wheel.

The people whom he had successively met and overthrown in his course, picking themselves up and getting into the village, reported that there was a furious madman broke loose, who attacked every one he met.

And soon every man and boy in the village who could mount a horse started in pursuit. Only race horses would have beaten the speed with which Wool ran, urged on by fear. It was nine miles on the turnpike road from Tip Top that the horsemen overtook and surrounded Wool, who, seeing himself hopelessly environed, fell down upon the ground and rolled and kicked, swearing that he would not be taken alive to have his eyelids cut off!

It was not until after a desperate resistance that he was finally taken, bound, put in a wagon and carried back to the village, where he was recognized as Major Warfield's man and a messenger was despatched for his master.

And not until he had been repeatedly assured that no harm should befall him did Wool gain composure enough to say, amid tears of cruel grief and fear:

"Oh, marsers! my young missus, Miss Black, done been captured and bewitched and turned into somebody else, right afore my own two looking eyes and gone off in dat coach! 'deed she is! and ole marse kill me!'deed he will, gemmen! He went and ordered me not to take my eyes offen her, and no more I didn't! But what good that do, when she turned to somebody else, and went off right afore my two looking eyes? But ole marse won't listen to reason. He kill me, I know he will!" whimpered Wool, refusing to be comforted.

CHAPTER X
CAP IN CAPTIVITY

I lingered here and rescue planned
For Clara and for me.

—SCOTT.

Meanwhile how fared it with Capitola in the Hidden House?

"I am in for it now!" said Cap, as she closed the door behind Clara; "I am in for it now! This is a jolly imprudent adventure! What will Wool do when he discovers that he has 'lost sight' of me? What will uncle say when he finds out what I've done? Whe-ew! Uncle will explode! I wonder if the walls at Hurricane Hall will be strong enough to stand it! Wool will go mad! I doubt if he will ever do a bit more good in this world!"

"But above all, I wonder what the Le Noirs, father and son, will say when they find that the heiress is flown and a 'beggar,' as uncle flatters me by calling me, will be here in her place! Whe-ew-ew-ew! There will be a tornado! Cap, child, they'll murder you! That's just what they'll do! They'll kill and eat you, Cap, without any salt! or they may lock you up in the haunted room to live with the ghost, Cap, and that would be worse!"

"Hush! here comes Dorcas Knight! Now I must make believe I'm Clara, and do the sentimental up brown!" concluded Capitola, as she seated herself near the door where she could be heard, and began to sob softly.

Dorcas rapped.

Cap sobbed in response.

"Are you coming to luncheon, Miss Day?" inquired the woman.

"Ee-hee! Ee-hee! Ee-hee! I do not want to eat," sobbed Cap, in a low and smothered voice. Any one would have thought she was drowned in tears.

"Very well; just as you like," said the woman harshly, as she went away.

"Well, I declare," laughed Cap, "I did that quite as well as an actress could! But now what am I to do? How long can I keep this up? Heigh-ho 'let the world slide!' I'll not reveal myself until I'm driven to it, for when I do-! Cap, child, you'll get chawed right up!"

A little later in the day Dorcas Knight came again and rapped at the door.

"Ee-hee! Ee-hee! Ee-hee!" sobbed Cap.

"Miss Day, your cousin, Craven Le Noir, wishes to speak with you alone."

"Ee-hee! Ee-hee! Ee-hee! I cannot see him!" sobbed Cap, in a low and suffocating voice.

The woman went away, and Cap suffered no other interruption until six o'clock, when Dorcas Knight once more rapped saying:

"Miss Day, your uncle is at the front door with the carriage, and he wishes to know if you are ready to obey him."

"Ee-hee! Ee-hee! Ee—hee!-te-te-tell him yes!" sobbed Cap, as if her heart would break.

The woman went off with this answer, and Capitola hastily enveloped her form in Clara's large, black shawl, put on Clara's black bonnet and tied her thick mourning veil closely over her face.

"A pretty bridal dress, this; but, however, I suppose these men are no more particular about my costume than they are about their own conduct," said Cap.

She had just drawn on her gloves when she heard the footsteps of two men approaching. They rapped at the door.

"Come in," she sobbed, in a low, broken voice, that might have belonged to any girl in deep distress, and she put a white cambric handkerchief up to her eyes and drew her thick veil closely over her face.

The two Le Noirs immediately entered the room. Craven approached her and whispered, softly:

"You will forgive me this, my share in these proceedings after awhile, sweet Clara! The Sabine women did not love the Roman youths the less that they were forcibly made wives by them."

"Ee-hee! Ee-hee! Ee-hee!" sobbed Cap, entirely concealing her white cambric handkerchief under her impenetrable veil.

"Come, come! we lose time!" said the elder Le Noir "Draw her arm within yours, Craven, and lead her out."

The young man did as he was directed and led Cap from the room. It was now quite dark—the long, dreary passage was only dimly lighted by a hanging lamp, so that with the care she took there was scarcely a possibility of Capitola's being discovered. They went on, Craven Le Noir whispering hypocritical apologies and Cap replying only by low sobs.

When they reached the outer door they found a close carriage drawn up before the house.

To this Craven Le Noir led Capitola, placed her within and took the seat by her side. Colonel Le Noir followed and placed himself in the front seat opposite them. And the carriage was driven rapidly off.

An hour's ride brought the party to an obscure church in the depths of the forest, which Capitola recognized by the cross on its top to be a Roman Catholic chapel.

Here the carriage drew up and the two Le Noirs got out and assisted Capitola to alight.

They then led her into the church, which was dimly illumined by a pair of wax candles burning before the altar. A priest in his sacerdotal robes was in attendance. A few country people were scattered thinly about among the pews, at their private devotions.

Guarded by Craven Le Noir on the right and Colonel Le Noir on the left, Capitola was marched up the aisle and placed before the altar.

Colonel Le Noir then went and spoke apart to the officiating priest, saying, in a tone of dissatisfaction:

"I told you, sir, that as our bride was an orphan, recently bereaved, and still in deep mourning, we wished the marriage ceremony to be strictly private, and you gave me to understand, sir, that at this hour the chapel was most likely to be vacant. Yet, here I find a half a score of people! How is this?"

"Sir," replied the priest, "it is true that at this hour of the evening the chapel is most likely to be vacant, but it is not therefore certain to be so! nor did I promise as much! Our chapel is, as you know, open at all hours of the day and night, that all who please may come and pray. These people that you see are hard-working farm laborers, who have no time to come in the day, and who are now here to offer up their evening prayers, and also, some of them, to examine their consciences preparatory to confession! They can certainly be no interruption to this ceremony."

"Egad, I don't know that!" muttered Colonel Le Noir between his teeth.

As for Cap, the sight of other persons present in the chapel filled her heart with joy and exultation, inasmuch as it insured her final safety. And so she just abandoned herself to the spirit of frolic that possessed her, and anticipated with the keenest relish the denouement of her strange adventure.

"Well, what are we waiting for? Proceed, sir, proceed!" said Colonel Le Noir as he took Cap by the shoulders and placed her on the left side of his son, while he himself stood behind ready to "give the bride away."

The ceremony immediately commenced.

The prologue beginning, "Dearly beloved, we are gathered together here," etc., etc., etc., was read.

The solemn exhortation to the contracting parties, commencing "I require and charge ye both, as ye shall answer in the dreadful day of judgment when the secrets of all hearts shall be disclosed, that if either of you know any just cause or impediment why ye may not lawfully be joined together," etc., etc., etc., followed.

Capitola listened to all this with the deepest attention, saying to herself: "Well, I declare, this getting married is really awfully interesting! If it were not for Herbert Greyson, I'd just let it go right straight on to the end and see what would happen next!"

While Cap was making these mental comments the priest was asking the bridegroom:

"Wilt thou have this woman to be thy wedded wife," etc., etc., etc., "so long as ye both shall live?"

To which Craven Le Noir, in a sonorous voice responded: "I will."

"Indeed you will? We'll see that presently!" said Cap to herself.

The priest then turning toward the bride, inquired:

"Wilt thou have this man to be thy wedded husband, etc., etc., etc., so long as ye both shall live?"

To which the bride, throwing aside her veil, answered firmly:

"No! not if he were the last man and I the last woman on the face of the earth and the human race was about to become extinct and the angel of Gabriel came down from above to ask it of me as a personal favor."

The effect of this outburst, this revelation, this explosion, may be imagined but can never be adequately described.

The priest dropped his book and stood with lifted hands and open mouth and staring eyes as though he had raised a ghost!

The two Le Noirs simultaneously sprang forward, astonishment, disappointment and rage contending in their blanched faces.

"Who are you, girl?" exclaimed Colonel Le Noir.

"Capitola Black, your honor's glory!" she replied, making a deep curtsey.

"What the foul fiend is the meaning of all this?" in the same breath inquired the father and son.

Cap put her thumb on the side of her nose, and, whirling her four fingers, replied:

"It means, your worships' excellencies, that—you—can't come it! it's no go!' this chicken won't fight It means that the fat's in the fire, and the cat's out of the bag! It means confusion! distraction! perdition! and a tearing off of our wigs! It means the game's up, the play's over, villainy is about to be hanged and virtue about to be married, and the curtain is going to drop and the principal performer—that's I-is going to be called out amid the applause of the audience!" Then, suddenly changing her mocking tone to one of great severity, she said:

"It means that you have been outwitted by a girl! It means that your purposed victim has fled, and is by this time in safety! It means that you two, precious father and son, would be a pair of knaves if you had sense enough; but, failing in that, you are only a pair of fools!"

By this time the attention of the few persons in the church was aroused. They all arose to their feet to look and listen, and some of them left their places and approached the altar. And to these latter Capitola now suddenly turned and said aloud:

"Good people, I am Capitola Black, the niece and ward of Major Ira Warfield, of Hurricane Hall, whom you all know, and now I claim your protection while I shall tell you the meaning of my presence here!"

"Don't listen to her. She is a maniac!" cried Colonel Le Noir.

"Stop her mouth!" cried Craven, springing upon Capitola and holding her tightly in the grasp of his right arm, while he covered her lips and nostrils with his large left hand.

Capitola struggled so fiercely to free herself that Craven had enough to do to hold her, and so was not aware of a ringing footstep coming up the aisle, until a stunning blow dealt from a strong arm covered his face with blood and stretched him out at Capitola's feet.

Cap flushed, breathless and confused, looked up and was caught to the bosom of Herbert Greyson, who, pale with concentrated rage, held her closely and inquired:

"Capitola! What violence is this which has been done you? Explain! who is the aggresor?"

"Wai, wai, wait until I get my breath! There! that was good! That villain has all but strangled me to death? Oh, Herbert, I'm so delighted you've come! How is it that you always drop right down at the right time and on the right spot?" said Cap, while gasping for breath.

"I will tell you another time! Now I want an explanation."

"Yes, Herbert, I also wish to explain—not only to you but to these gaping, good people! Let me have a hearing!" said Cap.

"She is mad! absolutely mad!" cried Colonel Le Noir, who was assisting his son to rise.

"Silence, sir!" thundered Herbert Greyson, advancing toward him with uplifted and threatening hand.

"Gentlemen! gentlemen! pray remember that you are within the walls of a church!" said the distressed priest.

"Craven, this is no place for us; let us go and pursue our fugitive ward," whispered Colonel Le Noir to his son.

"We might as well; for it is clear that all is over here!" replied Craven. And the two baffled villains turned to leave the place. But Herbert Greyson, speaking up, said:

"Good people, prevent the escape of those men until we hear what this young lady has to say! that we may judge whether to let them go or to take them before a magistrate."

The people flew to the doors and windows and secured them, and then surrounded the two Le Noirs, who found themselves prisoners.

"Now, Capitola, tell us how it is that you are here!" said Herbert Greyson.

"Well, that elder man" said Cap, "is the guardian of a young heiress who was betrothed to a worthy young man, one Doctor Traverse Rocke."

"My friend!" interrupted Herbert.

"Yes, Mr. Greyson, your friend! Their engagement was approved by the young lady's father, who gave them his dying blessing. Nevertheless, in the face of all this, this 'guardian' here, appointed by the Orphans' Court to take charge of the heiress and her fortune, undertakes, for his own ends, to compel the young lady to break her engagement and marry his own son! To drive her to this measure, he does not hesitate to use every species of cruelty. This night he was to have forced her to this altar! But in the interval, to-day, I chanced to visit her at the house where she was confined. Being informed by her of her distressing situation, and having no time to help her in any better way, I just changed clothes with her. She escaped unsuspected in my dress. And those two heroes there, mistaking me for her, forced me into a carriage and dragged me hither to be married against my will. And instead of catching an heiress, they caught a Tartar, that's all! And now, Herbert, let the two poor wretches go hide their mortification, and do you take me home, for I am immensely tired of doing the sentimental, making speeches and piling up the agonies!"

While Cap was delivering this long oration, the two Le Noirs had made several essays to interrupt and contradict her, but were effectually prevented by the people, whose sympathies were all with the speaker. Now, at Herbert Greyson's command, they released the culprits, who, threatening loudly took their departure.

Herbert then led Capitola out and placed her upon her own pony, Gyp, which, to her unbounded astonishment, she found there in charge of Wool, who was also mounted upon his own hack.

Herbert Greyson threw himself into the saddle of a third horse, and the three took the road to Hurricane Hall.

"And now," said Capitola, as Herbert rode up to her side, "for mercy sake tell me, before I go crazy with conjecture, how it happened that you dropped down from the sky at the very moment and on the very spot where you were needed? and where did you light upon Wool and the horses?"

"It is very simple when you come to understand it," said Herbert, smiling. "In the first place, you know, I graduated at the last commencement."

"Yes."

"Well, I have just received a lieutenant's commission in a regiment that is ordered to join General Scott in Mexico."

"Oh, Herbert, that is news, and I don't know whether to be in despair or in ecstasy!" said Cap, ready to laugh or cry, as a feather's weight might tip the scales in which she balanced Herbert's new honors with his approaching perils.

"If there's any doubt about it, I decidedly recommend the latter emotion," said Herbert, laughing.

"When do you go?" inquired Cap.

"Our regiment embarks from Baltimore on the first of next month. Meanwhile I got leave of absence to come and spend a week with my friends at home!"

"Oh, Herbert, I—I am in a quandary! But you haven't told me yet how you happened to meet Wool and to come here just in the nick of time!"

"I am just going to do so. Well, you see Capitola, I came down in the stage to Tip Top, which I reached about three o'clock. And there I found Wool in the hands of the Philistines, suspected of being mad, from the manner in which he raved about losing sight of you. Well, of course, like a true knight, I delivered my lady's squire, comforted and reassured him and made him mount his own horse and take charge of yours. After which I mounted the best beast that I had hired to convey me to Hurricane Hall, and we all set off thither. I confess that I was excessively anxious upon your account, for I could make nothing whatever of Wool's wild story of your supposed metamorphosis! I thought it best to make a circuit and take the Hidden House in our course, to make some inquiries there as to what had really happened. I had got a little bewildered between the dark night and the strange road, and, seeing the light in the church, I had just ridden up to inquire my way, when to my astonishment I saw you within, before the altar, struggling in the grasp of that ruffian. And you know the rest! And now let us ride on quickly, for I have a strong presentiment that Major Warfield is suffering the tortures of a lost soul through anxiety upon your account," concluded Herbert Greyson.

"Please, Marse Herbert and Miss Cap, don't you tell ole marse nuffin 'tall 'bout my loosin' sight of you!" pleaded Wool.

"We shall tell you old master all about it, Wool, for I would not have him miss the pleasure of hearing this adventure upon any account; but I promise to bear you harmless through it," said Herbert, as they galloped rapidly toward home.

They reached Hurricane Hall by eight o'clock, and in good time for supper. They found Old Hurricane storming all over the house, and ordering everybody off the premises in his fury of anxiety upon Capitola's account. But when the party arrived, surprise at seeing them in the company of Herbert Greyson quite revolutionized his mood, and, forgetting to rage, he gave them all a hearty welcome.

And when after supper was over and they were all gathered around the comfortable fireside, and Herbert related the adventures and feats of

Capitola at the Hidden House, and in the forest chapel, the old man grasped the hand of his favorite and with his stormy old eyes full of rain said:

"You deserve to have been a man, Cap! Indeed you do, my girl!"

That was his highest style of praise.

Then Herbert told his own little story of getting his commission and being ordered to Mexico.

"God bless you, lad, and save you in the battle and bring you home with victory!" was old Hurricane's comment.

Then seeing that the young people were quite worn out with fatigue, and feeling not averse to his own comfortable couch, Old Hurricane broke up the circle and they all retired to rest.

CHAPTER XI
AN UNEXPECTED VISITOR AT MARAH'S COTTAGE

"Friend wilt thou give me shelter here?
The stranger meekly saith
My life is hunted! evil men
Are following on my path."

Marah Rocke sat by her lonely fireside.

The cottage was not changed in any respect since the day upon which we first of all found her there. There was the same bright, little wood fire; the same clean hearth and the identical faded carpet on the floor. There was the dresser with its glistening crockery ware on the right, and the shelves with Traverse's old school books on the left of the fireplace.

The widow herself had changed in nothing except that her clean black dress was threadbare and rusty, and her patient face whiter and thinner than before.

And now there was no eager restlessness: no frequent listening and looking toward the door. Alas! she could not now expect to hear her boy's light and springing step and cheerful voice as he hurried home at eventide from his daily work. Traverse was far away at St. Louis undergoing the cares and trials of a friendless young physician trying to get into practice. Six months had passed since he took leave of her, and there was as yet no hope of his returning even, to pay a visit.

So Marah sat very still and sad, bending over her needlework without ever turning her head in the direction of the door. True, he wrote to her every week. No Wednesday ever passed without bringing her a letter written in a strong, buoyant and encouraging strain. Still she missed Traverse very sadly. It was dreary to rise up in the empty house every morning; dreary to sit down to her solitary meals, and drearier still to go to bed in her lonely room without having received her boy's kiss and heard his cheerful good-night. And it was her custom every night to read over Traverse's last letter before retiring to bed.

It was getting on toward ten o'clock when she folded up her work and put it away and drew her boy's latest epistle from her bosom to read. It ran as follows:

St. Louis, Dec. 1st, 184—.

My dearest Mother—I am very glad to hear that you continue in good health, and that you do not work too hard, or miss me too sadly. It is the greatest comfort of my life to hear good news of you, sweet mother. I count the days from one letter to another, and read every last letter over daily until I get a new one. You insist upon my telling you how I am getting on, and whether I am out of money. I am doing quite well, ma'am, and have some funds left! I have quite a considerable practice. It is true that my professional services are in request only among the very poor, who pay me with their thanks and good wishes. But I am very glad to be able to pay off a small part of the great debt of gratitude I owe to the benevolent of this world by doing all that I can in my turn for the needy. And even if I had never myself been the object of a good man's benevolence, I should still have desired to serve the indigent; "for whoso giveth to the poor lendeth to the Lord," and I "like the security." Therefore, sweet mother of mine, be at ease; for I am getting on swimmingly—with one exception. Still I do not hear from our Clara! Six months have now passed, during which, despite of her seeming silence, I have written to her every week; but not one letter or message have I received from her in return! And now you tell me also that you have not received a single letter from her either! I know not what to think. Anxiety upon her account is my one sole trouble! Not that I wrong the dear girl by one instant's doubt of her constancy—no! my soul upon her truth! if I could do that, I should be most unworthy of her love! No, mother, you and I know that Clara is true! But ah, we do not know to what sufferings she may be subjected by Le Noir, who I firmly believe has intercepted all our letters. Mother, I am about to ask a great, perhaps an unreasonable, favor of you! It is to go down into the neighborhood of the Hidden House and make inquiries and try to find out Clara's real condition. If it be possible, put yourself into communication with her, and tell her that I judge her heart by my own, and have the firmest faith in her constancy, even though I have written to her every week for six months without ever having received an answer. I feel that I am putting you to expense and trouble, but my great anxiety about Clara, which I am sure you share, must be my excuse. I kiss your dear and honored hands, and remain ever your loving son and faithful servant.

TRAVERSE ROCKE.

"I must try to go. It will be an awful expense, because I know no one down there, and I shall have to board at the tavern at Tip Top while I am making inquiries—for I dare not approach the dwelling of Gabriel Le Noir!" said Marah Rocke, as she folded up her letter and replaced it in her bosom.

Just at that moment she heard the sound of wheels approach and a vehicle of some sort draw up to the gate and some one speaking without.

She went to the door, and, listening, heard a girlish voice say:

"A dollar? Yes, certainly here it is. There, you may go now."

She recognized the voice, and with a cry of joy jerked the door open just as the carriage rolled away. And the next instant Clara Day was in her arms.

"Oh, my darling! my darling! my darling! is this really you? Really, really you, and no dream?" cried Marah Rocke, all in a flutter of excitement, as she strained Clara to her bosom.

"Yes, it is I, sweet friend, come to stay with you a long time, perhaps," said Clara, softly, returning her caresses.

"Oh, my lamb! my lamb! what a joyful surprise! I do think I shall go crazy! Where did you come from, my pet? Who came with you? When did you start? Did Le Noir consent to your coming? And how did it all happen? But, dear child, how worn and weary you look! You must be very tired! Have you had supper? Oh, my darling, come and lie down on this soft lounge while I put away your things and get you some refreshment," said Marah Rocke, in a delirium of joy, as she took off Clara's hat and sack and laid her down to rest on the lounge, which she wheeled up near the fire.

"Oh, my sweet, we have been so anxious about you! Traverse and myself! Traverse is still at St. Louis, love, getting on slowly. He has written to you every week, and so, indeed have I, but we neither of us have had so much as one letter in reply. And yet neither of us ever doubted your true heart, my child. We knew that the letters must have been lost, miscarried or intercepted," said Marah, as she busied herself putting on the tea-kettle.

"They must, indeed, since my experience in regard to letters exactly corresponds with yours! I have written every week to both of you, yet never received one line in reply from either," said Clara.

"We knew it! We said so! Oh, those Le Noirs! Those Le Noirs! But, my darling, you are perfectly exhausted, and though I have asked you a half an hundred questions you shall not reply to one of them, nor talk a bit more until you have rested and had refreshment. Here, my love; here is Traverse's last letter. It will amuse you to lie and read it while I am getting tea," said Marah, taking the paper from her bosom and handing it to Clara, and then placing the stand with the light near the head of her couch that she might see to read it without rising.

And while Clara, well pleased perused and smiled over her lover's letter, Marah Rocke laid the cloth and spread a delicate repast of tea, milk toast and poached eggs, of which she tenderly pressed her visitor to partake.

And when Clara was somewhat refreshed by food and rest, she said:

"Now, dear mamma, you will wish to hear how it happens that I am with you to-night."

"Not unless you feel quite rested, dear girl."

"I am rested sufficiently for the purpose; besides, I am anxious to tell you. And oh, dear mamma! I could just now sit in your lap and lay my head upon your kind, soft bosom so willingly!"

"Come, then, Clara! Come, then, my darling." said Marah, tenderly, holding out her arms.

"No, no, mamma; you are too little; it would be a sin!" said Clara, smiling; "but I will sit by you and put my hand in yours and rest my head against your shoulder while I tell you all about it."

"Come, then, my darling!" said Marah Rocke.

Clara took the offered seat, and when she was fixed to her liking she commenced and related to her friend a full history of all that had occurred to her at the Hidden House from the moment that she had first crossed its threshold to the hour in which, through the courage and address of Capitola, she was delivered from imminent peril.

"And now," said Clara, in conclusion, "I have come hither in order to get Doctor Williams to make one more appeal for me to the Orphans' Court. And when it is proved what a traitor my guardian has been to his trust I have no doubt that the judge will appoint some one else in his place, or at least see that my father's last wish in regard to my residence is carried into effect."

"Heaven grant it, my child! Heaven grant it! Oh, those Le Noirs! those Le Noirs! Were there ever in the world before such ruthless villains and accomplished hypocrites?" said Marah Rocke, clasping her hands in the strength of her emotions.

A long time yet they talked together, and then they retired to bed, and still talked until they fell asleep in each other's arms.

The next morning the widow arose early, gazed a little while with delight upon the sleeping daughter of her heart, pressed a kiss upon her cheek so softly as not to disturb her rest, and then, leaving her still in the deep, sweet sleep of wearied youth, she went down-stairs to get a nice breakfast.

Luckily a farmer's cart was just passing the road before the cottage on its way to market.

Marah took out her little purse from her pocket, hailed the driver and expended half her little store in purchasing two young chickens, some eggs and some dried peaches, saying to herself:

"Dear Clara always had a good appetite, and healthy young human nature must live substantially in spite of all its little heart-aches."

While Marah was preparing the chicken for the gridiron the door at the foot of the stairs opened and Clara came in, looking, after her night's rest, as fresh as a rosebud.

"What! up with the sun, my darling?" said Marah, going to meet her.

"Yes, mamma! Oh! it is so good to be here with you in this nice, quiet place, with no one to make me shudder! But you must let me help you, mamma! See! I will set the table and make the toast!"

"Oh, Miss Clara—"

"Yes, I will! I have been ill used and made miserable, and now you must pet me, mamma, and let me have my own way and help you to cook our little meals and to make the house tidy and afterward to work those buttonholes in the shirts you were spoiling your gentle eyes over last night. Oh! if they will only let me stay here with you and be at peace, we shall be very happy together, you and I!" said Clara, as she drew out the little table and laid the cloth.

"My dear child, may the Lord make you as happy as your sweet affection would make me!" said Marah.

"We can work for our living together," continued Clara, as she gaily flitted about from the dresser to the table, placing the cups and saucers and plates. "You can sew the seams and do the plain hemming, and I can work the buttonholes and stitch the bosoms, collars and wristbands! And 'if the worst comes to the worst,' we can hang out our little shingle before the cottage gate, inscribed with:"

MRS. ROCKE AND DAUGHTER
Shirt Makers
Orders executed with neatness and dispatch

"We'd drive a thriving business, mamma, I assure you," said Clara, as she sat down on a low stool at the hearth and began to toast the bread.

"I trust in heaven that it will never come to that with you, my dear!"

"Why? Why, mamma? Why should I not taste of toil and care as well as others a thousand times better than myself? Why should not I work as well as you and Traverse, mamma? I stand upon the broad platform of human rights, and I say I have just as good a right to work as others!" said Clara, with a pretty assumption of obstinacy, as she placed the plate of toast upon the board.

"Doubtless, dear Clara, you may play at work just as much as you please; but heaven forbid you should ever have to work at work!" replied Mrs. Rocke as she placed the coffee pot and the dish of broiled chicken on the table.

"Why, mamma, I do not think that is a good prayer at all! That is a wicked, proud prayer, Mrs. Marah Rocke! Why shouldn't your daughter really toil as well as other people's daughters, I'd like to be informed?" said Clara, mockingly, as they both took their seats at the table.

"I think, dear Clara, that you must have contracted some of your eccentric little friend Capitola's ways, from putting on her habit! I never before saw you in such gay spirits!" said Mrs. Rocke, as she poured out the coffee.

"Oh, mamma; it is but the glad rebound of the freed bird! I am so glad to have escaped from that dark prison of the Hidden House and to be here with you. But tell me, mamma, is my old home occupied?"

"No, my dear; no tenant has been found for it. The property is in the hands of an agent to let, but the house remains quite vacant and deserted."

"Why is that?" asked Clara.

"Why, my love, for the strangest reason! The foolish country people say that since the doctor's death the place has been haunted!"

"Haunted!"

"Yes, my dear, so the foolish people say, and they get wiser ones to believe them."

"What exactly do they say? I hope—I hope they do not trifle with my dear father's honored name and memory?"

"Oh, no, my darling! no! but they say that although the house is quite empty and deserted by the living strange sights and sounds are heard and seen by passers-by at night. Lights appear at the upper windows from which pale faces look out."

"How very strange!" said Clara.

"Yes, my dear, and these stories have gained such credence that no one can be found to take the house."

"So much the better, dear mamma, for if the new judge of the Orphans' Court should give a decision in our favor, as he must, when he hears the evidence, old and new, you and I can move right into it and need not then enter the shirt-making line of business!"

"Heaven grant it, my dear! But now, Clara, my love, we must lose no time in seeing Doctor Williams, lest your guardian should pursue you here and give you fresh trouble."

Clara assented to this, and they immediately arose from the table, cleared away the service, put the room in order and went up-stairs to put on their bonnets, Mrs. Rocke lending Clara her own best bonnet and shawl. When they were quite ready they locked up the house and set out for the town.

It was a bright, frosty, invigorating winter's morning, and the two friends walked rapidly until they reached Doctor Williams' house.

The kind old man was at home, and was much surprised and pleased to see his visitors. He invited them into his parlor, and when he had heard their story, he said: "This is a much more serious affair than the other. We must employ counsel. Witnesses must be brought from the neighborhood of the Hidden House. You are aware that the late judge of the Orphans' Court has been appointed to a high office under the government at Washington. The man that has taken his place is a person of sound integrity, who will do his duty. It remains only for us to prove the justice of our cause to his satisfaction, and all will be well."

"Oh, I trust in heaven that it will be," said Marah, fervently.

"You two must stay in my house until the affair is decided. You might possibly be safe from real injury; but you could not be free from molestation in your unprotected condition at the cottage," said Doctor Williams.

Clara warmly expressed her thanks.

"You had better go home now and pack up what you wish to bring, and put out the fire and close up the house and come here immediately. In the mean time I will see your dear father's solicitor and be ready with my report by the time you get back," said Doctor Williams, promptly taking his hat to go.

Mrs. Rocke and Clara set out for the cottage, which they soon reached.

Throwing off her bonnet and shawl, Clara said:

"Now, mamma, the very first thing I shall do will be to write to Traverse, so that we can send the letter by to-day's mail and set his mind at rest. I shall simply tell him that our mutual letters have failed to reach their destination, but that I am now on a visit to you, and that while I remain here nothing can interrupt our correspondence. I shall not speak of the coming suit until we see how it will end."

Mrs. Rocke approved this plan, and placed writing materials on the table. And while the matron employed herself in closing up the rooms, packing up what was needful to take with them to the doctor's and putting out the fire, Clara wrote and sealed her letter. They then put on their bonnets, locked up the house, and set out. They called at the post-office just in time to mail their letter, and they reached the doctor's house just as he himself walked up to the door, accompanied by the lawyer. The latter greeted the daughter of his old client and her friend, and they all went into the house together.

In the doctor's study the whole subject of Clara's flight and its occasion was talked over, and the lawyer agreed to commence proceedings immediately.

CHAPTER XII
CAP "RESTS ON HER LAURELS" AND "SPOILS FOR A FIGHT"

'Tis hardly in a body's power,
To keep at times frae being sour,
To see how things are shared;
How best o' chiels are whiles in want,
While coofs on countless thousands rant,
And ken na how to wear't.

—BURNS.

Leaving Clara Day and Marah Rocke in a home of safety, plenty and kindness, in the old doctor's house, we must run down to Hurricane Hall to see what mischief Cap has been getting into since we left her! In truth, none! Cap had had such a surfeit of adventures that she was fain to lie by and rest upon her laurels. Besides, there seemed just now nothing to do—no tyrants to take down, no robbers to capture, no distressed damsels to deliver, and Cap was again in danger of "spoiling for a fight." And then Herbert Greyson was at the Hall—Herbert Greyson whom she vowed always did make a Miss Nancy of her! And so Cap had to content herself for a week with quiet mornings of needlework at her workstand, with Herbert to read to or talk with her; sober afternoon rides, attended by Herbert and Old Hurricane; and humdrum evenings at the chess board, with the same Herbert, while Major Warfield dozed in a great "sleepy hollow" of an armchair.

One afternoon when they were out riding through the woods beyond the Demon's Run, a Sheriff's officer rode up, and bowing to the party, presented a suspicious-looking document to Capitola and a similar one to Herbert Greyson. And while Old Hurricane stared his eyes half out, the parties most interested opened the papers, which they found to be rather pressing invitations to present at a certain solemnity at Staunton. In a word, they were subpoenaed to give testimony in the case of Williams vs. Le Noir.

"Here's a diabolical dilemma!" said Old Hurricane to himself, as soon as he learned the purport of these documents.

"Here I shall have to bring Cap into court face to face with that demon to bear witness against him! Suppose losing one ward, he should lay claim to another! Ah, but he can't, without foully criminating himself! Well, well, we shall see!"

While Old Hurricane was cogitating Cap was exulting.

"Oh, won't I tell all I know! Yes, and more, too!" she exclaimed, in triumph.

"'More, too!' Oh, hoity-toity! Never say more, too!" said Herbert laughing.

"I will, for I'll tell all I suspect!" said Cap, galloping on ahead, in her eagerness to get home and pack up for her journey.

The next day Old Hurricane, Herbert Greyson, Capitola, Pitapat and Wool went by stage to Staunton. They put up at the Planters' and Farmers' Hotel, whence Herbert Greyson and Capitola soon sallied forth to see Clara and Mrs. Rocke. They soon found the doctor's house, and were ushered into the parlor in the presence of their friends.

The meeting between Capitola and Clara and between Mrs. Rocke and Herbert was very cordial. And then Herbert introduced Capitola to Mrs. Rocke and Cap presented Herbert to Clara. And they all entered into conversation upon the subject of the coming lawsuit, and the circumstances that led to it. And Clara and Capitola related to each other all that had happened to each after their exchanging clothes and parting. And when they had laughed over their mutual adventures and misadventures, Herbert and Capitola took leave and returned to their hotel.

Herbert Greyson was the most serious of the whole family. Upon reaching the hotel he went to his own room and fell into deep reflection. And this was the course of his thought:

"Ira Warfield and Marah Rocke are here in the same town—brought hither upon the same errand—to-morrow to meet in the same court-room! And yet not either of them suspects the presence of the other! Mrs. Rocke does not know that in Capitola's uncle she will behold Major Warfield! He does not foresee that in Clara's matronly friend he will behold Marah Rocke! And Le Noir, the cause of all their misery, will be present also! What will be the effect of this unexpected meeting? Ought I not to warn one or the other? Let me think—no! For were I to warn Major Warfield he would absent himself. Should I drop a hint to Marah she would shrink from the meeting!

No, I will leave it all to Providence—perhaps the sight of her sweet, pale face and soft, appealing eyes, so full of constancy and truth, may touch that stern old heart! Heaven grant it may!" concluded Herbert Greyson.

The next day the suit came on.

At an early hour Doctor Williams appeared, having in charge Clara Day, who was attended by her friend Mrs. Rocke. They were accommodated with seats immediately in front of the judge.

Very soon afterward Major Warfield, Herbert Greyson and Capitola entered, and took their places on the witness's bench, at the right side of the court-room.

Herbert watched Old Hurricane, whose eyes were spellbound to the bench where sat Mrs. Rocke and Clara. Both were dressed in deep mourning, with their veils down and their faces toward the judge. But Herbert dreaded every instant that Marah Rocke should turn her head and meet that fixed, wistful look of Old Hurricane. And he wondered what strange instinct it could be that riveted the old man's regards to that unrecognized woman.

At last, to Herbert's great uneasiness, Major Warfield turned and commenced questioning him:

"Who is that woman in mourning?"

"Hem—m—that one with the flaxen curls under her bonnet is Miss Day."

"I don't mean the girl, I mean the woman sitting by her?"

"That is—hem—hem—that is Doctor Williams sitting—"

Old Hurricane turned abruptly around and favored his nephew with a severe, scrutinizing gaze, demanding:

"Herbert, have you been drinking so early in the morning? Demmy, sir, this is not the season for mint juleps before breakfast! Is that great, stout, round-bodied, red-faced old Doctor Williams a little woman? I see him sitting on the right of Miss Day. I didn't refer to him! I referred to that still, quiet little woman sitting on her left, who has never stirred hand or foot since she sat down there. Who is she?"

"That woman? Oh, she?—yes—ah, let me see—she is a—Miss Day's companion!" faltered Herbert.

"To the demon with you! Who does not see that? But who is she? What is her name?" abruptly demanded Old Hurricane.

"Her name is a—a—did you ever see her before, sir?"

"I don't know! That is what I am trying to remember; but, sir, will you answer my question?"

"You seem very much interested in her."

"You seem very much determined not to let me know who she is! Hang it, sir, will you or will you not tell me that woman's name?"

"Certainly," said Herbert. "Her name is"—He was about to say Marah Rocke, but moral indignation overpowered him and he paused.

"Well, well, her name is what?" impatiently demanded Old Hurricane.

"Mrs. Warfield!" answered Herbert, doggedly.

And just at that unfortunate moment Marah turned her pale face and beseeching eyes around and met the full gaze of her husband!

In an instant her face blanched to marble and her head sank upon the railing before her bench. Old Hurricane was too dark to grow pale, but his bronzed cheek turned as gray as his hair, which fairly lifted itself on his head. Grasping his walking stick with both his hands, he tottered to his feet, and, muttering:

"I'll murder you for this, Herbert!" he strode out of the court-room.

Marah's head rested for about a minute on the railing before her and when she lifted it again her face was as calm and patient as before.

This little incident had passed without attracting attention from any one except Capitola, who, sitting on the other side of Herbert Greyson, had heard the little passage of words between him and her uncle, and had seen the latter start up and go out, and who now, turning to her companion, inquired:

"What is the meaning of all this, Herbert?"

"It means—Satan! And now attend to what is going on! Mr. Sauter has stated the case, and now Stringfellow, the attorney for the other side, is just telling the judge that he stands there in the place of his client, Lieutenant-Colonel Le Noir, who, being ordered to join General Taylor in Mexico, is upon the eve of setting out and cannot be here in person!"

"And is that true? Won't he be here?"

"It seems not. I think he is ashamed to appear after what has happened, and just takes advantage of a fair excuse to absent himself."

"And is he really going to Mexico?"

"Oh, yes! I saw it officially announced in this morning's papers. And, by the bye, I am very much afraid he is to take command of our regiment, and be my superior officer!"

"Oh, Herbert, I hope and pray not! I think there is wickedness enough packed up in that man's body to sink a squadron or lose an army!"

"Well, Cap, such things will happen. Attention! There's Sauter, ready to call his witnesses!" And, in truth, the next moment Capitola Black was called to the stand.

Cap took her place and gave her evidence con amore, and with such vim and such expressions of indignation, that Stringfellow reminded her she was there to give testimony, and not to plead the cause.

Cap rejoined that she was perfectly willing to do both! And so she continued not only to tell the acts, but to express her opinions as to the motives of Le Noir, and give her judgment as to what should be the decision of the court.

Stringfellow, the attorney for Colonel Le Noir, evidently thought that in this rash, reckless, spirited witness he had a fine subject for sarcastic cross-examination! But he reckoned "without his host." He did not know Cap! He, too, "caught a Tartar." And before the cross-examination was concluded, Capitola's apt and cutting replies had overwhelmed him with ridicule and confusion, and done more for the cause of her friend than all her partisans put together!

Other witnesses were called, to corroborate the testimony of Capitola, and still others were examined to prove the last expressed wishes of the late William Day, in regard to the disposal of his daughter's person during the period of her minority.

There was no effective rebutting evidence, and after some hard arguing by the attorneys on both sides, the case was closed, and the judge deferred his decision until the third day thereafter.

The parties then left the court and returned to their several lodgings.

Old Hurricane gave no one a civil word that day. Wool was an atrocious villain, an incendiary scoundrel, a cut-throat, and a black demon. Cap was a beggar, a vagabond and a vixen. Herbert Greyson was another beggar, besides being a knave, a fop and an impudent puppy. The inn-keeper was a swindler, the waiters thieves, the whole world was going to ruin, where it well deserved to go, and all mankind to the demon—as he hoped and trusted they would!

And all this tornado of passion and invective arose just because he had unexpectedly met in the court-room the purient face and beseeching eyes of a woman, married and forsaken, loved and lost, long ago!

Was it strange that Herbert, who had so resented his treatment of Marah Rocke, should bear all his fury, injustice and abuse of himself and others with such compassionate forbearance? But he not only forbore to resent his own affronts, but so besought Capitola to have patience with the old man's temper and apologised to the host by saying that Major Warfield had been very severely tried that day, and when calmer would be the first to regret the violence of his own words.

Marah Rocke returned with Clara to the old doctor's house. She was more patient, silent and quiet than before. Her face was a little paler, her eyes softer, and her tones lower—that was the only visible effect of the morning's unexpected encounter.

The next day but one all the parties concerned assembled at the court-house to hear the decision of the judge. It was given, as had been anticipated, in favor of Clara Day, who was permitted, in accordance with her father's approved wishes, to reside in her patrimonial home under the care of Mrs. Rocke. Colonel Le Noir was to remain trustee of the property, with directions from the court immediately to pay the legacies left by the late Doctor Day to Marah Rocke and Traverse Rocke, and also to pay to Clara Day, in quarterly instalments, from the revenue of her property, an annual sum of money sufficient for her support.

This decision filled the hearts of Clara and her friends with joy. Forgetting time, and place, she threw herself into the arms of Marah Rocke and wept with delight. All concerned in the trial then sought their lodgings.

Clara and Mrs. Rocke returned to the cottage to make preparations for removing to Willow Heights.

Doctor Williams went to the agent of the property to require him to give up the keys, which he did without hesitation.

Old Hurricane and his party packed up to be ready for the stage to take them to Tip-Top the next day.

But that night a series of mysterious events were said to have taken place at the deserted house at Willow Heights that filled the whole community with superstitious wonder. It was reported by numbers of gardeners and farmers, who passed that road, on their way to early market, that a perfect witches' sabbath had been held in that empty house all night; that lights had appeared, flitting from room to room; that strange, weird faces had looked out from the windows; and wild screams had pierced the air!

The next day when this report reached the ears of Clara, and she was asked by Doctor Williams whether she would not be afraid to live there, she laughed gaily and bade him try her.

Cap, who had come over to take leave of Clara, joined her in her merriment, declared that she, for her part, doted on ghosts, and that after Herbert Greyson's departure she should come and visit Clara and help her to entertain the specters.

Clara replied that she should hold her to her promise. And so the friends kissed and separated.

That same day saw several removals.

Clara and Mrs. Rocke took up their abode at Willow Heights and seized an hour even of that busy time to write to Traverse and apprise him of their good fortune.

Old Hurricane and his party set out for their home, where they arrived before nightfall.

And the next day but one Herbert Greyson took leave of his friends and departed to join his company on their road to glory.

CHAPTER XIII
BLACK DONALD

Feared, shunned, belied ere youth had lost her force,
He hated men too much to feel remorse,
And thought the vice of wrath a sacred call,
To pay the injuries of some on all.

There was a laughing devil in his sneer,
That caused emotions both of rage and fear:
And where his frown of hatred darkly fell,
Hope, withering fled and mercy sighed farewell!

—BYRON.

Herbert Greyson had been correct in his conjecture concerning the cause of Colonel Le Noir's conduct in absenting himself from the trial, or appearing there only in the person of his attorney. A proud, vain, conceited man, full of Joseph Surfacisms, he could better have borne to be arraigned upon the charge of murder than to face the accusation of baseness that was about to be proved upon him. Being reasonably certain as to what was likely to be the decision of the Orphan's Court, he was not disappointed in hearing that judgment had been rendered in favor of his ward and her friends. His one great disappointment had been upon discovering the flight of Clara. For when he had ascertained that she had fled, he knew that all was lost—and lost through Capitola, the hated girl for whose destruction he had now another and a stronger motive—revenge!

In this mood of mind three days before his departure to join his regiment he sought the retreat of the outlaw. He chose an early hour of the evening as that in which he should be most likely to find Black Donald.

It was about eight o'clock when he wrapped his large cloak around his tall figure, pulled his hat low over his sinister brow and set out to walk alone to the secret cavern in the side of the Demon's Punch Bowl.

The night was dark and the path dangerous; but his directions had been careful, so that when he reached the brink of that awful abyss he knew precisely where to begin his descent with the least danger of being precipitated to the bottom.

And by taking a strong hold upon the stunted saplings of pine and cedar that grew down through the clefts of the ravine, and placing his feet firmly upon the points of projecting rocks, he contrived to descend the inside of that horrible abyss, which from the top seemed to be fraught with certain death to any one daring enough to make the attempt.

When about half-way down the precipice he reached the clump of cedar bushes growing in the deep cleft, and concealing the hole that formed the entrance to the cavern.

"Here he paused, and, looking through the entrance into a dark and apparently fathomless cavern, he gave the peculiar signal whistle, which was immediately answered from within by the well-known voice of the outlaw chief, saying:"

"All right, my colonel! Give us your hand! Be careful, now, the floor of this cavern is several feet below the opening."

Le Noir extended his hand into the darkness within and soon felt it grasped by that of Black Donald, who, muttering; "Slowly, slowly, my colonel!" succeeded in guiding him down the utter darkness of the subterranean descent until they stood upon the firm bottom of the cavern.

They were still in the midst of a blackness that might be felt, except that from a small opening in the side of the rock a light gleamed. Toward this second opening Black Donald conducted his patron.

And stooping and passing before him, led him into an inner cavern, well lighted and rudely fitted up. Upon a large natural platform of rock, occupying the center of the space, were some dozen bottles of brandy or whisky, several loaves of bread and some dried venison. Around this rude table, seated upon fragments of rock, lugged thither for the purpose, were some eight or ten men of the band, in various stages of intoxication. Along the walls were piles of bearskins, some of which served as couches for six or seven men, who had thrown themselves down upon them in a state of exhaustion or drunken stupor.

"Come, boys, we have not a boundless choice of apartments here, and I want to talk to my colonel! Suppose you take your liquor and bread and meat into the outer cavern and give us the use of this one for an hour," said the outlaw.

The men sullenly obeyed and began to gather up the viands. Demon Dick seized one of the lights to go after them.

"Put down the glim! Satan singe your skin for you! Do you want to bring a hue and cry upon us? Don't you know a light in the outer cavern can be seen from the outside?" roared Black Donald.

Dick sulkily set down the candle and followed his comrades.

"What are you glummering about, confound you! You can see to eat and drink well enough and find your way to your mouth, in the dark, you brute!" thundered the captain. But as there was no answer to this and the men had retreated and left their chief with his visitor alone, Black Donald turned to Colonel Le Noir and said:

"Well, my patron, what great matter is it that has caused you to leave the company of fair Clara Day for our grim society?"

"Ah, then, it appears you are not aware that Clara Day has fled from us—has made a successful appeal to the Orphans' Court, and been taken out of our hands?" angrily replied Colonel Le Noir.

"Whe—ew! My colonel, I think I could have managed that matter better! I think if I had had that girl in my power as you had, she should not have escaped me!"

"Bah! bah! bah! Stop boasting, since it was through your neglect— yours! yours! that I lost this girl!"

"Mine!" exclaimed Black Donald, in astonishment.

"Aye, yours! for if you had done your duty, performed your engagement, kept your word, and delivered me from this fatal Capitola, I had not lost my ward, nor my son his wealthy bride!" exclaimed Le Noir, angrily.

"Capitola! Capitola again! What on earth had she to do with the loss of Clara Day?" cried Black Donald, in wonder.

"Everything to do with it, sir! By a cunning artifice she delivered Clara from our power—actually set her free and covered her flight until she was in security!"

"That girl again! Ha, ha, ha, ha, ha! Ho, ho, ho ho, ho!" laughed and roared Black Donald, slapping his knees.

Le Noir ground and gnashed his teeth in rage, muttering hoarsely:

"Yes, you may laugh, confound you, since it is granted those who win to do so! You may laugh; for you have done me out of five thousand dollars, and what on earth have you performed to earn it?"

"Come, come, my colonel, fair and easy! I don't know which is vulgarest, to betray loss of temper or love of money, and you are doing both. However, it is between friends. But how the demon did that girl, that capital Capitola, get Clara off from right under your eyes?"

"By changing clothes with her, confound you! I will tell you all about it," replied Le Noir, who thereupon commenced and related the whole stratagem by which Capitola freed Clara, including the manner in which she accompanied them to the church and revealed herself at the altar.

Black Donald threw himself back and roared with laughter, vigorously slapping his knees and crying:

"That girl! that capital Capitola! I would not sell my prospect of possessing her for double your bribe."

"Your 'prospect!' Your prospect is about as deceptive as a fata morgana! What have you been doing, I ask you again, toward realizing this prospect and earning the money you have already received?"

"Fair and easy, my colonel! Don't let temper get the better of justice! What have I been doing toward earning the money you have already paid me? In the first place, I lost time and risked my liberty watching around Hurricane Hall. Then, when I had identified the girl and the room she slept in by seeing her at the window, I put three of my best men in jeopardy to capture her. Then, when she, the witch, had captured them, I sacrificed all my good looks, transmogrifying myself into a frightful old field preacher, and went to the camp-meeting to watch, among other things, for an opportunity of carrying her off. The sorceress! she gave me no such opportunity. I succeeded in nothing except in fooling the wiseacres and getting admitted to the prison of my comrades, whom I furnished with instruments by which they made their escape. Since that time we have had to lie low—yes, literally to lie low—to keep out of sight, to burrow under ground; in a word, to live in this cavern."

"And since which you have abandoned all intention of getting the girl and earning the five thousand dollars," sneered Le Noir.

"Earning the remaining five thousand, you mean, colonel. The first five thousand I consider I have already earned. It was the last five thousand that I was to get when the girl should be disposed of."

"Well?"

"Well, I have not given up either the intention of earning the money or the hope of getting the girl; in truth, I had rather lose the money than the girl. I have been on the watch almost continually; but, though I suppose she rides out frequently, I have not yet happened to hit upon her in any of her excursions. At last, however, I have fixed upon a plan for getting the witch into my power. I shall trust the execution of my plan to no one but myself. But I must have time."

"Time! perdition, sir! delay in this matter is fraught with danger! Listen, sir! How Warfield got possession of this girl or the knowledge of her history I do not know, except that it was through the agency of that accursed hag Nancy Grewell. But that he has her and that he knows all about her is but too certain. That he has not at present legal proof enough to establish her identity and her rights before a court of justice I infer from the fact of his continuing inactive in the matter. But who can foresee how soon he may obtain all the proof that is necessary to establish Capitola's claims and wrest the whole of this property from me? Who can tell whether he is not now secretly engaged in seeking and collecting such proof? Therefore, I repeat that the girl must immediately be got rid of! Donald, rid me of that creature and the day that you prove to me her death I will double your fee!"

"Agreed, my colonel, agreed! I have no objection to your doubling, or even quadrupling, my fee. You shall find me in that, as in all other matters, perfectly amenable to reason. Only I must have time. Haste would ruin us. I repeat that I have a plan by which I am certain to get the girl into my possession—a plan the execution of which I will entrust to no other hands but my own. But I conclude as I began—I must have time."

"And how much time?" exclaimed Le Noir, again losing his patience.

"Easy, my patron. That I cannot tell you. It is imprudent to make promises, especially to you, who will take nothing into consideration when they cannot be kept," replied Black Donald, coolly.

"But, sir, do you not know that I am ordered to Mexico, and must leave within three days? I would see the end of this before I go," angrily exclaimed Le Noir.

"Softly, softly, my child the colonel! 'Slow and sure!' 'Fair and easy goes far in a day!'"

"In a word, will you do this business for me and do it promptly?"

"Surely, surely, my patron! But I insist upon time."

"But I go to Mexico in three days."

"All honor go with you, my colonel. Who would keep his friend from the path of glory?"

"Perdition, sir, you trifle with me."

"Perdition, certainly, colonel; there I perfectly agree with you. But the rest of your sentence is wrong; I don't trifle with you."

"What in the fiend's name do you mean?"

"Nothing in the name of any absent friend of ours. I mean simply that you may go to—Mexico!"

"And—my business—"

"—Can be done just as well, perhaps better, without you. Recollect, if you please, my colonel, that when you were absent with Harrison in the West your great business was done here without you! And done better for that very reason! No one even suspected your agency in that matter. The person most benefited by the death of Eugene Le Noir was far enough from the scene of his murder."

"Hush! Perdition seize you! Why do you speak of things so long past?" exclaimed Le Noir, growing white to his very lips.

"To jog your worship's memory and suggest that your honor is the last man who ought to complain of this delay, since it will be very well for you to be in a distant land serving your country at the time that your brother's heiress, whose property you illegally hold, is got out of your way."

"There is something in that," mused Le Noir.

"There is all in that!"

"You have a good brain, Donald."

"What did I tell you? I ought to have been in the cabinet—and mean to be, too! But, colonel, as I mean to conclude my part of the engagement, I should like, for fear of accidents, that you conclude yours—and settle with me before you go."

"What do you mean?"

"That you should fork over to me the remaining five thousand."

"I'll see you at the demon first," passionately exclaimed Le Noir.

"No, you won't, for in that case you'd have to make way with the girl yourself, or see Old Hurricane make way with all your fortune."

"Wretch that you are!"

"Come, come, colonel, don't let's quarrel. The Kingdom of Satan divided against itself cannot stand. Do not let us lose time by falling out. I will get rid of the girl. You, before you go, must hand over the tin, lest you should fall in battle and your heirs dispute the debt! Shell out, my colonel! Shell out and never fear! Capitola shall be a wife and Black Donald a widower before many weeks shall pass."

"I'll do it! I have no time for disputation, as you know, and you profit by the knowledge. I'll do it, though under protest," muttered Le Noir, grinding his teeth.

"That's my brave and generous patron!" said Black Donald, as he arose to attend Le Noir from the cavern; "that's my magnificent colonel of cavalry! The man who runs such risks for you should be very handsomely remunerated!"

CHAPTER XIV
GLORY

"What Alexander sighed for,
What Caesar's soul possessed,
What heroes, saints have died for,
Glory!"

Within three days after his settlement with Black Donald, Colonel Le Noir left home to join his regiment, ordered to Mexico.

He was accompanied by his son Craven Le Noir as far as Baltimore, from which port the reinforcements were to sail for New Orleans, en route for the seat of war.

Here, at the last moment, when the vessel was about to weigh anchor, Craven Le Noir took leave of his father and set out for the Hidden House.

And here Colonel Le Noir's regiment was joined by the company of new recruits in which Herbert Greyson held a commission as lieutenant, and thus the young man's worst forebodings were realized in having for a traveling companion and superior officer the man of whom he had been destined to make a mortal enemy, Colonel Le Noir. However, Herbert soon marked out his course of conduct, which was to avoid Le Noir as much as was consistent with his own official duty, and, when compelled to meet him, to deport himself with the cold ceremony of a subordinate to a superior officer.

Le Noir, on his part, treated Herbert with an arrogant scorn amounting to insult, and used every opportunity afforded him by his position to wound and humiliate the young lieutenant.

After a quick and prosperous voyage they reached New Orleans, where they expected to be farther reinforced by a company of volunteers who had come down the Mississippi river from St. Louis. These volunteers were now being daily drilled at their quarters in the city, and were only waiting the arrival of the vessel to be enrolled in the regiment.

One morning, a few days after the ship reached harbor, Herbert Greyson went on shore to the military rendezvous to see the new recruits exercised. While he stood within the enclosure watching their evolutions under the orders of an officer, his attention became concentrated upon the form of a young man of the rank and file who was marching in a line with many others having their backs turned toward him. That form and gait seemed familiar—the circumstances in which he saw them again—painfully familiar. And yet he could not identify the man. While he gazed, the recruits, at the word of command, suddenly wheeled and faced about. And Herbert could scarcely repress an exclamation of astonishment and regret.

That young man in the dress of a private soldier was Clara Day's betrothed, the widow's only son, Traverse Rocke! While Herbert continued to gaze in surprise and grief, the young recruit raised his eyes, recognized his friend, flushed up to his very temples and cast his eyes down again. The rapid evolutions soon wheeled them around, and the next order sent them into their quarters.

Herbert's time was also up, and he returned to his duty.

The next day Herbert went to the quarters of the new recruits and sought out his young friend, whom he found loitering about the grounds. Again Traverse blushed deeply as the young lieutenant approached. But Herbert Greyson, letting none of his regret appear, since now it would be worse than useless in only serving to give pain to the young private, went up to him cordially and shook his hands, saying:

"Going to serve your country, eh, Traverse? Well, I am heartily glad to see you, at any rate."

"But heartily sorry to see me here, enlisted as a private in a company of raw recruits, looking not unlike Falstaff's ragged regiment?"

"Nay; I did not say that, Traverse. Many a private in the ranks has risen to be a general officer," replied Herbert, encouragingly.

Traverse laughed good humoredly, saying:

"It does not look much like that in my case. This dress," he said, looking down at his coarse, ill-fitting uniform, cowhide shoes, etc.; "this dress, this drilling, these close quarters, coarse food and mixed company are enough to take the military ardor out of any one!"

"Traverse, you talk like a petit maitre, which is not at all your character. Effeminacy is not your vice."

"Nor any other species of weakness, do you mean? Ah, Herbert, your aspiring hopeful, confident old friend is considerably taken down in his ideas of himself, his success and life in general! I went to the West with high hopes. Six months of struggling against indifference, neglect and accumulated debts lowered them down! I carried out letters and made friends, but their friendship began and ended in wishing me well. While trying to get into profitable practice I got into debt. Meanwhile I could not hear from my betrothed in all those months. An occasional letter from her might have prevented this step. But troubles gathered around me, debts increased and—"

"—Creditors were cruel. It is the old story; my poor boy!"

"No; my only creditors were my landlady and my laundress, two poor widows who never willingly distressed me, but who occasionally asked for 'that little amount' so piteously that my heart bled to lack it to give them. And as victuals and clean shirts were absolute necessaries of life, every week my debts increased. I could have faced a prosperous male creditor, and might, perhaps, have been provoked to bully such an one, had he been inclined to be cruel; but I could not face poor women who, after all, I believe, are generally the best friends a struggling young man can have; and so, not to bore a smart young lieutenant with a poor private's antecedents—"

"Oh, Traverse—"

"—I will even make an end of my story. 'At last there came a weary day when hope and faith beneath the weight gave way.' And, hearing that a company of volunteers was being raised to go to Mexico, I enlisted, sold my citizen's wardrobe and my little medical library, paid my debts, made my two friends, the poor widows, some acceptable presents, sent the small remnant of the money to my mother, telling her that I was going farther south to try my fortune, and—here I am."

"You did not tell her that you had enlisted?"

"No."

"Oh, Traverse, how long ago was it that you left St. Louis?"

"Just two weeks."

"Ah! if you had only had patience for a few days longer!" burst unaware from Herbert's bosom. In an instant he was sorry for having spoken thus, for Traverse, with all his soul in his eyes, asked eagerly:

"Why—why, Herbert? What do you mean?"

"Why, you should know that I did not come direct from West Point, but from the neighborhood of Staunton and Hurricane Hall."

"Did you? Oh, did you? Then you may be able to give me news of Clara and my dear mother," exclaimed Traverse, eagerly.

"Yes, I am—pleasant news," said Herbert, hesitating in a manner which no one ever hesitated before in communicating good tidings.

"Thank heaven! oh, thank heaven! What is it, Herbert? How is my dear mother getting on? Where is my best Clara?"

"They are both living together at Willow Heights, according to the wishes of the late Doctor Day. A second appeal to the Orphans' Court made in behalf of Clara by her next friend, Doctor Williams, about a month ago, proved more successful. And if you had waited a few days longer before enlisting and leaving St. Louis, you would have received a letter from Clara to the same effect, and one from Doctor Williams apprizing you that your mother had received her legacy, and that the thousand dollars left you by Doctor Day had been paid into the Agricultural Bank, subject to your orders."

"Oh, heaven! had I but waited three days longer!" exclaimed Traverse, in such acute distress that Herbert hastened to console him by saying:

"Do not repine, Traverse; these things go by fate. It was your destiny—let us hope it will prove a glorious one."

"It was my impatience!" exclaimed Traverse. "It was my impatience! Doctor Day always faithfully warned me against it; always told me that most of the errors, sins and miseries of this world arose from simple impatience, which is want of faith. And now I know it! and now I know it! What had I, who had an honorable profession, to do with becoming a private soldier?"

"Well, well, it is honorable at least to serve your country," said Herbert, soothingly.

"If a foreign foe invaded her shores, yes; but what had I to do with invading another's country?—enlisting for a war of the rights and wrongs of which I know no more than anybody else does? Growing impatient because fortune did not at once empty her cornucopia upon my head! Oh, fool!"

"You blame yourself too severely, Traverse. Your act was natural enough and justifiable enough, much as it is to be regretted," said Herbert, cheerfully.

"Come, come, sit on this plank bench beside me—if you are not ashamed to be seen with a private who is also a donkey—and tell me all about it. Show me the full measure of the happiness I have so recklessly squandered away," exclaimed Traverse, desperately.

"I will sit beside you and tell you everything you wish to know, on condition that you stop berating yourself in a manner that fills me with indignation," replied Herbert, as they went to a distant part of the dusty enclosure and took their seats upon a rude bench.

"Oh, Herbert, bear with me; I could dash my wild, impatient head against a stone wall!"

"That would not be likely to clear or strengthen your brains," said Herbert, who thereupon commenced and told Traverse the whole history of the persecution of Clara Day at the Hidden House; the interception of her letters; the attempt made to force her into a marriage with Craven Le Noir; her deliverance from her enemies by the address and courage of Capitola; her flight to Staunton and refuge with Mrs. Rocke; her appeal to the court, and finally her success and her settlement under the charge of her matronly friend at Willow Heights.

Traverse had not listened patiently to this account. He heard it with many bursts of irrepressible indignation and many involuntary starts of wild passion. Toward the last he sprang up and walked up and down, chafing like an angry lion in his cage.

"And this man," he exclaimed, as Herbert concluded; "this demon! this beast! is now our commanding officer—the colonel of our regiment."

"Yes," replied Herbert, "but as such you must not call him names; military rules are despotic; and this man, who knows your person and knows you to be the betrothed of Clara Day, whose hand and fortune he covets for his son! will leave no power with which his command invests him untried to ruin and destroy you! Traverse, I say these things to you that being 'forewarned' you may be 'forearmed.' I trust that you will remember your mother and your betrothed, and for their dear sakes practise every sort of self-control, patience and forbearance under the provocations you may receive from our colonel. And in advising you to do this I only counsel that which I shall myself practise. I, too, am under the ban of Le Noir for the part I played in the church in succoring Capitola, as well as for happening to be 'the nephew of my uncle,' Major Warfield, who is his mortal enemy."

"I? Will I not be patient, after the lesson I have just learned upon the evils of the opposite? Be easy on my account, dear old friend, I will be as patient as Job, meek as Moses and long-suffering as—my own sweet mother!" said Traverse, earnestly.

The drum was now heard beating to quarters, and Traverse, wringing his friend's hand, left him.

Herbert returned to his ship full of one scheme, of which he had not spoken to Traverse lest it should prove unsuccessful. This scheme was to procure his free discharge before they should set sail for the Rio Grande. He had many influential friends among the officers of his regiment, and he was resolved to tell them as much as was delicate, proper and useful for them to know of the young recruit's private history, in order to get their cooperation.

Herbert spent every hour of this day and the next, when off duty, in this service of his friend. He found his brother officers easily interested, sympathetic and propitious. They united their efforts with his own to procure the discharge of the young recruit, but in vain; the power of Colonel Le Noir was opposed to their influence and the application was peremptorily refused.

Herbert Greyson did not sit down quietly under this disappointment, but wrote an application embodying all the facts of the case to the Secretary of War, got it signed by all the officers of the regiment and despatched it by the first mail.

Simultaneously he took another important step for the interest of his friend. Without hinting any particular motive, he had begged Traverse to let him have his photograph taken, and the latter, with a laugh at the lover-like proposal, had consented. When the likeness was finished Herbert sent it by express to Major Warfield, accompanied by a letter describing the excellent character and unfortunate condition of Traverse, praying the major's interest in his behalf and concluding by saying:

"You cannot look upon the accompanying photograph of my friend and any longer disclaim your own express image in your son."

How this affected the action of Old Hurricane will be seen hereafter.

Traverse, knowing nothing of the efforts that had been and were still being made for his discharge, suffered neither disappointment for failure of the first nor anxiety for the issue of the last.

He wrote to his mother and Clara, congratulating them on their good fortune; telling them that he, in common with many young men of St. Louis, had volunteered for the Mexican War; that he was then in New Orleans, en route for the Rio Grande, and that they would be pleased to know that their mutual friend, Herbert Greyson, was an officer in the same regiment of which he himself was at present a private, but with strong hopes of soon winning his epaulettes. He endorsed an order for his mother to draw the thousand dollars left him by Doctor Day, and he advised her to re-deposit the sum in her own name for her own use in case of need. Praying God's blessing upon them all, and begging their prayers for himself, Traverse concluded his letter, which he mailed the same evening.

And the next morning the company was ordered on board and the whole expedition set sail for the Rio Grande.

Now, we might just as easily as not accompany our troops to Mexico and relate the feats of arms there performed with the minuteness and fidelity of an eye-witness, since we have sat at dinner-tables where the heroes of that war have been honored guests, and where we have heard them fight their battles o'er till "thrice the foe was slain and thrice the field was won."

We might follow the rising star of our young lieutenant, as by his own merits and others' mishaps he ascended from rank to rank, through all the grades of military promotion, but need not because the feats of Lieutenant—Captain—Major and Colonel Greyson, are they not written in the chronicles of the Mexican War?

We prefer to look after our little domestic heroine, our brave little Cap, who, when women have their rights, shall be a lieutenant-colonel herself. Shall she not, gentlemen?

In one fortnight from this time, while Mrs. Rocke and Clara were still living comfortably at Willow Heights and waiting anxiously to hear from Traverse, whom they still supposed to be practising his profession at St Louis, they received his last letter written on the eve of his departure for the seat of war. At first the news overwhelmed them with grief, but then they sought relief in faith, answered his letter cheerfully and commended him to the infinite mercy of God.

CHAPTER XV
CAP CAPTIVATES A CRAVEN

"He knew himself a villain, but he deemed
The rest no better than the thing he seemed;
And scorned the best as hypocrites who hid
Those deeds the bolder spirits plainly did.
He knew himself detested, but he knew
The hearts that loathed him crouched and—dreaded, too."

The unregenerate human heart is, perhaps, the most inconsistent thing in all nature; and in nothing is it more capricious than in the manifestations of its passions; and in no passion is it so fantastic as in that which it miscalls love, but which is really often only appetite.

From the earliest days of manhood Craven Le Noir had been the votary of vice, which he called pleasure. Before reaching the age of twenty-five he had run the full course of dissipation, and found himself ruined in health, degraded in character and disgusted with life.

Yet in all this experience his heart had not been once agitated with a single emotion that deserved the name of passion. It was colder than the coldest.

He had not loved Clara, though, for the sake of her money, he had courted her so assiduously. Indeed, for the doctor's orphan girl he had from the first conceived a strong antipathy. His evil spirit had shrunk from her pure soul with the loathing a fiend might feel for an angel. He had found it repugnant and difficult, almost to the extent of impossibility, for him to pursue the courtship to which he was only reconciled by a sense of duty to—his pocket.

It was reserved for his meeting with Capitola at the altar of the Forest Chapel to fire his clammy heart, stagnant blood and sated senses with the very first passion that he had ever known. Her image, as she stood there at the altar with flashing eyes and flaming cheeks and scathing tongue defying him, was ever before his mind's eye. There was something about that girl so spirited, so piquant and original that she impressed even his apathetic nature as no other woman had ever been able to do. But what most of all attracted him to Capitola was her diablerie. He longed to catch that little savage to his bosom and have her at his mercy. The aversion she had exhibited toward him only stimulated his passion.

Craven Le Noir, among his other graces, was gifted with inordinate vanity. He did not in the least degree despair of over-coming all Capitola's dislike to his person and inspiring her with a passion equal to his own.

He knew well that he dared not present himself at Hurricane Hall, but he resolved to waylay her in her rides and there to press his suit. To this he was urged by another motive almost as strong as love—namely, avarice.

He had gathered thus much from his father, that Capitola Black was supposed to be Capitola Le Noir, the rightful heiress of all that vast property in land, houses, iron and coal mines, foundries and furnaces, railway shares, etc., and bank stocks, from which his father drew the princely revenue that supported them both in their lavish extravagance of living.

As the heiress—or, rather, the rightful owner—of all this vast fortune. Capitola was a much greater "catch" than poor Clara, with her modest estate, had been. And Mr. Craven Le Noir was quite willing to turn the tables on his father by running off with the great heiress, and step from his irksome position of dependent upon Colonel Le Noir's often ungracious bounty to that of the husband of the heiress and the master of the property. Added to that was another favorable circumstance—namely, whereas he had had a strong personal antipathy to Clara he had as strong an attraction to Capitola, which would make his course of courtship all the pleasanter.

In one word, he resolved to woo, win and elope with, or forcibly abduct, Capitola Le Noir, marry her and then turn upon his father and claim the fortune in right of his wife. The absence of Colonel Le Noir in Mexico favored his projects, as he could not fear interruption.

Meanwhile our little madcap remained quite unconscious of the honors designed her. She had cried every day of the first week of Herbert's absence; every alternate day of the second; twice in the third; once in the fourth; not at all in the fifth, and the sixth week she was quite herself again, as full of fun and frolic and as ready for any mischief or deviltry that might turn up.

She resumed her rides, no longer followed by Wool, because Old Hurricane, partly upon account of his misadventure in having had the misfortune inadvertently "to lose sight of" his mistress upon that memorable occasion of the metamorphosis of Cap into Clara and partly because of the distant absence of Le Noir, did not consider his favorite in danger.

He little knew that a subtle and unscrupulous agent had been left sworn to her destruction, and that another individual, almost equally dangerous, had registered a secret vow to run off with her.

Neither did poor Cap when, rejoicing to be free from the dogging attendance of Wool, imagine the perils to which she was exposed; nor is it even likely that if she had she would have cared for them in any other manner than as promising piquant adventures. From childhood she had been inured to danger, and had never suffered harm; therefore, Cap, like the Chevalier Bayard, was "without fear and without reproach."

Craven Le Noir proceeded cautiously with his plans, knowing that there was time enough and that all might be lost by haste. He did not wish to alarm Capitola.

The first time he took occasion to meet her in her rides he merely bowed deeply, even to the flaps of his saddle and, with a melancholy smile, passed on.

"Miserable wretch! He is a mean fellow to want to marry a girl against her will, no matter how much he might have been in love with her, and I am very glad I balked him. Still, he looks so ill and unhappy that I can't help pitying him," said Cap, looking compassionately at his white cheeks and languishing eyes, and little knowing that the illness was the effect of dissipation and that the melancholy was assumed for the occasion.

A few days after this Cap again met Craven Le Noir, who again, with a deep bow and sad smile, passed her.

"Poor fellow! he richly deserves to suffer, and I hope it may make him better, for I am right-down sorry for him; it must be so dreadful to lose one we love; but it was too base in him to let his father try to compel her to have him. Suppose, now, Herbert Greyson was to take a fancy to another girl, would I let uncle go to him and put a pistol to his head and say, 'Cap is fond of you, you varlet! and demmy, sir, you shall marry none but her, or receive an ounce of lead in your stupid brains'? No, I'd scorn it; I'd forward the other wedding; I'd make the cake and dress the bride and—then maybe I'd break—no, I'm blamed if I would! I'd not break my heart for anybody. Set them up with it, indeed! Neither would my dear, darling, sweet, precious Herbert treat me so, and I'm a wretch to think of it!" said Cap, with a rich, inimitable unction as, rejoicing in her own happy love, she cheered Gyp and rode on.

Now, Craven Le Noir had been conscious of the relenting and compassionate looks of Capitola, but he did not know that they were only the pitying regards of a noble and victorious nature over a vanquished and suffering wrong-doer. However, he still determined to be cautious, and not ruin his prospects by precipitate action, but to "hasten slowly."

So the next time he met Capitola he raised his eyes with one deep, sad, appealing gaze to hers, and then, bowing profoundly, passed on.

"Poor man," said Cap to herself, "he bears no malice toward me for depriving him of his sweetheart; that's certain. And, badly as he behaved, I suppose it was all for love, for I don't know how any one could live in the same house with Clara and not be in love with her. I should have been so myself if I'd been a man, I know!"

The next time Cap met Craven and saw again that deep, sorrowful, appealing gaze as he bowed and passed her, she glanced after him, saying to herself:

"Poor soul, I wonder what he means by looking at me in that piteous manner? I can do nothing to relieve him. I'm sure if I could I would. But 'the way of the transgressor is hard,' Mr. Le Noir, and he who sins must suffer."

For about three weeks their seemingly accidental meetings continued in this silent manner, so slowly did Craven make his advances. Then, feeling more confidence, he made a considerably long step forward.

One day, when he guessed that Capitola would be out, instead of meeting her as heretofore, he put himself in her road and, riding slowly toward a five-barred gate, allowed her to overtake him.

He opened the gate and, bowing, held it open until she had passed.

She bowed her thanks and rode on; but presently, without the least appearance of intruding, since she had overtaken him, he was at her side and, speaking with downcast eyes and deferential manner, he said:

"I have long desired an opportunity to express the deep sorrow and mortification I feel for having been hurried into rudeness toward an estimable young lady at the Forest Chapel. Miss Black, will you permit me now to assure you of my profound repentance of that act and to implore your pardon?"

"Oh, I have nothing against you, Mr. Le Noir. It was not I whom you were intending to marry against my will; and as for what you said and did to me, ha! ha! I had provoked it, you know, and I also afterwards paid it in kind. It was a fair fight, in which I was the victor, and victors should never be vindictive," said Cap, laughing, for, though knowing him to have been violent and unjust, she did not suspect him of being treacherous and deceitful, or imagine the base designs concealed beneath his plausible manner. Her brave, honest nature could understand a brute or a despot, but not a traitor.

"Then, like frank enemies who have fought their fight out, yet bear no malice toward each other, we may shake hands and be friends, I hope," said Craven, replying in the same spirit in which she had spoken.

"Well, I don't know about that, Mr. Le Noir. Friendship is a very sacred thing, and its name should not be lightly taken on our tongues. I hope you will excuse me if I decline your proffer," said Cap, who had a well of deep, true, earnest feeling beneath her effervescent surface.

"What! you will not even grant a repentant man your friendship, Miss Black?" asked Craven, with a sorrowful smile.

"I wish you well, Mr. Le Noir. I wish you a good and, therefore, a happy life; but I cannot give you friendship, for that means a great deal."

"Oh, I see how it is! You cannot give your friendship where you cannot give your esteem. Is it not so?"

"Yes," said Capitola; "that is it; yet I wish you so well that I wish you might grow worthy of higher esteem than mine."

"You are thinking of my—yes, I will not shrink from characterizing that conduct as it deserves—my unpardonable violence toward Clara. Miss Black, I have mourned that sin from the day that I was hurried into it until this. I have bewailed it from the very bottom of my heart," said Craven, earnestly, fixing his eyes with an expression of perfect truthfulness upon those of Capitola.

"I am glad to hear you say so," said Cap.

"Miss Black, please hear this in palliation—I would not presume to say in defense—of my conduct: I was driven to frenzy by a passion of contending love and jealousy as violent and maddening as it was unreal and transient. But that delusive passion has subsided, and among the unmerited mercies for which I have to be thankful is that, in my frantic pursuit of Clara Day, I was not cursed with success! For all the violence into which that frenzy hurried me I have deeply repented. I can never forgive myself, but—cannot you forgive me?"

"Mr. Le Noir, I have nothing for which to forgive you. I am glad that you have repented toward Clara and I wish you well, and that is really all that I can say."

"I have deserved this and I accept it," said Craven, in a tone so mournful that Capitola, in spite of all her instincts, could not choose but pity him.

He rode on, with his pale face, downcast eyes and melancholy expression, until they reached a point at the back of Hurricane Hall, where their paths diverged.

Here Craven, lifting his hat and bowing profoundly, said, in a sad tone:

"Good evening, Miss Black," and, turning his horse's head, took the path leading down into the Hidden Hollow.

"Poor young fellow! he must be very unhappy down in that miserable place; but I can't help it. I wish he would go to Mexico with the rest," said Cap, as she pursued her way homeward.

Not to excite her suspicion, Craven Le Noir avoided meeting Capitola for a few days, and then threw himself in her road and, as before, allowed her to overtake him.

Very subtly he entered into conversation with her, and, guarding every word and look, took care to interest without alarming her. He said no more of friendship, but a great deal of regret for wasted years and wasted talents in the past and good resolutions for the future.

And Cap listened good humoredly. Capitola, being of a brave, hard, firm nature, had not the sensitive perceptions, fine intuitions and true insight into character that distinguished the more refined nature of Clara Day—or, at least, she had not these delicate faculties in the same perfection. Thus, her undefined suspicions of Craven's sincerity were overborne by a sort of noble benevolence which determined her to think the best of him which circumstances would permit.

Craven, on his part, having had more experience, was much wiser in the pursuit of his object. He also had the advantage of being in earnest. His passion for Capitola was sincere, and not, as it had been in the case of Clara, simulated. He believed, therefore, that, when the time should be ripe for the declaration of his love, he would have a much better prospect of success, especially as Capitola, in her ignorance of her own great fortune, must consider his proposal the very climax of disinterestedness.

After three more weeks of riding and conversing with Capitola he had, in his own estimation, advanced so far in her good opinion as to make it perfectly safe to risk a declaration. And this he determined to do upon the very first opportunity.

Chance favored him.

One afternoon Capitola, riding through the pleasant woods skirting the back of the mountain range that sheltered Hurricane Hall, got a fall, for which she was afterwards inclined to cuff Wool.

It happened in this way: She had come to a steep rise in the road and urged her pony into a hard gallop, intending as she said to herself, to "storm the height," when suddenly, under the violent strain, the girth, ill-fastened, flew apart and Miss Cap was on the ground, buried under the fallen saddle.

With many a blessing upon the carelessness of grooms, Cap picked herself up, put the saddle on the horse, and was engaged in drawing under the girth when Craven Le Noir rode up, sprang from his horse and, with anxiety depicted on his countenance, ran to the spot inquiring:

"What is the matter? No serious accident, I hope and trust, Miss Black?"

"No; those wretches in uncle's stables did not half buckle the girth, and, as I was going in a hard gallop up the steep, it flew apart and gave me a tumble; that's all," said Cap, desisting a moment from her occupation to take breath.

"You were not hurt?" inquired Craven, with deep interest in his tone.

"Oh, no; there is no harm done, except to my riding skirt, which has been torn and muddied by the fall," said Cap, laughing and resuming her efforts to tighter the girth.

"Pray permit me," said Craven, gently taking the end of the strap from her hand; "this is no work for a lady, and, besides, is beyond your strength."

Capitola, thanking him, withdrew to the side of the road, and, seating herself upon the trunk of a fallen tree, began to brush the dirt from her habit.

Craven adjusted and secured the saddle with great care, patted and soothed the pony and then, approaching Capitola in the most deferential manner, stood before her and said: "Miss Black, you will pardon me, I hope, if I tell you that the peril I had imagined you to be in has so agitated my mind as to make it impossible for me longer to withhold a declaration of my sentiments—" Here his voice, that had trembled throughout this disclosure, now really and utterly failed him.

Capitola looked up with surprise and interest; she had never in her life before heard an explicit declaration of love from anybody. She and Herbert somehow had always understood each other very well, without ever a word of technical love-making passing between them; so Capitola did not exactly know what was coming next.

Craven recovered his voice, and encouraged by the favorable manner in which she appeared to listen to him, actually threw himself at her feet and, seizing one of her hands, with much ardor and earnestness and much more eloquence than any one would have credited him with, poured forth the history of his passion and his hopes.

"Well, I declare!" said Cap, when he had finished his speech and was waiting in breathless impatience for her answer; "this is what is called a declaration of love and a proposal of marriage, is it? It is downright sentimental, I suppose, if I had only sense enough to appreciate it! It is as good as a play; pity it is lost upon me!"

"Cruel girl! how you mock me!" cried Craven, rising from his knees and sitting beside her.

"No, I don't; I'm in solemn earnest. I say it is first rate. Do it again; I like it!"

"Sarcastic and merciless one, you glory in the pain you give! But if you wish again to hear me say I love you, I will say it a dozen—yes, a hundred—times over if you will only admit that you could love me a little in return."

"Don't; that would be tiresome; two or three times is quite enough. Besides, what earthly good could my saying 'I love you' do?"

"It might persuade you to become the wife of one who will adore you to the last hour of his life."

"Meaning you?"

"Meaning me; the most devoted of your admirers."

"That isn't saying much, since I haven't got any but you."

"Thank fortune for it! Then I am to understand, charming Capitola, that at least your hand and your affections are free," cried Craven, joyfully.

"Well, now, I don't know about that! Really, I can't positively say; but it strikes me, if I were to get married to anybody else, there's somebody would feel queerish!"

"No doubt there are many whose secret hopes would be blasted, for so charming a girl could not have passed through this world without having won many hearts who would keenly feel the loss of hope in her marriage. But what if they do, my enchanting Capitola? You are not responsible for any one having formed such hopes."

"Fudge!" said Cap, "I'm no belle; never was; never can be; have neither wealth, beauty nor coquetry enough to make me one. I have no lovers nor admirers to break their hearts about me, one way or another; but there is one honest fellow—hem! never mind; I feel as if I belonged to somebody else; that's all. I am very much obliged to you, Mr. Le Noir, for your preference, and even for the beautiful way in which you have expressed it, but—I belong to somebody else."

"Miss Black," said Craven, somewhat abashed but not discouraged. "I think I understand you. I presume that you refer to the young man who was your gallant champion in the Forest Chapel."

"The one that made your nose bleed," said the incorrigible Cap.

"Well, Miss Black, from your words it appears that this is by no means an acknowledged but only an understood engagement, which cannot be binding upon either party. Now, a young lady of your acknowledged good sense—"

"I never had any more good sense than I have had admirers," interrupted Cap.

Craven smiled.

"I would not hear your enemy say that," he replied; then, resuming his argument, he said:

"You will readily understand, Miss Black, that the vague engagement of which you speak, where there is want of fortune on both sides, is no more prudent than it is binding. On the contrary, the position which it is my pride to offer you is considered an enviable one; even apart from the devoted love that goes with it. You are aware that I am the sole heir of the Hidden House estate, which, with all its dependencies, is considered the largest property, as my wife would be the most important lady, in the county."

Cap's lip curled a little; looking askance at him she answered:

"I am really very much obliged to you Mr. Le Noir, for the distinguished honor that you designed for me. I should highly appreciate the magnanimity of a young gentleman, the heir of the wealthiest estate in the neighborhood who deigns to propose marriage to the little beggar that I acknowledge myself to be. I regret to be obliged to refuse such dignities, but—I belong to another," said Capitola, rising and advancing toward her horse.

Craven would not risk his success by pushing his suit further at this sitting.

Very respectfully lending his assistance to put Capitola into her saddle, he said he hoped at some future and more propitious time to resume the subject. And then, with a deep bow, he left her, mounted his horse and rode on his way.

He did not believe that Capitola was more than half in earnest, or that any girl in Capitola's circumstances would do such a mad thing as to refuse the position he offered her.

He did not throw himself in her way often enough to excite her suspicion that their meetings were preconcerted on his part, and even when he did overtake her or suffer her to overtake him, he avoided giving her offense by pressing his suit until another good opportunity should offer. This was not long in coming.

One afternoon he overtook her and rode by her side for a short distance when, finding her in unusually good spirits and temper, he again renewed his declaration of love and offer of marriage.

Cap turned around in her saddle and looked at him with astonishment for a full minute before she exclaimed: "Why, Mr. Le Noir, I gave you an answer more than a week ago. Didn't I tell you 'No'? What on earth do you mean by repeating the question?"

"I mean, bewitching Capitola, not to let such a treasure slip out of my grasp if I can help it."

"I never was in your grasp, that I know of," said Cap, whipping up her horse and leaving him far behind.

Days passed before Craven thought it prudent again to renew and press his suit. He did so upon a fine September morning, when he overtook her riding along the banks of the river. He joined her and in the most deprecating manner besought her to listen to him once more. Then he commenced in a strain of the most impassioned eloquence and urged his love and his proposal.

Capitola stopped her horse, wheeled around and faced him, looking him full in the eyes while she said:

"Upon my word, Mr. Le Noir, you remind me of an anecdote told of young Sheridan. When his father advised him to take a wife and settle, he replied by asking whose wife he should take. Will nobody serve your purpose but somebody else's sweetheart? I have told you that I belong to a brave young soldier who is fighting his country's battles in a foreign land, while you are lazing here at home, trying to undermine him. I am ashamed of you, sir, and ashamed of myself for talking with you so many times! Never do you presume to accost me on the highway or anywhere else again! Craven by name and Craven by nature, you have once already felt the weight of Herbert's arm! Do not provoke its second descent upon you! You are warned!" and with that Capitola, with her lips curled, her eyes flashing and her cheeks burning, put whip to her pony and galloped away.

Craven Le Noir's thin, white face grew perfectly livid with passion.

"I will have her yet! I have sworn it, and by fair means or by foul I will have her yet!" he exclaimed, as he relaxed his hold upon his bridle and let his horse go on slowly, while he sat with his brows gathered over his thin nose, his long chin buried in his neckcloth and his nails between his teeth, gnawing like a wild beast, as was his custom when deeply cogitating.

Presently he conceived a plan so diabolical that none but Satan himself could have inspired it! This was to take advantage of his acquaintance and casual meetings with Capitola so to malign her character as to make it unlikely that any honest man would risk his honor by taking her to wife; that thus the way might be left clear for himself; and he resolved, if possible, to effect this in such a manner—namely, by jests, innuendos and sneers—that it should never be directly traced to a positive assertion on his part. And in the mean time he determined to so govern himself in his deportment toward Capitola as to arouse no suspicion, give no offense and, if possible, win back her confidence.

It is true that even Craven Le Noir, base as he was, shrank from the idea of smirching the reputation of the woman whom he wished to make a wife; but then he said to himself that in that remote neighborhood the scandal would be of little consequence to him, who, as soon as he should be married, would claim the estate of the Hidden House in right of his wife, put it in charge of an overseer and then, with his bride, start for Paris, the paradise of the epicurean, where he designed to fix their principal residence.

Craven Le Noir was so pleased with his plan that he immediately set about putting it in execution. Our next chapter will show how he succeeded.

CHAPTER XVI
CAP'S RAGE

Is he not approved to the height of a villain, who hath
slandered, scorned, dishonored thy kinswoman. Oh! that I
were a man for his sake, or had a friend who would be
one for mine!

—SHAKESPEARE.

Autumn brought the usual city visitors to Hurricane Hall to spend the
sporting season and shoot over Major Warfield's grounds. Old Hurricane
was in his glory, giving dinners and projecting hunts.

Capitola also enjoyed herself rarely, enacting with much satisfaction to
herself and guests her new role of hostess, and not unfrequently joining her
uncle and his friends in their field sports.

Among the guests there were two who deserve particular attention, not
only because they had been for many years annual visitors of Hurricane
Hall, but more especially because there had grown up between them and
our little madcap heroine, a strong mutual confidence and friendship. Yet
no three persons could possibly be more unlike than Capitola and the two
cousins of her soul, as she called these two friends. They were both distant
relatives of Major Warfield, and in right of this relationship invariably
addressed Capitola as "Cousin Cap."

John Stone, the elder of the two, was a very tall, stout, squarely built
young man, with a broad, good-humored face, fair skin, blue eyes and light
hair. In temperament he was rather phlegmatic, quiet and lazy. In character
he was honest, prudent and good-tempered. In circumstances he was a safe
banker, with a notable wife and two healthy children. The one thing that
was able to excite his quiet nerves was the chase, of which he was as fond
as he could possibly be of any amusement. The one person who agreeably
stirred his rather still spirits was our little Cap, and that was the secret of his
friendship for her.

Edwin Percy, the other, was a young West Indian, tall and delicately formed, with a clear olive complexion, languishing dark hazel eyes and dark, bright chestnut hair and beard. In temperament he was ardent as his clime. In character, indolent, careless and self-indulgent. In condition he was the bachelor heir of a sugar plantation of a thousand acres. He loved not the chase, nor any other amusement requiring exertion. He doted upon swansdown sofas with springs, French plays, cigars and chocolate. He came to the country to find repose, good air and an appetite. He was the victim of constitutional ennui that yielded to nothing but the exhilaration of Capitola's company; that was the mystery of his love for her, and doubtless the young Creole would have proposed for Cap, had he not thought it too much trouble to get married, and dreaded the bustle of a bridal. Certainly Edwin Percy was as opposite in character to John Stone, as they both were to Capitola, yet great was the relative attraction among the three. Cap impartially divided her kind offices as hostess between them.

John Stone joined Old Hurricane in many a hard day's hunt, and Capitola was often of the party.

Edwin Percy spent many hours on the luxurious lounge in the parlor, where Cap was careful to place a stand with chocolate, cigars, wax matches and his favorite books.

One day Cap had had what she called "a row with the governor," that is to say, a slight misunderstanding with Major Warfield; a very uncommon occurrence, as the reader knows, in which that temperate old gentleman had so freely bestowed upon his niece the names of "beggar, foundling, brat, vagabond and vagrant," that Capitola, in just indignation, refused to join the birding party, and taking her game bag, powder flask, shot-horn and fowling piece, and calling her favorite pointer, walked off, as she termed it, "to shoot herself." But if Capitola's by no means sweet temper had been tried that morning, it was destined to be still more severely tested before the day was over.

Her second provocation came in this way: John Stone, another deserter of the birding party had that day betaken himself to Tip-top upon some private business of his own. He dined at the Antlers in company with some sporting gentlemen of the neighborhood, and when the conversation naturally turned upon field sports, Mr. John Stone spoke of the fine shooting that was to be had around Hurricane Hall, when one of the gentlemen, looking straight across the table to Mr. Stone, said:

"Ahem! That pretty little huntress of Hurricane Hall—that niece or ward, or mysterious daughter of Old Hurricane, who engages with so much enthusiasm in your field sports over there, is a girl of very free and easy manners I understand—a Diana in nothing but her love of the chase!"

"Sir, it is a base calumny! And the man who endorses it is a shameless slanderer! There is my card! I may be found at my present residence, Hurricane Hall," said John Stone, throwing his pasteboard across the table, and rising to leave it.

"Nay, nay," said the stranger, laughing and pushing the card away. "I do not endorse the statement—I know nothing about it! I wash my hands of it," said the young man. And then upon Mr. Stone's demanding the author of the calumny, he gave the name of Mr. Craven Le Noir, who, he said, had "talked in his cups," at a dinner party recently given by one of his friends.

"I pronounce—publicly, in the presence of all these witnesses, as I shall presently to Craven Le Noir himself—that he is a shameless miscreant, who has basely slandered a noble girl! You, sir, have declined to endorse those words; henceforth decline to repeat them! For after this I shall call to a severe account any man who ventures, by word, gesture or glance to hint this slander, or in any other way deal lightly with the honorable name and fame of the lady in question. Gentlemen, I am to be found at Hurricane Hall, and I have the honor of wishing you a more improving subject of conversation, and—a very good afternoon," said John Stone, bowing and leaving the room.

He immediately called for his horse and rode home.

In crossing the thicket of woods between the river and the rising ground in front of Hurricane Hall, he overtook Capitola, who, as we have said, had been out alone with her gun and dog, and was now returning home with her game bag well laden.

Now, as John Stone looked at Capitola, with her reckless, free and joyous air, he thought she was just the sort of girl, unconsciously, to get herself and friends into trouble. And he thought it best to give her a hint to put an abrupt period to her acquaintance, if she had even he slightest, with the heir apparent of the Hidden House.

While still hesitating how to begin the conversation, he came up with the young girl, dismounted, and, leading his horse, walked by her side, asking carelessly:

"What have you bagged, Cap?"

"Some partridges! Oh, you should have been out with me and Sweetlips! We've had such sport! But, anyhow, you shall enjoy your share of the spoils! Come home and you shall have some of these partridges broiled for supper, with currant sauce—a dish of my own invention for uncle's sake, you know! He's such a gourmand!"

"Thank you, yes—I am on my way home now. Hem—m! Capitola, I counsel you to cut the acquaintance of our neighbor, Craven Le Noir."

"I have already done so; but—what in the world is the matter that you should advise me thus?" inquired Capitola, fixing her eyes steadily upon the face of John Stone, who avoided her gaze as he answered:

"The man is not a proper associate for a young woman."

"I know that, and have cut him accordingly; but, Cousin John, there is some reason for your words, that you have not expressed; and as they concern me, now I insist upon knowing what they are!"

"Tut! it is nothing!" said the other evasively.

"John Stone, I know better! And the more you look down and whip your boot the surer I am that there is something I ought to know, and I will know!"

"Well, you termagant! Have your way! He has been speaking lightly of you—that's all! Nobody minds him—his tongue is no scandal."

"John Stone—what has he said?" asked Capitola, drawing her breath hardly between her closed teeth.

"Oh, now, why should you ask? It is nothing—it is not proper that I should tell you," replied that gentleman, in embarrassment.

"'It is nothing,' and yet 'it is not proper that you should tell me!' How do you make that out? John Stone, leave off lashing the harmless bushes and listen to me! I have to live in the same neighborhood with this man, after you have gone away, and I insist upon knowing the whole length and breadth of his baseness and malignity, that I may know how to judge and punish him!" said Capitola, with such grimness of resolution that Mr. Stone, provoked at her perversity, answered:

"Well, you wilful girl, listen!" And commencing, he mercilessly told her all that had passed at the table.

To have seen our Cap then! Face, neck and bosom were flushed with the crimson tide of indignation!

"You are sure of what you tell me, Cousin John?"

"The man vouches for it!"

"He shall bite the dust!"

"What?"

"The slanderer shall bite the dust!"

Without more ado, down was thrown gun, game bag, powder flask and shot-horn, and, bounding from point to point over all the intervening space, Capitola rushed into Hurricane Hall, and without an instant's delay ran straight into the parlor, where her epicurean friend, the young Creole, lay slumbering upon the lounge.

With her face now livid with concentrated rage, and her eyes glittering with that suppressed light peculiar to intense passion, she stood before him and said:

"Edwin! Craven Le Noir has defamed your cousin! Get up and challenge him!"

"What did you say, Cap?" said Mr. Percy, slightly yawning.

"Must I repeat it? Craven Le Noir has defamed my character—challenge him!"

"That would be against the law, coz; they would indict me sure!"

"You—you—you lie there and answer me in that way! Oh that I were a man!"

"Compose, yourself, sweet coz, and tell me what all this is about! Yaw-ooo!—really I was asleep when you first spoke to me!"

"Asleep! Had you been dead and in your grave, the words that I spoke should have roused you like the trump of the archangel!" exclaimed Capitola, with the blood rushing back to her cheeks.

"Your entrance was sufficiently startling, coz, but tell me over again—what was the occasion?"

"That caitiff, Craven Le Noir, has slandered me! Oh, the villain! He is a base slanderer! Percy, get up this moment and challenge Le Noir! I cannot breathe freely until it is done!" exclaimed Capitola, impetuously.

"Cousin Cap, duelling is obsolete; scenes are passe; law settles everything; and here there is scarcely ground for action for libel. But be comforted, coz, for if this comes to Uncle Hurricane's ears, he'll make mince-meat of him in no time, It is all in his line; he'll chaw him right up!"

"Percy, do you mean to say that you will not call out that man?" asked Capitola, drawing her breath hardly.

"Yes, coz."

"You won't fight him?"

"No, coz."

"You won't?"

"No."

"Edwin Percy, look me straight in the face!" said Cap, between her closed teeth.

"Well, I am looking you straight in the face—straight in the two blazing gray eyes, you little tempest in a teapot—what then?"

"Do I look as though I should be in earnest in what I am about to speak?"

"I should judge so."

"Then listen, and don't take your eyes off mine until I am done speaking!"

"Very well, don't be long, though, for it rather agitates me."

"I will not! Hear me, then! You say that you decline to challenge Le Noir. Very good! I, on my part, here renounce all acquaintance with you! I will never sit down at the same table—enter the same room, or breathe the same air with you—never speak to you—listen to you, or recognize you in any manner, until my deep wrongs are avenged in the punishment of my slanderer, so help me—"

"Hush—sh! don't swear, Cap—it's profane and unwomanly; and nothing on earth but broken oaths would be the result!"

But Cap was off! In an instant she was down in the yard, where her groom was holding her horse, ready in case she wished to take her usual ride.

"Where is Mr. John Stone?" she asked.

"Down at the kennels, miss," answered the boy.

She jumped into her saddle, put whip to her horse and flew over the ground between the mansion house and the kennels.

She pulled up before the door of the main building, sprang from her saddle, threw the bridle to a man in attendance, and rushed into the house and into the presence of Mr. John Stone, who was busy in prescribing for an indisposed pointer.

He looked up in astonishment, exclaiming: "Hilloe! All the witches! Here's Cap! Why, where on earth did you shoot from? What's up now? You look as if you were in a state of spontaneous combustion and couldn't stand it another minute."

"And I can't—and I won't! John Stone, you must call that man out!"

"What man, Cap—what the deuce do you mean?"

"You know well enough—you do this to provoke me! I mean the man of whom you cautioned me this afternoon—the wretch who slandered me—the niece of your host!"

"Whe—ew!"

"Will you do it?"

"Where's Percy?"

"On the lounge with an ice in one hand and a novel in the other! I suppose it is no use mincing the matter, John—he is a—mere epicure—there is no fight in him! It is you who must vindicate your cousin's honor!"

"My cousin's honor cannot need vindication! It is unquestioned and unquestionable!"

"No smooth words, if you please, cousin John! Will you, or will you not fight that man?"

"Tut, Cap, no one really questions your honor—that man will get himself knocked into a cocked hat if he goes around talking of an honest girl!"

"A likely thing, when her own cousins and guests take it so quietly."

"What would you have them do, Cap? The longer an affair of this sort is agitated, the more offensive it becomes! Besides, chivalry is out of date! The knights-errant are all dead."

"The men are all dead! If any ever really lived!" cried Cap, in a fury. "Heaven knows I am inclined to believe them to have been a fabulous race like that of the mastodon or the centaur! I certainly never saw a creature that deserved the name of man! The very first of your race was the meanest fellow that ever was heard of—ate the stolen apple and when found out laid one half of the blame on his wife and the other on his Maker—'The woman whom thou gavest me' did so and so—pah! I don't wonder the Lord took a dislike to the race and sent a flood to sweep them all off the face of the earth! I will give you one more chance to retrieve your honor—in one word, now—will you fight that man?"

"My dear little cousin, I would do anything in reason to vindicate the assailed manhood of my whole sex, but really, now—"

"Will you fight that man? One word—yes or no?"

"Tut, Cap! you are a very reckless young woman! You—it's your nature—you are an incorrigible madcap! You bewitch a poor wretch until he doesn't know his head from his heels—puts his feet into his hat and covers his scalp with his boots! You are a will-o'-the-wisp who lures a poor fellow on through woods, bogs and briars, until you land him in the quicksands! You whirl him around and around until he grows dizzy and delirious, and talks at random, and then you'd have him called out, you blood-thirsty little vixen! I tell you, Cousin Cap, if I were to take up all the quarrels your hoydenism might lead me into, I should have nothing else to do!"

"Then you won't fight!"

"Can't, little cousin! I have a wife and family, which are powerful checks upon a man's duelling impulses!"

"Silence! You are no cousin of mine—no drop of your sluggish blood stagnates in my veins—no spark of the liquid fire of my life's current burns in your torpid arteries, else at this insult would it set you in a flame! Never dare to call me cousin again." And so saying, she flung herself out of the building and into her saddle, put whip to her horse and galloped away home.

Now, Mr. Stone had privately resolved to thrash Craven Le Noir; but he did not deem it expedient to take Cap into his confidence. As Capitola reached the horse block, her own groom came to take the bridle.

"Jem," she said, as she jumped from her saddle, "put Gyp up and then come to my room, I have a message to send by you."

And then, with burning cheeks and flashing eyes, she went to her own sanctum, and after taking off her habit, did the most astounding thing that ever a woman of the nineteenth or any former century attempted— she wrote a challenge to Craven Le Noir—charging him with falsehood in having maligned her honor—demanding from him "the satisfaction of a gentleman," and requesting him as the challenged party to name the time, place and weapons with which he would meet her.

By the time she had written, sealed and directed this warlike defiance, her young groom made his appearance.

"Jem," she asked, "do you know the way to the Hidden House?"

"Yes, miss, sure."

"Then take this note thither, ask for Mr. Le Noir, put it into his hands, and say that you are directed to wait an answer. And listen! You need not mention to any one in this house where you are going—nor when you return, where you have been; but bring the answer you may get directly to this room, where you will find me."

"Yes, miss," said the boy, who was off like a flying Mercury.

Capitola threw herself into her chair to spend the slow hours until the boy's return as well as her fierce impatience and forced inaction would permit.

At tea time she was summoned; but excused herself from going below upon the plea of indisposition.

"Which is perfectly true," she said to herself, "since I am utterly indisposed to go. And besides, I have sworn never again to sit at the same table with my cousins, until for the wrongs done me I have received ample satisfaction."

CHAPTER XVII
CAPITOLA CAPS THE CLIMAX

Oh! when she's angry, she is keen and shrewd
She was a vixen when she went to school;
And though she is but little she is fierce.

—SHAKESPEARE

It was quite late in the evening when Jem, her messenger, returned.

"Have you an answer?" she impetuously demanded, rising to meet him as he entered.

"Yes, miss, here it is," replied the boy, handing a neatly folded, highly perfumed little note.

"Go," said Cap, curtly, as she received it.

And when the boy had bowed and withdrawn, she threw herself into a chair, and with little respect for the pretty device of the pierced heart with which the note was sealed, she tore it open and devoured its contents.

Why did Capitola's cheeks and lips blanch white as death? Why did her eyes contract and glitter like stilettoes? Why was her breath drawn hard and laboriously through clenched teeth and livid lips?

That note was couched in the most insulting terms.

Capitola's first impulse was to rend the paper to atoms and grind those atoms to powder beneath her heel. But a second inspiration changed her purpose.

"No—no—no! I will not destroy you, precious little note! No legal document involving the ownership of the largest estate, no cherished love letter filled with vows of undying affection, shall be more carefully guarded! Next to my heart shall you lie. My shield and buckler shall you be! My sure defense and justification! I know what to do with you, my precious little jewel! You are the warrant for the punishment of that man, signed by his own hand." And so saying Capitola carefully deposited the note in her bosom.

Then she lighted her chamber lamp, and, taking it with her, went downstairs to her uncle's bedroom.

Taking advantage of the time when she knew he would be absorbed in a game of chess with John Stone, and she would be safe from interruption for several hours if she wished, she went to Major Warfield's little armory in the closet adjoining his room, opened his pistol case and took from it a pair of revolvers, closed and locked the case, and withdrew and hid the key that they might not chance to be missed until she should have time to replace them.

Then she hurried back into her own chamber, locked the pistols up in her own drawer, and, wearied out with so much excitement, prepared to go to rest. Here a grave and unexpected obstacle met her; she had always been accustomed to kneel and offer up to heaven her evening's tribute of praise and thanksgiving for the mercies of the day, and prayers for protection and blessing through the night.

Now she knelt as usual, but thanksgiving and prayer seemed frozen on her lips! How could she praise or pray with such a purpose as she had in her heart?

For the first time Capitola doubted the perfect righteousness of that purpose which was of a character to arrest her prayers upon her lips.

With a start of impatience and a heavy sigh, she sprang up and hurried into bed.

She did not sleep, but lay tossing from side to side in feverish excitement the whole night—having, in fact, a terrible battle between her own fierce passions and her newly awakened conscience.

Nevertheless, she arose by daybreak in the morning, dressed herself, went and unlocked her drawer, took out the pistols, carefully loaded them, and laid them down for service.

Then she went down-stairs, where the servants were only just beginning to stir, and sent for her groom, Jem, whom she ordered to saddle her pony, and also to get a horse for himself, to attend her in a morning ride.

After which she returned up-stairs, put on her riding habit, and buckled around her waist a morocco belt, into which she stuck the two revolvers. She then threw around her shoulders a short circular cape that concealed the weapons, and put on her hat and gloves and went below.

She found her little groom already at the door with the horses. She sprang into her saddle, and, bidding Jem follow her, took the road toward Tip-Top.

She knew that Mr. Le Noir was in the habit of riding to the village every morning, and she determined to meet him. She knew, from the early hour of the day, that he could not possibly be ahead of her, and she rode on slowly to give him an opportunity to overtake her.

Probably Craven Le Noir was later that morning than usual, for Capitola had reached the entrance of the village before she heard the sound of his horse's feet approaching behind her.

She did not wish that their encounter should be in the streets of the village, so she instantly wheeled her horse and galloped back to meet him.

As both were riding at full speed, they soon met.

She first drew rein, and, standing in his way, accosted him with:

"Mr. Le Noir!"

"Your most obedient, Miss Black!" he said, with a deep bow.

"I happen to be without father or brother to protect me from affront, sir, and my uncle is an invalid veteran whom I will not trouble! I am, therefore, under the novel necessity of fighting my own battles! Yesterday, sir, I sent you a note demanding satisfaction for a heinous slander you circulated against me! You replied by an insulting note. You do not escape punishment so! Here are two pistols; both are loaded; take either one of them; for, sir, we have met, and now we do not part until one of us falls from the horse!"

And so saying, she rode up to him and offered him the choice of the pistols.

He laughed—partly in surprise and partly in admiration, as he said, with seeming good humor:

"Miss Black, you are a very charming young woman, and delightfully original and piquant in all your ideas; but you outrage all the laws that govern the duello. You know that, as the challenged party, I have the right to the choice of time, place and arms. I made that choice yesterday. I renew it to-day. When you accede to the terms of the meeting I shall endeavor to give you all the satisfaction you demand! Good-morning, miss."

And with a deep bow, even to the flaps of his saddle, he rode past her.

"That base insult again!" cried Capitola, with the blood rushing to her face.

Then lifting her voice, she again accosted him: "Mr. Le Noir!"

He turned, with a smile.

She threw one of the pistols on the ground near him, saying: "Take that up and defend yourself."

He waved his hand in negation, bowed, smiled, and rode on.

"Mr. Le Noir!" she called, in a peremptory tone.

Once more he turned.

She raised her pistol, took deliberate aim at his white forehead, and fired—

Bang! bang! bang! bang! bang! bang!

Six times without an instant's intermission, until her revolver was spent.

When the smoke cleared away, a terrible vision met her eyes!

It was Craven Le Noir with his face covered with blood, reeling in his saddle, from which he soon dropped to the ground.

In falling his foot remained in the hanging stirrup. The well-trained cavalry horse stood perfectly still, though trembling in a panic of terror, from which he might at any moment start to run, dragging the helpless body after him.

Capitola saw this danger, and not being cruel, she tempered justice with mercy, threw down her spent pistol, dismounted from her horse, went up to the fallen man, disengaged his foot from the stirrup, and, taking hold of his shoulders, tried with all her might to drag the still breathing form from the dusty road where it lay in danger of being run over by wagons, to the green bank, where it might lie in comparative safety.

But that heavy form was too much for her single strength. And, calling her terrified groom to assist her, they removed the body.

Capitola then remounted her horse and galloped rapidly into the village, and up to the "ladies' entrance" of the hotel, where, after sending for the proprietor she said:

"I have just been shooting Craven Le Noir for slandering me; he lies by the roadside at the entrance of the village; you had better send somebody to pick him up."

"Miss!" cried the astonished inn-keeper.

Capitola distinctly repeated her words and then, leaving the inn-keeper, transfixed with consternation, she crossed the street and entered a magistrate's office, where a little, old gentleman, with a pair of green spectacles resting on his hooked nose, sat at a writing-table, giving some directions to a constable, who was standing hat in hand before him.

Capitola waited until this functionary had his orders and a written paper, and had left the office, and the magistrate was alone, before she walked up to the desk and stood before him.

"Well, well, young woman! Well, well, what do you want?" inquired the old gentleman, impatiently looking up from folding his papers.

"I have come to give myself up for shooting Craven Le Noir, who slandered me," answered Capitola, quietly.

The old man let fall his hands full of papers, raised his head and stared at her over the tops of his green spectacles.

"What did you say, young woman?" he asked, in the tone of one who doubted his own ears.

"I say that I have forestalled an arrest by coming here to give myself up for the shooting of a dastard who slandered, insulted and refused to give me satisfaction," answered Capitola, very distinctly.

"Am I awake? Do I hear aright? Do you mean to say that you have killed a man?" asked the dismayed magistrate.

"Oh, I can't say as to the killing! I shot him off his horse and then sent Mr. Merry and his men to pick him up, while I came here to answer for myself!"

"Unfortunate girl! And how can you answer for such a dreadful deed?" exclaimed the utterly confounded magistrate.

"Oh, as to the dreadfulness of the deed, that depends on circumstances," said Cap, "and I can answer for it very well! He made addresses to me. I refused him. He slandered me. I challenged him. He insulted me. I shot him!"

"Miserable young woman, if this be proved true, I shall have to commit you!"

"Just as you please," said Cap, "but bless your soul, that won't help Craven Le Noir a single bit!"

As she spoke several persons entered the office in a state of high excitement—all talking at once, saying:

"That is the girl!"

"Yes, that is her!"

"She is Miss Black, old Warfield's niece."

"Yes, he said she was," etc., etc., etc.

"What is all this, neighbors, what is all this?" inquired the troubled magistrate, rising in his place.

"Why, sir, there's been a gentleman, Mr. Craven Le Noir, shot. He has been taken to the Antlers, where he lies in articulus mortis, and we wish him to be confronted with Miss Capitola Black, the young woman here present, that he may identify her, whom he accuses of having shot six charges into him, before his death. She needn't deny it, because he is ready to swear to her!" said Mr. Merry, who constituted himself spokesman.

"She accuses herself," said the magistrate, in dismay.

"Then, sir, had she not better be taken at once to the presence of Mr. Le Noir, who may not have many minutes to live?"

"Yes, come along," said Cap. "I only gave myself up to wait for this; and as he is already at hand, let's go and have it all over, for I have been riding about in this frosty morning air for three hours, and I have got a good appetite, and I want to go home to breakfast."

"I am afraid, young woman, you will scarcely get home to breakfast this morning," said Mr. Merry.

"We'll see that presently," answered Cap, composedly, as they all left the office, and crossed the street to the Antlers.

They were conducted by the landlord to a chamber on the first floor, where upon a bed lay stretched, almost without breath or motion, the form of Craven Le Noir. His face was still covered with blood, that the bystanders had scrupulously refused to wash off until the arrival of the magistrate. His complexion, as far as it could be seen, was very pale. He was thoroughly prostrated, if not actually dying.

Around his bed were gathered the village doctor, the landlady and several maid-servants.

"The squire has come, sir; are you able to speak to him?" asked the landlord, approaching the bed.

"Yes, let him swear me," feebly replied the wounded man, "and then send for a clergyman."

The landlady immediately left to send for Mr. Goodwin, and the magistrate approached the head of the bed, and, speaking solemnly, exhorted the wounded man, as he expected soon to give an account of the works done in his body, to speak the truth, the whole truth, and nothing but the truth, without reserve, malice or exaggeration, both as to the deed and its provocation.

"I will I will—for I have sent for a minister and I intend to try to make my peace with heaven," replied Le Noir.

The magistrate then directed Capitola to come and take her stand at the foot of the bed, where the wounded man, who was lying on his back, could see her without turning.

Cap came as she was commanded and stood there with some irrepressible and incomprehensible mischief gleaming out from under her long eye-lashes and from the corners of her dimpled lips.

The magistrate then administered the oath to Craven Le Noir, and bade him look upon Capitola and give his evidence.

He did so, and under the terrors of a guilty conscience and of expected death, his evidence partook more of the nature of a confession than an accusation. He testified that he had addressed Capitola, and had been rejected by her; then, under the influence of evil motives, he had circulated insinuations against her honor, which were utterly unjustifiable by fact; she, seeming to have heard of them, took the strange course of challenging him—just as if she had been a man. He could not, of course, meet a lady in a duel, but he had taken advantage of the technical phraseology of the challenged party, as to time, place and weapons, to offer her a deep insult; then she had waylaid him on the highway, offered him his choice of a pair of revolvers, and told him that, having met, they should not part until one or the other fell from the horse; he had again laughingly refused the encounter except upon the insulting terms he had before proposed. She had then thrown him one of the pistols, bidding him defend himself. He had laughingly passed her when she called him by name, he had turned and she fired—six times in succession, and he fell. He knew no more until he was brought to his present room. He said in conclusion he did not wish that the girl should be prosecuted, as she had only avenged her own honor; and that he hoped his death would be taken by her and her friends as a sufficient expiation of his offenses against her; and, lastly he requested that he might be left alone with the minister.

"Bring that unhappy young woman over to my office, Ketchum," said the magistrate, addressing himself to a constable. Then turning to the landlord, he said:

"Sir, it would be a charity in you to put a messenger on horseback and send him to Hurricane Hall for Major Warfield, who will have to enter into a recognizance for Miss Black's appearance at court."

"Stop," said Cap, "don't be too certain of that! 'Be always sure you're right—then go ahead!' Is not any one here cool enough to reflect that if I had fired six bullets at that man's forehead and every one had struck, I should have blown his head to the sky? Will not somebody at once wash his face and see how deep the wounds are?"

The doctor who had been restrained by others now took a sponge and water and cleaned the face of Le Noir, which was found to be well peppered with split peas!

Cap looked around, and seeing the astonished looks of the good people, bust into an irrepressible fit of laughter, saying, as soon as she had got breath enough:

"Upon my word, neighbors, you look more shocked, if not actually more disappointed, to find that, after all he is not killed, and there'll be no spectacle, than you did at first when you thought murder had been done."

"Will you be good enough to explain this, young woman?" said the magistrate, severely.

"Certainly, for your worship seems as much disappointed as others!" said Cap. Then turning toward the group around the bed, she said:

"You have heard Mr. Le Noir's 'last dying speech and confession,' as he supposed it to be; and you know the maddening provocations that inflamed my temper against him. Last night, after having received his insulting answer to my challenge, there was evil in my heart, I do assure you! I possessed myself of my uncle's revolvers and resolved to waylay him this morning and force him to give me satisfaction, or if he refused— well, no matter! I tell you, there was danger in me! But, before retiring to bed at night, it is my habit to say my prayers; now the practice of prayer and the purpose of 'red-handed violence' cannot exist in the same person at the same time! I wouldn't sleep without praying, and I couldn't pray without giving up my thoughts of fatal vengeance upon Craven Le Noir. So at last I made up my mind to spare his life, and teach him a lesson. The next morning I drew the charges of the revolvers and reloaded them with poor powder and dried peas! Everything else has happened just as he has told you! He has received no harm, except in being terribly frightened, and in having his beauty spoiled! And as for that, didn't I offer him one of the pistols, and expose my own face to similar damage? For I'd scorn to take advantage of any one!" said Cap, laughing.

Craven Le Noir had now raised himself up in a sitting posture, and was looking around with an expression of countenance which was a strange blending of relief at this unexpected respite from the grave, and intense mortification at finding himself in the ridiculous position which the address of Capitola and his own weak nerves, cowardice and credulity had placed him.

Cap went up to him and said, in a consoling voice:

"Come, thank heaven that you are not going to die this bout! I'm glad you repented and told the truth; and I hope you may live long enough to offer heaven a truer repentance than that which is the mere effect of fright! For I tell you plainly that if it had not been for the grace of the Lord, acting upon my heart last night, your soul might have been in Hades now!"

Craven Le Noir shut his eyes, groaned and fell back overpowered by the reflection.

"Now, please your worship, may I go home?" asked Cap, demurely, popping down a mock courtesy to the magistrate.

"Yes—go! go! go! go! go!" said that officer, with an expression as though he considered our Cap an individual of the animal kingdom whom neither Buffon nor any other natural philosopher had ever classified, and who, as a creature of unknown habits, might sometimes be dangerous.

Cap immediately availed herself of the permission, and went out to look for her servant and horses.

But Jem, the first moment he had found himself unwatched, had put out as fast as he could fly to Hurricane Hall, to inform Major Warfield of what had occurred.

And Capitola, after losing a great deal of time in looking for him, mounted her horse and was just about to start, when who should ride up in hot haste but Old Hurricane, attended by Wool.

"Stop there!" he shouted, as he saw Cap.

She obeyed, and he sprang from his horse with the agility of youth, and helped her to descend from hers.

Then drawing her arm within his own, he led her into the parlor, and, putting an unusual restraint upon himself, he ordered her to tell him all about the affair.

Cap sat down and gave him the whole history from beginning to end.

Old Hurricane could not sit still to hear. He strode up and down the room, striking his stick upon the floor, and uttering inarticulate sounds of rage and defiance.

When Cap had finished her story he suddenly stopped before her, brought down the point of his stick with a resounding thump upon the floor and exclaimed:

"Demmy, you New York newsboy! Will you never be a woman? Why the demon didn't you tell me, sirrah? I would have called the fellow out and chastised him to your heart's content! Hang it, miss, answer me and say!"

"Because you are on the invalid list and I am in sound condition and capable of taking my own part!" said Cap.

"Then, answer me this, while you were taking your own part, why the foul fiend didn't you pepper him with something sharper than dried peas?"

"I think he is quite as severely punished in suffering from extreme terror and intense mortification and public ridicule," said Cap.

"And now, uncle, I have not eaten a single blessed mouthful this morning, and I am hungry enough to eat up Gyp, or to satisfy Patty."

Old Hurricane, permitting his excitement to subside in a few expiring grunts, rang the bell and gave orders for breakfast to be served.

And after that meal was over he set out with his niece for Hurricane Hall.

And upon arriving at home he addressed a letter to Mr. Le Noir, to the effect that as soon as the latter should have recovered from the effect of his fright and mortification, he, Major Warfield, should demand and expect satisfaction.

CHAPTER XVIII
BLACK DONALD'S LAST ATTEMPT

Who can express the horror of that night,
When darkness lent his robes to monster fear?
And heaven's black mantle, banishing the light,
Made everything in fearful form appear.

—BRANDON.

Let it not be supposed that Black Donald had forgotten his promise to Colonel Le Noir, or was indifferent to its performance.

But many perilous failures had taught him caution.

He had watched and waylaid Capitola in her rides. But the girl seemed to bear a charmed safety; for never once had he caught sight of her except in company with her groom and with Craven Le Noir. And very soon by eavesdropping on these occasions, he learned the secret design of the son to forestall the father, and run off with the heiress.

And as Black Donald did not foresee what success Craven Le Noir might have with Capitola, he felt the more urgent necessity for prompt action on his own part.

He might, indeed, have brought his men and attacked and overcome Capitola's attendants, in open day; but the enterprise must needs have been attended with great bloodshed and loss of life, which would have made a sensation in the neighborhood that Black Donald, in the present state of his fortunes, was by no means ambitious of daring.

In a word, had such an act of unparalleled violence been attempted, the better it succeeded the greater would have been the indignation of the people, and the whole country would probably have risen and armed themselves and hunted the outlaws, as so many wild beasts, with horses and hounds.

Therefore, Black Donald preferred quietly to abduct his victim, so as to leave no trace of her "taking off," but to allow it to be supposed that she had eloped.

He resolved to undertake this adventure alone, though to himself personally this plan was even more dangerous than the other.

He determined to gain access to her chamber, secrete himself anywhere in the room (except under the bed, where his instincts informed him that Capitola every night looked), and when the household should be buried in repose, steal out upon her, overpower, gag and carry her off, in the silence of the night, leaving no trace of his own presence behind.

By means of one of his men, who went about unsuspected among the negroes, buying up mats and baskets, that the latter were in the habit of making for sale, he learned that Capitola occupied the same remote chamber, in the oldest part of the house; but that a guest slept in the room next, and another in the one opposite hers. And that the house was besides full of visitors from the city, who had come down to spend the sporting season, and that they were hunting all day and carousing all night from one week's end to another.

On hearing this, Black Donald quickly comprehended that it was no time to attempt the abduction of the maiden, with the least probability of success. All would be risked and most probably lost in the endeavor.

He resolved, therefore, to wait until the house should be clear of company, and the household fallen into their accustomed carelessness and monotony.

He had to wait much longer than he had reckoned upon—through October and through November, when he first heard of and laughed over Cap's "duel" with Craven Le Noir, and congratulated himself upon the fact that that rival was no longer to be feared. He had also to wait through two-thirds of the month of December, because a party had come down to enjoy a short season of fox-hunting. They went away just before Christmas.

And then at last came Black Donald's opportunity! And a fine opportunity it was! Had Satan himself engaged to furnish him with one to order, it could not have been better!

The reader must know that throughout Virginia the Christmas week, from the day after Christmas until the day after New-year, is the negroes' saturnalia! There are usually eight days of incessant dancing, feasting and frolicking from quarter to quarter, and from barn to barn. Then the banjo, the fiddle and the "bones" are heard from morning until night, and from night until morning.

And nowhere was this annual octave of festivity held more sacred than at Hurricane Hall. It was the will of Major Warfield that they should have their full satisfaction out of their seven days' carnival. He usually gave a dinner party on Christmas day, after which his people were free until the third of January.

"Demmy, mum!" he would say to Mrs. Condiment, "they wait on us fifty-one weeks in the year, and it's hard if we can't wait on ourselves the fifty-second!"

Small thanks to Old Hurricane for his self-denial! He did nothing for himself or others, and Mrs. Condiment and Capitola had a hot time of it in serving him. Mrs. Condiment had to do all the cooking and housework. And Cap had to perform most of the duties of Major Warfield's valet. And that was the way in which Old Hurricane waited on himself.

It happened, therefore, that about the middle of the Christmas week, being Wednesday, the twenty-eighth of December, all the house-servants and farm laborers from Hurricane. Hall went off in a body to a banjo break-down given at a farm five miles across the country.

And Major Warfield, Mrs. Condiment and Capitola were the only living beings left in the old house that night.

Black Donald, who had been prowling about the premises evening after evening, watching his opportunity to effect his nefarious object, soon discovered the outward bound stampede of the negroes, and the unprotected state in which the old house, for that night only, would be left. And he determined to take advantage of the circumstance to consummate his wicked purpose.

In its then defenceless condition he could easily have mustered his force and carried off his prize without immediate personal risk. But, as we said before, he eschewed violence, as being likely to provoke after effects of a too fatal character.

He resolved rather at once to risk his own personal safety in the quieter plan of abduction which he had formed.

He determined that as soon as it should be dark he would watch his opportunity to enter the house, steal to Cap's chamber, secrete himself in a closet, and when all should be quiet, "in the dead waste and middle of the night," he would come out, master her, stop her mouth and carry her off.

When it became quite dark he approached the house, and hid himself under the steps beneath the back door leading from the hall into the garden, to watch his opportunity of entering. He soon found that his enterprise required great patience as well as courage. He had to wait more than two hours before he heard the door unlocked and opened.

He then peered out from his hiding-place and saw old Hurricane taking his way out towards the garden.

Now was his time to slip unperceived into the house. He stealthily came out from his hiding-place, crept up the portico stairs to the back door, noiselessly turned the latch, entered and closed it behind him. He had just time to open a side door on his right hand and conceal himself in a wood closet under the stairs, when he heard the footsteps of Old Hurricane returning.

The old man came in and Black Donald laughed to himself to hear with what caution he locked, bolted and barred the doors to keep out house-breakers!

"Ah, old fellow, you are fastening the stable after the horse has been stolen!" said Black Donald to himself.

As soon as old Hurricane had passed by the closet in which the outlaw was concealed, and had gone into the parlor, Black Donald determined to risk the ascent into Capitola's chamber. From the description given by his men, who had once succeeded in finding their way thither, he knew very well where to go.

Noiselessly, therefore, he left his place of concealment and crept out to reconnoitre the hall, which he found deserted.

Old Hurricane's shawl, hat and walking stick were deposited in one corner. In case of being met on the way, he put the hat on his head, wrapped the shawl around his shoulders, and took the stick in his hand.

His forethought proved to be serviceable. He went through the hall and up the first flight of stairs without interruption; but on going along the hall of the second story he met Mrs. Condiment coming out of Old Hurricane's room.

"Your slippers are on the hearth, your gown is at the fire and the kettle is boiling to make your punch, Major Warfield," said the old lady in passing.

"Umph! umph! umph!" grunted Black Donald in reply.

The housekeeper then bade him good-night, saying that she was going at once to her room.

"Umph!" assented Black Donald. And so they parted and this peril was passed.

Black Donald went up the second flight of stairs and then down a back passage and a narrow staircase and along a corridor and through several untenanted rooms, and into another passage, and finally through a side door leading into Capitola's chamber.

Here he looked around for a safe hiding-place—there was a high bedstead curtained; two deep windows also curtained; two closets, a dressing bureau, workstand, washstand and two arm chairs. The forethought of little Pitapat had caused her to kindle a fire on the hearth and place a waiter of refreshments on the workstand, so as to make all comfortable before she had left with the other negroes to go to the banjo breakdown.

Among the edibles Pitapat had been careful to leave a small bottle of brandy, a pitcher of cream, a few eggs and some spice, saying to herself, "Long as it was Christmas time Miss Caterpillar might want a sup of egg nog quiet to herself, jes' as much as old marse did his whiskey punch"—and never fancying that her young mistress would require a more delicate lunch than her old master.

Black Donald laughed as he saw this outlay, and remarking that the young occupant of the chamber must have an appetite of her own, he put the neck of the brandy bottle to his lips and took what he called "a heavy swig."

Then vowing that old Hurricane knew what good liquor was, he replaced the bottle and looked around to find the best place for his concealment.

He soon determined to hide himself behind the thick folds of the window curtain, nearest the door, so that immediately after the entrance of Capitola he could glide to the door, lock it, withdraw the key and have the girl at once in his power.

He took a second "swig" at the brandy bottle and then went into his place of concealment to wait events.

That same hour Capitola was her uncle's partner in a prolonged game of chess. It was near eleven o'clock before Cap, heartily tired of the battle, permitted herself to be beaten in order to get to bed.

With a satisfied chuckle, Old Hurricane arose from his seat, lighted two bed-chamber lamps, gave one to Capitola, took the other himself, and started off for his room, followed by Cap as far as the head of the first flight of stairs, where she bade him good night.

She waited until she saw him enter his room, heard him lock his door on the inside and throw himself down heavily into his arm chair, and then she went on her own way.

She hurried up the second flight of stairs and along the narrow passages, empty rooms, and steep steps and dreary halls, until she reached the door of her own dormitory.

She turned the latch and entered the room.

The first thing that met her sight was the waiter of provisions upon the stand. And at this fresh instance of her little maid's forethought, she burst into a uncontrollable fit of laughter.

She did not see a dark figure glide from behind the window curtains, steal to the door, turn the lock and withdraw the key!

But still retaining her prejudice against the presence of food in her bed-chamber, she lifted up the waiter in both hands to cany it out into the passage, turned and stood face to face with—Black Donald!

CHAPTER XIX
THE AWFUL PERIL OF CAPITOLA

Out of this nettle, danger,
I'll pluck the flower, safety!

—SHAKESPEARE.

Capitola's blood seemed turned to ice, and her form to stone by the sight! Her first impulse was to scream and let fall the waiter! She controlled herself and repressed the scream though she was very near dropping the waiter.

Black Donald looked at her and laughed aloud at her consternation, saying with a chuckle:

"You did not expect to see me here to-night, did you now, my dear?"

She gazed at him in a silent panic for a moment.

Then her faculties, that had been suddenly dispersed by the shock, as suddenly rallied to her rescue.

In one moment she understood her real position.

Black Donald had locked her in with himself and held the key—so she could not hope to get out.

The loudest scream that she might utter would never reach the distant chamber of Major Warfield, or the still more remote apartment of Mrs. Condiment; so she could not hope to bring any one to her assistance.

She was, therefore, entirely in the power of Black Donald. She fully comprehended this, and said to herself:

"Now, my dear Cap, if you don't look sharp your hour is come! Nothing on earth will save you, Cap, but your own wits! For if ever I saw mischief in any one's face, it is in that fellow's that is eating you up with his great eyes at the same time that he is laughing at you with his big mouth! Now, Cap, my little man, be a woman! Don't you stick at trifles! Think of Jael and Sisera! Think of Judith and Holofernes! And the devil and Doctor Faust, if necessary, and don't you blanch! All stratagems are fair in love and war—especially in war, and most especially in such a war as this is likely to be—a contest in close quarters for dear life!"

All this passed through her mind in one moment, and in the next her plan was formed.

Setting her waiter down upon the table and throwing herself into one of the armchairs, she said:

"Well, upon my word! I think a gentleman might let a lady know when he means to pay her a domiciliary visit at midnight!"

"Upon my word, I think you are very cool!" replied Black Donald, throwing himself into the second armchair on the other side of the stand of refreshments.

"People are likely to be cool on a December night, with the thermometer at zero, and the ground three feet under the snow," said Cap, nothing daunted.

"Capitola, I admire you! You are a cucumber! That's what you are, a cucumber!"

"A pickled one?" asked Cap.

"Yes, and as pickled cucumbers are good to give one an appetite, I think I shall fall to and eat."

"Do so," said Cap, "for heaven forbid that I should fail in hospitality!"

"Why, really, this looks as though you had expected a visitor—doesn't it?" asked Black Donald, helping himself to a huge slice of ham, and stretching his feet out toward the fire.

"Well, yes, rather; though, to say the truth, it was not your reverence I expected," said Cap.

"Ah! somebody else's reverence, eh? Well, let them come! I'll be ready for them!" said the outlaw, pouring out and quaffing a large glass of brandy. He drank it, set down the glass, and turning to our little heroine, inquired:

"Capitola did you ever have Craven Le Noir here to supper with you?"

"You insult me! I scorn to reply!" said Cap.

"Whe—ew! What long whiskers our Grimalkin's got! You scorn to reply! Then you really are not afraid of me?" asked the robber, rolling a great piece of cheese in his mouth.

"Afraid of you? No, I guess not!" replied Cap, with a toss of her head.

"Yet, I might do you some harm."

"But, you won't!"

"Why won't I?"

"Because it won't pay!"

"Why wouldn't it?"

"Because you couldn't do me any harm, unless you were to kill me, and you would gain nothing by my death, except a few trinkets that you may have without."

"Then, you are really not afraid of me?" he asked, taking another deep draught of brandy.

"Not a bit of it—I rather like you!"

"Come, now, you're running a rig upon a fellow," said the outlaw, winking and depositing a huge chunk of bread in his capacious jaws.

"No, indeed! I liked you, long before I ever saw you! I always did like people that make other people's hair stand on end! Don't you remember when you first came here disguised as a peddler, though I did not know who you were, when we were talking of Black Donald, and everybody was abusing him, except myself? I took his part and said that for my part I liked Black Donald and wanted to see him."

"Sure enough, my jewel, so you did! And didn't I bravely risk my life by throwing off my disguise to gratify your laudable wish?"

"So you did, my hero!"

"Ah, but well as you liked me, the moment you thought me in your power didn't you leap upon my shoulders like a catamount and cling there, shouting to all the world to come and help you, for you had caught Black Donald and would die before you would give him up? Ah! you little vampire, how you thirsted for my blood! And you pretended to like me!" said Black Donald, eying her from head to foot, with a sly leer.

Cap returned the look with interest. Dropping her head on one side, she glanced upward from the corner of her eye, with an expression of "infinite" mischief and roguery, saying:

"Lor, didn't you know why I did that?"

"Because you wanted me captured, I suppose."

"No, indeed, but, because—"

"Well, what?"

"Because I wanted you to carry me off!"

"Well, I declare! I never thought of that!" said the outlaw, dropping his bread and cheese, and staring at the young girl.

"Well, you might have thought of it then! I was tired of hum-drum life, and I wanted to see adventures!" said Cap.

Black Donald looked at the mad girl from head to foot and then said, coolly:

"Miss Black, I am afraid you are not good."

"Yes I am—before folks!" said Cap.

"And so you really wished me to carry you off?"

"I should think so! Didn't I stick to you until you dropped me?"

"Certainly! And now if you really like me as well as you say you do, come give me a kiss."

"I won't!" said Cap, "until you have done your supper and washed your face! Your beard is full of crumbs!"

"Very well, I can wait awhile! Meantime just brew me a bowl of egg-nog, by way of a night-cap, will you?" said the outlaw, drawing off his boots and stretching his feet to the fire.

"Agreed, but it takes two to make egg-nog; you'll have to whisk up the whites of the eggs into a froth, while I beat the yellows, and mix the other ingredients," said Cap.

"Just so," assented the outlaw, standing up and taking off his coat and flinging it upon the floor.

Cap shuddered, but went on calmly with her preparations. There were two little white bowls setting one within the other upon the table. Cap took them apart and set them side by side and began to break the eggs, letting the whites slip into one bowl and dropping the yellows into the other.

Black Donald sat down in his shirt sleeves, took one of the bowls from Capitola and began to whisk up the whites with all his might and main.

Capitola beat up the yellows, gradually mixing the sugar with it. In the course of her work she complained that the heat of the fire scorched her face, and she drew her chair farther to-wards the corner of the chimney, and pulled the stand after her.

"Oh, you are trying to get away from me," said Black Donald, hitching his own chair in the same direction, close to the stand, so that he sat immediately in front of the fireplace.

Cap smiled and went on beating her eggs and sugar together. Then she stirred in the brandy and poured in the milk and took the bowl from Black Donald and laid on the foam. Finally, she filled a goblet with the rich compound and handed it to her uncanny guest.

Black Donald untied his neck cloth, threw it upon the floor and sipped his egg-nog, all the while looking over the top of the glass at Capitola.

"Miss Black," he said, "it must be past twelve o'clock."

"I suppose it is," said Cap.

"Then it must be long past your usual hour of retiring."

"Of course it is," said Cap.

"Then what are you waiting for?"

"For my company to go home," replied Cap.

"Meaning me?"

"Meaning you."

"Oh, don't mind me, my dear."

"Very well," said Cap, "I shall not trouble myself about you," and her tones were steady, though her heart seemed turned into a ball of ice, through terror.

Black Donald went on slowly sipping his egg-nog, filling up his goblet when it was empty, and looking at Capitola over the top of his glass. At last he said:

"I have been watching you, Miss Black."

"Little need to tell me that," said Cap.

"And I have been reading you."

"Well, I hope the page was entertaining."

"Well, yes, my dear, it was, rather so. But why don't you proceed?"

"Proceed—with what?"

"With what you are thinking of, my darling."

"I don't understand you!"

"Why don't you offer to go down-stairs and bring up some lemons?"

"Oh, I'll go in a moment," said Cap, "if you wish."

"Ha—ha—ha—ha—ha! Of course you will, my darling! And you'd deliver me into the hands of the Philistines, just as you did my poor men when you fooled them about the victuals! I know your tricks and all your acting has no other effect on me than to make me admire your wonderful coolness and courage; so, my dear, stop puzzling your little head with schemes to baffle me! You are like the caged starling! You can't—get—out!" chuckled Black Donald, hitching his chair nearer to hers. He was now right upon the center of the rug.

Capitola turned very pale, but not with fear, though Black Donald thought she did, and roared with laughter.

"Have you done your supper?" she asked, with a sort of awful calmness.

"Yes my duck," replied the outlaw, pouring the last of the egg-nog into his goblet, drinking it at a draught and chuckling as he set down the glass.

Capitola then lifted the stand with the refreshments to remove it to its usual place.

"What are you going to do, my dear?" asked Black Donald.

"Clear away the things and set the room in order," said Capitola, in the same awfully calm tone.

"A nice little housewife you'll make, my duck!" said Black Donald.

Capitola set the stand in its corner and then removed her own armchair to its place before the dressing bureau.

Nothing now remained upon the rug except Black Donald seated in the armchair!

Capitola paused; her blood seemed freezing in her veins; her heart beat thickly; her throat was choked; her head full nearly to bursting, and her eyes were veiled by a blinding film.

"Come—come—my duck—make haste; it is late; haven't you done setting the room in order yet?" said Black Donald, impatiently.

"In one moment," said Capitola, coming behind his chair and leaning upon the back of it.

"Donald," she said, with dreadful calmness, "I will not now call you Black Donald! I will call you as your poor mother did, when your young soul was as white as your skin, before she ever dreamed her boy would grow black with crime! I will call you simply Donald, and entreat you to hear me for a few minutes."

"Talk on, then, but talk fast, and leave my mother alone! Let the dead rest!" exclaimed the outlaw, with a violent convulsion of his bearded chin and lip that did not escape the notice of Capitola, who hoped some good of this betrayal of feeling.

"Donald," she said, "men call you a man of blood; they say that your hand is red and your soul black with crime!"

"They may say what they like—I care not!" laughed the outlaw.

"But I do not believe all this of you! I believe that there is good in all, and much good in you; that there is hope for all, and strong hope for you!"

"Bosh! Stop talking poetry! 'Tain't in my line, nor yours either!" laughed Black Donald.

"But truth is in all our lines. Donald, I repeat it, men call you a man of blood! They say that your hands are red and your soul black with sin. Black Donald, they call you! But, Donald, you have never yet stained your soul with a crime as black as that which you think of perpetrating to-night!"

"It must be one o'clock, and I'm tired," replied the outlaw, with a yawn.

"All your former acts," continued Capitola, in the same voice of awful calmness, "have been those of a bold, bad man. This act would be that of a base one!"

"Take care, girl—no bad names! You are in my power—at my mercy!"

"I know my position, but I must continue. Hitherto you have robbed mail coaches and broken into rich men's houses. In doing thus you have always boldly risked your life, often at such fearful odds that men have trembled at their firesides to hear of it. And even women, while deploring your crimes, have admired your courage."

"I thank 'em kindly for it! Women always like men with a spice of the devil in them!" laughed the outlaw.

"No, they do not!" said Capitola, gravely. "They like men of strength, courage and spirit—but those qualities do not come from the Evil One, but from the Lord, who is the giver of all good. Your Creator, Donald, gave you the strength, courage and spirit that all men and women so much admire; but He did not give you these great powers that you might use them in the service of his enemy, the devil!"

"I declare there is really something in that! I never thought of that before."

"Nor ever thought, perhaps, that however misguided you may have been, there is really something great and good in yourself that might yet be used for the good of man and the glory of God!" said Capitola, solemnly.

"Ha, ha, ha! Oh, you flatterer! Come, have you done? I tell you it is after one o'clock, and I am tired to death!"

"Donald, in all your former acts of lawlessness your antagonists were strong men; and as you boldly risked your life in your depredations, your acts, though bad, were not base! But now your antagonist is a feeble girl, who has been unfortunate from her very birth; to destroy her would be an act of baseness to which you never yet descended."

"Bosh! Who talks of destruction? I am tired of all this nonsense! I mean to carry you off and there's an end of it!" said the outlaw, doggedly, rising from his seat.

"Stop!" said Capitola, turning ashen pale. "Stop—sit down and hear me for just five minutes—I will not tax your patience longer."

The robber, with a loud laugh, sank again into his chair, saying:

"Very well, talk on for just five minutes, and not a single second longer; but if you think in that time to persuade me to leave this room to-night without you, you are widely out of your reckoning, my duck, that's all."

"Donald, do not sink your soul to perdition by a crime that heaven cannot pardon! Listen to me! I have jewels here worth several thousand dollars! If you will consent to go I will give them all to you and let you quietly out of the front door and never say one word to mortal of what has passed here to-night."

"Ha, ha, ha! Why, my dear, how green you must think me! What hinders me from possessing myself of your jewels, as well as of yourself!" said Black Donald, impatiently rising.

"Sit still! The five minutes' grace are not half out yet," said Capitola, in a breathless voice.

"So they are not! I will keep my promise," replied Black Donald, laughing, and again dropping into his seat.

"Donald, Uncle pays me a quarterly sum for pocket money, which is at least five times as much as I can spend in this quiet country place. It has been accumulating for years until now. I have several thousand dollars all of my own. You shall have it if you will only go quietly away and leave me in peace!" prayed Capitola.

"My dear, I intend to take that anyhow—take it as your bridal dower, you know! For I'm going to carry you off and make an honest wife of you!"

"Donald, give up this heinous purpose!" cried Capitola, in an agony of supplication, as she leaned over the back of the outlaw's chair.

"Yes, you know I will—ha—ha—ha!" laughed the robber.

"Man, for your own sake give it up!"

"Ha, ha, ha! for my sake!"

"Yes, for yours! Black Donald, have you ever reflected on death?" asked Capitola, in a low and terrible voice.

"I have risked it often enough; but as to reflecting upon it—it will be time enough to do that when it comes! I am a powerful man, in the prime and pride of life," said the athlete, stretching himself exultingly.

"Yet it might come—death might come with sudden overwhelming power, and hurl you to destruction! What a terrible thing for this magnificent frame of yours, this glorious handiwork of the Creator, to be hurled to swift destruction, and for the soul that animates it to be cast into hell!"

"Bosh again! That is a subject for the pulpit, not for a pretty girl's room. If you really think me such a handsome man, why don't you go with me at once and say no more about it," roared the outlaw laughing.

"Black Donald—will you leave my room?" cried Capitola, in an agony of prayer.

"No!" answered the outlaw, mocking her tone.

"Is there no inducement that I can hold out to you to leave me?"

"None!"

Capitola raised herself from her leaning posture, took a step backward, so that she stood entirely free from the trap-door, then slipping her foot under the rug, she placed it lightly on the spring-bolt, which she was careful not to press; the ample fall of her dress concealed the position of her foot.

Capitola was now paler than a corpse, for hers was the pallor of a living horror! Her heart beat violently, her head throbbed, her voice was broken as she said:

"Man, I will give you one more chance! Oh, man, pity yourself as I pity you, and consent to leave me!"

"Ha, ha, ha! It is quite likely that I will! Isn't it, now? No, my duck, I haven't watched and planned for this chance for this long time past to give it up, now that you are in my power! A likely story indeed! And now the five minutes' grace are quite up!"

"Stop! Don't move yet! Before you stir, say: 'Lord, have mercy on me!'" said Capitola, solemnly.

"Ha, ha, ha! That's a pretty idea! Why should I say that?"

"Say it to please me! Only say it, Black Donald!"

"But why to please you?"

"Because I wish not to kill both your body and soul—because I would not send you prayerless into the presence of your Creator! For, Black Donald, within a few seconds your body will be hurled to swift destruction, and your soul will stand before the bar of God!" said Capitola, with her foot upon the spring of the concealed trap.

She had scarcely ceased speaking before he bounded to his feet, whirled around and confronted her, like a lion at bay, roaring forth:

"You have a revolver there, girl—move a finger and I shall throw myself upon you like an avalanche?"

"I have no revolver—watch my hands as I take them forth, and see!" said Capitola, stretching her arms out toward him.

"What do you mean, then, by your talk of sudden destruction?" inquired Black Donald, in a voice of thunder.

"I mean that it hangs over you—that it is imminent! That it is not to be escaped! Oh, man, call on God, for you have not a minute to live!"

The outlaw gazed on her in astonishment.

Well he might, for there she stood paler than marble—sterner than fate—with no look of human feeling about her, but the gleaming light of her terrible eyes, and the beading sweat upon her death-like brow.

For an instant the outlaw gazed on her in consternation, and then, recovering himself he burst into a loud laugh, exclaiming:

"Ha, ha, ha! Well, I suppose this is what people would call a piece of splendid acting! Do you expect to frighten me, my dear, as you did Craven Le Noir, with the peas!"

"Say 'Lord have mercy on my soul'—say it. Black Donald—say it. I beseech you!" she prayed.

"Ha, ha, ha, my dear! You may say it for me! And to reward you, I will give you, such a kiss! It will put life into those marble cheeks of yours!" he laughed.

"I will say it for you! May the Lord pity and save Black Donald's soul, if that be yet possible, for the Saviour's sake!" prayed Capitola, in a broken voice, with her foot upon the concealed and fatal spring.

He laughed aloud, stretched forth his arms and rushed to clasp her.

She pressed the spring.

The drop fell with a tremendous crash!

The outlaw shot downwards—there was an instant's vision of a white and panic-stricken face, and wild, uplifted hands as he disappeared, and then a square, black opening, was all that remained where the terrible intruder had sat.

No sight or sound came up from that horrible pit, to hint of the secrets of the prison house.

One shuddering glance at the awful void and then Capitola turned and threw herself, face downward, upon the bed, not daring to rejoice in the safety that had been purchased by such a dreadful deed, feeling that it was an awful, though a complete victory!

CHAPTER XX
THE NEXT MORNING

Oh, such a day!
So fought, so followed and so fairly won
Came not till now to dignify the times.
Since Caesar's fortunes.

—SHAKESPEARE.

Capitola lay upon the bed, with her face buried in the pillow, the greater portion of the time from two o'clock until day. An uncontrollable horror prevented her from turning lest she should see the yawning mystery in the middle of the floor, or hear some awful sound from its unknown depths. The very shadows on the walls thrown up wildly by the expiring firelight were objects of grotesque terror. Never—never—in her whole youth of strange vicissitude, had the nerves of this brave girl been so tremendously shaken and prostrated.

It was late in the morning when at last nature succumbed, and she sank into a deep sleep. She had not slept long when she was aroused from a profound state of insensibility by a loud, impatient knocking at her door.

She started up wildly and gazed around her. For a minute she could not remember what were the circumstances under which she had laid down, or what was that vague feeling of horror and alarm that possessed her. Then the yawning trapdoor, the remnants of the supper, and Black Donald's coat, hat and boots upon the floor, drove in upon her reeling brain the memory of the night of terror!

The knocking continued more loudly and impatiently, accompanied by the voice of Mrs. Condiment, crying:

"Miss Capitola—Miss Capitola—why, what can be the matter with her? Miss Capitola!"

"Eh? What? Yes!" answered Capitola, pressing her hands to her feverish forehead, and putting back her dishevelled hair.

"Why, how soundly you sleep, my dear! I've been calling and rapping here for a quarter of an hour! Good gracious, child what made you oversleep yourself so?"

"I—did not get to bed till very late," said Capitola, confusedly.

"Well, well, my dear, make haste now, your uncle is none of the patientest, and he has been waiting breakfast for some time! Come, open the door and I will help you to dress, so that you may be ready sooner."

Capitola rose from the side of the bed, where she had been sitting, and went cautiously around that gaping trap door to her chamber door, when she missed the key, and suddenly remembered that it had been in Black Donald's pocket when he fell. A shudder thrilled her frame at the thought of that horrible fall.

"Well—well—Miss Capitola, why don't you open the door?" cried the old lady, impatiently.

"Mrs. Condiment, I have lost the key—dropped it down the trap-door. Please ask uncle to send for some one to take the lock off—and don't wait breakfast for me."

"Well, I do think that was very careless, my dear; but I'll go at once," said the old lady, moving away.

She had not been gone more than ten minutes, when Old Hurricane was heard, coming blustering along the hall and calling:

"What now, you imp of Satan? What mischief have you been at now? Opening the trap-door, you mischievous monkey! I wish from the bottom of my soul you had fallen into it, and I should have got rid of one trial! Losing your key, you careless baggage! I've a great mind to leave you locked up there forever."

Thus scolding, Old Hurricane reached the spot and began to ply screwdrivers and chisels until at length the strong lock yielded, and he opened the door.

There a vision met his eyes that arrested his steps upon the very threshold; the remains of a bacchanalian supper; a man's coat and hat and boots upon the floor; in the midst of the room the great, square, black opening; and beyond it standing upon the hearth, the form of Capitola, with disordered dress, dishevelled hair and wild aspect!

"Oh, uncle, see what I have been obliged to do!" she exclaimed, extending both her arms down toward the opening with a look of blended horror and inspiration, such as might have sat upon the countenance of some sacrificial priestess of the olden time.

"What—what—what!" cried the old man, nearly dumb with amazement.

"Black Donald was in my room last night. He stole from his concealment and locked the door on the inside and withdrew the key, thus locking me in with himself, and—" She ceased and struck both hands to her face, shuddering from head to foot.

"Go on, girl!" thundered Old Hurricane, in an agony of anxiety.

"I escaped harmless—oh, I did, sir—but at what a fearful price!"

"Explain! Explain!" cried Old Hurricane, in breathless agitation.

"I drew him to sit upon the chair on the rug, and"—again she shuddered from head to foot, "and I sprang the trap and precipitated him to—oh, heaven of heavens!—where? I know not!"

"But you—you were unharmed?"

"Yes—yes!"

"Oh, Cap! Oh, my dear Cap! Thank heaven for that!"

"But, uncle, where—oh, where did he go?" inquired Capitola, almost wildly.

"Who the demon cares? To perdition. I hope and trust, with all my heart and soul!" cried Old Hurricane, with emphasis, as he approached and looked down the opening.

"Uncle, what is below there?" asked Capitola anxiously, pointing down the abyss.

"An old cellar, as I have told you long ago, and Black Donald, as you have just told me. Hilloe there! Are you killed, as you deserve to be, you atrocious villain?" roared Old Hurricane, stooping down into the opening.

A feeble distant moan answered him.

"Oh, heaven! He is living! He is living! I have not killed him!" cried Capitola, clasping her hands.

"Why, I do believe you are glad of it!" exclaimed Old Hurricane, in astonishment.

"Oh, yes, yes, yes! For it was a fearful thought that I had been compelled to take a sacred life! to send an immortal soul unprepared to its account!"

"Well! his neck isn't broken, it appears, or he couldn't groan; but I hope and trust every other bone in his body is! Mrs. Condiment, mum! I'll trouble you to put on your bonnet and walk to Ezy's and tell him to come here directly! I must send for the constable," said Old Hurricane, going to the door and speaking to his housekeeper, who, with an appalled countenance had been a silent spectator of all that had passed.

As soon as the old woman had gone to do her errand he turned again, and stooping down the hole, exclaimed:

"I say, you scoundrel down there! What do you think of yourself now? Are you much hurt, you knave? Is everyone of your bones broken, as they deserve to be, you villain? Answer me, you varlet!"

A low, deep moan was the only response.

"If that means yes, I'm glad to hear it, you wretch. You'll go to the camp-meeting with us again, won't you, you knave? You'll preach against evil passions and profane swearing, looking right straight at me all the time, until you bring the eyes of the whole congregation upon me as a sinner above all sinners, you scoundrel? You'll turn me out of my own bed and away from my own board, won't you, you villain? Won't you, precious Father Grey? Oh, we'll Father Grey you! Demmy, the next time a trap-door falls under you, you rascal, there shall be a rope around your neck to keep you from the ground, precious Father Grey!"

"Uncle! Uncle! that is cowardly!" exclaimed Capitola.

"What is cowardly, Miss Impertinence?"

"To insult and abuse a fallen man who is in your power! The poor man is badly hurt, may be dying, for aught you know, and you stand over him and berate him when he cannot even answer you!"

"Umph, umph, umph; Demmy, you're—umph, well, he is fallen, fallen pretty badly, eh? and if he should come round after this, the next fall he gets will be likely to break his neck, eh?—I say, you gentleman below there—Mr. Black Donald—precious Father Grey—you'll keep quiet, won't you, while we go and get our breakfast? do, now! Come, Cap, come down and pour out my coffee, and by the time we get through, Old Ezy will be here."

Capitola complied, and they left the room together.

The overseer came in while they were at breakfast, and with his hair standing on end, listened to the account of the capture of the outlaw by our heroine.

"And now saddle Fleetfoot and ride for your life to Tip-Top and bring a pair of constables," were the last orders of Old Hurricane.

While Mr. Ezy was gone on his errand, Major Warfield, Capitola and Mrs. Condiment remained below stairs.

It was several hours before the messenger returned with the constables, and with several neighbors whom interest and curiosity had instigated to join the party.

As soon as they arrived, a long ladder was procured and carried up into Capitola's chamber, and let down through the trap-door. Fortunately it was long enough, for when the foot of the ladder found the floor of the cellar, the head rested securely against the edge of the opening.

In a moment the two constables began singly to descend, the foremost one carrying a lighted candle in his hand.

The remaining members of the party, consisting of Major Warfield, Capitola, Mrs. Condiment, and some half dozen neighbors, remained gathered around the open trap-door, waiting, watching, and listening for what might next happen.

Presently one of the constables called out:

"Major Warfield, sir!"

"Well!" replied Old Hurricane.

"He's a-breathing still, sir; but seems badly hurt, and may be a-dying, seeing as he's unsensible and unspeakable. What shall we do long of him?"

"Bring him up! let's have a look at the fellow, at any rate!" exclaimed Old Hurricane, peremptorily.

"Just so, sir! but some of the gem-men up there'll have to come down on the ladder and give a lift. He's a dead weight now, I tell your honor!"

Several of the neighbors immediately volunteered for the service, and two of the strongest descended the ladder to lend their aid.

On attempting to move the injured man he uttered a cry of pain, and fainted, and then it took the united strength and skill of four strong men to raise the huge insensible form of the athlete, and get him up the ladder. No doubt the motion greatly inflamed his inward wounds, but that could not be helped. They got him up at last, and laid out upon the floor a ghastly, bleeding, insensible form, around which every one gathered to gaze. While they were all looking upon him as upon a slaughtered wild beast, Capitola alone felt compassion.

"Uncle, he is quite crushed by his fall. Make the men lay him upon the bed. Never think of me; I shall never occupy this room again; its associations are too full of horrors. There, uncle, make them at once lay him upon the bed."

"I think the young lady is right, unless we mean to let the fellow die," said one of the neighbors.

"Very well! I have particular reasons of my own for wishing that the man's life should be spared until he could be brought to trial and induced to give up his accomplices," said Old Hurricane. Then, turning to his ward, he said:

"Come along, Capitola. Mrs. Condiment will see that your effects are transferred to another apartment."

"And you, friends," he continued, addressing the men present, "be so good, so soon as we have gone, to undress that fellow and put him to bed, and examine his injuries while I send off for a physician; for I consider it very important his life should be spared sufficiently long to enable him to give up his accomplices." And so saying, Old Hurricane drew the arm of Capitola within his own and left the room.

It was noon before the physician arrived. When he had examined the patient he pronounced him utterly unfit to be removed, as besides other serious contusions and bruises, his legs were broken and several of his ribs fractured.

In a word. It was several weeks before the strong constitution of the outlaw prevailed over his many injuries, and he was pronounced well enough to be taken before a magistrate and committed to prison to await his trial. Alas! his life, it was said, was forfeit by a hundred crimes, and there could be no doubt as to his fate. He maintained a self-possessed good-humored and laughingly defiant manner, and when asked to give up his accomplices, he answered gaily:

That treachery was a legal virtue which outlaws could not be expected to know anything about.

Capitola was everywhere lauded for her brave part in the capture of the famous desperado. But Cap was too sincerely sorry for Black Donald to care for the applause.

CHAPTER XXI
A FATAL HATRED

"Oh, heaven and all its hosts, he shall not die!"
"By Satan and his fiends, he shall not live!
This is no transient flash of fugitive passion,
His death has been my life for years of misery,
Which, else I had not lived,
Upon that thought, and not on food, I fed,
Upon that thought, and not on sleep, I rested,
I came to do the deed that must be done,
Nor thou, nor the sheltering angels could prevent me."

—MATURIN.

The United States army, under General Scott, invested the city of Mexico.

A succession of splendid victories had marked every stage of their advance, from the seacoast to the capital. Vera Cruz had fallen; Cerro-Gordo had been stormed and passed: Xalapa taken; the glorious triumph of Churubusco had been achieved. The names of Scott, Worth, Wool, Quitman, Pillow and others were crowned with honor. Others again, whose humble names and unnoticed heroism have never been recorded, endured as nobly, suffered as patiently, and fought as bravely. Our own young hero, Herbert Greyson, had covered himself with honor.

The war with Mexico witnessed, perhaps, the most rapid promotions of any other in the whole history of military affairs.

The rapid ascent of our young officer was a striking instance of this. In two years from the time he had entered the service, with a lieutenant's commission, he held the rank of major, in the—Regiment of Infantry.

Fortune had not smiled upon our other young friend, Traverse Rocke—partly because, being entirely out of his vocation, he had no right to expect success; but mostly because he had a powerful enemy in the Colonel of his regiment—an unsleeping enemy, whose constant vigilance was directed to prevent the advancement and insure the degradation and ruin of one whom he contemptuously termed the "gentleman private."

Now, it is known that by the rules of military etiquette, a wide social gulf lies between the Colonel of the regiment and the private in the ranks.

Yet, Colonel Le Noir continually went out of his way to insult Private Rocke, hoping to provoke him to some act of fatal insubordination.

And very heavy was this trial to a high spirited young man like Traverse Rocke, and very fortunate was it for him that he had early been imbued with that most important truth, that "He who ruleth his own spirit is greater than he who taketh a city."

But, if Colonel Le Noir crossed the gulf of military etiquette to harass the poor young soldier, Major Greyson did the same thing for the more honorable purpose of soothing and encouraging him.

And both Herbert and Traverse hoped that the designs of their Colonel would be still frustrated by the self-command and patience of the young private.

Alas! they did not know the great power of evil! They did not know that nothing less than Divine Providence could meet and overcome it.

They fondly believed that the malignity of Le Noir had resulted in no other practical evil than in preventing the young soldier's well-merited advancement, and in keeping him in the humble position of a private in the ranks.

They were not aware that the discharge of Traverse Rocke had long ago arrived, but that it had been suppressed through the diabolical cunning of Le Noir. That letters, messages and packets, sent by his friends to the young soldier, had found their way into his Colonel's possession and no further.

And so, believing the hatred of that bad man to have been fruitless of serious, practical evil, Herbert encouraged his friend to be patient for a short time longer, when they should see the end of the campaign, if not of the war.

It was now that period of suspense and of false truce between the glorious 20th of August and the equally glorious 8th of September, 1847—between the two most brilliant actions of the war, the battle of Churubusco and the storming of Chapultepec.

The General-in-Chief of the United States forces in Mexico was at his headquarters in the Archiepiscopal palace of Tacubaya, on the suburbs, or in the full sight of the city of the Montezumas, awaiting the issue of the conference between the commissioners of the hostile governments, met to arrange the terms of a treaty of peace—that every day grew more hopeless.

General Scott, who had had misgivings as to the good faith of the Mexicans, had now his suspicions confirmed by several breaches on the part of the enemy of the terms of the armistice.

Early in September he despatched a letter to General Santa Anna, complaining of these infractions of the truce, and warning him that if some satisfactory explanations were not made within forty-eight hours he should consider the armistice at an end, and renew hostilities.

And not to lose time, he began on the same night a series of reconnaisances, the object of which was to ascertain their best approach to the city of Mexico, which, in the event of the renewal of the war, he purposed to carry by assault.

It is not my intention to pretend to describe the siege and capture of the capital, which has been so often and eloquently described by grave and wise historians, but rather to follow the fortunes of an humble private in the ranks, and relate the events of a certain court-martial, as I learned them from the after-dinner talk of a gallant officer who had officiated on the occasion.

It was during these early days in September, while the illustrious General-in-Chief was meditating concluding the war by the assault of the city of Mexico, that Colonel Le Noir also resolved to bring his own private feud to an end, and ruin his enemy by a coup-de-diable.

He had an efficient tool for his purpose in the Captain of the company to which Traverse Rocke belonged. This man, Captain Zuten, was a vulgar upstart thrown into his command by the turbulence of war, as the scum is cast up to the surface by the boiling of the cauldron.

He hated Traverse Rocke, for no conceivable reason, unless it was that the young private was a perfect contrast to himself, in the possession of a handsome person, a well cultivated mind, and a gentlemanly deportment— cause sufficient for the antagonism of a mean and vulgar nature.

Colonel Le Noir was not slow to see and to take advantage of this hatred.

And Captain Zuten became the willing coadjutor and instrument of his vengeance. Between them they concocted a plot to bring the unfortunate young man to an ignominious death.

One morning, about the first of September, Major Greyson, in going his rounds, came upon Traverse, standing sentry near one of the outposts. The aspect of the young private was so pale, haggard and despairing that his friend immediately stopped and exclaimed:

"Why Traverse, how ill you look! More fitted for the sick list than the sentry's duties. What the deuce is the matter?"

The young soldier touched his hat to his superior and answered sadly, "I am ill, ill in body and mind, sir."

"Pooh!—leave off etiquette when we are alone, Traverse, and call me Herbert, as usual. Heaven knows, I shall be glad when all this is over and we fall back into our relative civil positions towards each other. But what is the matter now, Traverse? Some of Le Noir's villainy again, of course."

"Of course. But I did not mean to complain, Herbert; that were childish. I mus' endure this slavery, these insults and persecutions patiently since I have brought them upon myself."

"Take comfort, Traverse. The war is drawing to a close. Either this armistice will end in a permanent peace, or when hostilities are renewed our General will carry the city of Mexico by storm, and dictate the terms of a treaty from the grand square of the capital. In either event the war will soon be over, the troops disbanded, and the volunteers free to go about their business, and Doctor Traverse Rocke at liberty to pursue his legitimate profession," said Herbert, cheerfully.

"It may be so; I do not know. Oh, Herbert, whether it be from want of sleep and excessive fatigue—for I have been on duty for three days and nights—or whether it be from incipient illness, or all these causes put together, I cannot tell, but my spirits are dreadfully depressed! There seems to be hanging over me a cloud of fate I cannot dispel. Every hour seems descending lower and blacker over my head, until it feels like some heavy weight about to suffocate or crush me," said Traverse, sadly.

"Pooh, pooh! hypochondria! cheer up! Remember that in a month we shall probably be disbanded, and in a year—think of it, Traverse Rocke—Clara Day will be twenty-one, and at liberty to give you her hand. Cheer up!"

"Ah, Herbert, all that seems now to be more unsubstantial than the fabric of a dream. I cannot think of Clara or of my mother without despair. For oh, Herbert, between me and them there seems to yawn a dishonored grave! Herbert, they talk, you know, of an attack upon the Molino-del-Rey, and I almost hope to fall in that charge!"

"Why?" inquired Major Greyson, in dismay.

"To escape being forced into a dishonored grave! Herbert, that man has sworn my ruin, and he will accomplish it!" said Traverse, solemnly.

"For Heaven's sake, explain yourself!" said Herbert.

"I will. Listen! I will tell you the history of the last three days," said Traverse; but before he could add another word the sentry that was to relieve his guard approached and said:

"Captain Zuten orders you to come to his tent instantly."

With a glance of significance, Traverse bowed to Herbert and walked off, while the sentinel took his place.

Herbert saw no more of Traverse that day. At night he went to inquire for him, but learned that he had been sent with a reconnoitering party to the Molino-del-Rey.

The next day, on seeking Traverse, he understood that the young private had been despatched on a foraging expedition. That night, upon again inquiring for him, he was told that he had been sent in attendance upon the officers who had borne secret despatches to General Quitman, at his quarters on the Acapulco road.

"Traverse is right. They mean to ruin him. I see how it is, exactly. When I saw Traverse on guard, two days ago, he looked like a man exhausted and crazed for want of sleep, and since that time he has been night and day engaged in harassing duty. That demon, Le Noir, with Zuten to help him, has determined to keep Traverse from sleep, until nature is thoroughly exhausted, and then set him upon guard, that he may be found sleeping on his post. That was what the boy meant when he talked of the cloud that was hanging over him, and of being forced into a dishonored grave, and when he hoped, poor fellow, to fall in the approaching assault upon the Molino-del-Rey! I see it all now. They have decided upon the destruction of Traverse. He can do nothing. A soldier's whole duty is comprised in one word—obedience, even if, as in this instance, he is ordered to commit suicide. Let them hatch their diabolical plots. We will see if the Lord does not still reign, and the devil is not a fool. It shall go hard, but that they are 'hoist with their own petard!'" said Herbert, indignantly.

Early the next morning he went to the tent of Captain Zuten and requested to see Private Traverse Rocke, in whom, he said, he felt a warm interest.

The answer of Colonel Le Noir's tool confirmed Herbert's worse suspicions.

Touching his cap with an air of exaggerated deference, he said:

"As you think so much of the young fellow, Major, I am very sorry to inform you, sir, that he is under arrest."

"Upon what charge?" inquired Herbert, calmly, concealing the suspicion and indignation of his bosom.

"Upon a rather bad one, Major—sleeping on his post," replied the officer, masking his exultation with a show of respect.

"Rather bad! The penalty is death," said Herbert, dryly.

"Yes, sir—martial law is rather severe."

"Who charges him?" asked Herbert, curtly.

"The Colonel of our regiment, sir," replied the man, scarcely able to conceal his triumph.

"An accusation from a high quarter. Is his charge supported by other testimony?"

"Beg pardon, Major, but is that necessary?"

"You have answered my question by asking another one, sir. I will trouble you for a direct reply," said Herbert with dignity.

"Then, Major, I must reply—yes."

"What testimony? I would know the circumstances?"

"Well, sir, I will tell you about it," said the officer, with ill-concealed triumph. "Private Traverse Rocke had the early morning watch—"

"After his return from the night ride to Acapulco?"

"Yes, sir. Well, Colonel Le Noir and myself in going our rounds this morning, just before sunrise, came full upon the young fellow, fast asleep on his post. In fact, sir, it required a hearty shake to awaken him."

"After ninety-six hours' loss of sleep, I should not wonder."

"I know nothing about that, sir. I only know that Colonel Le Noir and myself found him fast asleep on his post. He was immediately arrested."

"Where is he now?" inquired Herbert.

"In one of the Colonel's extra tents, under guard," replied the officer.

Herbert immediately went to the tent in question, where he found two sentinels, with loaded muskets, on duty before the door. They grounded arms on the approach of their superior officer.

"Is Private Traverse Rocke confined within there?" he inquired.

"Yes, sir,"

"I must pass in to see him."

"I beg your pardon, sir, but our orders are strict, not even to admit an officer, without a written order from our Colonel," said the sentinel.

"Where is the Colonel?"

"In his tent, sir."

Herbert immediately went on to the fine marquee occupied by Colonel Le Noir.

The sentinel on duty there at once admitted him, and he passed on into the presence of the Colonel.

He saluted his superior officer with cold military etiquette, and said:

"I have come, sir, to ask of you an order to see Private Traverse Rocke, confined under the charge of sleeping on his post."

"I regret to say, Major Greyson, that it cannot be done," replied Le Noir, with ironical politeness.

"Will you have the kindness to inform me, sir, upon what pretext my reasonable request is refused?" asked Herbert, coldly.

"I deem it quite unnecessary to do so, sir," answered the Colonel, haughtily.

"Then I have no more to do here," replied Herbert, leaving the tent.

He immediately threw himself into his saddle and rode off to the Archiepiscopal palace of Tacubaya, where the General-in-Chief had fixed his headquarters.

Here he had to wait some little time before he was admitted to the presence of the gallant commander, who received him with all the stately courtesy for which that renowned officer is distinguished.

Herbert mentioned the business that had brought him to the general's presence, the request of a written order to see a prisoner in strict confinement for sleeping on his post.

The commander whose kind heart was interested in the welfare of all his soldiers, made some inquiries into the affair, of which Herbert proceeded to give him a short history, without, however, venturing, as yet, directly to charge the Captain or the Colonel with intentional foul play; indeed to have attempted to criminate the superior officers of the accused man would then have been most unwise, useless and hurtful.

The General immediately wrote the desired order and passed it to the young officer.

Herbert bowed and was about to retire from the room, when he was called back by the General, who placed a packet of letters in his hand, saying that they had arrived among his despatches, and were for the prisoner, to whom Major Greyson might as well take them at once.

Herbert received them with avidity, and on his way back to the Colonel's tent he examined their superscription.

There were three letters—all directed to Traverse Rocke. On two of them, he recognized the familiar handwriting of Marah Rocke, on the other he saw the delicate Italian style of a young lady's hand, which he readily believed to be that of Clara.

In the midst of his anxiety on his friend's account rejoiced to have this one little ray of comfort to carry him. He knew that many months had elapsed since the young soldier had heard from his friends at home—in fact, Travers never received a letter unless it happened to come under cover to Herbert Greyson. And well they both knew the reason.

"How very fortunate," said Herbert, as he rode on, "that I happened to be at the General's quarters to receive these letters just when I did; for if they had been sent to Colonel Le Noir's quarters or to Captain Z.'s, poor traverse would never have heard of them. However, I shall no distract Traverse's attention by showing him these letters until he has told me the full history of his arrest, for I wish him to give me a cool account of the whole thing, so that I may know if I can possible server him. Ah, it is very unlikely that nay power of mine will be ale to save him if indeed, and in truth, he did sleep upon his post," ruminated Herbert, as he rode up to the tent where the prisoner was confined.

Another pair of sentinels were on duty in place of those who had refused him admittance.

He alighted from his horse, was challenged, showed his order, and passed into the tent.

There a sight met him that caused the tears to rush to his eyes—for the bravest is always the tenderest heart.

Thrown down on the mat at the back of the tent lay Traverse Rocke, pale, haggard and sunken in the deep, deep sleep of utter exhaustion. Even in that state of perfect abandonment, prostration and insensibility, the expression of great mental anguish remained upon his deathly countenance; a mortal pallor overspread his face; his thick, black curls, matted with perspiration, clung to his hollow temples and cheeks; great drops of sweat beaded upon his corrugated brow; a quiver convulsed his mouth and chin; every circumstance betrayed how severely, even in that swoonlike state, he suffered.

Herbert drew a camp-stool and sat down beside his mat, resolving not to break that greatly needed rest, but to wait patiently until the sleeper should awake.

Again, I say that I know nothing about mesmerism, but I have seen strange effects produced quite unconsciously by the presence of one person upon another. And in a few minutes after Herbert took his seat beside Traverse, it was noticeable that the face of the sleeper lost its look of pain, and his rest grew deep and calm.

Herbert sat watching that pale, calm, intellectual face, thanking heaven that his mother, in her distant home, knew nothing of her boy's deadly peril and praying heaven that its justice might be vindicated in the deliverance of this victim from the snares of those who sought his life.

For more than an hour longer Traverse slept the deep sleep of exhaustion, and then calmly awoke. On seeing Herbert sitting beside him, he smiled sadly, saying:

"You here, Herbert? How kind of you to come. Well, Herbert, you see they have succeeded, as I knew they would. That was what I wished to tell you about when I was abruptly ordered away. I do believe it was done on purpose to prevent my telling you. I really think I have been surrounded by spies to report and distort every word and look and gesture. If our company had only watched die enemy with half the vigilance with which they watched me, that party of emigrants would not have been cut off on the plains."

"Traverse," said Herbert solemnly taking the hand of his friend, "were you caught sleeping on your post?"

"Ah, sleeping like death, Herbert."

Herbert dropped the hand of his friend, covered his face with his own, and groaned aloud, "He could not help it!"

"I told you that they had resolved upon my death, Herbert. I told you that I should be pushed into a shameful grave!"

"Oh, no, no, the Lord forbid! But tell me all about it, Traverse, that I may understand and know how to proceed," said Herbert, in a broken voice.

"Well, I need not tell you how I have been insulted, oppressed and persecuted by those two men, for you know that already."

"Yes, yes!"

"It really soon became apparent to me that they were resolved, if possible, to exasperate to desert, to retort, or to commit some other fatal act of insubordination or violence. Yet, for the sake of my dear mother and of Clara, I did violence only to my own natural manhood, and bore it all with the servility of a slave."

"With the submission of a saint, dear Traverse; and in doing so you followed the divine precept and example of Our Saviour, who, when accused, railed upon and buffeted, 'opened not his mouth.' And in His forbearance, dear Traverse, there was as much of God-like dignity as there was of saintly patience. Great self-respect is as often manifested in forbearance as in resentment," said Herbert, soothingly.

"But you see it availed me nothing. Here I am, under a charge to which I plead guilty, and the penalty of which is—death!" replied Traverse in despair.

"Tell me how it was, Traverse. Your persecutions and your patience I knew before, but what are the circumstances that led to your present position? That your misfortune is the result of a concerted plan on the part of Le Noir and his tool, I partly see, but I wish you to put me in possession of all the facts, that I may see in what manner I may be able to assist you."

"Ah, Herbert, I thank you, most faithful of friends, but I doubt whether you can assist me in any other manner than in being kind to my poor mother and my dear Clara when I am gone—for ah, old playmate, the act can be too surely proved upon me, and the penalty is certain—and it is death!" said the poor boy, deeply sighing.

Herbert groaned, and said:

"But tell me, at least, the history of the four days preceding your arrest."

"I will. Let me see—this is Friday. Well, until this morning's fatal sleep, I had not slept since Sunday night. Monday was passed in the usual routine of military duty. Monday evening I was sent on a reconnoitering expedition to the old castellated Spanish fort of the Casa de Mata, that occupied the whole night. On Tuesday morning I was selected to attend the messenger who went with the flag of truce into the city to carry our General's letter of expostulation to Santa Anna, which employed the whole day. On Tuesday night, without having had an hour's rest in the interval, I was put on guard. Wednesday morning I was sent with a party to escort an emigrant caravan across the marsh to the village of Churubusco. Wednesday afternoon you saw me on guard and I told you that I had not slept one hour for three days and nights."

"Yes, you looked ill enough to be ordered on the sick list."

"Yet, listen. Thoroughly exhausted as I was, on Wednesday night I was ordered to join a party to go on a secret reconnoitering expedition to the Molina-del-Rey. On Thursday morning I was sent out with another party on a foraging tour. On Thursday night I was sent in attendance upon the officer who carried despatches to General Quitman. On Friday morning I was set on guard between the hours of four and eight!"

"Oh, heaven, what an infamous abuse of military authority!" exclaimed Herbert, indignantly.

"Herbert, in my life I have sometimes suffered with hunger, cold and pain, and have some idea of what starving, freezing and torture may be, but among all the ills to which flesh is heir, I doubt if there is one so trying to the nerves and brain of man as enforced and long-continued vigilance, when all his failing nature sinks for want of sleep. Insanity and death must soon be the result."

"Humph! Go on. Tell me about the manner of their finding you," said Herbert, scarcely able to repress his indignation.

"Well, when after—let me see—eighty-four—ninety—ninety six hours of incessant watching, riding and walking, I was set on guard to keep the morning watch between four o'clock and eight, 'my whole head was sick and my whole heart faint'; my frame was sinking; my soul could scarcely hold my body upright. In addition to this physical suffering was the mental anguish of feeling that these men had resolved upon my death, and thinking of my dear mother and Clara, whose hearts would be broken by my fall. Oh! the thought of them at this moment quite unmans me. I must not reflect. Well, I endeavored with all the faculties of my mind and body to keep awake. I kept steadily pacing to and fro, though I could scarcely drag one limb after the other, or even stand upright; sleep would arrest me while in motion, and I would drop my musket and wake up in a panic, with the impression of some awful, overhanging ruin appalling my soul. Herbert, will you think me a miserably weak wretch if I tell you that that night was a night of mental and physical horrors? Brain and nerves seemed in a state of disorganization; thought and emotion were chaos; the relations of soul and body broken up. I had but one strong, clear idea, namely, that I must keep awake at all costs, or bring shameful death upon myself and disgrace upon my family. And even In the very midst of thinking this I would fall asleep."

"No power within yourself could have prevented it; indeed, you had to drop into sleep or death!"

"I pinched myself, I cut my flesh, I burned my skin, but all in vain. Nothing could withstand the overwhelming power of sleep that finally conquered me, about five o'clock this morning. Then, in the midst of a delightful dream of mother and Clara and home, I was roused up by a rude shake, and awoke to find my musket fallen from my hands, and my Captain and Colonel standing over me. It was several minutes before I could travel back from the pleasant land of sleep and dreams and realize my real position. When I did I had nothing to say. The inevitable ruin I felt had come, and crushed me into a sort of dumb despair. Nor did my superior officers reproach me—their revenge was too perfect. The captain called a sergeant to take my gun, and I was marched off to my present prison. And, Herbert, no sooner was I left alone here than sleep overcame me again, like a strong man, and despite all the gloom and terror of my situation, despite all of my thoughts of home and mother and Clara, I slept like a tired child. But this awakening. Oh! this awakening. Herbert!"

"Be of good courage. Let us hope that heaven will enable us to confound the plots of the evil, and save you!"

"Ah, Herbert, that will be impossible. The duty of a soldier is clear and stern; his punishment if he fails in it, swift and sure. At the word of command he must march into the very jaws of death, as is right. He must die or madden for the want of rest, rather than fall asleep on his post, for if he does, his punishment is certain and shameful death. Oh, my mother! Oh, Clara! Would heaven I had fallen at Vera Cruz or Churubusco, rather than live to bring this dreadful sorrow upon you," cried Traverse, covering his convulsed face with his hands.

"Cheer up, cheer up, old comrade. All is not lost that is endangered, and we shall save you yet!"

"Herbert, you know it is impossible."

"No, I do not know any such thing!"

"You know that I shall be tried to-day and shot tomorrow! Oh, Herbert, never let my dear ones at home know how I shall die. Tell them that I fell before Chepultepec—which will be literally true, you know. Oh, my mother! Oh, my dear Clara, shall I never see you more? Never hear your sweet voices calling me? Never feel the kind clasp of your hands again? Is this the end of a life of aspiration and endeavor? Is this the comfort and happiness I was to bring you?—early bereavement, dishonored names and broken hearts?"

"I tell you, no! You shall be saved! I say it!"

"Ah, it is impossible."

"No, it is only very difficult—so very difficult that I shall be sure to accomplish it!"

"What a paradox."

"It is a truth. Things difficult—almost to impossibility—can always be accomplished. Write that upon your tables, for it is a valuable truth. And no cheer up, for I bring you letters from Clara and your mother."

"Letters! from Clara! and mother! Oh, give them to me!" exclaimed the young man eagerly.

Herbert handed them, and Traverse eagerly broke the seals, one after another, and devoured the contents.

"They are well! They are well and happy! Oh, thank God they are so. Oh, Herbert, never let them know how I shall die! If they think I fell honorably in battle, they will get over it in time, but if they know I died a convict's death it will break their hearts. Oh, Herbert, my dear friend, by all our boyhood's love, never let my poor mother and dear Clara know the manner of my death!" cried Traverse, in an imploring voice.

Before he could say another word or Herbert could answer, an orderly sergeant entered and put into Major Greyson's hands a paper that proved to be a summons for him to attend immediately at headquarters to serve upon a court-martial, to try Private Traverse Rocke upon the charge of sleeping on his post.

"This is done on purpose to prevent me becoming a witness for the defense!" whispered Herbert to his friend, "but take courage. We will see yet whether you shall succeed!"

CHAPTER XXII
THE COURT-MARTIAL

I wish I could
Meet all accusers with as good excuse,
As well as I am certain I can clear
Myself of this.

—SHAKESPEARE.

Pursuant with the general orders issued from headquarters, the court-martial, consisting of thirteen officers, convened at Tacubaya, for the trial of Traverse Rocke, private in the—Regiment of Infantry, accused of sleeping on his post.

It was a sultry morning, early in September, and by seven o'clock the drum was heard beating before the Archiepiscopal palace, where it was understood the trial, involving life or death, would come off.

The two sentinels on guard before the doors and a few officers off duty, loitering about the verandas, were the only persons visible near the well-ordered premises, until the members of the court-martial, with the prosecutors and witnesses, began to assemble and pass in.

Within a lofty apartment of the building, which was probably at one time the great dining-hall of the priests, were collected some twenty persons, comprising the court-martial and its attendants.

An extension table covered with green cloth occupied the middle of the long room.

At the head of this table sat General W., the president of the court. On his right and left, at the sides of the table, were arranged the other members according to their rank.

At a smaller table, near the right hand of the President, stood the Judge Advocate or prosecutor on behalf of the United States.

At the door stood a sentinel on guard, and near him two or three orderly sergeants in attendance upon the officers.

The Judge Advocate opened the court by calling over the names of the members, beginning with the President and ending with the youngest officer present, and recording them as they responded. This preliminary settled, orders were despatched to bring the prisoner, prosecutor and witnesses into court.

And in a few minutes entered Colonel Le Noir, Captain Zuten, Ensign Allen and Sergeant Baker. They were accommodated with seats near the left hand of the President.

Lastly, the prisoner was brought in guarded, and placed standing at the foot of the table.

Traverse looked pale, from the severe effects of excessive fatigue and anxiety, but he deported himself with firmness and dignity, bowed respectfully to the court, and then drew his stately form up to its fullest height, and stood awaiting the proceedings.

The Judge Advocate at the order of the President, commenced and read the warrant for holding the court. He then read over the names of the members, commencing as before, with the President, and descending through the gradations of rank to the youngest officer, and demanded of the prisoner whether he had any cause of challenge, or took any exception to any member present, and if so, to declare it, as was his privilege.

Traverse lifted his noble head and keen eyes, and looked slowly around, in turn, upon each officer of the court-martial.

They might all be said to be strangers to him, since he knew them only by sight—all except his old acquaintance, Herbert Greyson, who sat first at the left hand of the President, and who returned his look of scrutiny with a gaze full of encouragement.

"I find no cause of challenge, and take no exception to any among the officers composing this court," answered Traverse, again bowing with such sweetness and dignity in tone and gesture that the officers, in surprise, looked first at the prisoner and then at each other. No one could doubt that the accused, in the humble garb of a private soldier, was nevertheless a man of education and refinement—a true gentleman, both in birth and breeding.

As no challenge was made, the Judge Advocate proceeded to administer to each of the members of the court the oath prescribed in the Articles of War, to the intent that they should "try the matter before them, between the prisoner and the United States, according to the evidence, without fear, favor or affection."

This oath was taken by each member holding up his right hand and repeating the words after the officer.

The court then being regularly constituted, and every preliminary form observed, the Judge Advocate arose and directed the prisoner to listen to the charge brought against him, and preferred by the Colonel of his Regiment, Gabriel Le Noir.

Traverse raised his head and fixed his eagle eyes upon the prosecutor, who stood beside the Judge Advocate, while the latter in an audible voice read the accusation, charging the prisoner with wilful neglect of duty, in that he, the said Traverse Rocke, on the night of the first of September, being placed on guard at the northwestern outpost of the Infantry quarters, at Tacubaya, did fall asleep upon his post, thereby endangering the safety of the quarters, and violating the 46th Article of War.

To which charge the prisoner, in a firm voice, replied:

"Not guilty of wilful neglect of duty, though found sleeping upon my post."

The Judge Advocate then cautioned all witnesses to withdraw from the court and come only as they were called. They withdrew, and he then arranged some preliminaries of the examination, and called in—Captain Zuten, of the—Regiment of Infantry.

This witness was a short, coarse-featured, red-haired person of Dutch extraction, without intellect enough to enable him to conceal the malignity of his nature.

He testified that on Thursday, the first of September, Traverse Rocke, private in his company, was ordered on guard at the northwestern out post of the quarters, between the hours of four and eight a.m. That about five o'clock on the same morning, he, Joseph Zuten, in making his usual rounds, and being accompanied on that occasion by Colonel Gabriel Le Noir, Lieutenant Adams and Ensign Baker, did surprise Private Traverse Rocke asleep on his post leaning against the sentry box with his musket at his feet.

This witness was cross-examined by the Judge Advocate, who, it is known, combines in his own person the office of prosecutor on the part of the United States and counsel for the prisoner, or rather, if he be honest, he acts as impartial inquirer and arbiter between the two.

As no new facts were gained by the cross-examination, the Judge Advocate proceeded to call the next witness, Colonel Le Noir.

Here, then, was a gentleman of most prepossessing exterior, as well as of most irreproachable reputation.

In brief, his testimony corroborated that of the foregoing witness, as to the finding of the prisoner asleep on his post at the time and place specified. In honor of his high social and military standing, this witness was not cross-examined.

The next called was Lieutenant Adams, who corroborated the evidence of former witnesses. The last person examined was Ensign Baker, whose testimony corresponded exactly to that of all who had gone before him.

The Judge Advocate then briefly summed up the case on the part of the United States—first by reading the 46th Article of War, to wit, that:

"Any sentinel who shall be found sleeping on his post, or shall leave it before he shall be regularly relieved, shall suffer death," etc., etc., etc.

And secondly, by reading the recorded evidence to the effect that:

Traverse Rocke had been found by competent witnesses sleeping on his post.

And concluded by saying:

"Gentlemen, officers of the court-martial, here is the law and here is the fact both proven, and it remains for the court to find a verdict in accordance with both."

The prisoner was then put upon his defence.

Traverse Rocke drew himself up and said, that the truth, like the blessed sun, must, on its shining forth, dispel all clouds of error; that, trusting in the power of truth, he should briefly relate the history of the preceding seven days. And then he commenced and narrated the facts with which the reader is, already acquainted.

Traverse was interrupted several times in the course of his narrative by the President, General W., a severe martinet, who reminded him that an attempt to criminate his superior Officers would only injure his cause before the court.

Traverse, bowing, as in duty bound to the President at every fresh interruption, nevertheless proceeded straight on with his narrative to its conclusion.

The defence being closed, the Judge Advocate arose, as was his privilege, to have the last word. He stated that if the prisoner had been oppressed or aggrieved by his superior officer, his remedy lay in the 35th of the Articles of War, providing that any soldier who shall feel himself wronged by his captain shall complain thereof to the Colonel of his Regiment.

To this the prisoner begged to reply that he had considered the Colonel of his Regiment his personal enemy, and as such could have little hope of the issue, even if he had had opportunity afforded him, of appealing to that authority.

The Judge Advocate expressed his belief that this complaint was vexatious and groundless.

And here the evidence was closed, the prosecutor, prisoner and witnesses dismissed, and the court adjourned to meet again to deliberate with closed doors.

It was a period of awful suspense with Traverse Rocke. The prospect seemed dark for him.

The fact of the offence and the law affixing the penalty of death to that offence was established, and as the Judge Advocate truly said, nothing remained but for the court to find their verdict in accordance to both.

Extenuating circumstances there were certainly; but extenuating circumstances were seldom admitted in courts-martial, the law and practice of which were severe to the extent of cruelty.

Another circumstance against him was the fact that it did not require an unanimous vote to render a legal verdict, but that if a majority of two-thirds should vote for conviction, the fate of the prisoner would be sealed. Traverse had but one friend in the court, and what could his single voice do against so many? Apparently nothing: yet, as the prisoner on leaving the court-room, raised his eyes to that friend, Herbert Greyson returned the look with a glance of more than encouragement—of triumph.

CHAPTER XXIII
THE VERDICT

We must not make a scare-crow of the law,
Setting it up to frighten birds of prey;
And let it keep one shape till custom makes it,
Their perch and not their terror.

—SHAKESPEARE.

The members of a court-martial sit in the double capacity of jurors and judges; as jurors they find the facts, and as judges they award the punishment. Yet their session with closed doors was without the solemn formality that the uninitiated might have supposed to attend a grave deliberation upon a matter of guilt or innocence involving a question of life or death.

No sooner were the doors closed that shut out the "vulgar" crowd, than the "high and mighty" officials immediately fell into easy attitudes, and disengaged conversation upon the weather, the climate, yesterday's dinner at General Cushion's quarters, the claret, the cigars and the Mexican signoritas.

They were presently recalled from this easy chat by the President, a severe disciplinarian, who reminded them rather sharply of the business upon which they had convened.

The officers immediately wheeled themselves around in the chairs, facing the table, and fell into order.

The Judge Advocate seated himself at his detached stand, opened his book, called the attention of the court, and commenced and read over the whole record of the evidence and the proceedings up to this time.

The President then said:

"For my own part, gentlemen, I think this quite a simple matter, requiring but little deliberation. Here is the fact of the offence proved, and here is the law upon that offence clearly defined. Nothing seems to remain for us to do but to bring in a verdict in accordance with the law and the fact."

Several of the elder officers and sterner disciplinarians agreed with the President, who now said:

"I move that the vote be immediately made upon this question."

To this, also, the elder officers assented. And the Judge Advocate was preparing to take the ballot, when one of the younger members arose and said:

"Mr. President and gentlemen, there are mitigating circumstances attending this offence, which, in my opinion, should be duly weighed before making up our ballot."

"Lieutenant Lovel, when your hair has grown white in the service of your country, as mine has, and when your skin is mottled with the scars of a score of well-fought fields, you will find your soft theories corrected by hard experience, and you will know that in the case of a sentinel steeping upon, his post there can be no mitigating circumstances; that nothing can palliate such flagrant and dangerous neglect, involving the safety of the whole army; a crime that martial law and custom have very necessarily made punishable by death," said the President, sternly.

The young lieutenant sat down abashed, under the impression that he had betrayed himself into some act of gross impropriety. This was his first appearance in the character of juror and judge; he was literally unaccustomed to public speaking, and did not hazard a reply.

"Has any other gentleman any views to advance before we proceed to a general ballot?" inquired the President.

Several of the officers whispered together, and then some one replied that there seemed to be no reason why the vote should not be immediately taken.

Herbert Greyson remained perfectly silent. Why he did not speak then, in reply to this adjuration—why, indeed, he had not spoken before, in support of Lieutenant Lovel's views in favor of his friend, I do not know to this day, though I mean to ask him the first time I have the opportunity. Perhaps he wished to "draw the enemy's fire," perhaps he was inclined to dramatic effects; but whatever might have been the motive, he continued silent, offering no obstacle to the immediate taking of the vote.

The Judge Advocate then called the court to order for the taking of the ballot, and proceeded to question the members in turn, commencing with the youngest.

"How say you, Lieutenant Lovel, is the prisoner on trial guilty or not guilty of the offence laid to his charge?"

"Guilty," responded the young officer, as his eyes filled with tears of pity for the other young life against which he had felt obliged to record this vote.

"If that is the opinion of one who seems friendly to him, what will be the votes of the other stern judges?" said Herbert Greyson to himself, in dismay.

"What say you, Lieutenant Adams—is the prisoner guilty or not guilty?" said the Judge Advocate, proceeding with the ballot.

"Guilty!"

"Lieutenant Cragin?"

"Guilty!"

"Lieutenant Evans?"

"Guilty!"

"Lieutenant Goffe?"

"Guilty!"

"Lieutenant Hesse?"

"Guilty!"

"Captain Kingsley?"

"Guilty!"

"Captain McConkey?"

"Guilty!"

"Captain Lucas?"

"Guilty!"

"Captain O'Donnelly?"

"Guilty!"

"Captain Rozencrantz?"

"Guilty!"

"Major Greyson?"

"NOT GUILTY!"

Every officer sprang to his feet and gazed in astonishment, consternation and indignant inquiry upon the renderer of this unprecedented vote.

The President was the first to speak, breaking out with:

"Sir! Major Greyson! your vote, sir, in direct defiance of the fact and the law upon it, is unprecedented, sir, in the whole history of court-martial!"

"I record it as uttered, nevertheless," replied Herbert.

"And your oath, sir! What becomes of your oath as a judge, of this court?"

"I regard my oath in my vote!"

"What, sir?" inquired Captain McConkey, "do you mean to say that you have rendered that vote in accordance with the facts elicited in evidence, as by your oath you were bound to do?"

"Yes."

"How, sir, do you mean to say that the prisoner did not sleep upon his post?"

"Certainly I do not; on the contrary, I grant that he did sleep upon his post, and yet I maintain that in doing so he was not guilty!"

"Major Greyson plays with us," said the President.

"By no means, sir! I never was in more solemn earnest than at present! Your honor, the President and gentlemen judges of the court, as I am not counsel for the prisoner, nor civil officer, nor lawyer, of whose interference courts-martial are proverbially jealous, I beg you will permit me to say a few words in support, or at least, I will say, in explanation of the vote which you have characterized as an opinion in opposition to fact and law, and unprecedented in the whole history of courts-martial."

"Yes, it is! it is!" said General W., shifting uneasily in his seat.

"You heard the defense of the prisoner," continued Herbert; "you heard the narrative of his wrongs and sufferings, to the truth of which his every aspect bore testimony. I will not here express a judgment as to the motives that prompted his superior officers, I will merely advert to the facts themselves, in order to prove that the prisoner, under the circumstances, could not, with his human power, have done otherwise than he did."

"Sir, if the prisoner considered himself wronged by his captain, which is very doubtful, he could have appealed to the Colonel of his Regiment!"

"Sir, the Articles of War accord him that privilege. But is it ever taken advantage of? Is there a case on record where a private soldier ventures to make a dangerous enemy of his immediate superior by complaining of his Captain to his Colonel? Nor in this case would it have been of the least use, inasmuch as this soldier had well-founded reasons for believing the Colonel of his regiment his personal enemy, and the Captain as the instrument of this enmity."

"And you, Major Greyson, do you coincide in the opinion of the prisoner? Do you think that there could have been anything in common between the Colonel of the regiment and the poor private in the ranks, to explain such an equalizing sentiment as enmity?" inquired Captain O'Donnelly.

"I answer distinctly, yes, sir! In the first place, this poor private is a young gentleman of birth and education, the heir of one of the most important estates in Virginia, and the betrothed of one of the most lovely girls in the world. In both these capacities he has stood in the way of Colonel Le Noir, standing between him and the estate on the one hand, and between him and the young lady on the other. He has disappointed Le Noir both in love and ambition. And he has thereby made an enemy of the man who has, besides, the nearest interest in his destruction. Gentlemen, what I say now in the absence of Colonel Le Noir, I am prepared to repeat in his presence, and maintain at the proper time and place."

"But how came this young gentleman of birth and expectations to be found in the ranks?" inquired Captain Rosencrantz.

"How came we to have headstrong sons of wealthy parents, fast young men of fortune, and runaway students from the universities and colleges of the United States in our ranks? In a burst of boyish impatience the youth enlisted. Destiny gave him as the Colonel of his regiment his mortal enemy. Colonel Le Noir found in Captain Zuten a ready instrument for his malignity. And between them both they have done all that could possibly be effected to defeat the good fortune and insure the destruction of Traverse Rocke. And I repeat, gentlemen, that what I feel constrained to affirm here in the absence of those officers, I shall assuredly reassert and maintain in their presence, upon the proper occasion. In fact I shall bring formal charges against Colonel Le Noir and Captain Zuten, of conduct unworthy of officers and gentlemen!"

"But it seems to me that this is not directly to the point at issue," said Captain Kingsley.

"On the contrary, sir, it is the point, the whole point, and only point, as you shall presently see by attending to the facts that I shall recall to your memory. You and all present must, then, see that there was a deliberate purpose to effect the ruin of this young man. He is accused of having been found sleeping on his post, the penalty of which, in time of war, is death. Now listen to the history of the days that preceded his fault, and tell me if human nature could have withstood the trial?"

"Sunday night was the last of repose to the prisoner until Friday morning, when he was found asleep on his post."

"Monday night he was sent with the reconnoitering party to Casa-de-Mata."

"Tuesday he was sent with the officer that carried our General's expostulation to Santa Anna. At night he was put on guard."

"Wednesday he was sent with another party to protect a band of emigrants crossing the marshes. At night he was sent with still another party to reconnoiter Molina-del-Rey."

"Thursday he was sent in attendance upon the officer that carried despatches to General Quitman, and did not return until after midnight, when, thoroughly worn out, driven indeed to the extreme degree of mortal endurance, he was again on a sultry, oppressive night, in a still, solitary place, set on guard where a few hours later he was found asleep upon his post—by whom? The Colonel of his regiment and the Captain of his company, who seemed bent upon his ruin—as I hold myself bound to establish before another court-martial."

"This result had been intended from the first! If five nights' loss of sleep would not have effected this, fifteen probably would; if fifteen would not, thirty would; or if thirty wouldn't sixty would!—and all this Captain Zuten had the power to enforce until his doomed victim should fall into the hands of the provost-marshal, and into the arms of death!"

"And now, gentlemen, in view of all these circumstances, I ask you—was Traverse Rocke guilty of wilful neglect of duty in dropping asleep on his post? And I move for a reconsideration, and a new ballot!"

"Such a thing is without precedent, sir! These mitigating circumstances may be brought to bear on the Commander-in-Chief, and may be embodied in a recommendation to mercy! They should have no weight in the finding of the verdict," said the President, "which should be in accordance with the fact and the law."

"And with justice and humanity! to find a verdict against this young man would be to place an unmerited brand upon his spotless name, that no after clemency of the Executive could wipe out! Gentlemen, will you do this! No! I am sure that you will not! And again I move for a new ballot!"

"I second the motion!" said Lieutenant Lovel, rising quite encouraged to believe in his own first instincts, which had been so favorable.

"Gentlemen," said the President sternly, "this thing is without precedent! In all the annals of courts-martial, without precedent!"

"Then, if there is no such precedent, it is quite time that such a one were established, so that the iron car of literal law should not always roll over and crush justice! Gentlemen, shall we have a new ballot?"

"Yes! yes! yes!" were the answers.

"It is irregular! It is illegal! It is unprecedented! A new ballot? Never heard of such a thing in forty years of military life! Lord bless my soul, what is the service coming to!"

"A new ballot! a new ballot! a new ballot!" was the unanimous cry.

The President groaned in spirit, and recorded a vow never to forgive Herbert Greyson for this departure from routine.

The new ballot demanded by acclamation had to be held.

The Judge Advocate called the court to order and began anew. The votes were taken as before, commencing with the young lieutenant, who now responded sonorously:

"Not guilty!"

And so it ran around the entire circle.

"Not guilty!" "Not guilty!" "Not guilty!" were the hearty responses of the court.

The acquittal was unanimous. The verdict was recorded.

The doors were then thrown open to the public, and the prisoner called in and publicly discharged from custody.

The court then adjourned.

Traverse Rocke threw himself upon the bosom of his friend, exclaiming in a broken voice:

"I cannot sufficiently thank you! My dear mother and Clara will do that!"

"Nonsense!" said Herbett laughing; "didn't I tell you that the Lord reigns, and the devil is a fool? This is only the beginning of victories!"

CHAPTER XXIV
THE END OF THE WAR

Now are our brows bound with victorious wreaths,
Our bruised arms hung up for monuments;
Our stern alarums changed to merry meetings,
Our dreadful marches to delightful measures.
Grim-visaged war hath smoothed his wrinkled front,
And now instead of mounting barbed steeds,
To fright the souls of fearful adversaries,
He capers nimbly in a lady's chamber,
To the lascivious pleasing of a lute.

—SHAKESPEARE.

Ten days later Molina-del-Rey, Casa-de-Mata, and Chapultepec had fallen! The United States forces occupied the city of Mexico, General Scott was in the Grand Plaza, and the American standard waved above the capital of the Montezumas!

Let those who have a taste for swords and muskets, drums and trumpets, blood and fire, describe the desperate battles and splendid victories that led to this final magnificent triumph!

My business lies with the persons of our story, to illustrate whom I must pick out a few isolated instances of heroism in this glorious campaign.

Herbert Greyson's division was a portion of the gallant Eleventh that charged the Mexican batteries on Molina-del-Rey. He covered his name with glory, and qualified himself to merit the command of the regiment, which he afterwards received.

Traverse Rocke fought like a young Paladin. When they were marching into the very mouths of the cannon they were vomiting fire upon them, and when the young ensign of his company was struck down before him, Traverse Rocke took the colors from his falling hand, and crying "Victory!" pressed onward and upward over the dead and the dying, and springing upon one of the guns which continued to belch forth fire, he thrice waved the flag over his head and then planted it upon the battery. Captain Zuten fell in the subsequent assault upon Chapultepec.

Colonel Le Noir entered the city of Mexico with the victorious army, but on the subsequent day, being engaged in a street skirmish with the leperos, or liberated convicts, he fell mortally wounded by a copper bullet, and he was now dying by inches at his quarters near the Grand Cathedral.

It was on the evening of the 20th of September, six days from the triumphant entry of General Scott into the capital, that Major Greyson was seated at supper at his quarters, with some of his brother officers, when an orderly entered and handed a note to Herbert, which proved to be a communication from the surgeon of their regiment, begging him to repair without delay to the quarters of Colonel Le Noir, who, being in extremity, desired to see him.

Major Greyson immediately excused himself to his company, and repaired to the quarters of the dying man.

He found Colonel Le Noir stretched upon his bed in a state of extreme exhaustion and attended by the surgeon and chaplain of his regiment.

As Herbert advanced to the side of his bed, Le Noir stretched out his pale hand and said:

"You bear no grudge against a dying man, Greyson?"

"Certainly not," said Herbert, "especially when he proposes doing the right thing, as I judge you do, from the fact of your sending for me."

"Yes, I do; I do!" replied Le Noir, pressing the hand that Herbert's kindness of heart could not withhold.

Le Noir then beckoned the minister to hand him two sealed packets, which he took and laid upon the bed before him.

Then taking up the larger of the two packets, he placed it in the hands of Herbert Greyson, saying:

"There, Greyson, I wish you to hand that to your friend, young Rocke, who has received his colors, I understand?"

"Yes, he has now the rank of ensign."

"Then give this parcel into the hands of Ensign Rocke, with the request, that being freely yielded up, they may not be used in any manner to harass the last hours of a dying man."

"I promise, on the part of my noble young friend, that they shall not be so used," said Herbert as he took possession of the parcel.

Le Noir then took up the second packet, which was much smaller, but much more firmly secured, than the first, being in an envelope of parchment, sealed with three great seals.

Le Noir held it in his hand for a moment, gazing from the surgeon to the chaplain, and thence down upon the mysterious packet, while spasms of pain convulsed his countenance. At length he spoke:

"This second packet, Greyson, contains a—well, I may as well call it a narrative. I confide it to your care upon these conditions—that it shall not be opened until after my death and funeral, and that, when it has served its purpose of restitution, it may be, as far as possible, forgotten. Will you promise me this?"

"On my honor, yes," responded the young man, as he received the second parcel.

"This is all I have to say, except this—that you seemed to me, upon every account, the most proper person to whom I could confide this trust. I thank you for accepting it, and I believe that I may safely promise that you will find the contents of the smaller packet of great importance and advantage to yourself and those dear to you."

Herbert bowed in silence.

"That is all, good-by. I wish now to be alone with our chaplain," said Colonel Le Noir, extending his hand.

Herbert pressed that wasted hand; silently sent up a prayer for the dying wrong-doer, bowed gravely and withdrew.

It was almost eight o'clock, and Herbert thought that he would scarcely have time to find Traverse before the drum should beat to quarters.

He was more fortunate than he had anticipated, for he had scarcely turned the Grand Cathedral when he came full upon the young ensign.

"Ah! Traverse, I am very glad to meet you! I was just going to look for you. Come immediately to my rooms, for I have a very important communication to make to you. Colonel Le Noir is supposed to be dying. He has given me a parcel to be handed to you, which I shrewdly suspect to contain your intercepted correspondence for the last two years," said Herbert.

Traverse started and gazed upon his friend in amazement, and was about to express his astonishment, when Herbert, seeing others approach, drew the arm of his friend within his own, and they hurried silently on toward Major Greyson's quarters.

They had scarcely got in and closed the door and stricken a light before Traverse exclaimed impatiently:

"Give it me!" and almost snatched the parcel from Herbert's hands.

"Whist! don't be impatient! I dare say it is all stale news!" said Herbert, as he yielded up the prize.

They sat down together on each side of a little stand supporting a light.

Herbert watched with sympathetic interest while Traverse tore open the envelope and examined its contents.

They were, as Herbert had anticipated, letters from the mother and the betrothed of Traverse—letters that had arrived and been intercepted, from time to time, for the preceding two years.

There were blanks, also, directed in a hand strange to Traverse, but familiar to Herbert as that of Old Hurricane, and those blanks inclosed drafts upon a New Orleans bank, payable to the order of Traverse Rocke.

Traverse pushed all these latter aside with scarcely a glance and not a word of inquiry, and began eagerly to examine the long-desired, long-withheld letters from the dear ones at home.

His cheek flamed to see that every seal was broken, and the fresh aroma of every heart-breathed word inhaled by others, before they reached himself.

"Look here, Herbert! look here! Is not this insufferable? Every fond word of my mother, every delicate and sacred expression of—of regard from Clara, all read by the profane eyes of that man!"

"That man is on his deathbed, Traverse, and you must forgive him! He has restored your letters."

"Yes, after their sacred privacy has been profaned! Oh!"

Traverse handed his mother's letters over to Herbert, that his foster brother might read them, but Clara's "sacred epistles" were kept to himself.

"What are you laughing at?" inquired Traverse, looking up from his page, and detecting Herbert with a smile upon his face.

"I am thinking that you are not as generous as you were some few years since, when you would have given me Clara herself; for now you will not even let me have a glimpse of her letters!"

"Have they not been already sufficiently published?" said Traverse, with an almost girlish smile and blush.

When those cherished letters were all read and put away, Traverse stooped down and "fished up" from amidst envelopes, strings and waste paper another set of letters which proved to be the blanks inclosing the checks, of various dates, which Herbert recognized as coming anonymously from Old Hurricane.

"What in the world is the meaning of all this, Herbert? Have I a nabob uncle turned up anywhere, do you think? Look here!—a hundred dollars—and a fifty, and another—all drafts upon the Planters' Bank, New Orleans, drawn in my favor and signed by Largent Dor, bankers!—I, that haven't had five dollars at a time to call my own for the last two years! Here, Herbert, give me a good, sharp pinch to wake me up! I may be sleeping on my post again?" said Traverse in perplexity.

"You are not sleeping, Traverse!"

"Are you sure?"

"Perfectly," replied Herbert, laughing.

"Well, then, do you think that crack upon the crown of my head that I got upon Chapultepec has not injured my intellect?"

"Not in the slightest degree!" said Herbert, still laughing at his friend's perplexity.

"Then I am the hero of a fairy tale, that is all—a fairy tale in which waste paper is changed into bank notes and private soldiers prince palatines! Look here!" cried Traverse, desperately, thrusting the bank checks under the nose of his friend, "do you see those things and know what they are, and will you tell me that everything in this castle don't go by enchantment?"

"Yes, I see what they are, and it seems to me perfectly natural that you should have them!"

"Humph!" said Traverse, looking at Herbert with an expression that seemed to say that he thought the wits of his friend deranged.

"Traverse," said Major Greyson, "did it never occur to you that you must have other relatives in the world besides your mother? Well, I suspect that those checks were sent by some relative of yours or your mother's, who just begins to remember that he has been neglecting you."

"Herbert, do you know this?" inquired Traverse, anxiously.

"No, I do not know it; I only suspect this to be the case," said Herbert, evasively. "But what is that which you are forgetting."

"Oh! this—yes, I had forgotten it. Let us see what it is!" said Traverse, examining a paper that had rested unobserved upon the stand.

"This is an order for my discharge, signed by the Secretary of War, and dated—ha-ha-ha—two years ago! Here I have been serving two years illegally, and if I had been convicted of neglect of duty in sleeping on my post, I should have been shot unlawfully, as that man, when he prosecuted me, knew perfectly well!" exclaimed Traverse.

"That man, as I said before, lies upon his deathbed! Remember, nothing against him! But that order for a discharge! now that you are in the way of promotion and the war is over, will you take advantage of it?"

"Decidedly, yes! for though I am said to have acquitted myself passably well at Chapultepec—"

"Gloriously, Traverse! You won your colors gloriously!"

"Yet for all that my true mission is not to break men's bones, but to set them when broken. Not to take men's lives, but to save them when endangered! So to-morrow morning, please Providence, I shall present this order to General Butler and apply for my discharge."

"And you will set out immediately for home?"

The face of Traverse suddenly changed.

"I should like to do so! Oh, how I should like to see my dear mother and Clara, if only for a day! but I must not indulge the longing of my heart. I must not go home until I can do so with honor!"

"And can you not do so now? You, who triumphed over all your personal enemies and who won your colors at Chapultepec?"

"No, for all this was in my legitimate profession! Nor will I present myself at home until, by the blessing of the Lord, I have done what I set out to do, and established myself in a good practice. And so, by the help of heaven, I hope within one week to be on my way to New Orleans to try my fortune in that city."

"To New Orleans! And a new malignant fever of some horrible, unknown type, raging there!" exclaimed Herbert.

"So much the more need of a physician! Herbert, I am not the least uneasy on the subject of infection! I have a theory for its annihilation."

"I never saw a clever young professional man without a theory!" laughed Herbert.

The drum was now heard beating the tattoo, and the friends separated with hearts full of revived hope.

The next morning Traverse presented the order of the Secretary to the Commander-in-Chief and received his discharge.

And then, after writing long, loving and hopeful letters to his mother and his betrothed, and entreating the former to try to find out who was the secret benefactor who had sent him such timely aid, Traverse took leave of his friends, and set out for the Southern Queen of Cities, once more to seek his fortune.

Meantime the United States army continued to occupy the City of Mexico, through the whole of the autumn and winter. General Butler, who temporarily succeeded the illustrious Scott in the chief command, very wisely arranged the terms of an armistice with the enemy that was intended to last two months from the beginning of February, but which happily lasted until the conclusion of the treaty of peace between the two countries.

Colonel Le Noir had not been destined soon to die; his wound, an inward canker from a copper bullet, that the surgeon had at length succeeded in extracting, took the form of a chronic fester disease. Since the night, upon which he had been so extremely ill to be supposed dying, and yet had rallied, the doctors felt no apprehensions of his speedy death, though they gave no hopes of his final recovery.

Under these circumstances there were hours in which Le Noir bitterly regretted his precipitation in permitting those important documents to go out of his own hands. And he frequently sent for Herbert Greyson in private to require assurances that he would not open the packet confided to him before the occurrence of the event specified.

And Herbert always soothed the sufferer by reiterating his promise that so long as Colonel Le Noir should survive the seals of that packet should not be broken.

Beyond the suspicion that the parcel contained an important confession, Herbert Greyson was entirely ignorant of its contents.

But the life of Gabriel Le Noir was prolonged beyond all human calculus of probabilities.

He was spared to experience a more effectual repentance than that spurious one into which he had been frightened by the seeming rapid approach of death. And after seven months of lingering illness and gradual decline, during the latter portions of which he was comforted by the society of his only son, who had come at his summons to visit him, in May, 1848, Gabriel Le Noir expired a sincere penitent, reconciled to God and man.

And soon afterward, in the month of May, the treaty of peace having been ratified by the Mexican Congress at Queretaro, the American army evacuated the city and territory of Mexico.

And our brave soldiers, their "brows crowned with victorious wreaths," set out upon their return to home and friends.

CHAPTER XXV
THE FORTUNATE BATH

Heaven has to all allotted soon or late
Some lucky revolution of their fate;
Whose motions if we watch and guide with skill
(For human good depends on human will)
Our fortune rolls as from a smooth descent.
And from the first impression takes its bent.
Now, now she meets you with a glorious prize,
And spreads her locks before her as she flies.

—DRYDEN.

Meanwhile, what had our young adventurer been doing in all these months between September and June!

Traverse, with his two hundred dollars, had set out for New Orleans about the first of October.

But by the time he had paid his traveling expenses and fitted himself out with a respectable suit of professional black and a few necessary books, his little capital had diminished three-quarters.

So that when he found himself settled in his new office, in a highly respectable quarter of the city, he had but fifty dollars and a few dimes left.

A portion of this sum was expended in a cheap sofa-bedstead, a closed washstand and a spirit lamp coffee boiler, for Traverse determined to lodge in his office and board himself—"which will have this additional advantage," said the cheerful fellow to himself—"for besides saving me from debt, it will keep me always on hand for calls."

The fever, though it was October, had scarcely abated; indeed, on the contrary, it seemed to have revived and increased in virulency in consequence of the premature return of many people who had fled on its first appearance, and who in coming back too soon to the infected atmosphere, were less able to withstand contagion than those who remained.

That Traverse escaped the plague was owing not so much to his favorite "theory" as to his vigorous constitution, pure blood and regular habits of temperance, cleanliness and cheerful activity of mind and body.

Just then the demand was greater than the supply of medical service. Traverse found plenty to do, and his pleasant, young face and hopeful and confident manners won him great favor in sick rooms, where, whether it were to be ascribed to his "theory," his "practice" or to the happy, inspiring influence of his personal presence, or to all these together, with the blessing of the Lord upon them, it is certain that he was very successful in raising the sick. It is true that he did not earn five dollars in as many days, for his practice, like that of almost every very young professional man, was among the indigent.

But what of that? What if he were not running up heavy accounts against wealthy patrons? He was "giving to the poor," not money, for he himself was as poor as any of them; but his time, labor and professional skill; he was "giving to the poor;" he was "lending to the Lord," and he "liked the security." And the most successful speculator that ever made a fortune on 'change never, never invested time, labor or money to a surer advantage.

And this I would say for the encouragement of all young persons in similar circumstances—do not be impatient if the "returns" are a little while delayed, for they are so sure and so rich that they are quite worth waiting for, nor will the waiting be long. Give your services cheerfully, also, for "the Lord loveth a cheerful giver."

Traverse managed to keep out of debt; he regularly paid his office rent and his laundress' bill; he daily purchased his mutton chop or pound of beefsteak and broiled it himself; he made his coffee, swept and dusted his office, put up his sofa-bed, blacked his boots; and oh! miracle of independence, he mended his own gloves and sewed on his own shirt buttons, for you may depend that the widow's son knew how to do all these things; nor was there a bit of hardship in his having so to wait upon himself, though if his mother and Clara, in their well-provided and comfortable home at Willow Heights, had only known how destitute the young man was of female aid and comfort, how they would have cried!

"No one but himself to mend his poor dear gloves! Oh—oh-boo-hoo-oo!"

Traverse never alluded to his straitened circumstances, but boasted of the comfort of his quarters and the extent of his practice, and declared that his income already exceeded his outlay, which was perfectly true, since he was resolved to live within it, whatever it might be.

As the fever began to subside Traverse's practice declined, and about the middle of November his "occupation was gone."

We said that his office was in the most respectable locality in the city; it was, in fact, on the ground floor of a first-class hotel.

It happened that one night, near the close of winter, Traverse lay awake on his sofa-bedstead, turning over in his mind how he should contrive to make both ends meet at the conclusion of the present term and feeling as near despondency as it was possible for his buoyant and God-trusting soul to be, when there came a loud ringing at his office bell.

This reminded him of the stirring days and nights of the preceding autumn. He started up at once to answer the summons.

"Who's there?"

"Is Doctor Rocke in?"

"Yes, what's wanted?"

"A gentleman, sir, in the house here, sir, taken very bad, wants the doctor directly, room number 555."

"Very well, I will be with the gentleman immediately," answered Traverse, plunging his head into a basin of cold water and drying it hastily.

In five minutes Traverse was in the office of the hotel, inquiring for a waiter to show him up into 555.

One was ordered to attend him, who led the way up several flights of stairs and around divers galleries, until he opened a door and ushered the doctor immediately into the sick room.

There was a little, old, dried-up Frenchman in a blue nightcap, extended on a bed in the middle of the room and covered with a white counterpane that clung close to his rigid form as to a corpse.

And there was a little, old, dried-up Frenchwoman in a brown merino gown and a high-crowned muslin cap who hopped and chattered about the bed like a frightened magpie.

"Ou! Monsieur le Docteur!" she screamed, jumping at Traverse in a way to make him start back; "Ou, Monsieur le Docteur, I am very happy you to see! Voila mon frere! Behold my brother! He is ill! He is verra ill! He is dead! He is verra dead!"

"I hope not," said Traverse, approaching the bed.

"Voila, behold! Mon dieu, he is verra still! He is verra cold! He is verra dead! What can you, mon frere, my brother to save?"

"Be composed, madam, if you please, and allow me to examine my patient," said Traverse.

"Ma foi! I know not what you speak 'compose.' What can you my brother to save?"

"Much, I hope, madam, but you must leave me to examine my patient and not interrupt me," said Traverse, passing his hand over the naked chest of the sick man.

"Mon Dieu! I know not 'exam' and 'interrup'! and I know not what can you mon frere to save!"

"If you don't hush parley-vooing, the doctor can do nothink, mum," said the waiter, in a respectful tone.

Traverse found his patient in a bad condition—in a stupor, if not in a state of positive insensibility. The surface of his body was cold as ice, and apparently without the least vitality. If he was not, as his sister had expressed it, "very dead," he was certainly "next to it."

By close questioning, and by putting his questions in various forms, the doctor learned from the chattering little magpie of a Frenchwoman that the patient had been ill for nine days; that he had been under the care of Monsieur le Doctor Cartiere; that there had been a consultation of physicians; that they had prescribed for him and given him over: that le Docteur Cartiere still attended him, but was at this instant in attendance as accoucheur to a lady in extreme danger, whom he could not leave; but Doctor Cartiere had directed them, in his unavoidable absence, to call in the skilful, the talented, the soon to be illustrious young Docteur Rocque, who was also near at hand.

The heart of Traverse thrilled with joy. The Lord had remembered him! His best skill spent upon the poor and needy who could make him no return, but whose lives he had succeeded in saving, had reached the ears of the celebrated Dr. C., who had with the unobtrusive magnanimity of real genius quietly recommended him to his own patrons.

Oh! well, he would do his very best, not only to advance his own professional interests, and to please his mother and Clara, but also to do honor to the magnanimous Doctor C.'s recommendation!

Here, too, was an opportunity of putting in practise his favorite theory; but first of all it was necessary to be informed of the preceding mode of treatment and its results.

So he further questioned the little, restless magpie, and by ingeniously framed inquiries succeeded in gaining from her the necessary knowledge of his patient's antecedents. He examined all the medicines that had been used, and informed himself of their effects upon the disease. But the most serious difficulty of all seemed to be the impossibility of raising vital action upon the cold, dead skin.

The chattering little woman informed him that the patient had been covered with blisters that would not "pull," that would not "delineate," that would not, what call you it—"draw!"

Traverse could easily believe this, for not only the skin, but the very flesh of the old doctor seemed bloodless and lifeless.

Now for his theory! What would kill a healthy man with a perfect circulation might save the life of this dying one, whose whole surface, inch deep, seemed already dead.

"Put him in a bath of mustard water, as hot as you can bear your own hand in and continue to raise the temperature slowly, watching the effect, for about five minutes. I will go down and prepare a cordial draught to be taken the moment he gets back to bed," said Doctor Rocke, who immediately left the room.

His directions were all but too well obeyed. The bathing tub was quickly brought into the chamber and, filled with water as hot as the nurse could bear her hand in then the invalid was hastily invested in a slight bathing gown and lifted by two servants and laid in the hot bath.

"Now, bring quickly, water boiling," said the little, old woman, imperatively. And when a large copper kettleful was forthcoming, she took it and began to pour a stream of hissing, bubbling water in at the foot of the bath.

The skin of the torpid patient had been reddening for a few seconds, so as to prove that its sensibility was returning, and now when the stream from the kettle began to mix with the already very hot bath, and to raise its temperature almost to boiling, suddenly there was heard a cry from the bath, and the patient, with the agility of youth and health, skipped out of the tub and into his bed, kicking vigorously and exclaiming:

"Brigands! Assassins! You have scalded my legs to death!"

"Glory be to the Lord, he's saved!" cried one of the waiters, a devout Irishman.

"Ciel! he speaks! he moves! he lives! mon frere!" cried the little Frenchwoman, going to him.

"Ah, murderers! bandits! you've scalded me to death! I'll have you all before the commissaire!"

"He scolds! he threatens! he swears! he gets well! mon frere!" cried the old woman, busying herself to change his clothes and put on his flannel nightgown. They then tucked him up warmly in bed and put bottles of hot water all around, to keep up this newly stimulated circulation.

At that moment Dr. Rocke came in, put his hand into the bath-tub and could scarcely repress a cry of pain and of horror—the water scalded his fingers! What must it have done to the sick man?

"Good heavens, madam! I did not tell you to parboil your patient!" exclaimed Traverse, speaking to the old woman. Traverse was shocked to find how perilously his orders had been exceeded.

"Eh bien, Monsieur! he lives! he does well! voila mon frere!" exclaimed the little old woman.

It was true: the accidental "boiling bath" as it might almost be called, had effected what perhaps no other means in the world could—a restored circulation.

The disease was broken up, and the convalescence of the patient was rapid. And as Traverse kept his own secret concerning the accidental high temperature of that bath, which every one considered a fearful and successful experiment, the fame of Dr. Rocke spread over the whole city and country.

He would soon have made a fortune in New Orleans, had not the hand of destiny beckoned him elsewhere. It happened thus:

The old Frenchman whose life Traverse had, partly by accident and partly by design, succeeded in saving, comprehended perfectly well how narrow his escape from death had been, and attributed his restoration solely to the genius, skill and boldness of his young physician, and was grateful accordingly with all a Frenchman's noisy demonstration.

He called Traverse his friend, his deliverer, his son.

One day, as soon as he found himself strong enough to think of pursuing his journey, he called his "son" into the room and explained to him that he, Doctor Pierre St. Jean, was the proprietor of a private insane asylum, very exclusive, very quiet, very aristocratic, indeed, receiving none but patients of the highest rank; that this retreat was situated on the wooded banks of a charming lake in one of the most healthy and beautiful neighborhoods of East Feliciana; that he had originally come down to the city to engage the services of some young physician of talent as his assistant, and finally, that he would be delighted, enraptured if "his deliverer, his friend, his son," would accept the post.

Now Traverse particularly wished to study the various phases of mental derangement, a department of his professional education that had hitherto been opened to him only through books.

He explained this to his old friend, the French physician, who immediately went off into ecstatic exclamations of joy as, "Good! Great! Grand!" and "I shall now repay my good child! my dear son! for his so excellent skill!"

The terms of the engagement were soon arranged, and Traverse prepared to accompany his new friend to his "beautiful retreat," the private madhouse. But Traverse wrote to his mother and to Clara in Virginia, and also to Herbert Greyson in Mexico, to apprise them of his good fortune.

CHAPTER XXVI
THE MYSTERIOUS MANIAC

Stay, jailer, stay, and hear my woe;
She is not mad, who kneels to thee,
For what I am, full well I know,
And what I was, and what should be;
I'll rave no more in proud despair—
My language shall be calm tho' sad
But yet I'll truly, firmly swear,
I am not mad! no, no, not mad!

—M.G. LEWIS

It was at the close of a beautiful day in early spring that Traverse Rocke, accompanying the old doctor and the old sister, reached the grove on the borders of the beautiful lake upon the banks of which was situated the "Calm Retreat."

A large, low, white building surrounded with piazzas and shaded by fragrant and flowering southern trees, it looked like the luxurious country seat of some wealthy merchant or planter rather than a prison for the insane.

Doctor St. Jean conducted his young assistant into a broad and cool hall on each side of which doors opened into spacious rooms, occupied by the proprietor and his household. The cells of the patients, as it appeared were up-stairs. The country doctor and the matron who had been in charge during the absence of the proprietor and his sister now came forward to welcome the party and report the state of the institution and its inmates.

All were as usual, the country doctor said, except "Mademoiselle."

"And what of her—how is Mademoiselle—?"

"A patient most interesting, Doctor Rocke," said the old Frenchman, alternately questioning his substitute and addressing Traverse.

"She has stopped her violent ravings, and seems to me to be sinking into a state of stupid despair," replied the substitute.

"A patient most interesting, my young friend! A history most pathetic! You shall hear of it some time. But come into the parlor, and you, Angele, my sister, ring and order coffee," said the old Frenchman, leading the way into a pleasant apartment on the right of the hall, furnished with straw matting upon the floor and bamboo settees and chairs around the walls.

Here coffee was presently served to the travelers, who soon after retired for the night.

Traverse's room was a large, pleasant apartment at the end of a wide, long hall, on each side of which were the doors opening into the cells of the patients.

Fatigued by his journey, Traverse slept soundly through the night; but early in the morning he was rudely awakened by the sounds of maniac voices from the cells. Some were crying, some laughing aloud some groaning and howling and some holding forth in fancied exhortations.

He dressed himself quickly and left his room to walk down the length of the long hall and observe the cells on each side. The doors were at regular intervals, and each door had in its center a small opening to enable the proprietor to look in upon the patients.

As these were all women, and some of them delicate and refined even in their insanity, Traverse felt shocked at this necessary, if it were necessary, exposure of their sanctuary.

The cells were, in fact, small bedrooms that with their white-washed walls and white-curtained beds and windows looked excessively neat, clean and cool, but also, it must be confessed, very bare, dreary and cheerless.

"Even a looking-glass would be a great benefit to those poor girls, for I remember that even Clara, in her violent grief, and mother in her lifelong sorrow, never neglected their looking-glass and personal appearance," said Traverse to himself, as he passed down the hall and resolved that this little indulgence should be afforded the patients.

And except those first involuntary glances he scrupulously avoided looking in through the gratings upon those helpless women who had no means of secluding themselves.

But as he turned to go down the stairs his eyes went full into an opposite cell and fell upon a vision of beauty and sorrow that immediately riveted his gaze.

It was a small and graceful female figure, clothed in deep black, seated by the window, with her elbow resting upon the sill and her chin supported on her hand. Her eyes were cast down until her eyelashes lay like inky lines upon her snow-white cheek. Her face, of classic regularity and marble whiteness, bore a ghastly contrast to the long eyelashes, arched eyebrows and silken ringlets black as midnight. She might have been a statue or a picture, so motionless she sat.

Conscious of the wrong of gazing upon this solitary woman, Traverse forced his looks away and passed on down-stairs, where he again met the old doctor and Mademoiselle Angele at breakfast.

After breakfast Doctor St. Jean invited his young assistant to accompany him on a round of visits to the patients, and they went immediately up to the hall, at the end of which Traverse had slept.

"There are our incurables, but they are not violent; incurables never are! Poor Mademoiselle! She has just been conveyed to this ward," said the doctor, opening the door of the first cell on the right at the head of the stairs and admitting Traverse at once into the presence of the beautiful, black-haired, snow-faced woman, who had so much interested him.

"This is my friend, Doctor Rocke, Mademoiselle; Doctor, this is my friend, Mademoiselle Mont de St. Pierre!"

Traverse bowed profoundly, and the lady arose, curtsied and resumed her seat, saying, coldly:

"I have told you, Monsieur, never to address me as Mademoiselle; you persist in doing so, and I shall never notice the insult again."

"Ten thousand pardons, madame! But if madame will always look so young, so beautiful, can I ever remember that she is a widow?"

The classic lip of the woman curled in scorn, and she disdained a reply.

"I take an appeal to Monsieur Le Docteur—is not madame young and beautiful?" asked the Frenchman, turning to Traverse, while the splendid, black eyes of the stranger passed from the one to the other.

Traverse caught the glance of the lady and bowed gravely. It was the most delicate and proper reply.

She smiled almost as gravely, and with a much kinder expression than any she had bestowed upon the Frenchman.

"And how has madame fared during my absence so long? The servants—have they been respectful? Have they been observant? Have they been obedient to the will of madame? Madame has but to speak!" said the doctor, bowing politely.

"Why should I speak when every word I utter you believe, or affect to believe, to be the ravings of a maniac? I will speak no more," said the lady, turning away her superb dark eyes and looking out of the window.

"Ah, madame will not so punish her friend, her servant, her slave!"

A gesture of fierce impatience and disgust was the only reply deigned by the lady.

"Come away; she is angry and may become dangerously excited," said the old doctor, leading the way from the cell.

"Did you tell me this lady is one of the incurables?" inquired Traverse, when they had left her apartment.

"Bah! yes, poor girl, vera incurable, as my sister would say."

"Yet she appears to me to be perfectly sane, as well as exceedingly beautiful and interesting."

"Ah, bah; my excellent, my admirable, my inexperienced young friend, that is all you know of lunatics! With more or less violence of assertion, they every one insist upon their sanity, just as criminals protest their innocence. Ah, bah! you shall go into every cell in this ward and find not one lunatic among them," sneered the old doctor, as he led the way into the next little room.

It was indeed as he had foretold, and Traverse Rocke found himself deeply affected by the melancholy, the earnest and sometimes the violent manner in which the poor unfortunates protested their sanity and implored or demanded to be restored to home and friends.

"You perceive," said the doctor, with a dry laugh, "that they are none of them crazy?"

"I see," said Traverse, "but I also detect a very great difference between that lovely woman in the south cell and these other inmates."

"Bah! bah! bah! She is more beautiful, more accomplished, more refined than the others, and she is in one of her lucid intervals! That is all; but as to a difference between her insanity and that of the other patients, it lies in this, that she is the most hopelessly mad of the whole lot! She has been mad eighteen years!"

"Is it possible?" exclaimed Traverse, incredulously.

"She lost her reason at the age of sixteen, and she is now thirty-four; you can calculate!"

"It is amazing and very sorrowful! How beautiful she is!"

"Yes; her beauty was a fatal gift. It is a sad story. Ah, it is a sad story. You shall hear it when we get through."

"I can connect no idea of woman's frailty with that refined and intellectual face," said Traverse coldly.

"Ah, bah! you are young! you know not the world! you, my innocent, my pious young friend!" said the old doctor, as they crossed the hall to go into the next wing of the building, in which were situated the men's wards.

Traverse found nothing that particularly interested him in this department, and when they had concluded their round of visits and were seated together in the old doctor's study, Traverse asked him for the story of his beautiful patient.

The doctor shrugged his shoulders.

"It is a story miserable, as I told you before. A gentleman, illustrious, from Virginia, an officer high in the army, and distinguished in the war, he brought this woman to me nearly three years ago. He informed me that— oh, bien! I had better tell you the story in my own manner. This young lady, Mademoiselle Mont de St. Pierre, is of a family noble and distinguished—a relative of this officer, illustrious and brave. At fifteen Mademoiselle met a man, handsome and without honor. Ah, bah! you understand! at sixteen the child became a fallen angel! She lost her reason through sorrow and shame. This relative—this gentleman, illustrious and noble, tender and compassionate—took her to the seclusion of his country house, where she lived in elegance, luxury and honor. But as the years passed her malady increased; her presence became dangerous; in a word, the gentleman, distinguished and noble, saw the advertisement of my 'Calm Retreat,' my institution incomparable, and he wrote to me. In a word, he liked my terms and brought to me his young relative, so lovely and so unfortunate. Ah! he is a good man, this officer, so gallant, so chivalrous; but she is ungrateful!"

"Ungrateful!"

"Ah, bah! yes; it is the way of lunatics! They ever imagine their best friends to be their worst enemies. The poor, crazed creature fancies that she is the sister-in-law of this officer illustrious! She thinks that she is the widow of his elder brother, whom she imagines he murdered, and that she is the mother of children, whom she says he has abducted or destroyed, so that he may enjoy the estate that is her widow's dower and their orphans' patrimony. That is the reason why she insists on being called madame instead of mademoiselle, and we indulge her when we think of it!"

"But all this is very singular!"

"Ah, bah! who can account for a lunatic's fancies? She is the maddest of the whole lot. Sometimes she used to become so violent that we would have to restrain her. But lately, Doctor Wood tells me, she is quite still; that we consider a bad sign; there is always hope for a lunatic until they begin to sink into this state," said the doctor, with an air of competency.

CHAPTER XXVII
THE MANIAC'S STORY,

A scheming villain forged the tale
That chains me in this dreary cell,
My fate unknown, my friends bewail,
Oh, doctor, haste that fate to tell!
Oh, haste my daughter's heart to cheer,
Her heart, at once, 'twill grieve and glad
To know, tho' chained and captive here,
I am not mad! I am not mad!

—M. G. LEWIS.

There is some advantage in having imagination, since that visionary faculty opens the mental eyes to facts that more practical and duller intellects could never see.

Traverse was young and romantic, and deeply interested in the doctor's beautiful patient. He, therefore, did not yield his full credulity to the tale told by the "relative illustrious" to the old doctor, as to the history and cause of the lady's madness, or even take it for granted that she was mad. He thought it quite possible that the distinguished officer's story might be a wicked fabrication, to conceal a crime, and that the lady's "crazy fancy" might be the pure truth.

And Travers had heard to what heinous uses private madhouses were sometimes put by some unscrupulous men, who wished to get certain women out of their way, yet who shrank from bloodshed.

And he thought it not impossible that this "gentleman so noble, so compassionate and tender," might be just such a man, and this "fallen angel" such a victim. And he determined to watch and observe. And he further resolved to treat the interesting patient with all the studious delicacy and respect due to a refined and accomplished woman in the full possession of her faculties. If she were really mad, this demeanor would not hurt her, and if she were not mad it was the only proper conduct to be observed toward her, as any other must be equally cruel and offensive. Her bodily health certainly required the attendance of a physician, and Traverse had therefore a fair excuse for his daily visits to her cell.

His respectful manners, his grave bow, and his reverential tone in saying—

"I hope I find you stronger to-day, Madam," seemed to gratify one who had few sources of pleasure.

"I thank you," she would answer, with a softened tone and look, adding, "Yes" or "No," as the truth might be.

One day, after looking at the young physician some time, she suddenly said:

"You never forget. You always address me by my proper title of Madam, and without the touch of irony which others indulge in when 'humoring' me, as they call it! Now, pray explain to me why, in sober earnest, you give me this title?"

"Because, Madam, I have heard you lay claim to that title, and I think that you yourself, of all the world, have the best right to know how you should be addressed," said Traverse, respectfully.

The lady looked wistfully at him and said:

"But my next-door neighbor asserts that she is a queen; she insists upon being called 'your majesty.' Has she, then, the best right to know how she should be addressed?"

"Alas! no, Madam, and I am pained that you should do yourself the great wrong to draw such comparisons."

"Why? Am not I and the 'queen' inmates of the same ward of incurables, in the same lunatic asylum?"

"Yes, but not with equal justice of cause. The 'queen' is a hopelessly deranged, but happy lunatic. You, Madam, are a lady who has retained the full possession of your faculties amid circumstances and surroundings that must have overwhelmed the reason of a weaker mind."

The lady looked at him in wonder and almost in joy.

"Ah! it was not the strength of my mind; it was the strength of the Almighty upon whom my mind was stayed, for time and for eternity, that has saved my reason in all these many years! But how did you know that I was not mad? How do you know that this is anything more than a lucid interval of longer duration than usual?" she asked.

"Madam, you will forgive me for having looked at you so closely, and watched you so constantly, but I am your physician, you know—"

"I have nothing to forgive and much to thank you for, young man. You have an honest, truthful, frank, young face! the only one such that I have seen in eighteen years of sorrow! But why, then, did you not believe the doctor? Why did you not take the fact of my insanity upon trust, as others did?" she asked, fixing her glorious, dark eyes inquiringly upon his face.

"Madam, from the first moment in which I saw you, I disbelieved the story of your insanity, and mentioned my doubts to Doctor St. Jean—"

"Who ridiculed your doubts, of course. I can readily believe that he did. Doctor St. Jean is not a very bad man, but he is a charlatan and a dullard; he received the story of my reported insanity as he received me, as an advantage to his institution, and he never gave himself the unprofitable trouble to investigate the circumstances. I told him the truth about myself as calmly as I now speak to you, but somebody else had told him that this truth was the fiction of a deranged imagination, and he found it more convenient and profitable to believe somebody else. But again I ask you, why were not you, also, so discreetly obtuse?"

"Madam," said Traverse, blushing ingenuously, "I hope you will forgive me for saying that it is impossible any one could see you without becoming deeply interested in your fate. Your face, Madam, speaks equally of profound sorrows and of saintly resignation. I saw no sign of madness there. In the calm depths of those sad eyes, lady, I knew that the fires of insanity never could have burned. Pardon me that I looked at you so closely; I was your physician, and was most deeply anxious concerning my patient."

"I thank you; may the Lord bless you! Perhaps he has sent you here for my relief, for you are right, young friend—you are altogether right; I have been wild with grief, frantic with despair, but never for one hour in the whole course of my life have I been insane."

"I believe you, Madam, on my sacred honor I do!" said Traverse, fervently.

"And yet you could get no one about this place to believe you! They have taken my brother-in-law's false story, indorsed as it is by the doctor-proprietor, for granted. And just so long as I persist in telling my true story, they will consider me a monomaniac, and so often as the thought of my many wrongs and sorrows combines with the nervous irritability to which every woman is occasionally subject, and makes me rave with impatience and excitement, they will report me a dangerous lunatic, subject to periodical attacks of violent frenzy; but, young man, even at my worst, I am no more mad than any other woman, wild with grief and hysterical through nervous irritation, might at any time become without having her sanity called in question."

"I am sure that you are not, nor ever could have been, Madam. The nervous excitement of which you speak is entirely within the control of medicine, which mania proper is not. You will use the means that I prescribe and your continued calmness will go far to convince even these dullards that they have been wrong."

"I will do everything you recommend; indeed, for some weeks before you came, I had put a constraint upon myself and forced myself to be very still; but the effect of that was, that acting upon their theory they said that I was sinking into the last or 'melancholy-mad' state of mania, and they put me in here with the incurables."

"Lady," said Traverse, respectfully taking her hand, "now that I am acquainted in some slight degree with the story of your heavy wrongs, do not suppose that I will ever leave you until I see you restored to your friends."

"Friends! ah, young man, do you really suppose that if I had had friends I should have been left thus long unsought? I have no friends, Doctor Rocke, except yourself, newly sent me by the Lord; nor any relatives except a young daughter whom I have seen but twice in my life!—once upon the dreadful night when she was born and torn away from my sight and once about two years ago, when she must have been sixteen years of age. My little daughter does not know that she has a poor mother living, and I have no friend upon earth but you, whom the Lord has sent."

"And not in vain!" said Traverse, fervently, "though you have no other friends, yet you have the law to protect you. I will make your case known and restore you to liberty. Then, lady, listen: I have a good mother, to whom suffering has taught sympathy with the unfortunate, and I have a lovely betrothed bride, whom you will forgive her lover for thinking an angel in woman's form; and we have a beautiful home among the hills of Virginia, and you shall add to our happiness by living with us."

The lady looked at Traverse Rocke with astonishment and incredulity.

"Boy," she said, "do you know what you are promising—to assume the whole burden of the support of a useless woman for her whole life? What would your mother or your promised wife say to such a proposition?"

"Ah! you do not know my dear mother nor my Clara—no, nor even me. I tell you the truth when I say that your coming among us would make us happier. Oh. Madam, I myself owe so much to the Lord and to His instruments, the benevolent of this world, for all that has been done for me. I seize with gratitude the chance to serve in my turn any of His suffering children. Pray believe me!"

"I do! I do, Doctor Rocke! I see that life has not deprived you of a generous, youthful enthusiasm," said the lady, with the tears welling up into her glorious black eyes.

After a little, with a smile, she held out her hand to him, saying:

"Young friend, if you should succeed in freeing me from this prison and establishing my sanity before a court of justice, I and my daughter will come into the immediate possession of one of the largest estates in your native Virginia! Sit you down, Doctor Rocke, while I tell you my true story, and much, very much more of it than I have ever confided to any human being."

"Lady, I am very impatient to hear your history, but I am your physician, and must first consider your health. You have been sufficiently excited for one day; it is late; take your tea and retire early to bed. To-morrow morning, after I have visited the wards and you have taken your breakfast, I will come, and you shall tell me the story of your life."

"I will do whatever you think best," said the lady.

Traverse lifted her hand to his lips, bowed and retreated from the cell.

That same night Traverse wrote to his friend Herbert Greyson, in Mexico, and to his mother and Clara, describing his interesting patient, though as yet he could tell but little of her, not even in fact her real name, but promising fuller particulars next time, and declaring hi intention of bringing her home for the present to their house.

CHAPTER XXVIII
END OF THE LADY'S STORY

Of the present naught is bright,
But in the coming years I see
A brilliant and a cheerful light,
Which burns before thee constantly.

—W. D. GALLAGHER

At the appointed hour the next morning Traverse Rocke repaired to the cell of his mysterious patient.

He was pleased to find her up, dressed with more than usual care and taste and looking, upon the whole, much better in health and spirits than upon the preceding day.

"Ah, my young hero, it is you; you see that I am ready for you," she said, holding out her hand.

"You are looking very well this morning," said Traverse, smiling.

"Yes, hope is a fine tonic, Doctor Rocke."

She was seated by the same window at which Traverse had first seen her, and she now beckoned the young doctor to come and take a seat near her.

"My story is almost as melodramatic as a modern romance, Doctor Rocke," she said.

Traverse bowed gravely and waited.

"My father was a French patriot, who suffered death in the cause of liberty when I, his only child, was but fourteen years of age. My mother, broken-hearted by his loss, followed him within a few months. I was left an orphan and penniless, for our estate was confiscated."

"Ah, your sorrows came early and heavily indeed," said Traverse.

"Yes; well, a former servant of my father held an humble situation of porter on the ground floor of a house, the several floors of which were let out to different lodgers. This poor man and his wife gave me a temporary home with themselves. Among the lodgers of the house there was a young Virginian gentleman of fortune, traveling for pleasure and improvement; his name was Mr. Eugene Le Noir."

"Le Noir!" cried Traverse, with a violent start.

"Yes—what is the matter?"

"It is a familiar Virginia name, Madam, that is all; pray go on."

"Mr. Le Noir was as good and kind as he was wise and cultivated. He used to stop to gossip with old Cliquot every time he stopped at the porter's room to take or to leave his key. There he heard of the poor little orphan of the guillotine, who had no friend in the world but her father's old servant. He pitied me, and after many consultations with Father and Mother Cliquot, he assumed the position of guardian to me, and placed me at one of the best schools in Paris. He lingered in the city and came to see me very often; but always saw me in the presence of Madame, the directress. I clung to him with affection as to a father or an elder brother, and I knew he loved me with the tender, protecting affection that he would have given a younger sister, had he possessed one. Ah! Doctor Rocke, tell me, besides yourself, are there many other men in your State like him?"

"I knew but one such; but go on, dear Madam."

"When I had been to school some months he came to me one day scarcely able to conceal his woe. He told me that his father was ill and that he should have to sail in the first packet from Havre, and that, in fact, he had then come to take leave of me. I was wild with grief, not only upon his account but upon my own, at the prospect of losing him, my only friend. I was but a child, and a French child to boot. I knew nothing of the world; I regarded this noble gentleman, who was so much my superior in years as in everything else, as a father, guardian or elder brother; so in an agony of grief I threw myself into his arms, sobbing and weeping bitterly and imploring him not to break my heart by leaving me. It was in vain Madame the Directress exclaimed and expostulated at these improprieties. I am sure I did not hear a word until he spoke. Putting me out of his arms, he said:"

"I must go, my child; duty calls me."

"Then take me with you; take your poor little one with you, and do not pull her out of your warm, good heart, or she will wither and die like a flower torn up by the roots!" I cried, between my sobs and tears.

"He drew me back to his bosom and whispered:"

"There is but one way in which I can take you with me, my child. Will you be my wife, little Capitolie?"

"Capitola!" cried Traverse, with another great start.

"Yes! Why? What is the matter now?"

"Why, it is such an odd name, that is all! Pray proceed, Madam."

"We were married the same day, and sailed the third morning thereafter from Havre for the United States, where we arrived, alas! only to find the noble gentleman, my Eugene's father, laid in his grave. After Mr. Le Noir's natural grief was over we settled down peaceably to our country life at the Hidden House—"

"The Hidden House!" again exclaimed Traverse Rocke.

"Yes! that is another odd name, isn't it? Well, I was very happy. At first when I understood my real position, I had been afraid that my husband had married me only from compassion; but he soon proved to me that his love was as high, as pure and as noble as himself. I was very happy. But one day, in the midst of my exultant joy, a thunderbolt fell and shattered my peace to destruction forever! Oh, Doctor Rocke, my husband was murdered by some unknown hand in his own woods, in open day! I cannot talk of this!" cried the widow, breaking down, overwhelmed with the rush of terrible recollections.

Traverse poured out a glass of water and handed it to her.

She drank it, made an effort at self-control, and resumed:

"Thus, scarcely sixteen years of age, I was a widow, helpless, penniless and entirely dependent—upon my brother-in-law, Colonel Gabriel Le Noir, for by the terms of their father's will, if Eugene died without issue the whole property descended to his younger brother, Gabriel. To speak the truth, Colonel Le Noir was exceedingly kind to me after, my awful bereavement, until a circumstance was discovered that changed all our relations. It was two months after my husband's death that I discovered, with mingled emotions of joy and sorrow, that heaven had certainly destined me to become a mother! I kept my cherished secret to myself as long as it was possible, but it could not indeed be long concealed from the household. I believe that my brother-in-law was the first to suspect it. He called me into his study one day, and I obeyed like a child. And there he rudely questioned me upon the subject of my sacred mother-mystery. He learned the truth more from my silence than from my replies, for I could not answer him."

"The brute! the miserable hound!" ejaculated Traverse.

"Oh, Doctor Rocke, I could not tell you the avalanche of abuse, insult and invective that he hurled upon my defenseless head. He accused me of more crimes than I had ever heard talk of. He told me that my condition was an impossible one unless I had been false to the memory of his brother; that I had dishonored his name, disgraced his house and brought myself to shame; that I should leave the roof, leave the neighborhood and die as I deserved to die, in a ditch! I made no reply. I was crushed into silence under the weight of his reproaches."

"The caitiff! The poltroon! Ah, poor stranger, why did you not leave the house at once and throw yourself upon the protection of the minister of your parish or some other kind neighbor?"

"Alas! I was a child, a widow and a foreigner all in one! I did not know your land or your laws or your people. I was not hopeful or confident; I had suffered so cruelly and I was overwhelmed by his abuse."

"But did you not know, dear lady, that all his rage was aroused only by the fact that the birth of your child would disinherit him?"

"Ah, no! I was not aware, at that time, that Gabriel Le Noir was a villain. I thought his anger honest, though unjust, and I was as ignorant as a child. I had no mother nor matronly friend to instruct me. I knew that I had broken no command of God or man; that I had been a faithful wife, but when Gabriel Le Noir accused me with such bitter earnestness I feared that some strange departure from the usual course of nature had occurred for my destruction. And I was overwhelmed by mortification, terror and despair!"

"Ah, the villain!" exclaimed Traverse, between his teeth.

"He told me at last that to save the memory of his dead brother he would hide my dishonor, and he ordered me to seclude myself from the sight of all persons. I obeyed him like a slave, grateful even for the shelter of his roof."

"A roof that was your own, as he very well knew. And he knew, also, the caitiff! that if the circumstance became known the whole State would have protected you in your rights, and ejected him like a cur."

"Nay, even in that case no harm should have reached him on my account. He was my husband's brother."

"And worst enemy! But proceed, dear lady."

"Well, I secluded myself as he commanded. For four months I never left the attic to which he had ordered me to retreat. At the end of that time I became the mother of twins—a boy and a girl. The boy only opened his eyes on this world to close them again directly. The girl was living and healthy. The old nurse who attended me had an honest and compassionate face; I persuaded her to secrete and save the living child, and to present the dead babe to Colonel Le Noir as the only one, for the suspicions that had never been awakened for myself were alarmed for my child. I instinctively felt that he would have destroyed it."

"The mother's instinct is like inspiration," said Traverse.

"It may be so. Well, the old woman pitied me and did as I desired. She took the dead child to Colonel Le Noir, who carried it off, and afterward buried it as the sole heir of his elder brother. The old woman carried off my living child and my wedding ring, concealed under her ample shawl. Anxiety for the 'fate of my child caused me to do what nothing else on earth would have tempted me to do—to creep about the halls and passages on tiptoe and under cover of the night and listen at keyholes," said the lady, blushing deeply at the recollection.

"You—you were perfectly right, Mrs. Le Noir! In a den of robbers, where your life and honor were always at stake, you could have done no otherwise!" exclaimed Traverse, warmly.

"I learned by this means that my poor old nurse had paid with her liberty for her kindness to me. She had been, abducted and forced from her native country together with a child found in her possession, which they evidently suspected, and I knew, to be mine. Oh, heaven! the agony then of thinking of what might be her unknown fate, worse than death, perhaps! I felt that I had only succeeded in saving her life-doubtful good!"

Here Mrs. Le Noir paused in thought for a few moments and then resumed.

"It is the memory of a long, dreary and hopeless imprisonment, my recollection of my residence in that house! In the same manner in which I gained all my information, I learned that it was reported in the neighborhood that I had gone mad with grief for the loss of my husband and that I was an inmate of a madhouse in the North! It was altogether false! I never left the Hidden House in all those years until about two years ago. My life there was dreary beyond all conception. I was forbidden to go out or to appear at a window. I had the whole attic, containing some eight or ten rooms, to rove over, but I was forbidden to descend. An ill-looking woman called Dorcas Knight, between whom and the elder Le Noir there seemed to have been some sinful bond was engaged ostensibly as my attendant, but really as my jailer. Nevertheless, when the sense of confinement grew intolerable I sometimes eluded her vigilance and wandered about the house at night."

"Thence, no doubt," said Traverse, "giving rise to the report that the house was haunted."

Mrs. Le Noir smiled, saying:

"I believe the Le Noirs secretly encouraged that report. I'll tell you why. They gave me a chamber lamp inclosed in an intense blue, shade, that cast a strange, unearthly light around. Their ostensible reason was to insure my safety from fire. Their real reason was that this light might be seen from without in what was reputed to be an uninhabited portion of the house, and give color to its bad reputation among the ignorant of being haunted."

"So much for the origin of one authenticated ghost story," said Traverse.

"Yes, and there was still more circumstantial evidence to support this ghostly reputation of the house. As the years passed I had, even in my confined state, gathered knowledge in one way and another—picking up stray books and hearing stray conversation; and so, in the end I learned how gross a deception and how great a wrong had been practised upon me. I was not wise or cunning. I betrayed constantly to my attendant my knowledge of these things. In consequence of which my confinement became still more restricted."

"Yes, they were afraid of you, and fear is always the mother of cruelty," said Traverse.

"Well, from the time that I became enlightened as to my real position, all my faculties were upon the alert to find means of escaping and making my condition known to the authorities. One night they had a guest, Colonel Eglen, of the army, Old Dorcas had her hands full, and forgot her prisoner. My door was left unlocked. So, long after Colonel Eglen had retired to rest, and when all the household were buried in repose, I left my attic and crept down to the chamber of the guest, with no other purpose than to make known my wrongs and appeal to his compassion. I entered his chamber, approached his bed to speak to him, when this hero of a hundred fields started up in a panic, and at the sight of the pale woman who drew his curtains in the dead of the night, he shrieked, violently rang his bell and fainted prone away."

"Ha! ha! ha! he could brave an army or march into a cannon's mouth easier than meet a supposed denizen of another world! Well, Doctor Johnson believed in ghosts," laughed Traverse.

"It remained for me to retreat as fast as possible to my room to avoid the Le Noirs, who were hurrying with head-long speed to the guest-chamber. They knew of course, that I was the ghost, although they affected to treat their visitor's story as a dream. After that my confinement was so strict that for years I had no opportunity of leaving my attic. At last the strict espionage was relaxed. Sometimes my door would be left unlocked. Upon one such occasion, in creeping about in the dark, I learned, by overhearing a conversation between Le Noir and his housekeeper, that my long lost daughter, Capitola, had been found and was living at Hurricane Hall! This was enough to comfort me for years. About three years ago the surveillance over me was so modified that I was left again to roam about the upper rooms of the house at will, until I learned that they had a new inmate, young Clara Day, a ward of Le Noir! Oh, how I longed to warn that child to fly! But I could not; alas, again I was restricted to my own room, lest I should be seen by her. But again, upon one occasion, old Dorcas forgot to lock my door at night. I stole forth from my room and learned that a young girl, caught out in the storm, was to stay all night at the Hidden House. Young girls were not plentiful in that neighborhood, I knew. Besides, some secret instinct told me that this was my daughter: I knew that she would sleep in the chamber under mine, because that was the only habitable guest-room in the whole house. In the dead of night I left my room and went below and entered the chamber of the young girl. I went first to the toilet table to see if among her little girlish ornaments, I could find any clue to her identity. I found it in a plain, gold ring—the same that I had intrusted to the old nurse. Some strange impulse caused me to slip the ring upon my finger. Then I went to the bed and threw aside the curtains to gaze upon the sleeper. My girl—my own girl! With what strange sensations I first looked upon her face! Her eyes were open and fixed upon mine in a panic of terror. I stooped to press my lips to her's and she closed her eyes in mortal fear, I carried nothing but terror with me! I withdrew from the room and went back, sobbing, to my chamber. My poor girl next morning unconsciously betrayed her mother. It had nearly cost me my life."

"When the Le Noirs came home, the first night of their arrival they entered my room, seized me in my bed and dragged me shrieking from it!"

"Good heaven! What punishment is sufficient for such wretches!" exclaimed Traverse, starting up and pacing the narrow limits of the cell.

"Listen! They soon stopped both my shrieks and my breath at once. I lost consciousness for a time, and when I awoke I found myself in a close carriage, rattling over a mountain road, through the night. Late the next morning we reached an uninhabited country house, where I was again imprisoned, in charge of an old dumb woman, whom Le Noir called Mrs. Raven. This I afterwards understood to be Willow Heights, the property of the orphan heiress, Clara Day. And here, also, for the term of my stay, the presence of the unknown inmate got the house the reputation of being haunted."

"The old dumb woman was a shade kinder to me than Dorcas Knight had been, but I did not stay in her charge very long. One night the Le Noirs came in hot haste. The young heiress had been delivered from their charge by a degree, of the Orphans' Court, and they had to give up her house. I was drugged and hurried away. Some narcotic sedative must have been insinuated into all my food, for I was in a state of semi-sensibility and mild delirium during the whole course of a long journey by land and sea, which passed to me like a dream, and at the end of which I found myself here. No doubt, from the excessive use of narcotics, there was something wild and stupid in my manner and appearance that justified the charge of madness. And when I found that I was a prisoner in a lunatic asylum, far, far away from the neighborhood where at least I had once been known I gave way to the wilder grief that further confirmed the story of my madness. I have been here two years, occasionally giving way to outbursts of wild despair, that the doctor calls frenzy. I was sinking into an apathy, when one day I opened the little Bible that lay upon the table of my cell. I fixed upon the last chapters in the gospel of John. That narrative of meek patience and divine love. It did for me what no power under that of God could have done. It saved me! It saved me from madness! It saved me from despair! There is a time for the second birth of every soul; that time had collie fur me. From that hour, this book has been my constant companion and comfort. I have learned from its pages how little it matters how or where this fleeting, mortal life is passed, so that it answers its purpose of preparing the soul for another. I have learned patience with sinners, forgiveness of enemies, and confidence in God. In a word, I trust I have learned the way of salvation, and in that have learned everything. Your coming and your words, young friend, have stirred within my heart the desire to be free, to mingle again on equal terms with my fellow beings, and above all, to find and to embrace my child. But not wildly anxious am I even for these earthly blessings. These, as well as all things else, I desire to leave to the Lord, praying that His will may be mine. Young friend, my story is told."

"Madam," said Traverse, after a thoughtful pause, "our fates have been more nearly connected than you could have imagined. Those Le Noirs have been my enemies as they are yours. That young orphan heiress, who appealed from their cruelty to the Orphans' Court, was my own betrothed. Willow Heights was her patrimony and is now her quiet home where she lives with my mother, and where in their names I invited you to come. And take this comfort also; your enemy no longer lives: months ago I left him ill with a mortal wound. This morning the papers announce his death. There remains, therefore, but little for me to do, but to take legal measures to free you from this place, and restore you to your home. Within an hour I shall set out for New Orleans, for the purpose of taking the initiatory steps. Until my return then, dear lady," said Traverse, respectfully taking her hand— "farewell, and be of good cheer!"

CHAPTER XXIX
PROSPECTS BRIGHTEN

Thus far our fortune keeps an onward course,
And we are graced with wreaths of victory.

—SHAKESPEARE.

Leaving Mrs. Le Noir, Traverse went down to the stable, saddled the horse that had been allotted to his use, and set off for a long day's journey to New Orleans, where late at night he arrived, and put up at the St. Charles.

He slept deeply from fatigue until late the next morning, when he was awakened by the sounds of trumpets, drums and fifes, and by general rejoicing.

He arose and looked from his windows to ascertain the cause, and saw the square full of people in a state of the highest excitement, watching for a military procession coming up the street.

It was the United States troops under their gallant commanders, who had landed from the steamboats that morning and were now marching from the quays up to their quarters at the St. Charles.

As they advanced, Traverse, eagerly upon the lookout, recognized his own regiment.

Traverse withdrew from the window, hurriedly completed his toilet, and hastened down-stairs, where he soon found himself face to face with Herbert, who warmly grasping his hand, exclaimed:

"You here, old friend? Why, I thought you were down in East Feliciana, with your interesting patient!"

"It is for the interest of that 'interesting patient' that I am here, Herbert! Did I tell you, she was one of the victims of that demon Le Noir?"

"No: but I know it from another source. I know as much, or more of her, perhaps, than you do!"

"Ah!" exclaimed Traverse, in surprise.

"Yes! I know, for instance, that she is Capitola's mother, the long-lost widow of Eugene Le Noir, the mistress of the Hidden House, and the ghost who drew folks' curtains there at night."

"Then you do know something about her, but how did you arrive at the knowledge?"

"By the 'last dying speech and confession' of Gabriel Le Noir, confided to me to be used in restitution after his decease. But, come! There is the second bell. Our mess are going in to breakfast; join us and afterwards you and I will retire and compare notes," said Herbert, taking the arm of his friend as they followed the moving crowd into the breakfast parlor.

After the morning meal was concluded the friends withdrew together to the chamber occupied by Traverse Rocke, where they sat down for mutual explanations.

Herbert first related to Traverse all that had occurred from the time that the latter left the city of Mexico, including the arrival of Craven Le Noir at the dying bed of his father, the subsequent death and funeral of Colonel Le Noir, and the late emigration of Craven, who to avoid the shame of the approaching revelation, joined a party of explorers bound for the recently discovered gold mines in California.

"The civilized world is then rid of two villains at once," said the uncompromising Traverse.

Herbert took from his pocket the confession of Colonel Le Noir, which he said he was now at liberty to use as he thought proper for the ends of justice. That certain parts of the disclosure intimately concerned Traverse Rocke, to whom he should therefore read the whole. The confession may be briefly summed up as follows:

The first item was that he had sought to win the affections of Marah Rocke, the supposed wife of Major Ira Warfield; he had sedulously waylaid and followed her with his suit during the whole summer; she had constantly repulsed and avoided him; he, listening to his own evil passions, had bribed her maid to admit him in the dark to Marah's cabin, upon a certain night when her husband was to be absent; that the unexpected return of Major Warfield who had tracked him to the house, had prevented the success of his evil purpose, but had not saved the reputation of the innocent wife, whose infuriated husband would not believe her ignorant of the presence of the villain in her house; that he, Gabriel Le Noir, in hatred as well as in shame, had forborne until now to make the explanation, which he hoped might now, late in life as it was, bring the long-severed pair together, and establish Marah Rocke and her son in their legal and social rights.

The second item in the black list of crime was the death of his elder brother, whom he declared he had not intended to kill. He said that, having contracted large debts which he was unable to pay he had returned secretly from his distant quarters to demand the money from his brother, who had often helped him; that, meeting his brother in the woods, he made this request. Eugene reproached him for his extravagance and folly, and refused to aid him; an encounter ensued, in which Eugene fell. He, Gabriel Le Noir, fled pursued by the curse of Cain, and reached his own quarters before even his absence had been suspected. His agency in the death of his brother was not suspected even by his accomplice in other crimes, the outlaw called Black Donald, who, thinking to gain an ascendency over one whom he called his patron, actually pretended to have made way with Eugene Le Noir for the sake of his younger brother.

The third item of confession was the abduction of the nurse and babe of the young widow of Eugene, the circumstances of which are already known to the reader.

The fourth in the dreadful list comprised the deceptions, wrongs and persecutions practised upon Madame Eugene Le Noir, and the final false imprisonment of that lady under the charge of insanity, in the private madhouse kept by Doctor Pierre St. Jean, in East Feliciana.

In conclusion, he spoke of the wrongs done to Clara Day, whose pardon, with that of others, he begged. And he prayed that in consideration of his son, as little publicity as was possible might be given to these crimes.

During the reading of this confession, the eyes of Traverse Rocke were fixed in wonder and half incredulity upon the face of Herbert, and at its conclusion he said:

"What a mass of crime! But that we may not dare to question the mercy of the Lord, I should ask if these were sins that he would ever pardon! Herbert, it appals me to think of it!"

Then, after deep thought, he added:

"This, then, was the secret of my dear mother's long unhappiness. She was Major Warfield's forsaken wife. Herbert, I feel as though I never, never could forgive my father!"

"Traverse, if Major Warfield had wilfully and wantonly forsaken your mother, I should say that your resentment was natural and right. Who should be an honorable woman's champion if not her own son? But Major

Warfield, as well as his wife, was more sinned against than sinning. Your parents were both victims of a cruel conspiracy, and he suffered as much in his way as she did in hers," said Herbert.

"I always thought, somehow, that my dear mother was a forsaken wife. She never told me so, but there was some-thing about her circumstances and manners, her retired life, her condition, so much below her deserts, her never speaking of her husband's death, which would have been natural for her to do, had she been a widow—all, somehow, went to give me the impression that my father had abandoned us. Lately I had suspected Major Warfield had something to do with the sad affair, though I never once suspected him to be my father. So much for natural instincts," said Traverse, with a melancholy smile.

"Traverse," said Herbert, with the design of drawing him off from sad remembrances of his mother's early trials. "Traverse, this confession, signed and witnessed as it is, will wonderfully simplify your course of action in regard to the deliverance of Madame Le Noir."

"Yes; so it will," said Traverse, with animation. "There will be no need now of applying to law, especially if you will come down with me to East Feliciana and bring the confession with you."

"I will set out with you this very morning, if you wish, as I am on leave. What! To hasten to the release of Capitola's mother, I would set out at midnight and ride straight on for a week!"

"Ah! there is no need of such extravagant feats of travel. It is now ten o'clock; if we start within an hour we can reach the 'Calm Retreat' by eleven o'clock to-night."

"En avant, then," exclaimed Herbert, rising and ringing the bell.

Traverse ordered horses, and in twenty minutes the friends were on the road to East Feliciana.

They reached the "Calm Retreat" so late that night that there was none but the porter awake to admit them.

Traverse took his friend up to his own dormitory, saying, laughingly:

"It is an unappreciable distance of time since you and I occupied the same bed, Herbert."

"Yes; but it is not the first, by five hundred times. D' you remember, Traverse, the low attic where we used to sleep and how on stormy nights we used to listen to the rain pattering on the roof, within two or three inches of our faces, and how we used to be half afraid to turn over for fear that we should bump our heads against the timbers of the ceiling?"

"Yes, indeed," said Traverse.

And thereupon the two friends launched into a discussion of old times, when the two widows and their sons lived together—the two women occupying one bed, and the two boys the other. And this discussion they kept up until long after they retired, and until sleep overtook them.

The next morning Traverse conducted his friend down to the breakfast parlor, to introduce him to Doctor St. Jean, who, as soon as he perceived his young medical assistant, sprang forward exclaiming:

"Grand ciel! Is this then you? Have you then returned? What for did you run away with my horse?"

"I went to New Orleans in great haste, upon very important business, sir."

"Grand Dieu! I should think so, when you ride off on my horse without saying a word. If it had been my ambling pony I should have been in despair, I! Your business so hasty and so important was accomplished, I hope."

"Yes; I did my errand with less trouble than I had anticipated, owing to the happy circumstance of meeting my friend here, who has come down hither connected with the same business."

"Ah! vera happy to see your friend. In the medical profession, I suppose?"

"No, sir; in the army. Allow me to present him. Major Herbert Greyson, of the -th Regiment of Cavalry."

"Ou! ay! Grand ciel! This is the brave, the distinguished, the illustrious officer, so honorably mentioned in the dispatches of the invincible Taylor and the mighty Scott!" said the little Frenchman, bowing his night-capped head down to his slippery toes.

Herbert smiled as he returned the bow. And then the little French doctor, turning to Traverse said:

"But your business, so important and so hasty, which has brought this officer so illustrious down here—what is it, my friend?"

"We will have the honor of explaining to Monsieur le Docteur, over our coffee, if he will oblige us by ordering the servant to retire," said Traverse, who sometimes adopted, in speaking to the old Frenchman, his own formal style of politeness. "Go, then, John!"

"Oui, oui, certainement! Allez donc, John!"

As soon as the man had gone, Traverse said:

"I propose to discuss this business over our coffee, because it will save time without interfering with our morning meal, and I know that immediately afterwards you will go your usual round of visits to your patients."

"Eh bien! proceed, my son! proceed!"

Traverse immediately commenced and related all that was necessary concerning the fraud practised upon the institution by introducing into it an unfortunate woman, represented to be mad, but really only sorrowful, nervous and excitable. And to prove the truth of his words, Traverse desired Herbert to read from the confession the portion relating to this fraud, and to show the doctor the signature of the principal and the witness.

To have seen the old French doctor then! I rejoice in a Frenchman, for the frank abandon with which he gives himself up to his emotions! Our doctor, after staring at the confession, took hold of the top of his blue tasseled night-cap, pulled it off his head and threw it violently upon the floor! Then remembering that he was exposing a cranium as bald as a peeled potato, he suddenly caught it up again, clapped it upon his crown and exclaimed:

"Sacre! Diable!" and other ejaculations dreadful to translate, and others again which it would be profane to set down in French or English.

Gabriel Le Noir was no longer an officer illustrious, a gentleman noble and distinguished, compassionate and tender; he was a robber infamous! a villain atrocious, a caitiff ruth, and without remorse!

After breakfast the doctor consented that his young hero, his little knight-errant, his dear son, should go to the distressed lady and open the good news to her, while the great Major Greyson, the warrior invincible, should go around with himself to inspect the institution.

Traverse immediately repaired to the chamber of Mrs. Le Noir, whom he found sitting at the window, engaged in some little trifle of needlework, the same pale, patient woman that she had first appeared to him.

"Ah, you have come! I read good news upon your smiling face, my friend! Tell it! I have borne the worst of sorrows! Shall I not have strength to bear joy?"

Traverse told her all, and then ended by saying:

"Now, dear madame, it is necessary that we leave this place within two hours, as Major Greyson's regiment leaves New Orleans for Washington to-morrow, and it is advisable that you go under our protection. We can get you a female attendant from the St. Charles."

"Oh, I can be ready in ten minutes! Bless you, I have no fine lady's wardrobe to pack up!" replied Mrs. Le Noir, with a smile.

Traverse bowed and went out to procure a carriage from the next village. And in half an hour afterwards the whole party took leave of Doctor Pierre St. Jean and his "institution in-comparable," and set forth on their journey to New Orleans, whence in two days afterwards they sailed for the North. And now, dear reader, let you and I take the fast boat and get home before them, to see our little Cap, and find out what adventures she is now engaged in, and how she is getting on.

CHAPTER XXX
CAPITOLA A CAPITALIST

Plumed victory
Is truly painted with a cheerful look,
Equally distant from proud insolence
And sad dejection.

—MASSINGER.

How glad I am to get back to my little Cap, for I know very well, reader, just as well as if you had told me, that you have been grumbling for some time for the want of Cap. But I could not help it, for, to tell the truth, I was pining after her myself, which was the reason that I could not do half justice to the scenes of the Mexican War.

Well, now let us see what Cap has been doing—what oppressors she has punished—what victims she has delivered—in a word, what new heroic adventures she has achieved.

Well, the trial of Donald Bayne, alias Black Donald, was over. Cap, of course, had been compelled to appear against him. During the whole course of the trial the court-room was crowded with a curious multitude, "from far and near," eager to get sight of the notorious outlaw.

Black Donald, through the whole ordeal, deported himself with a gallant and joyous dignity, that would have better become a triumph than a trial.

He was indicted upon several distinct counts, the most serious of which—the murder of the solitary widow and her daughter in the forest cabin, and the assassination of Eugene Le Noir in the woods near the Hidden House—were sustained only by circumstantial evidence. But the aggregate weight of all these, together with his very bad reputation, was sufficient to convict him, and Black Donald was sentenced to death.

This dreadful doom, most solemnly pronounced by the judge was received by the prisoner with a loud laugh, and the words:

"You're out o' your reckoning now, cap'n! I never was a saint, the Lord knows, but my hands are free from blood guiltiness! There's an honest little girl that believes me—don't you?" he said, turning laughingly to our little heroine.

"Yes, I do!" said Cap, bursting into tears; "and I am sorry for you as ever I can be, Donald Bayne."

"Bother! It was sure to come to this first or last, and I knew it! Now, to prove you do not think this rugged hand of mine stained with blood, give it a friendly shake!" said the condemned man. And before Old Hurricane could prevent her, Capitola had jumped over two or three intervening seats and climbed up to the side of the dock, and reached up her hand to the prisoner, saying:

"God help you, Donald Bayne, in your great trouble, and I will do all I can to help you in this world. I will go to the Governor myself, and tell him I know you never did any murder."

"Remove the prisoner," said the judge, peremptorily.

The constables approached and led away Black Donald.

Old Hurricane rushed upon Cap, seized her, and, shaking her fiercely, exclaimed, under his breath:

"You—you—you—you New York hurrah boy! You foundling! You vagabond! You vagrant! You brat! You beggar! Will you never be a lady? To go and shake hands with that ruffian!"

"Sure, uncle, that's nothing new; I have shaken hands with you often enough!"

"Demmy, you—you—you New York trash, what do you mean by that?"

"Of course I mean, uncle, that you are as rough a ruffian as ever Donald Bayne was!"

"Demmy, I'll murder you!"

"Don't, uncle; they have an uncivilized way here of hanging murderers," said Cap, shaking herself free of Old Hurricane's grasp, and hastening out of the court-room to mount her horse and ride home.

One night after tea, Capitola and her uncle occupied their usual seats by the little bright wood fire, that the chilly evening and keen mountain air made agreeable, even in May.

Old Hurricane was smoking his pipe and reading his paper.

Cap was sitting with her slender fingers around her throat, which she, with a shudder, occasionally compressed:

"Well, that demon Black Donald will be hanged the 26th of July," said Old Hurricane, exultingly, "and we shall get rid of one villain, Cap."

"I pity Black Donald, and I can't bear to think of his being hanged! It quite breaks my heart to think that I was compelled to bring him to such a fate!"

"Oh, that reminds me! The reward offered for the apprehension of Black Donald, to which you were entitled, Cap, was paid over to me for you. I placed it to your account in the Agricultural Bank."

"I don't want it! I won't touch it! The price of blood! It would burn my fingers!" said Cap.

"Oh, very well! A thousand dollars won't go a-begging," said Old Hurricane.

"Uncle, it breaks my heart to think of Black Donald's execution! It just does! It must be dreadful, this hanging! I have put my finger around my throat and squeezed it, to know how it feels, and it is awful. Even a little squeeze makes my head feel as if it would burst, and I have to let go! Oh, it is horrible to think of!"

"Well, Cap, it wasn't intended to be as pleasant as tickling, you know. I wish it was twenty times worse! It would serve him right, the villain! I wish it was lawful to break him on the wheel—I do!"

"Uncle, that is very wicked in you! I declare I won't have it! I'll write a petition to the Governor to commute his sentence, and carry it all around the county myself!"

"You wouldn't get a soul to sign it to save your life, much less his."

"I'll go to the Governor myself, and beg him to pardon Donald Bayne!"

"Ha! ha! ha! the Governor would not do it to save all our lives, and if he were to do such an outrageous thing he might whistle for his reelection!"

"I declare, Donald Bayne shall not be hanged—and so there!" said Cap, passionately.

"Whe-ew! You'll deliver him by the strength of your arm, my little Donna Quixota."

"I'll save him one way or another, now mind I tell you! He sinned more against me than against anybody else, and so I have the best right of anybody in the world to forgive him, and I do forgive him! And he shan't be hanged I I say it!"

"You say it! Ha! ha! ha! Who are you, to turn aside the laws?"

"I, Capitola Black, say that Donald Bayne, not having deserved to be hanged, shall not be hanged! And in one way or another I'll keep my word!"

And Cap did her best to keep it. The next morning she mounted Gyp and rode up to Tip Top, where she employed the village lawyer to draw up a petition to the Governor for the commutation of Donald Bayne's sentence. And then she rode all over the county to try to get signatures to the document. But all in vain. People of every age and condition too thoroughly feared and hated the famous outlaw, and too earnestly wished to be entirely and forever rid of him, to sign any petition for a commutation of his sentence. If a petition for his instant execution had been carried around it would have stood a much better chance of success.

Cap spent many days in her fruitless enterprise, but at last gave it up— but by no means in despair, for—

"I'll save his life, yet! by one means or another! I can't change clothes with him as I did with Clara; he's too big, but one way or other I'll save him," said Cap, to herself. She said it to no one else, for the more difficult the enterprise the more determined she was to succeed, and the more secretive she grew as to her measures.

In the mean time the outlaw, double-ironed, was confined in the condemned cell, the strongest portion of the county jail. All persons were strictly prohibited from visiting him, except certain of the clergy.

They did all they could to bring the outlaw to a sense of his condition, to prepare him to meet his fate and to induce him to make a confession and give up the retreat of his band.

And Donald listened to them with respect, acknowledged himself a great sinner, and knelt with them when they knelt to pray for him.

But he denied that he was guilty of the murders for which he had been doomed to die, and he utterly refused to give up his old companions, replying to the ministers in something like these words:

"Poor wretches! They are no more fit to die than I am, and a condemned cell, with the thought of the scaffold before him, are not exactly the most favorable circumstances under which a man might experience sincere repentance, my masters!"

And so, while the convict listened with docility to all that the ministers had to say, he steadily persisted in asserting his own innocence of the crimes for which he was condemned, and in his refusal to deliver up his companions.

Meantime, Capitola, at Hurricane Hall, was doing all she could to discover or invent means to save the life of Black Donald. But still she said no more about it even to Old Hurricane.

One evening, while Cap was sitting by the fire with her thoughts busy with this subject, her uncle came in saying:

"Cap, I have got some curiosities to show you!"

"What are they?" said Cap, languidly.

"A set of burglar's tools, supposed to belong to some member of Black Donald's band! One of my negroes found them in the woods in the neighborhood of the Devil's Punch Bowl! I wrote to the sheriff concerning them, and he requested me to take care of them until he should have occasion to call for them. Look! Did you ever see such things?" said Old Hurricane, setting down a canvas bag upon the table and turning out from it all sorts of strange looking instruments—tiny saws, files, punches, screws, picks, etc., etc., etc.

Cap looked at them with the most curious interest, while Old Hurricane explained their supposed uses.

"It must have been an instrument of this sort, Cap, that that blamed demon, Donald, gave to the imprisoned men to file their fetters off with!" he said, showing a thin file of tempered steel.

"That!" said Cap. "Hand it here! Let me see it!" And she examined it with the deepest interest.

"I wonder what they force locks with?" she inquired.

"Why, this, and this, and this!" said Old Hurricane, producing a burglar's pick, saw and chisel.

Cap took them and scrutinized them so attentively that Old Hurricane burst out into a loud laugh, exclaiming:

"You'll dream of house-breakers to-night, Cap!" and taking the tools, he put them all back in the little canvas bag, and put the bag up on a high shelf of the parlor closet.

The next morning, while Cap was arranging flowers on the parlor mantelpiece, Old Hurricane burst in upon her with his hands full of letters and newspapers, and his heart full of exultation—throwing up his hat and cutting an alarming caper for a man of his age, he exclaimed:

"Hurrah, Cap! Hurrah! Peace is at last proclaimed and our victorious troops are on their way home! It's all in the newspapers, and here are letters from Herbert, dated from New Orleans! Here are letters for you, and here are some for me! I have not opened them yet! Hurrah, Cap! Hurrah!"

"Hurrah, Uncle! Hurrah!" cried Cap, tossing up her flowers and rushing into his arms.

"Don't squeeze me into an apoplexy, you little bear," said Old Hurricane, turning purple in the face, from the savage hug of Cap's joyful arms. "Come along and sit down with me, at this table, and let us see what the letters have brought us."

They took their seats opposite each other at a small table, and Old Hurricane threw the whole mail between them, and began to pick out the letters.

"That's for you, Cap. This is for me," he said, pitching out two in the handwriting of Herbert Greyson.

Cap opened hers and commenced reading. It was in fact Herbert's first downright, practical proposal of marriage, in which he begged that their union might take place as soon as he should return, and that as he had written to his uncle by the same mail, upon another subject, which he did not wish to mix up with his own marriage, she would, upon a proper opportunity, let her uncle know of their plans.

"Upon my word, he takes my consent very coolly as a matter of course, and even forces upon me the disagreeable duty of asking myself of my own uncle! Who ever heard of such proceedings? If he were not coming home from the wars, I declare I should get angry; but I won't get upon my dignity with Herbert—dear, darling, sweet Herbert. If it were anybody else, shouldn't they know the difference between their liege lady and Tom Trotter? However, as it's Herbert, here goes! Now, I suppose the best way to ask myself of uncle, for Herbert, will be just to hand him over this matter. The dear knows it isn't so over and above affectionate that I should hesitate. Uncle," said Cap, pulling Old Hurricane's coat sleeve.

"Don't bother me, Cap," exclaimed Major Warfield, who sat there, holding a large, closely written document in his hand, with his great round eyes strained from their sockets, as they passed along the lines with devouring interest.

"Well, I do declare! I do believe he has received a proposal of marriage himself," cried Cap, shooting much nearer the truth than she knew.

Old Hurricane did not hear her. Starting up with the document in his hand, he rushed from the room and went and shut himself up in his own study.

"I vow, some widow has offered to marry him," said Cap, to herself.

Old Hurricane did not come to dinner, nor to supper. But after supper, when Capitola's wonder was at its climax, and while she was sitting by the little wood fire that that chilly evening required, Old Hurricane came in, looking very unlike himself, in an humble, confused, deprecating, yet happy manner, like one who had at once a mortifying confession to make, and a happy secret to tell.

"Cap," he said, trying to suppress a smile, and growing purple in the face.

—"Oh, yes! You've come to tell me, I suppose, that you're going to put a step-aunt-in-law over my head, only you don't know how to announce it," answered Capitola, little knowing how closely she had come to the truth; when, to her unbounded astonishment, Old Hurricane answered:

"Yes, my dear, that's just it!"

"What! My eyes! Oh, crickey!" cried Cap, breaking into her newsboy's slang, from mere consternation.

"Yes, my dear, it is perfectly true!" replied the old man, growing furiously red, and rubbing his face.

"Oh! oh! oh! Hold me! I'm 'kilt!'" cried Cap, falling back in her chair in an inextinguishable fit of laughter, that shook her whole frame. She laughed until the tears ran down her cheeks. She wiped her eyes and looked at Old Hurricane, and every time she saw his confused and happy face she burst into a fresh paroxysm that seemed to threaten her life or her reason.

"Who is the happy—Oh, I can't speak! Oh, I'm 'kilt' entirely!" she cried, breaking off in the midst of her question and falling into fresh convulsions.

"It's no new love, Cap; it's my old wife!" said Old Hurricane, wiping his face.

This brought Capitola up with a jerk! She sat bolt upright gazing at him with her eyes fixed as if In death.

"Cap," said Old Hurricane, growing more and more confused, "I've been a married man more years than I like to think of! Cap, I've—I've a wife and grown-up son! Why do you sit there staring at me, you little demon? Why don't you say something to encourage me, you little wretch?"

"Go on!" said Cap, without removing her eyes.

"Cap, I was—a jealous—passionate—Demmy, confession isn't in my line. A diabolical villain made me believe that my poor little wife wasn't good!"

"There! I knew you'd lay it on somebody else. Men always do that," said Cap, to herself.

"He was mortally wounded in Mexico. He made a confession and confided it to Herbert, who has just sent me an attested copy. It was Le Noir. My poor wife lived under her girlhood's name of Marah Rocke." Old Hurricane made a gulp, and his voice broke down.

Cap understood all now, as well as if she had known it as long as Old Hurricane had. She comprehended his extreme agitation upon a certain evening, years ago, when Herbert Greyson had mentioned Marah Rocke's name, and his later and more lasting disturbance upon accidentally meeting Marah Rocke at the Orphans' Court.

This revelation filled her with strange and contradictory emotions. She was glad; she was angry with him; she was sorry for him; she was divided between divers impulses to hug and kiss him, to cry over him, and to seize him and give him a good shaking! And between them she did nothing at all.

Old Hurricane was again the first to speak,

"What was that you wished to say to me, Cap, when I ran ray from you this morning?"

"Why, uncle, that Herbert wants to follow your example, and—and—and—" Cap blushed and broke down.

"I thought as much. Getting married at his age! A boy of twenty-five!" said the veteran in contempt.

"Taking a wife at your age, uncle, an infant of sixty-six!"

"Bother, Cap! Let me see that fellow's letter to you."

Cap handed it to him and the old man read it.

"If I were to object, you'd get married all the same! Demmy! you're both of age. Do as you please!"

"Thank you, sir," said Cap, demurely.

"And now, Cap, one thing is to be noticed. Herbert says, both in your letter and in mine, that they were to start to return the day after these letters were posted. These letters have been delayed in the mail. Consequently we may expect our hero here every day. But Cap, my dear, you must receive them. For to-morrow morning, please the Lord, I shall set out for Staunton and Willow Heights, and go and kneel down at the feet of my wife, and ask her pardon on my knees!"

Cap was no longer divided between the wish to pull Old Hurricane's gray beard and to cry over Him. She threw herself at once into his arms and exclaimed:

"Oh, uncle! God bless you! God bless you! God bless you! It has come very late in life, but may you be happy with her through all the ages of eternity!"

Old Hurricane was deeply moved by the sympathy of his little madcap, and pressed her to his bosom, saying:

"Cap, my dear, if you had not set your heart upon Herbert, I would marry you to my son Traverse, and you two should inherit all that I have in the world! But never mind, Cap, you have an inheritance of your own. Cap, Cap, my dear, did it ever occur to you that you might have had a father and mother?"

"Yes! often! But I used to think you were my father, and that my mother was dead."

"I wish to the Lord that I had been your father, Cap, and that Marah Rocke had been your mother! But Cap, your father was a better man than I, and your mother as good a woman as Marah. And Cap, my dear, you vagabond, you vagrant, you brat, you beggar, you are the sole heiress of the Hidden House estate and all its enormous wealth! What do you think of that, now? What do you think of that, you beggar? cried Old Hurricane."

A shriek pierced the air, and Capitola starting up, stood before Old Hurricane, crying in an impassioned voice:

"Uncle! Uncle! Don't mock me! Don't overwhelm me! I do not care for wealth or power; but tell me of the parents who possessing both, cast off their unfortunate child—a girl, too! to meet the sufferings and perils of such a life as mine had been, if I had not met you!"

"Cap, my dear, hush! Your parents were no more to blame for their seeming abandonment of you, than I was to blame for the desertion of my poor wife. We are all the victims of one villain, who has now gone to his account, Capitola. I mean Gabriel Le Noir. Sit down, my dear, and I will read the copy of his whole confession, and afterwards, in addition, tell you all I know upon the subject!"

Capitola resumed her seat, Major Warfield read the confession of Gabriel Le Noir, and afterwards continued the subject by relating the events of that memorable Hallowe'en when he was called out in a snow storm to take the dying deposition of the nurse who had been abducted with the infant Capitola.

And at the end of his narrative Cap knew as much of her own history as the reader has known all along.

"And I have a mother, and I shall even see her soon! You told me she was coming home with the party—did you not, Uncle?" said Capitola.

"Yes, my child. Only think of it! I saved the daughter from the streets of New York, and my son saved the mother from her prison at the madhouse! And now, my dear Cap, I must bid you good night and go to bed, for I intend to rise to-morrow morning long before daylight, to ride to Tip Top to meet the Staunton stage," said the old man, kissing Capitola.

Just as he was about to leave the room he was arrested by a loud ringing and knocking at the door.

Wool was heard running along the front hall to answer the summons.

"Cap, I shouldn't wonder much if that was our party. I wish it may be, for I should like to welcome them before I leave home to fetch my wife," said Old Hurricane, in a voice of agitation.

And while they were still eagerly listening, the door was thrown open by Wool, who announced:

"Marse Herbert, which I mean to say, Major Herbert Greyson;" and Herbert entered and was grasped by the two hands of Old Hurricane, who exclaimed:

"Ah, Herbert, my lad! I have got your letters. It is all right, Herbert, or going to be so. You shall marry Cap when you like. And I am going to-morrow morning to throw myself at the feet of my wife."

"No need of your going so far, dear sir, no need. Let me speak to my own dear girl a moment, and then I shall have something to say to you," said Herbert, leaving the old man in suspense, and going to salute Capitola, who returned his fervent embrace by an honest, downright frank kiss, that made no secret of itself.

"Capitola! My uncle has told you all?"

"Every single bit! So don't lose time by telling it all over again! Is my mother with you?"

"Yes! and I will bring her in, in one moment; but first I must bring in some one else," said Herbert, kissing the hand of Capitola and turning to Old Hurricane, to whom he said:

"You need not travel far to find Marah. We took Staunton in our way and brought her and Clara along—Traverse!" he said going to the door—"bring in your mother."

And the next instant Traverse entered with the wife of Major Warfield upon his arm.

Old Hurricane started forward to meet her, exclaiming in a broken voice:

"Marah, my dear Marah, God may forgive me, but can you—can you ever do so?" And he would have sunk at her feet, but that she prevented, by meeting him and silently placing both her hands in his. And so quietly Marah's forgiveness was expressed, and the reconciliation sealed.

Meanwhile Herbert went out and brought in Mrs. Le Noir and Clara. Mrs. Le Noir, with a Frenchwoman's impetuosity, hurried to her daughter and clasped her to her heart.

Cap gave one hurried glance at the beautiful pale woman that claimed from her a daughter's love and then, returning the caress, she said:

"Oh, mamma! Oh, mamma! If I were only a boy instead of a girl, I would thrash that Le Noir within an inch of his life! But I forgot! He has gone to his account."

Old Hurricane was at this moment shaking hands with his son, Traverse, who presently took occasion to lead up and introduce his betrothed wife, Clara Day, to her destined father-in-law.

Major Warfield received her with all a soldier's gallantry, a gentleman's courtesy and a father's tenderness.

He next shook hands with his old acquaintance, Mrs. Le Noir.

And then supper was ordered and the evening was passed in general and comparative reminiscences and cheerful conversation.

CHAPTER XXXI
"THERE SHALL BE LIGHT AT THE EVENTIDE."—Holy Bible

They shall be blessed exceedingly, their store
Grow daily, weekly more and more,
And peace so multiply around,
Their very hearth seems holy ground.

—MARY HOWITT.

The marriage of Capitola and of Herbert and that of Clara and of Traverse was fixed to take place upon the first of August, which was the twenty-first birthday of the doctors daughter, and also the twenty-fifth anniversary of the wedding of Ira Warfield and Marah Rocke.

German husbands and wives have a beautiful custom of keeping the twenty-fifth anniversary of their marriage by a festival, which they call the "Silver Wedding." And thus Major Warfield and Marah resolved to keep this first of August, and further to honor the occasion by uniting the hands of their young people.

There was but one cloud upon the happiness of Capitola; this was the approaching execution of Black Donald.

No one else seemed to care about the matter, until a circumstance occurred which painfully aroused their interest.

This was the fact that the Governor, through the solicitation of certain ministers of the gospel who represented the condemned as utterly unprepared to meet his fate, had respited him until the first of August, at which time he wished the prisoner to be made to understand that his sentence would certainly, without further delay, be carried into effect.

This carried a sort of consternation into the heart of every member of the Hurricane Hall household!

The idea of Black Donald being hanged in their immediate neighborhood upon their wedding day was appalling!

Yet there was no help for it, unless their wedding was postponed to another occasion than that upon which Old Hurricane had set his heart. No one knew what to do.

Cap fretted herself almost sick. She had cudgeled her brains to no purpose. She had not been able to think of any plan by which she could deliver Black Donald. Meantime the last days of July were rapidly passing away.

Black Donald in the condemned cell maintained his firmness, resolutely asserting his innocence of any capital crime and persistently refusing to give up his band. As a last motive of confession, the paper written by Gabriel Le Noir upon his death-bed was shown him. He laughed a loud, crackling laugh, and said that was all true, but that he, for his part, never had intended to harm a hair of Capitola's head; that he had taken a fancy to the girl when he had first seen her, and had only wanted to carry her off and force her into a marriage with himself; that he had pretended to consent to her death only for the purpose of saving her life.

When Cap heard this she burst into tears and said she believed it was true.

The night before the wedding of Capitola and Herbert, and Clara and Traverse, and of the execution of Black Donald, came.

At Hurricane Hall the two prospective bridegrooms were busy with Old Hurricane over some papers that had to be prepared in the library.

The two intended brides were engaged, under the direction of Mrs. Warfield, in her dressing-room, consulting over certain proprieties of the approaching festival. But Capitola could give only a half attention to the discussion. Her thoughts were with the poor condemned man who was to die the next day.

And suddenly she flew out of the room, summoned her groom, mounted her horse, and rode away.

In his condemned cell Black Donald was bitterly realizing how unprepared he was to die, and how utterly impossible it was for him to prepare in the short hours left him. He tried to pray, but could form no other petition than that he might be allowed, if possible, a little longer to fit himself to meet his Creator. From his cell he could hear the striking of the great clock in the prison hall. And as every hour struck it seemed "a nail driven in his coffin."

At eight o'clock that night the warden sat in his little office, consulting the sheriff about some details of the approaching execution. While they were still in discussion, a turnkey opened the door, saying:

"A lady to see the warden."

And Capitola stood before them!

"Miss Black!" exclaimed both sheriff and warden, rising in surprise, gazing upon our heroine, and addressing her by the name under which they had first known her.

"Yes, gentlemen, it is I. The truth is, I cannot rest tonight without saying a few words of comfort to the poor man who is to die to-morrow. So I came hither, attended by my groom, to know if I may see him for a few minutes."

"Miss Black, here is the sheriff. It is just as he pleases. My orders were so strict that had you come to me alone I should have been obliged to refuse you."

"Mr. Keepe, you will not refuse me," said Capitola, turning to the sheriff.

"Miss Black, my rule is to admit no one but the officers of the prison and the ministers of the gospel, to see the condemned! This we have been obliged to observe as a measure of safety. This convict, as you are aware, is a man of consummate cunning, so that it is really wonderful he has not found means to make his escape, closely as he has been watched and strongly as he has been guarded."

"Ah, but Mr. Keepe, his cunning was no match for mine, you know!" said Capitola, smiling.

"Ha-ha-ha! so it was not! You took him very cleverly! Very cleverly, indeed! In fact, if it had not been for you, I doubt if ever we should have captured Black Donald at all. The authorities are entirely indebted to you for the capture of this notorious outlaw. And really that being the case, I do think it would be straining a point to refuse you admittance to see him. So, Miss Black, you have my authority for visiting the condemned man in his cell and giving him all the comfort you can. I would attend you thither myself, but I have got to go to see the captain of a militia company to be on the scene of action to-morrow," said the sheriff, who soon after took leave of the warden and departed.

The warden then called a turnkey and ordered him to attend Miss Black to the condemned cell.

The young turnkey took up a lamp and a great key and walked before, leading the way down-stairs to a cell in the interior of the basement, occupied by Black Donald.

He unlocked the door, admitted Capitola, and then walked off to the extremity of the lobby, as he was accustomed to do when he let in the preachers.

Capitola thanked heaven for this chance, for had he not done so she would have to invent some excuse for getting rid of him.

She entered the cell. It was very dimly lighted from the great lamp that hung in the lobby, nearly opposite the cell door.

By its light she saw Black Donald, not only doubly ironed but confined by a chain and staple to the wall. He was very pale and haggard from long imprisonment and great anxiety.

Cap's heart bled for the poor banned and blighted outlaw, who had not a friend in the world to speak a kind word to him in his trouble.

He also recognized her, and rising and coming to meet her as far as the length of the chain would permit, he held out his hand and said:

"I am very glad you have come, little one; it is very kind of you to come and see a poor fellow in his extremity! You are the first female that has been in this cell since my imprisonment. Think of that, child! I wanted to see you, too, I wanted to say to you yourself again, that I was never guilty of murder, and that I only seemed to consent to your death to save your life! Do you believe this? On the word of a dying man it is truth!"

"I do believe you, Donald Bayne," said Capitola, in a broken voice.

"I hear that you have come into your estate. I am glad of it. And they tell me that you are going to be married to-morrow! Well! God bless you, little one!"

"Oh, Donald Bayne! Can you say God bless me, when it was I who put you here?"

"Tut, child, we outlaws bear no malice. Spite is a civilized vice. It was a fair contest, child, and you conquered. It's well you did. Give me your hand in good will, since I must die to-morrow!"

Capitola gave her hand, and whilst he held it, she stooped and said:

"Donald, I have done everything in the world I could to save your life!"

"I know you have, child. May yours be long and happy."

"Donald, may your life be longer and better than you think. I have tried all other means of saving you in vain; there is but one means left!"

The outlaw started violently, exclaiming:

"Is there one?"

"Donald, yes! There is! I bring you the means of deliverance and escape. Heaven knows whether I am doing right—for I do not! I know many people would blame me very much, but I hope that He who forgave the thief upon the cross and the sinful woman at his feet, will not condemn me for following His own compassionate example! For Donald, as I was the person whom you injured most of all others, so I consider that I of all others have the best right to pardon you and set you free. Oh, Donald! Use well the life I am about to give you, else I shall be chargeable with every future sin you commit!"

"In the name of mercy, girl, do not hold out a false hope! I had nerved myself to die!'"

"But you were not prepared to meet your Maker! Oh, Donald! I hold out no false hope! Listen, for I must speak low and quick. I could never be happy again if on my wedding-day you should die a felon's death! Here! here are tools with the use of which you must be acquainted, for they were found in the woods near the Hidden House!" said Capitola, producing from her pockets a burglar's lock-pick, saw, chisel, file, etc.

Black Donald seized them as a famished wolf might seize his prey.

"Will they do?" inquired Capitola, in breathes anxiety.

"Yes—yes—yes! I can file off my irons, pick every lock, drive back every bolt, and dislodge every bar between myself and freedom with these instruments! But, child, there is one thing you have forgotten: suppose a turnkey or a guard should stop me? You have brought me no revolver!"

Capitola turned pale.

"Donald, I could easily have brought you a revolver; but I would not, even to save you from to-morrow's death! No, Donald, no! I give you the means of freeing yourself, if you can do it, as you may, without bloodshed! But, Donald, though your life is not justly forfeited, your liberty is, and so I cannot give you the means of taking any one's life for the sake of saving your own!"

"You are right," said the outlaw.

"Listen further, Donald. Here are a thousand dollars! I thought never to have taken it from the bank, for I would never have used the price of blood! But I drew it to-day for you. Take it—it will help you to live a better life! When you have picked your way out of this place, go to the great elm-tree at the back of the old mill, and you will find my horse, Gyp, which I shall have tied there. He is very swift. Mount him and ride for your life to the nearest seaport, and so escape by a vessel to some foreign country. And oh, try to lead a good life, and may God redeem you, Donald Bayne! There—conceal your tools and your money quickly, for I hear the guard coming. Good-by—and again, God redeem you, Donald Bayne!"

"God bless you, brave and tender girl! And God forsake me if I do not heed your advice!" and the outlaw pressed the hand she gave him while the tears rushed to his eyes.

The guard approached; Capitola turned to meet him. They left the cell together and Black Donald was locked in for the last time!

"Oh, I hope, I pray, that he may get off! Oh, what shall I do if he doesn't! How can I enjoy my wedding to-morrow! How can I bear the music and the dancing and the rejoicing, when I know that a fellow creature is in such a strait! Oh, Lord grant that Black Donald may get clear off to-night, for he isn't fit to die!" said Cap to herself, as she hurried out of the prison.

Her young groom was waiting for her and she mounted her horse and rode until they got to the old haunted church at the end of the village, when drawing rein, she said:

"Jem, I am very tired. I will wait here and you must just ride back to the village, to Mr. Cassell's livery stable, and get a gig, and put your horse into it, and come back here to drive me home, for I cannot ride."

Jem, who never questioned his imperious little mistress's orders, rode off at once to do her bidding.

Cap immediately dismounted from her pony and led him under the deep shadows of the elm tree, where she fastened him. Then taking his face between her hands, and looking him in the eyes, she said:

"Gyp, my son, you and I have had many a frolic together, but we've got to part now! It almost breaks my heart, Gyp, but it is to save a fellow creature's life, and it can't be helped! He'll treat you well, for my sake, dear Gyp. Gyp, he'll part with his life sooner than sell you! Good-by, dear, dear Gyp."

Gyp took all these caresses in a very nonchalant manner, only snorting and pawing in reply.

Presently the boy came back, bringing the gig. Cap once more hugged Gyp about the neck, pressed her cheek against his mane, and with a whispered "Good-by, dear Gyp," sprang into the gig and ordered the boy to drive home.

"An' leab the pony, miss?"

"Oh, yes, for the present; everybody knows Gyp—no one will steal him. I have left him length of line enough to move around a little and eat grass, drink from the brook, or lie down. You can come after him early to-morrow morning."

The little groom thought this a queer arrangement, but he was not in the habit of criticising his young mistress's actions.

Capitola got home to a late supper and to the anxious inquiries of her friends she replied that she had been to the prison to take leave of Black Donald, and begged that they would not pursue so painful a subject.

And, in respect to Cap's sympathies, they changed the conversation.

That night the remnant of Black Donald's band were assembled in their first old haunt, the Old Road Inn. They had met for a twofold purpose—to bury their old matron, Mother Raven, who, since the death of her patron and the apprehension of her captain, had returned to the inn to die—and to bewail the fate of their leader, whose execution was expected to come off the next day.

The men laid the poor old woman in her woodland grave, and assembled in the kitchen to keep a death watch in sympathy with their "unfortunate" captain. They gathered around the table, and, foaming mugs of ale were freely quaffed for "sorrow's dry," they said. But neither laugh, song nor jest attended their draughts. They were to keep that night's vigil in honor of their captain, and then were to disband and separate forever.

Suddenly, in the midst of their heavy grief and utter silence a familiar sound was heard—a ringing footstep under the back windows.

And every man leaped to his feet, with looks of wild delight and questioning.

And the next instant the door was flung wide open, and the outlaw chief stood among them!

Steve stopped rolling and curled himself around Black Donald's neck, exclaiming:

"It's you—it's you—it's you!—my dear, my darling—my adored—my sweetheart—my prince!—my lord!—my king!—my dear, dear captain!"

Steve, the lazy mulatto, rolled down upon the floor at his master's feet, and embraced him in silence.

While Demon Dick growled forth:

"How the foul fiend did you get out?"

And the anxious faces of all the other men silently repeated the question.

"Not by any help of yours, boys! But don't think I reproach you, lads! Well I know that you could do nothing on earth to save me! No one on earth could have helped me except the one who really freed me—Capitola!"

"That girl again!" exclaimed Hal, in the extremity of wonder.

Steve stopped rolling, and curled himself around the feet of his master and gazed up in stupid astonishment.

"It's to be hoped, then, you've got her at last, captain," said Demon Dick.

"No—heaven bless her!—she's in better hands. Now listen, lads, for I must talk fast! I have already lost a great deal too much time. I went first to the cave in the Punch Bowl, and, not finding you there, came here at a venture, where I am happy to meet you for the last time—for to-night we disband forever!"

"'Twas our intention, captain," said Hal, in a melancholy voice.

Black Donald then threw himself into a seat at the head of the table, poured out a mug of ale, and invited his band to pledge him. They gathered around the table, filled their mugs, pledged him standing, and then resumed their seats to listen to the last words of their chief.

Black Donald commenced and related the manner of his deliverance by Capitola; and then, taking from his bosom a bag of gold, he poured it upon the table and divided it two into equal portions, one of which he handed to "Headlong Hal," saying:

"There, Hal, take that and divide it among your companions, and scatter to distant parts of the country, where you may yet have a chance of earning an honest livelihood! As for me, I shall have to quit the country altogether, and it will take nearly half this sum to enable me to do it. Now I have not a minute more to give you! So once more pledge your captain and away!"

The men filled their mugs, rose to their feet, and pledged their leader in a parting toast and then:

"Good luck to you all!" exclaimed Black Donald, waving his hat thrice above his head with a valedictory hurrah. And the next moment he was gone!

That night, if any watchman had been on guard near the stables of Hurricane Hall, he might have seen a tall man mounted upon Capitola's pony, ride up in hot haste, dismount and pick the stable lock, take Gyp by the bridle and lead him in, and presently return leading out Fleetfoot, Old Hurricane's racer, upon which he mounted and rode away.

The next morning, while Capitola was dressing; her groom rapped at the door and, in great dismay, begged that he might speak to Miss Cap one minute.

"Well, what is it, Jem?" said Capitola.

"Oh, Miss Cap, you'll kill me! I done been got up long afore day and gone to Tip-Top arter Gyp, but somebody done been stole him away afore I got there!"

"Thank heaven!" cried Capitola, to little Jem's unspeakable amazement. For to Capitola the absence of her horse meant just the escape of Black Donald!

The next minute Cap sighed and said:

"Poor Gyp! I shall never see you again!"

That was all she knew of the future!

That morning while they were all at breakfast a groom from the stables came in with a little canvas bag in his hand, which he laid, with a bow, before his master.

Major Warfield took it up; it was full of gold, and upon its side was written, in red chalk:

"Three hundred dollars, to pay for Fleetfoot.—Black Donald, Reformed Robber."

While Old Hurricane was reading this inscription, the groom said that Fleetfoot was missing from his stall, and that Miss Cap's pony, that was supposed to have been stolen, was found in his place, with this bag of gold tied around his neck!

"It is Black Donald—he has escaped!" cried Old Hurricane, about to fling himself into a rage, when his furious eyes encountered the gentle gaze of Marah, that fell like oil on the waves of his rising passion.

"Let him go! I'll not storm on my silver wedding day," said Major Warfield.

As for Cap, her eyes danced with delight—the only little clouds upon her bright sky were removed. Black Donald had escaped, to commence a better life, and Gyp was restored!

That evening a magnificent old-fashioned wedding came off at Hurricane Hall.

The double ceremony was performed by the bishop of the diocese (then on a visit to the neighborhood) in the great salon of Hurricane Hall, in the presence of as large and splendid an assembly as could be gathered together from that remote neighborhood.

The two brides, of course, were lovely in white satin, Honiton lace, pearls and orange flowers. "Equally," of course, the bridegrooms were handsome and elegant, proud and happy.

To this old-fashioned wedding succeeded a round of dinners and evening parties, given by the wedding guests. And when all these old-time customs had been observed for the satisfaction of old friends, the bridal party went upon the new-fashioned tour, for their own delight. They spent a year in traveling over the eastern continent, and then returned home to settle upon their patrimonial estates.

Major Warfield and Marah lived at Hurricane Hall and as his heart is satisfied and at rest, his temper is gradually improving. As the lion shall be led by the little child, Old Hurricane is led by the gentlest woman that ever loved or suffered, and she is leading him in his old age to the Saviour's feet.

Clara and Traverse live at Willow Heights, which has been repaired, enlarged and improved, and where Traverse has already an extensive practice, and where both endeavor to emulate the enlightened goodness of the sainted Doctor Day.

Cap and Herbert, with Mrs. Le Noir, live at the Hidden House, which has been turned by wealth and taste into a dwelling of light and beauty. As the bravest are always the gentlest, so the most high-spirited are always the most forgiving. And thus the weak or wicked old Dorcas Knight finds still a home under the roof of Mrs. Le Noir. Her only retribution being the very mild one of having her relations changed in the fact that her temporary prisoner is now her mistress and sovereign lady.

I wish I could say "they all lived happy ever after." But the truth is I have reason to suppose that even Clara had sometimes occasion to administer to Doctor Rocke dignified curtain lectures, which no doubt did him good. And I know for a positive fact that our Cap sometimes gives her "dear, darling, sweet Herbert," the benefit of the sharp edge of her tongue, which, of course, he deserves.

But notwithstanding all this, I am happy to say that all enjoy a fair amount of human felicity.